Many Waters Cannot Quench Love

by Betty Leitner Reichert

PublishAmerica
Baltimore

ISBN: 1-4241-8936-5
PUBLISHED BY PUBLISHAMERICA, LLLP
www.publishamerica.com
Baltimore

Printed in the United States of America

MANY WATERS CANNOT QUENCH LOVE
is dedicated to my late parents

My mother, Ruth Washaw Leitner, was a brave, strong, energetic woman with a heart to serve others. She raised four children while managing a rooming-house. Fishing, crocheting, canning fruits and vegetables, playing Canasta, and reading her Bible were her favorite modes of relaxation. Mom taught me of the importance of family, God's love and the power of prayer.

My father, Perry Otto Leitner, a former newspaper reporter and an I.R.S. agent for many years, was a gentle, soft-spoken man who endowed me with his enthusiasm regarding books and journalism, and concocted stories for his children about the life of Daniel Boone. Dad had a great appreciation of nature in general, and thunderstorms in particular. He taught me to swim…

Acknowledgments

Much appreciation for my husband, George Reichert, who has been incredibly supportive and patient as he edited my book several times, made pertinent suggestions, and utilized his computer skills. What a blessing!

Our daughter, Angela Roetger, a beautiful young woman who will also be an author one day, and is even more excited about my book than I am.

My three siblings, Stan Leitner, Lilly Johnson, and Juanita Chilton: all have writing talents, and have been a constant source of encouragement.

My dear friend, Jackie Fisher shared her knowledge in an area of which I knew practically nothing, edited my book, and spurred me on in my quest.

Nannette Serra, a long-time friend and author, who said I could do it.

Geri Valentine and Mary Ann Kroner, who prayed for publication.

My two chums since childhood: Darlene Hopkins McDermott for sharing the traumas of a family member's bout with Alzheimer's; and Dorothy Moriarty Edrington regarding her memories of sailing at Carlyle Lake.

Paige Johnson, my great-niece, who attended a local Greek Church with me, as we learned together about one of the early roots of Christianity.

Harry Lemakis who told me stories pertaining to the Greece he loves, and to his sweet wife Christine, who gracefully participates in the Greek dance.

Father Joseph Strzelecki of the Assumption Greek Church in Des Peres, MO, who shared the beauty and rituals of Greek weddings with me.

Despena Stergen and Dessie Bellos, two lovely Greek ladies who patiently attempted to tutor me in the art of baking Greek pastries.

Robert L. Creel, author of "The Settlement," for his constant support.

The gracious Librarians at the Daniel Boone Branch of the St. Louis County Library, who were tireless in their assistance with my research.

All other family members, friends, neighbors and associates who wished me great success.

Last but certainly not least, my late, great friend Doris Lungwitz, with whom I discussed the plot several years ago when it was just a short-story.

CHAPTER I

Current Year—Early Springtime

Eve's beautiful green eyes appeared rather smoky, no longer having the bright, clear gaze they usually portrayed. Her mouth opened as if to speak, but she said nothing, and then slipped back into the land of oblivion. Adam patted and smoothed her tousled white hair, led her to the kitchen, and seated her. Handing her a spoon, he encouraged her to eat some of the homemade lentil soup he had prepared earlier that morning.

"Here darling, sit down and eat the soup I cooked for you. I even sprinkled it with some of the oyster crackers you enjoy so much."

No sooner was Eve seated, than she stood up and walked toward the front door. Adam followed her, took her hand, and gently walked her back to the kitchen. He placed the soup in front of her once again, all the while speaking to her in a calm, gentle manner as though attempting to guide a small child.

"Eve, you haven't eaten since noon yesterday. I know you must be hungry. Please try the soup I made for you."

Though their marriage of over 40 years produced no children, they had always felt fulfilled through one another and their careers in journalism. Joint-hobbies of sailing, swimming, tennis, gardening, walking, and reading brought much delight also. Had it really only been six months ago that Adam and Eve Alexander had retired and began to enjoy their free time, doing just as they wished each day after so many years of work? Could the diagnosis of their family doctor possibly be accurate? Some new tests for Alzheimer's had been administered to Eve just the day before. As part of the final test, drops were placed in her eyes to prompt dilation of the pupils. After completing his examination the doctor said, "Positive diagnosis…Alzheimer's Disease—No Cure"

For the past few months, there had been extreme changes in Eve's personality. Her temperament changed from fun-loving to tense and anxious, her calmness to confusion. Constant repetitions about trivial matters now marked the mood of their days together. After making a decision to keep track of how often she asked the same question in the space of several hours, Adam became exhausted. Once again she said, "Adam, isn't it time for bed yet?"

As her questioning began almost immediately after lunch, he kept patiently saying, "No, Eve. It isn't time for bed yet. Are you tired? Don't you feel well?"

And each time she responded, "I'm fine, but it must be my bedtime."

Ordinarily a very patient man, Adam was at his wit's end and decided to pay another visit to Dr. Childress the very next day. For now though, he realized that he must have a bit of time alone just to think about the situation and attempt to make plans for their future. Finally, he helped Eve prepare for bed, and when she was settled in for the night, he sat alone in their living room and began to reflect on the past, on the first time they met…

CHAPTER II

St. Louis—1964

Their first meeting occurred 40 years earlier on the campus of the community college they both attended while pursuing careers in journalism. Each of them had a natural gift of writing, and enjoyed expressing their thoughts on paper. Soon, they discovered that research was a very exciting and important tool also.

On that particular day however, career aspirations played no role in their mutual attraction. All Adam saw was a tall, shapely redhead with lively green eyes and a heart-warming smile walking down the pathway towards him. Eve observed a young man with the broadest shoulders she had ever seen. When her gaze lifted to his face, she was struck with the openness of his crystal-clear gray eyes. His black hair was blowing about in an untidy fashion. She attributed it to the wind, but Adam always said that she literally made his hair stand on end!

As soon as Eve realized that she was staring, she averted her gaze. Seconds later, she had to look back to see if Adam was still staring at her. He was! They both smiled as if reading one another's minds and said, "Hello."

From that moment on they became a twosome, and were almost always seen together on campus. Standard comments by their classmates were, "How appropriate that your names are Adam and Eve; you seem to have been created for one another."

Two months later, they decided that delaying marriage until after graduation was not an option. Now was the time! They notified the most important people in their lives, and everyone who knew them tried to change their minds and advised them to wait. However, true love could not be postponed. The following weekend was the beginning of spring-break; they eloped and spent the next week in a romantic little cottage set in the hills of the Missouri Ozarks.

Viewing the countryside from a lofty hillside, they began to make plans for their future together. Schooling would take several more years. Adam's grandparents, with whom he lived, were paying for his tuition. They had retired and planned to move to Florida after his graduation. The agreement was that he would pay them back after graduating and gaining a permanent job. Eve grew up in a local home for orphans and had obtained a partial-scholarship due to her exceptionally good grades in high school. She worked part-time to help pay for her expenses, and lived in a local Salvation Army home for women. Adam too, worked part-time to buy his clothing and other incidental items. A small apartment just five minutes from campus became their first home together.

Eve had been a vegetarian for as long as she could remember. The matron at the home where she grew up always said, "When I attempted to feed Gerber's pureed meat products to Eve when she was a toddler, she would spit it out on her tray. Even though I would sometimes mix it with vegetables or fruit, she would immediately detect it!"

Now, Eve convinced Adam that he might like to try a meat-free way of eating also. As she said, "You can also save a great deal of money." He agreed to try for the period of a month and found that his energy level and sense of well-being were even greater than before.

The next couple of years went by quickly as they both spent the majority of their time either in class, doing research, or studying. On graduation day, surrounded by classmates and friends, they felt the world was just one tremendous opportunity awaiting their exploration. They were both employed by a local newspaper, but their shifts were different, so their times together were somewhat limited. This only enhanced their pleasure when they were together.

Money was still scarce, so they spent their free time exploring the countryside, visiting museums, picnicking, walking, and playing tennis, anything at all just to be together. Endless hours of conversation took place about their hopes and plans for the future. They both had a great desire to bring pleasure to others through the written word. Talk of raising a family was very exciting too, but they agreed that having children would have to be delayed for a few more years.

Time passed and after graduation, they were both offered positions that would allow them to enjoy their chosen professions and pay the bills. Adam was employed by a St. Louis newspaper as a reporter who was sent out to interview people while gathering local news. Eve was on staff of a woman's magazine and was adept at researching the many avenues that interest women.

Once, they were invited to spend a week aboard a sailboat with friends in the Bahamas, and they became enchanted with sailing. They enjoyed setting anchor, diving overboard, and snorkeling their way through shimmering waters with brightly patterned fish and coral when they had money for vacations. As soon as possible, they put money down on a used sailboat and spent most of their free time afloat at a lake that was just an hour's drive from their apartment.

The only empty part about their life together was the absence of children. After five years of marriage, they started making plans to have a baby. Within the next three years, Eve suffered through two miscarriages. Afterwards, they visited a fertility specialist who put them both through the standard testing. The news was not good! The doctor advised them to adopt…something they never quite reached the point of investigating.

CHAPTER III

Current Year—Springtime

Once again, Adam found himself in the office of the doctor who had diagnosed Eve's affliction. Adam inquired, "Doctor Childress, I've heard of Alzheimer's but don't really know much about it."

"Adam, it's been around a long time. It was discovered in 1906 by a German physician named, Alois Alzheimer. He described the symptoms and conditions to his cohorts, and it was named after him."

"At what age does it usually occur, and what are the actual symptoms?"

"It doesn't usually occur until after 65 years of age, but younger people may sometimes suffer from it too. A slight loss of memory may mark the beginning, like forgetfulness, shortened attention-span, trouble with simple math, difficulty expressing thoughts, changing or unpredictable moods, and less desire to try new things or meet new people."

"Those are all changes I have noticed in my wife Eve, during the past several months, doctor. What causes this to happen?"

"Lots of research is going on and we have much to learn yet. A few of the things we think may contribute are genetic influences. If elder family members have been affected, you might inherit the tendency also. It could be from a virus that takes years to develop fully, but is not contagious to others. An abnormal amount of proteins have been found in some people afflicted with Alzheimer's who have been subjected to an autopsy after death. There can also be a shortage of vital chemicals in the brain and an overload of aluminum in the system. Less blood supply to the brain and the lack of ability to use oxygen in the blood can also be contributors."

"Doctor, will these symptoms remain or will they change and intensify?"

"They will become more intense. Memory loss can become more severe and include forgetting the names of close family members. Your wife may even forget you, her husband of many years. She may forget how to dress herself, neglect her personal hygiene, have outbursts of anger, and become suspicious and unable to concentrate."

"Should people with family members who have these symptoms just accept the changes, doctor?"

"No. Not at all! Many other things may cause these symptoms, some of which are depression, malnutrition, kidney problems, and, or reactions to drugs. All of these things can and do affect many elderly people."

"Could any of these have affected Eve, doctor?"

"They possibly could have, but we've run the basic tests and all the other health issues of which I just spoke test negative. As you know, Eve took very little medication through the years. No, we are almost certain that Alzheimer's is what is affecting Eve."

"What can I do to help her?"

"Try to act as though everything is normal. Continue to talk to her about the customary, everyday affairs. Keep her as active as possible. Take her to places she has enjoyed in the past. Daily exercise is important—both for her and for you. It is an amazing mood lifter-upper."

"What can she do, doctor?"

"What has she always enjoyed?"

"Well, she loves to read, but can't seem to concentrate any longer."

"Physically—what did she enjoy?"

"Roller-skating, swimming, walking, fishing, hiking, traveling…"

"Well…walking would probably be the safest and easiest. Could the two of you walk on a regular, daily basis?"

"Yes, of course. The problem seems to be that Eve doesn't want to get dressed, but prefers to wear a gown and robe all day long."

"Does she have trouble dressing?"

"Well, yes. She chooses outfits that don't match or are inappropriate. Yesterday, when we needed to visit the grocery store, she put on her holiday dress of red velvet. Her chosen footwear was blue and white walking shoes."

"Can you offer constructive criticism, like telling her that her attire doesn't fit the occasion?"

"Not really. She gets extremely upset and perplexed. When things seem appropriate to her, she can't understand it might not be okay."

"Are you telling me she has already begun to show symptoms of rage? That is usually a symptom that comes later."

"Evidently so…"

"Does it ever appear that she might be violent with you?"

"Not really. It seems to be more frustration with herself, rather than anger directed toward me. What could or should I have done to be aware of what was happening to Eve sooner? Could I have helped prevent it?"

"No, there is nothing you could have done to stop its onset. So often, families of those afflicted with Alzheimer's tend to blame themselves. At this time, nothing can be done to delay or turn the situation around. Love and consideration are of prime importance. There are support groups for the caregivers and you might consider becoming part of one. So many emotions of the caregiver come into play with the discovery of their loved one's affliction. Like guilt that you should have done something you've neglected to do. Fear about what is happening to your loved one; feelings of embarrassment when the person with Alzheimer's disease causes a scene in public or needs constant attention; anger and resentment regarding the cost of time and money to family members. All of these things can be very detrimental to your very own sense of well-being. Please don't be hard on yourself. It is not your fault."

Adam turned his head sideways and appeared to be in deep thought.

Dr. Childress continued: "Adam, it's very important to take time for yourself too. Time to do something you enjoy doing alone. Finding a reliable person to be a substitute or stand-in is critical. You can't take the whole responsibility on your own shoulders. You may know someone personally, or go through an agency to find an individual who is trained along these lines. These are agencies that offer daycare services and will care for a family member up to 9 hours a day. This too, offers relief to the caregiver. It's important that you acquire a wristband for yourself."

"A wristband?"

"Yes, a wristband. As you are the caregiver, and apparently have no other family member or friend who might care for Eve, it is important that identification is on your person at all times. If something might happen to you, no one would be aware that Eve is in your home. It could be a very long time before she is noticed and cared for."

"That makes sense. What about Eve? Shouldn't she have some type of identification also?"

"Yes, we will have a wristband made up for Eve too. Hers will be a bit more feminine, somewhat like a bracelet, so she won't object to wearing it. I will have my nurse arrange for you to get a wrist band also. Yours will resemble a military dog tag, but it will also be worn on your wrist."

"Well, Doctor Childress, I've learned so much today. Thank you for taking the time to make me aware of what to expect and what my options are. The thing that causes me the most grief is being aware how embarrassed and hurt Eve would be if she knew she was causing problems for others. She's always been so independent."

"I know, Adam. However, she will probably never realize the changes taking place in herself. During the earlier stages, she might have sensed that something was not quite right, but as of now, that time is evidently past. Adam, please feel free to call me if I can be of further assistance."

"Good day, Doctor Childress. I may take you up on that."

After leaving the doctor's office, Adam realized that he had to have some quality time alone to assess what he had just been told regarding Eve's current affliction. He drove to Carondelet Park, one of his favorite places to sit and meditate. Parking the car and walking up the pathway to the gazebo, he anticipated the peace and inspiration that always greeted him there. As Adam sat quietly reminiscing, he was instantly transported back in time to memories of how their lives together had always seemed to merge together so perfectly.

"What a good life we enjoyed together," Adam mused. Basking in the rays of sunlight streaming through the ornamental laced wooden strips adorning the sides of the gazebo, he allowed his thoughts to drift back to meaningful episodes in their years together. Once again, he thought of his other amazing family members and their effect on the lives of himself and Eve:

CHAPTER IV

St. Louis—Spring—1973

"Adam, please hurry home today. There is a personal, return-receipt-requested letter awaiting you at the post office," Eve breathed excitedly into the telephone receiver.

"Who's it from Eve?"

"I don't know, but the postal clerk said the return address shows Crete."

"Crete? You mean someone in Greece sent me a letter? It is probably one of those form letters that promise to do research on a family coat-of-arms using your surname. I understand their fees go on and on."

"Do you really think so? As your family chose to use a surname honoring Alexander the Great, the symbology might reference him."

"Could be. His emblems of war were probably a horse, sword and spear."

"Well Adam, we could discuss this all day dear, but we still won't know until you pick it up."

"Since you're home right now, can't you pick it up for me?"

"No. I told you it is return-receipt-requested and requires your personal signature."

"Okay. I'll try to leave work early. If not today, maybe I'll wait until tomorrow which is Saturday."

"No Adam! You know how curious I am. Today, please!"

"Okay. See you soon Eve."

As Adam's normal skin tones were of an olive hue, his face rarely picked up any additional color. But, today, his cheeks were brightly flushed as he charged into the front door of their home.

"Eve, Eve. Come quickly!"

"Adam, what's wrong? I've never seen you look like this. Are you ill? Do you have a fever? Your face is so animated and full of color. Let me feel your forehead. Shall I get the thermometer?"

"No Eve. Sit down and try to be patient until I tell you something life-changing."

Demurely, Eve sat down.

"Where shall I begin? You remember me telling you about my origins?"

"Yes dear. Your dad fell in love with a lovely, young Greek lady named Jenny while stationed in Crete during World War II."

"Yes, Eve. They were married, and he discovered after being shipped out that she was expecting their child."

"And that child was you!"

"Yes. Their plans were to live together in America after the war ended. That was in September of 1942. In June of 1943, I was born. My dad received a letter telling of my birth and also that Jenny died in childbirth. Dad was heart-broken but made arrangements for me to be brought to America. His parents hired a woman to make the trip and bring me to the states when I was 6 months old."

"Yes, she brought you to your grandparents, because by that time they had received the news that your father was killed while fighting on the frontlines in France."

"Okay. You know everything that I have known up to this point."

"Now Adam, tell me about the letter you just picked up from the post office."

"Just a bit more history, Eve: Jenny's father, my maternal grandfather, Andreas Alexander has never contacted me nor acknowledged my existence as far as I know."

"Right!"

"And…I received the double names of Alexander due to the surnames of both parents being the same. That is why I am called, Adam Alexander Alexander."

"Oh Adam, that's news to me. Now tell me of the letter, I can hardly wait!"

Adam stopped pacing the floor and flung himself on the sofa.

"This letter came through a detective agency. It seems they tried for some time to track my dad, Luke Alexander. As he was killed during the war while in France, it took a long time to trace his family. My grandparents moved to St. Louis from San Francisco, so the agency had to locate them, and finally…they reached me."

"Who hired them?"

"It seems I have a maternal aunt named Clarice Alexander Simion, sister to Andreas Alexander, my grandfather. Her letter states that she was present at my birth and there is a family secret she must share with me."

"A secret?"

"Yes Eve. She can no longer live with her conscience and must share what she knows about our family history."

"Did she write the letter personally?"

"No! She can converse in English and read it, but cannot write it."

"Then someone else acted as her scribe."

"Yes."

"What does she suggest? Are you going to converse over the phone?"

"Probably not. It is so important to her to get the matter resolved that she is willing to travel to the States, unless we can make time to visit her in Crete."

"This is a bad time of year for you to be away, isn't it Adam?"

"Yes. It really is. However, the letter indicates that Clarice Alexander Simion is 81 years of age. It could be a rough trip for her."

"How are we to communicate with her?"

"The detective from Crete gave his name and phone number. We are to make contact with him. I suppose she wants to know something about me before progressing any further."

"Shall we suggest she visit us here Adam?"

"Yes, I think so. It's really her call to make. Let's dial this number and see what happens."

As the time difference was 8 hours, Adam decided to call the next morning at 7:00 a.m. as it would then be approximately 3:00 p.m. in Crete. He assumed that either the detective or his secretary would be available at that time.

Adam tossed and turned all night, and was up long before 5:00 a.m. He put on a pot of coffee and attempted to read the early morning edition of the newspaper, but found his thoughts drifting. Recalling his growing-up years with his grandparents, he had always thought of them with great love and appreciation. They were in their mid-40's when they adopted him, and should have been at the point in their lives when they could enjoy traveling, but suddenly they were bound to a tiny baby named Adam. Adam was a living reminder of Luke, their only child. It was almost like starting all over again. Dirty diapers, formulas and night-time crying became their daily routine. All their friends were immersed in the growth of their grandchildren too, so they had something in common. The big difference was…their friend's little ones eventually went home.

Drifting and dreaming of days gone by, of ice-skating and sleighing with Grandpa Alexander and smells of fresh-baked cookies drifting through the house, Adam began to get hungry. He reached for a bag of store-bought cookies to have with his coffee, and threw them in the trash as he compared the taste with those of his granny's.

Suddenly, Adam sat up with a start and realized it was time to make the overseas phone call and get ready for work. Lots of numbers to dial he thought to himself. The immediate pick up on the other end was so abrupt; he thought his connection had been broken.

"Kalimera (Good Day), Ryan's Detective Agency. How may I help you?" a female voice queried.

"Hello. My name is Adam Alexander; I just received a letter from Nick Ryan regarding my maternal great-aunt."

"Oh yes. Nick is in. One moment please, I will call him to the phone."

"Hello, Mr. Alexander, this is Nick Ryan. You responded very quickly."

"Yes, I found the letter extremely interesting. You are in touch with my aunt?"

"Yes. She has been anxiously awaiting your response. Would you care to speak to her personally?"

"Of course. That is why I called."

"Very well, I will give you her phone number. My part in the reunion has probably been completed. I wish you the very best. Here is her number. As you are aware, her name is Clarice Alexander Simion."

"Thank you very much. Do you feel this is an appropriate time to call her?"

"I would suggest you wait several hours. This is siesta time, and she usually naps, as is our custom. If you call her around 4:30 p.m. our time, she should be refreshed. As you are aware, she is 81 years of age and enjoys her quiet time of day."

"Does she have family members who live nearby?"

"Sir, I am unable to share any of Mrs. Simion's business with you. She will confide in you as she sees fit."

"Of course, I wasn't thinking properly. Well, thank you and goodbye."

"Goodbye, Mr. Alexander."

"Eve, wake up. I got in touch with the detective from the agency in Greece. He recommended I call Mrs. Simion in two hours as she will be taking a siesta right now. I think I'll wait here until that time and just leave for work a bit later today."

"That's a good idea Adam. Shall I fix a hearty breakfast for you?"

"Yes, that store-bought cookie was not what I was looking for. How about fixing a vegetable omelet with melted cheese, and a whole wheat bagel?"

"Will do."

After breakfast, Adam and Eve discussed the probability of having a house guest soon.

"The guest bedroom has just been newly decorated and the daybed makes a comfortable full-sized bed at night, and can even be split into two twin sizes if she prefers to leave things on the other bed," Eve noted. "The southern exposure makes it a nice cheerful room, don't you think? The pale yellow walls emit such a lovely glow when the sun casts its beams through the window. It should be a cozy room for her, Adam."

"Okay, it's settled then. As you do your magazine periodicals from home anyway, someone can be with her at all times."

"Yes Adam, it will be very pleasant. Maybe she can teach me to cook some Greek dishes too. Most of all, I will be anxious to learn more of your mother."

"Oops, check the clock. It's almost 9:30 a.m., time for me to call. I hope we can understand one another."

"I'm sure you'll be able to communicate properly. Do you think we should check on available flights yet?"

"No. Let's wait to hear what she wants to do."

"Oh Adam, I'm so excited. Won't it be wonderful to make contact with someone from your mother's family?

"I'm excited too Eve, but also a bit nervous. We will probably have nothing in common but our DNA."

"Your Grandmother Alexander will be thrilled to meet her too. Even though they're from two different worlds, they are from the same basic generation. They are both aware of the international trauma caused by World War II."

"Well, here goes. See how many numbers you have to dial to place an inter-continental call?"

"One moment, dear. I'm going into the bedroom and will pick up the receiver to listen. Call in to me just as someone answers so I don't break your connection."

"OK. My heart is pounding!"

"Mine too!"

"Here goes."

Adam placed the paper containing the phone number given by the detective agency on the kitchen table and dialed. After just two rings, he heard a woman's response. Her cheerful greeting of "Hello" was very precise.

"Hello," Adam said. "Am I speaking with Mrs. Clarice Simion?"

"Yes you are," the woman on the other end confirmed.

"My name is Adam Alexander. I understand we are related."

Adam heard a gasp on the other end of the line. "Oh my, I've dreamed of this moment for years, and prayed so many times that we would eventually meet."

"I can't believe I've never been made aware of your existence, Mrs. Simion."

"That is much too formal. Would you mind calling me Aunt Clarice?"

"No, of course not Aunt Clarice. I understand you have some family secrets to share with me."

"Indeed I do, but I can't speak of them over the phone. It's much too important. I must speak to you face-to-face. Even though it's a long trip, I am willing to come to you."

"That will be fine with us. I have been married for the past nine years to my lovely wife, Eve. She is anxious to meet you too."

"And, I can't wait to meet her too. Would it be convenient for me to visit the two of you rather soon, possibly next week?"

"Of course. That is not too soon. We will look forward to meeting you. Let me give you our phone number. Please feel free to come when it's convenient. Just call and let me know of your travel arrangements so we can meet you at the airport."

"To which city will I be traveling?"

"Tell the travel agent you wish to fly into Lambert Field Airport in St. Louis, Missouri, U.S.A. I will give you our phone number and address. By the way, do you have a passport?"

"Oh yes. I applied for one several months ago, and waited until I received it before trying to contact you."

"Did you know how to find me then?"

"Yes, through the years I've been in touch with your father's parents."

"You don't mean it! How could that be? I was not aware of it."

"When we received word of your father's death, it seemed best for your grandparents to raise you. I couldn't begin to do so and that would have been your father's wishes."

"I am amazed. Your story makes me feel my life was more real to others than to myself."

"I'm sure that is true. Please, let's save the rest of the story until we meet in person."

"Very well, Aunt Clarice. Call us when you have made your travel plans."

"I shall. Goodbye for now Adam."

"Goodbye, Aunt Clarice."

"Adam," Eve asked, "Could you hear me breathing over the phone? I was so excited, but kept my hand over the mouthpiece so I would not distract you."

"No, Eve. I heard nothing but the voice of my aunt. Now, I must be off to work. Our conversation took a lot longer than I had anticipated."

The next morning at precisely 7:30 a.m., the phone rang. The voice of Aunt Clarice burst excitedly from the receiver as Eve answered the phone.

"Hello Eve, this is Aunt Clarice. Would you and Adam mind if I bring along a guest?"

"Of course not, Aunt Clarice. We have been very concerned about you traveling so far alone. That would be ideal. We have plenty room in our home, and we would welcome a friend of yours too. I assume it is a lady friend you are speaking of."

"Yes it is. I have known her for a very long time. She is very special to me."

"Good. She will certainly be most welcome. By the way, have you checked on the appropriate travel arrangements yet?"

"As a matter of fact, I have." Clarice quickly gave Eve the travel arrangements.

"Wonderful. We will be there to meet you. Adam will be pleased that you plan to arrive so soon."

CHAPTER V

To St. Louis from Greece—1973

Three days after the phone call from Aunt Clarice in Greece, Adam and Eve were driving along Route I-270 towards Lambert Field. Neither of them were able to contain their excitement that has been building for the past week.

"Adam, just think, we are going to learn so much about your Greek heritage from your aunt."

"You're right Eve, we certainly will. It still seems like a fairy tale. All through my childhood, I tried to imagine what it would be like to have my real parents. Gram and Gramps were just great, but not quite like having your very own family. They couldn't have loved me more than they did, nor raised me to have a more positive outlook on life than if I were their very own child."

"Don't you think it was hard on them to be responsible for a tiny baby at their age?"

"Their age? They certainly weren't old, just in their mid 40's."

"Yes, but what a change in their lifestyle. Grams quit her job and stayed home to care for you, didn't she?"

"Of course."

"Gramps had to relieve her after coming home from a hard day's work, right?"

"Right," Adam admitted.

"Well then, wasn't that quite a big commitment to raise you from babyhood to manhood? There were lots of years in-between…"

"Come on Eve, I'm not downgrading what they did for me, nor how much they gave up. I'm just saying there were parts of me that have always barren."

"Did they talk much about your father?"

"I suppose so. They have albums full of his pictures of course, and when they shared about his personality and talents, I could visualize him fairly easily."

"Why did he enlist at 20 years of age while residing in another country?"

"Well, he knew that part of his heritage was Greek. When he discovered that the Nazis were invading Greece and the United States had not yet become one of the allies helping them, he realized he wanted to go to England."

"What did that have to do with enlisting and aiding Greece?"

"Great Britain was sending troops to aid Greece when they found the Germans were trying to take over, and had already destroyed many villages there."

"Why is England called Great Britain?"

"In 1707, England and Scotland became one and assumed the name of Great Britain to solidify their oneness."

"Oh."

"Anyway, Dad had a few more years before he would graduate from college, but he felt such a strong urge to do something to help the Greek people. He went to Great Britain on spring-break and never returned"

"So, he went to Great Britain and joined the military. I'm surprised they accepted him," Eve said.

"Why? When people come to America from other lands and want to really be part of our country when we are at war, they quite often enlist in our armed forces."

"How long was your Dad in Greece?"

"Well, he left home in 1941, was in Greece until 1942, and was sent to France, where he was killed in battle."

"His medals were sent home, weren't they?"

"Yes, and later on he was awarded the Purple Heart for valor above and beyond the call of duty."

"That came after his death, didn't it?"

"Yes, they awarded it in a ceremony to my grandparents who later gave it to me."

"So…what was he really like?"

"It seems he was very serious about important things, but had a great sense of humor too."

"What did he enjoy?"

"My father enjoyed many, many things. He played the guitar and was part of a band that performed for parties. For a while, he practiced several hours daily while in high school. His voice was quite good also, he sang the lead in a school musical. Ice and roller-skating were several of his passions, and he was an avid tennis player. He was president of his senior class and editor of the yearbook."

"Darling, he sounds so much like you. You've inherited many of his outstanding qualities."

"Thank you. I suppose I have acquired some of his interests."

"What do you have of his that is personal?"

"I have a scrapbook that was put together by my grandparents. There are also letters my mother sent to him while pregnant with me and awaiting his return."

"Those should be interesting."

"I suppose so, but it's been very difficult to read them. I haven't looked at them for years."

"Why not, Adam?"

"They are part of the past. They contain things that were so private between the two of them. I felt almost like an intruder reading about the passion they enjoyed together."

"Oh Adam, how could you intrude while trying to learn more of the two people who loved one another enough to give you life?"

"I don't know, my dear. It just seemed to be rather pointless in a way since neither one of them are still around."

"Oh look, there's the sign that indicates our turnoff; the terminal is just ahead."

"Thank goodness the skimpy traffic allowed us to arrive early at the airport. Now we will have time for a cup of coffee, and the opportunity to sit and wait for passengers to disembark. We should be able to spot Aunt Clarice before she feels any dismay regarding identifying us."

"I think she'll be fine. From the tone of her voice, I would say she is used to being in charge."

Walking from the parking lot, they held hands and shared their excitement regarding the arrival of Adam's great-aunt and her traveling companion.

Relaxing at a tiny food stand close to the arrival gate, Adam and Eve sipped their cups of hot coffee and continued to chat nervously.

"Eve, I really feel this visit will be one of the highlights of my life. Isn't it amazing that her decision to get in touch took so long? My 32nd birthday is just around the corner. Even though she stumbled upon us by looking for information about my father, it seems she would have done so long before now."

"You're right Adam, but I expect her to fill us in on all the details very soon. Let's go in that gift shop and buy her some flowers."

"Good idea, Eve. Women always think of the right thing to do."

"I suppose that's because we know what would mean a lot to us also."

"Touché! Forgive me for not giving you flowers more often. I know how you love them. What kind shall we purchase for Aunt Clarice?"

"Those lovely pink rosebuds we just passed by would be perfect. We can get some ferns and baby's breath to surround them and have it all encased in that brilliant green waxed paper with a pink bow."

"Whatever you say, my dear."

After purchasing the delicate floral arrangement, they proceeded to the proper gate and sat down.

"Only fifteen minutes until their arrival, Adam. We've been on pins and needles awaiting this moment, and it's finally arrived."

Eve held the bouquet up to her nose to inhale its delightful fragrance. The pink roses enhanced the delicate pink flush on her smooth cheeks.

"My darling, how beautiful you are. I am so blessed to have you as my wife."

"And I am so blessed to have you as my husband, Adam."

"Wow! Sounds as though we have a 'mutual-admiration society' here."

"Indeed we do!"

Just then, the airline attendant at the desk called out the following information:

"Now landing: Flight #2077 from New York City. Please step back and allow the passengers to disembark."

The doors opened and one by one, weary-looking passengers began to flood into the waiting area. Several business men emerged who were obviously first as they had just left their first-class seats. Next, a young bejeweled woman stepped forward while hanging on the arm of her paunchy, middle-aged "sugar-daddy".

A distraught mother carrying a baby on one arm, and holding a toddler's hand with her other hand nervously looked about as though searching for someone who might be of help with the children. A young couple was obviously having a hard time walking forward as they continued to gaze sideways into one another's eyes. An elderly couple, one using a cane and the other a walker, appeared while walking at very tedious gaits. Then, in a rush, six teenagers appeared laughing and talking. On and on the parade went. Just when they thought Clarice may have missed the flight, an elegant-looking lady with snow-white hair, attired all in black, from her black leather shoes to the knotted black scarf on her head appeared. Her gaze shifted to and fro over the awaiting crowd as she was obviously seeking a familiar face.

Then, when her eyes caught those of Adam, she broke out into a beautiful smile. Quickly, in spite of her age, she seemed to skim across the floor as she hastened to quickly cover the distance that lay between them. Holding out both hands toward him, she exclaimed, "Adam!"

"Aunt Clarice," he said as he bent down to greet her with a kiss.

"Yes dear, it is I," she said as she encircled his neck with her outstretched arms, while kissing him on his cheek. "How handsome you are, and what a perfect blend of your father and mother! I thank God that I was able to locate you."

"I'm so grateful too, Aunt Clarice. Allow me to introduce my wife, Eve."

"My, how lovely she is. We don't often see hair that color in Greece. It reminds me of some of our flaming sunrises."

Eve held out the delicate bouquet of flowers they had chosen for Clarice and said, "Hello, Aunt Clarice. Thank you for the lovely compliment. We thought you might enjoy smelling these roses after being cooped-up on a plane with stale air for such a long time."

Lowering her head toward the flowers, Clarice began to inhale their delicate aroma. "Lovely," she said as she held out her arms to embrace Eve.

"Well, let's head for the luggage area and get your suitcases. Oh my, I almost forgot about your traveling companion. Did she come along?" queried Adam.

"Yes, she did. There she is, standing close to the doorway," affirmed Clarice.

Adam glanced over and noted a very lovely middle-aged woman who was also attired all in black. He strode over, introduced himself and shook her hand, while commenting how happy he was that she could accompany his aunt on the trip. It wasn't until later that he realized that she had not offered a response.

Eve maintained a lively chatter as she tried to make the two ladies feel welcome and at ease. After learning they experienced some turbulent weather during part of their journey, they assured her they were very happy to have their feet on solid ground once again. Meanwhile, Adam put their luggage on a cart and wheeled it to the garage where their car was parked. When he pulled the car in front of the terminal at the pre-arranged spot, they were still talking. All the way home, Eve and Clarice continued to talk.

After they pulled into their driveway and unloaded the car, the weary travelers were shown to their room with its adjoining bathroom so they could tidy up a bit, and become familiar with the room that would be theirs while in town.

After they had taken the house tour and become familiar with their new surroundings, Adam suddenly became aware that he was not being the best host. He had not even inquired as to the identity of the traveling companion of Clarice. Turning to her, he said, "Please forgive me. I neglected to ask your name."

"My name is Jenny Alexander Andropokis."

"That's interesting," he commented. "My mother's name was Jenny Alexander."

With tear-filled eyes, the lady said, "Adam…I *am* your mother!

CHAPTER VI

Current Year—Springtime (cont'd)

"Where are you, Eve?" Adam cried out. He had just entered their home and smelled a strong odor of something burning. Hurrying to the kitchen, he saw black smoke emanating from a wok full of stir-fried vegetables. He quickly removed it from the stove top burner and turned on the exhaust fan. With alarm, he noted the hot pink color of Eve's favorite robe lying on the deck outside the sliding kitchen door. Then, he saw Eve. She was standing on the deck totally nude.

Quickly, he opened the door, picked up the robe, and placed it around Eve's shoulders. As he did so, she turned ever so slightly and gave him a big smile although her eyes were filled with tears.

"Oh Adam, how can we help those little chipmunks? The neighbor's cat just caught and ate another one. Could we possibly transport them out of the area?"

"Darling," Adam said. "I think that's just the natural food-chain in nature."

"But why? Why must animals eat one another? Why can't we all live happily together? It's just not fair."

"Eve, you know why that sort of thing happens. When the original Adam and Eve disobeyed God by eating from the forbidden tree of good and evil, all of nature was thrown into chaos. God Himself, sacrificed the first animals by killing them to provide garments Adam and Eve to wear. Until then, they had no awareness of being naked."

"Oh Adam, wouldn't that be delightful not to wear clothing. Look! My name is Eve and I don't have to dress either."

With great glee, Eve untied the sash on her robe and once again, let the garment slide to the floor of the deck. "Does this mean we're in Eden?" she inquired.

Moving faster than he believed possible, Adam swooped her up in his arms and deposited her on the other side of the sliding glass door and into the kitchen. And, just as quickly, as he bent to retrieve her robe, Eve slid the bolt on the door and locked him out. With a hearty laugh, she gave him a wisp of a wave and vanished from his sight.

"Eve, open the door! Eve, it's cold out here, please open the door!"

No mater how hard he banged, there was no response or reappearance. Feeling in his pocket, Adam was relieved to find that the door keys were there. At times, he was prone to lay them on the pedestal table in the front hall where they always placed their current mail before reading it. As he had smelled the burning vegetables as soon as he opened the front door, he had not stopped to look at the mail, but had jammed the keys in his jacket pocket and hurried to the kitchen. Now, he ran down the steps of their deck, raced to the front door of their home and was inside within moments.

Opening the bedroom door, he discovered Eve sitting up in bed with the covers pulled up under her chin. As she shivered, she cried out, "Leave my bedroom. Who do you think you are? I'm going to call the police if you don't leave right now!"

With great alarm, Adam backed out of the room, closed the door and placed a call to Dr. Childress. As usual, the doctor was with a patient and the nurse promised she would have him return the call when he was free.

Fifteen minutes later, Dr. Childress called. "Hello, Adam. How can I help?"

"Doctor, it's about Eve. Her actions are frightening. I don't know how to handle her anymore."

"What is she doing?"

Adam described the situation, and the doctor agreed that firm measures must be taken. When Adam asked what he recommended, he said he would make a few calls and look for an agency that might be able to help.

"Thank you doctor, I really appreciate it."

When Dr. Childress called back, he indicated that a local nursing home by the name of Quiet Haven had a vacancy in their Alzheimer's unit, and would accept her in the morning.

Adam thanked him and breathed a sigh of relief. Although Eve didn't seem to mind being nude, the thought of her burning down their home and not being able to get out was even more frightening.

Just as Adam was going over the situation in his mind, the bedroom door opened and Eve appeared in a pair of summer shorts and a halter top. "Let's go play tennis, Adam. Do you know where my tennis shoes are?"

"No Eve, I don't. Do you realize it's only 52 degrees, and they're predicting rain for later this afternoon?"

"Oh pooh! You're no fun…"

Taking her by the arm, Adam steered her into the bedroom to change her attire.

CHAPTER VII

Spring 1973—(cont'd)

After the initial shock wore off, Adam said, "How can you be my mother, Jenny? She died when I was born!"

"Adam, that's obviously not true. After I gave birth to you, I was told that you were stillborn."

"Didn't you ask to see me?"

"Of course, but I was sedated when you were born. When I awoke, the midwife said you didn't make it. When I asked to see you, she said they took you away immediately so I would not suffer more trauma than necessary."

"Wasn't there someone you knew who would be truthful with you?"

"I was in a home for unwed mothers. There were others there who were just awaiting the birth of their child so they could get back to their normal life."

"Normal life?"

"Yes. They were unwed and planned to give their babies up for adoption."

"But you were married, married to my father, Luke Alexander."

"Yes, I was. But he had been shipped out. As you know, he was an infantryman. He never returned."

"Didn't you know he was killed in battle while serving in France?"

"No! I didn't know that at the time."

"Why not?"

"I wasn't informed."

"But, the military make families aware of their mates—whether dead or alive."

"Actually, our marriage was conducted by a Justice of the Peace. Evidently, Luke did not inform the U.S. Government of his marital status. He enlisted under the auspices of the British government, so they had his records."

"But surely they had enough information to notify his family of his death."

"They did, but the record of our wedding had not reached them."

"How did they know how to notify my dad's parents of my birth?"

"Well, my father, Andreas Alexander, told the people who ran the home for unwed mothers that my baby was to be cared for by a local couple in that area until the child was six month's old. Then, they were to contact your next of kin."

"Why would your father do that?"

"Oh my, it's such a long story."

Eve broke in to say, "Please, this is so totally overwhelming. Let's have a cup of hot tea to rid us of the chill."

"Adam, please put their luggage in the guest bedroom."

"Clarice and Jenny, you will find fresh towels, scented hand soap in the restroom, and hangers for your clothing in the closet. Please make yourselves comfortable and let me know if you need anything else. I'm putting the teapot on now. What is your favorite type of tea?"

"We enjoy all types. You choose for us."

As they drank the soothing chamomile tea, they resolved not to speak of the past until later, and tried to keep up a light banter talking of places in the St. Louis area which they might enjoy seeing during the following week.

Then Eve said, "It's almost 3:00 p.m., past-time for your siesta. We'll continue our conversation after you have both rested an hour or two."

Around 5:15 p.m., Clarice and Jenny emerged from the bedroom looking very refreshed. They had both showered and wore more casual garments, although they were still in black. Eve greeted them with a friendly, "Hello again. My, you look so rested; but you must be hungry."

"Yes, we certainly are," responded Jenny. "The food on the plane was not the best, and we were so anxious about our meeting that we didn't feel like eating."

The table had been set for four with colorful placemats and napkins to match. Filled wine glasses awaited the recipients.

"Please take your wine into the living room and relax as I finish preparing our meal."

"Yes," said Adam. "I'll join you and leave Eve to do the cooking."

As they entered the living room, the lights were turn low and lovely scented candles burned here and there. The stereo emitted soft sounds of classical music. The room was decorated with walls and drapes in soft cream. Accent colors of peach and pale mint green were displayed in throw rugs, pillows, and other decorations.

Adam sat down with a deep sigh as he lowered himself into his comfortable leather recliner. "Forgive me," he said, "I didn't mean to be so nosey by asking you so many personal questions. This has been an emotional day for me."

"We understand," said Clarice, as she and Jenny exchanged glances and smiles. "It has been an emotional time for us too. It's hard to believe we're really here with you and your lovely wife, Eve."

"There is so much to discuss, Aunt Clarice. Questions keep racing through my mind. Questions I want the answers to, but am almost afraid to know."

Jenny's eyes filled with tears as she gazed at Adam, and her lower lip trembled as she acknowledged his remark by saying, "Adam, I'm so sorry to turn up at this time of your life and disrupt things."

"Please Jenny, don't ever feel that way. There has always been a sense of lack in my life. I'm very glad to learn of the missing pieces of the puzzle. Even though the facts are not as I would have chosen, they're still the facts. I can live with truth much more easily than myth. Learning that I do indeed have a mother is very enlightening."

"Just then, Eve's cheerful voice broke into the conversation with, "Dinner's ready."

After a very tasty meal, they returned to the living room with their dessert and coffee. Adam took several logs from the hearth, placed them on the metal grate of the fireplace, and lit them. Soon a rosy glow from the flames illuminated their faces, and they allowed themselves to relax and relish one another's company.

Adam asked, "Where shall we begin? Who would like to share first?"

"Well," Clarice responded. "As I'm the oldest, I'll begin. Jenny's father, Andreas, was my twin brother."

"Was? Is he deceased?"

"Yes."

"My grandfather…" Adam swallowed a huge lump in his throat as he realized he could never spend time getting to know his maternal grandfather. "Forgive me for interrupting, please go on."

"Andreas and I were very close. Our parents were hard-working people who trained us to have a strong set of values. At age 19, I married a young man named Peter Simion. We had known one another all our lives, and at 10 years of age, decided we would marry one day."

"Did your parents approve of him?" queried Eve.

"Oh yes. Peter made everyone laugh at his antics. He was good-hearted and always willing to help others."

"How did he earn his living?" Adam asked.

"Peter was a fisherman. He reminded me of the Peter in the Bible who was an apostle of Jesus Christ and was called from his fishing nets to follow our Lord. My Peter was rough-hewn and looked more like a lumberjack than a fisherman. His coloring was rather unique for a Greek. He had blonde hair and blue eyes, which was the complete opposite of me, with my dark hair, brown eyes and olive complexion. People saw us as a study in contrasts."

"Do you have any children?"

"No, my dear. Before we married, we knew our chances of conceiving a baby were slim. Peter contacted mumps at age 17, and it obviously made him sterile."

"How sad, Aunt Clarice," said Adam, while reaching over to pat her hand.

"Thank you, but I would not have wanted any other man to be my husband. Being with him made it all worthwhile. We had one another."

"Are you still together?" Eve asked.

"No Eve. I lost Peter 17 years ago. He developed a bad cold, but went out to sea anyway as fishing had been bad for some time, and he was eager to make up for it financially. It turned out that the ship's main dragnet was frayed and developed a huge hole. As Peter's hands were extremely strong and he was well versed in repairing nets, he was chosen to restore it. However, a storm of gale force developed. Peter was forced to remain on deck and create knot after knot to knit it into one piece again. Soaked garments left on too long worsened his cold. By the time he returned home, the malady had turned into pneumonia. The local doctor and I did everything in our power for three days, and then…I lost him!"

The three listeners were all moved to the point of tears. However, Eve was the only one who physically reached out to Clarice. Springing to her feet, she quickly covered the area between their chairs, knelt at Clarice's feet, placed her head on the lap of their elderly house guest and cried.

Clarice patted her bright curls and said, "There, there, my darling. It's been many years ago."

"Yes Aunt Clarice, but we never stop missing our loved ones."

"That's true, Eve, but I know he is with our Lord and I shall see him again one day."

"How long did it take you to get that kind of peace about it?"

"God's peace came quickly, but I've never stopped missing my Peter."

Jenny stretched out her legs and then yawned deeply.

Eve stood to her feet and stretched out her hands, one to Clarice, the other to Jenny. "Please forgive me," she said, "We've been trying to have you both relive many years in several hours. It's already past 10:00 o'clock, and you must both be exhausted. Tomorrow is another day. During the next week, we will have time to catch up."

"Oh wait, before we retire for the night, there is something we would like you to see. It is a gift for your home. We hope you like it," said Jenny. When she returned, she had an elegant looking box in her arms. She handed it to Eve, who in turn handed it to Adam. They opened it together, and both emitted sounds of awe. Inside lay a gorgeous vase about 18" in height. Emblazed on it was the figure of an incredibly beautiful woman.

"How lovely," Eve exclaimed. "It looks very old. Is it an antique?"

"Yes, we think it is. The shop owner told us he purchased it from an estate sale the week before. The papers that accompanied it said it was to represent the Grecian queen, Helen of Troy. She was described as having, 'the face that sank a thousand ships!' Many, many men were supposed to have fallen in love with her. It is a long story, of course. Her father Zeus, was the father of gods, and the battle of Troy was fought over her. As it is probably mythology, one can use which ever of the stories, one likes. Even if we were not aware of whom the woman on the vase is to represent, it is a gorgeous thing to behold."

"Oh my, yes. Her hair appears to be the same beautiful shade of auburn as yours Eve. The cowl-neckline, full-length, sleeveless, scarlet gown enhances her creamy white face, throat and arms. What a beautiful wide lipped smile, and such radiant eyes of green. Her stance is so graceful too. She should be a pleasant addition to your home."

Adam rose and placed the precious vase on the fireplace mantle. He then stepped back to admire it, and just shook his head. "We've been looking for the perfect decoration for that area as we spend so much time in this room, but nothing ever seemed quite right. *It is* just perfect, isn't it Eve? Actually, it reminds me of you, my Darling!"

"You flatter me, Adam."

"Clarice and Jenny, we thank you both so much. It was obviously very costly, and we will certainly treasure it, and think of you each time we view it with pleasure," said Eve.

Adam invited them to join him for a moment in his study. He pointed out a framed, decorated caption that sat on his desk, and informed them that Eve had given it to him on their first wedding anniversary. It very simply said, 'Happiness is being married to your best friend.' They were deeply moved…

Eve took the opportunity during the silence to leave the room, go to the guest bedroom and turn down the coverlets on the twin beds created by separating the full-sized daybed. Adam had placed a night stand in-between with a lamp on top. As Eve turned on the table lamp, the two ladies who followed her regarded their room as a warm, welcoming haven.

"Is there something I can get for either of you before you retire for the night?" Eve inquired.

"The only thing I need is a glass of water by my bed. I always get thirsty during the night," said Clarice.

Adam who had trailed behind turned aside to get two glasses of water. "Ice or not?" he asked.

"No, room temperature water is best. Thank you, Adam"

"If the two of you get hungry during the night, feel free to go through the refrigerator and cabinets and help yourselves." Eve listed various options and then added, "Maybe you would like a snack before bedtime."

"Actually," said Clarice, "I do enjoy a cup of yogurt before retiring for the night. It seems to relax me and help me drift off to sleep."

"Do you like it plain?"

"A bit of honey makes it more palatable."

"Here. I have just the thing. It's a locally produced honey we purchase from the health food store. It is supposed to be more nourishing than most."

After they enjoyed the yogurt and honey combo, they all retired for the night.

Sunbeams peeked through the bedroom window shade framed by lace curtains, and rippled over the serene features of Adam Alexander. Eve leaned on her elbow while supporting her head with her right hand. She gazed at her husband who was still totally relaxed in sleep. As she mused over the events of the day before, she wondered if his dreams had been affected by what he had heard yesterday regarding his family. Realizing there was much more to learn, and a week could go by so quickly, she arose and donned a set of pale gray sweats, pushed her feet into furry gray scuffs and quietly opened the bedroom door.

"Well, good morning Aunt Clarice. How long have you been up?"

"Not long. I was too excited to sleep any longer and made myself a cup of hot tea."

"Oh, did you find a blend that you enjoy?"

"Yes, the one I chose is new to me. It's called Rooibos."

"Oh yes, it's an African red tea. It only grows in one region on earth. The producers credit it with powerful antioxidant qualities. It's our favorite both morning and evening as it is caffeine-free."

"Is Jenny still sleeping?"

"No, she showered and is getting dressed now."

Just as Eve was prepared to wake Adam, he peeked around the corner of the door with a hearty greeting of, "Good morning. Did you sleep well Aunt Clarice?"

Clarice's face softened as she noted the intimate title. "Yes, my dear. I slept better than I have in months."

"Great! Eve, what do you think about going to the Missouri Botanical Gardens today?"

"That's a great idea as Clarice and Jenny are both interested in flowers. If they find some different species other than what they have at home, we could ship some to them after they depart."

"Good idea! Let's eat something light for breakfast and enjoy one of the interesting lunches they serve in their tearoom. Cottage cheese with fruit and a toasted whole wheat bagel sound good to me."

Jenny appeared wearing a sturdy pair of walking shoes. They had a thick 2" heel and laced up the front. "These were recommended as the most comfortable, and are supposed to give you the most sure-footing, and the best support." she volunteered.

Clarice said, "I've had a problem with fallen arches and I purchased a pair just like that several months ago, and can attest to their comfort."

"The leather looks so soft, just like a pair of kid gloves," noted Eve. "I would love to have a pair. A friend of mine went hiking in Australia and New Zealand and wore the same type shoe while she was there. She was so pleased with them."

"We'll send you a pair when we return home Eve," Clarice offered. "What size do you wear?"

"Seven."

"Okay ladies, enough girl-talk. Let's get the show on the road. As the only male in the crowd, I don't know how to take part in this conversation."

"Yes Adam, we're ready to go."

En route to "Missouri Botanical Gardens," Jenny asked for a description of a botanical garden. Eve explained to the best of her ability:

"From what I have read, the Garden of Eden the Bible speaks of was a botanical garden. It was not a flower garden, although it had flowers. It was not a vegetable garden although it had herbs and vegetables. It was not an orchard, although it had fruit, and it was not truly a park, although it had trees."

"It sounds as though a botanical garden contains everything one might need to sustain life," noted Jenny.

"Yes, you might say that," Eve agreed.

After hearing Eve's description of botanical gardens, all were silent for several minutes. It was as though all their thoughts were drifting to the un-discussed topics pending, the matter of the lost years between mother and son.

As Adam pulled up in front of the entrance to the gardens, he stopped to allow the three ladies to disembark before parking the car.

"Adam, we'll meet you in the gift shop. You know I can't pass it up. There's always something unusual to purchase for that 'very special gift' you can't find elsewhere."

"Okay Eve, but remember we need to allow time to explore the gardens too. It takes hours to see everything."

"Okay."

When Adam entered the gift shop, he spied each of his ladies engrossed in separate interests. Eve could never resist testing the hanging wind chimes for a new melody. She was doing so again, going from one to the next, while gaily moving their tines like a small child at play.

Jenny discovered something she had never been exposed to. It appeared to be a wooden cylinder about 10 inches in diameter and 2 ½ feet in length gaily decorated with African tribal symbols. As she turned it perpendicular to the floor, it emitted the sounds of softly falling rain— then it stopped. As she turned it the other way, the rain sounds began again. She giggled like a small child and inquired, "Adam, what causes that delightful sound?"

"It comes from the shifting downward of many tiny dried seeds" he said.

"I must buy several and take them home for my grandchildren."

"Grandchildren?"

"Oh, yes, they comprise part of my story. I can't begin telling it now, it's too intense and lengthy."

"I understand, Jenny. Well, choose the items you wish to purchase, and leave them at the counter where we can pick them up on our way home. Where is Clarice?"

"She's over there, looking through all the plants. She truly has a green thumb and grows many flowers, and all the herbs we use in cooking too."

The foursome decided to tour the grounds and return to the gift shop later. They then walked up a flight of stairs, passed the restaurant on the upper level, and then walked down more stairs which led out of doors. Straight ahead was a huge garden with roses of every size, shape and color. To the right was an open-air tram with a conductor awaiting the next group of passengers. Walking a short distance brought them to the Climatron, a building with controlled temperatures and humidity which imitated a great rain forest waiting to envelop them in its almost liquid embrace.

"What a lot of choices. We plan to do it all—but must just choose which to view first."

"Adam, how about admiring the rose garden first, and then riding on the tram? That way, we can look over the entire park area, get off as we choose, and then re-board on the next tram. After that, it will be time for lunch, and then we can visit the Climatron."

"Sounds good, but we can't forget the Japanese Gardens."

"Of course not. There is so much to see."

"We must consider Aunt Clarice. That's a lot of walking for someone her age."

"Well then, let's reverse it. The Climatron first, then lunch, ride the tram, and get off at the Japanese Gardens, ride back to the gift shop, and then head for home."

"Let's go…"

The Climatron greeted them with hot, steamy, open arms. Huge tropical trees and plants seemed to bow down and stretch out their branches in welcome to the visitors. After about half an hour, they walked through the waterfall area and exited the other side.

Adam began to chuckle as he gazed at Eve. "Look at you my darling. Your hair appears as 'a blaze of glory.'"

Jenny and Clarice both glanced at Eve in utter amazement. Her auburn hair appeared to be several inches shorter than before and lay in tiny ringlets about her face. She looked like a crimson-haired doll. They noted that at times, Eve's hair appeared to be auburn, at other times, it had the appearance of red glowing coals of fire. Both Jenny and Clarice experienced the opposite effect. Their curls had disappeared and their hair hung in damp strands, clinging to their cheeks.

"Adam," Eve noted, "You're the only who hasn't changed. Your cowlick is still standing straight up."

They all laughed and decided to break for lunch.

After an interesting, delicious lunch, they stepped out-of-doors again and walked toward the awaiting tram. Adam purchased four tickets and they all climbed aboard. The English Countryside area contained many large trees, all of which had labeled explanations at their base containing the botanical names and also the layman's terms. A cool, refreshing aura was its main offering.

Then, they rode past a maze of tall, entwined bright green shrubs in circular shapes whose function was to entertain children as they explored and attempted to find their way out. Adjoining that was a large building with an information area where several volunteers known as "Master Gardeners" donated their time to encourage and aid potential gardening novices. Several large ponds boasted huge lily-pads on which were perched luscious looking flowers of every size and hue.

When the tram entered the Japanese Garden area, they decided to relax and breathe in the beauties of this natural habitat. Curved benches were scattered here and there. They spotted a young artist sketching a bridge which gracefully curved upward, almost in the shape of a horseshoe. Underneath the bridge rippled blue waters, which churned as huge goldfish thrashed about, sometimes leaping into the air as they sought to catch food tossed toward them by onlookers. For just twenty-five cents, fish food could be purchased from a nearby vending machine.

Goldfish is what they are usually called," Adam informed the ladies, "but they are actually carp. Note the colors; not just gold, but orange, red, white, green and blue. Rather amazing."

As it was near dinnertime when they returned home, Eve invited the ladies to freshen up while she prepared a meal. Knowing there wouldn't be much time to cook when they returned from the gardens, she had removed a tray of one of her specialties from the freezer. "Does everyone like vegetable lasagna?" she queried.

"I'm not sure," remarked Jenny, "we may have it but use a different name. We enjoy a dish called, 'moussaka,' that contains baked eggplant with a special sauce. However, it contains ground beef also. We are looking forward to eating American food while visiting you here."

"Well, we don't eat red meats, but the vegetable lasagna is a good hearty dish, even though it contains no meat. That is what we will have tonight, and I will make a fresh tossed vegetable salad with hot rolls. Those are some of our favorite foods," Eve remarked.

Adjourning to the living room after dinner, they each carried their coffee with them and sat down. Adam opened the conversation with, "Jenny, I feel the time is right to hear your story. What do you think?"

"Yes, Adam. It's a long one of course, as it covers many years, but I will try to condense it."

"That isn't necessary. Please relate it in the manner you wish."

"Very well, I shall."

"Aunt Clarice, there may be a few surprises for you too," Jenny said.

"I'm sure that's true, my dear. Knowing all the characters will help though."

Jenny took another sip of coffee and began. "Fifty years ago, I was born in Crete. My parents were Andreas and Vivian Alexander. Both grew up there. My father was what is called a 'whaler.' His employer operated a steam-driven ship and they would sometimes go to sea for weeks at a time until they were able to locate a sperm whale."

"How are whales captured?" queried Eve.

"They aren't actually captured, they are speared. Huge harpoons are used. Harpoons look somewhat like large lances with a barbed spear on the end attached to an incredibly heavy line. The line is anchored on the whaling ship, and after it is hurled at a whale and meets its target, the line is reeled in and the whale is captured and lifted on board. My father learned to be a whaler from a family friend who had his own business. By the time father was 17 years of age, he was classified as an experienced whaler. At that time sperm whales were still plentiful, and their blubber was in demand."

"Blubber? You mean whale fat?"

"Yes," Jenny continued, "Their blubber was used for many things, some of which were fuel and grease. Actually, some perfumers used it to combine with scents also."

"I thought sperm whales were almost extinct." queried Adam.

"That's right," Jenny responded, "but at that time, it was a thriving business. It was such a demanding job that my father worked almost constantly. They were at sea most of the time. When they finally docked, it took time to get rested and accomplish things of a business nature during their short time at home."

"Yes," said Clarice, "Andreas was always deeply tanned, very lean, and exhausted when he returned home."

"There's much more I could share about whaling, but for now, I want to relate the basic facts you need to know," said Jenny.

She continued. "Clarice, when I finish my story, you will probably also have things to share and revisions to make, as children and adults see things differently."

"Yes Jenny, I will just listen to you at this time."

Jenny's eyes seemed to darken as her thoughts shifted to days of long ago:

CHAPTER VIII

Jenny continued, "My father was over 30 years old when I was born. Prior to his marriage to my mother, he had given himself almost completely to the whaling business and had not taken time to court anyone and pursue a permanent relationship. You've heard the expression about sailors, 'They have a girlfriend in every port?' He dated quite a few ladies while on shore-leave, but none of them had a permanent place in his heart."

"Not until Vivian, that is," interjected Clarice. Then, quickly she said, "Forgive me Jenny, that just slipped out."

"I understand, Clarice. I've seen pictures of my Mom and she was so pretty."

"You look so much like her Jenny. However, your personalities are quite different. She was vivacious and fun-loving. We used to call her 'The Gypsy.' She had long straight black hair and black flashing eyes to match. She loved to sing and dance, and as she twirled about, her tiny feet tapped to the music's rhythm."

"Was she a cheerful mother too, Jenny? Did the two of you enjoy one another while you were growing up?" queried Eve.

Jenny's eyes turned darker still as she said, "I was not able to grow up with her…"

"Oh!" gasped Eve.

"She died when I was only three years of age."

"She died so young? What happened?" Adam asked in a shocked voice.

"No one seems to know. She was evidently there one day and gone the next!"

"There was no autopsy?"

"No!" Clarice said almost too quickly. "Andreas' heart was broken. He wanted to forget as soon as possible."

"How could he forget the mother of his child, the woman he had loved so passionately?" Eve gasped.

"Andreas was a very deep, private person. He got back into things as soon as possible afterwards. He would not allow himself to meditate on what had been."

"My father was a very harsh man. He was always strictly business. When I tried to ask about my mother, he just said, 'That part of our life is past. Let's concentrate on today and what must be accomplished right now.'"

"Who cared for you, a little three-year old, when he was away?"

"That's where my special relationship with Aunt Clarice comes in. She cared for me on a regular basis. She was what you would call my Nanny."

"Yes," interrupted Clarice, "At that time, Peter and I had been married for quite some time and were childless. As we had been trying to conceive, we found Jenny to be a delightful little companion."

"So…Jenny. You too, had no real mother while growing up. At least your father was your next of kin."

"He was, but I saw him so seldom."

"Is that why you always refer to him as Father, not as Dad?"

"Yes, I suppose it is. I always felt like an intruder in his home and was happy when he returned to the sea, and I could be alone with Aunt Clarice and Uncle Peter. They were always full of love and compassion. They enjoyed my company and showed it. The only ones to whom my Father ever showed any affection to in my presence were my children."

Adam, once again, felt a wave of…was it jealousy, he wasn't sure? Jenny let out a deep sigh and Eve, who had been listening so intently and with such deep emotional involvement said, "Jenny, you and Aunt Clarice were unable to take your siesta today. I know you must both be exhausted; would you care to retire for the evening?"

"Oh yes my dear, I'm a bit weary."

"Tomorrow is Sunday, do you usually attend church?"

"Yes we do, where do you go?"

"Well, we don't actually attend church as a rule. Occasionally, on holidays, our friends invite us to go with them, and we accompany them. Which denomination do you prefer?"

"We attend the Greek Orthodox Church at home. Is there one close by?"

Actually, a well-known one is rather near our home. We can all visit there tomorrow."

"Thank you, that sounds good."

"Good night."

"Good night, my dears," said Aunt Clarice.

On the way to church, Adam asked if his three ladies would care to drive to Carlyle Lake that afternoon. He gave a bit of explanation regarding the lake by telling them it was the largest manmade lake in Illinois, and was 26,000 acres in size. As it was only 50 miles east of St. Louis, the drive was not too far for a day of adventure. Many sailboat owners spent almost every weekend there in the summertime, as it was known to be one of the most challenging lakes for sailing. Races were held on weekends, and it was an excellent fish and wildlife area. Bird watchers quite often spotted bald eagles and great blue herons diving for fish. After his description of the lake, Adam left the decision up to the others.

"That's a great idea, Adam" Eve responded. "We could also acquaint Clarice and Jenny with 'The Land of Dreams.'"

"'The Land of Dreams,' what is that?" inquired Jenny.

"It's our sailboat. We've had it for several years and enjoy sailing most weekends during the summer. We chose that name because we pretend we're venturing into uncharted territories."

"Oh! Where would you like to explore?"

"Actually, we've talked for years about visiting Greece and sailing the Mediterranean."

"Oh!"

"Yes," said Adam. "As you know of course, both my parents are of

Greek origin. Aside from enjoying sailing, I have always wanted to view the land of my birth."

"Well then, why don't you visit us? We would love to share our country with you."

"Maybe we could discuss it before you return."

"Look, is that the church we are going to attend today?" asked Eve.

"Yes, quite beautiful, isn't it?" Adam agreed. As you know, I called the church office yesterday, and they said the service starts at 8:30 a.m., but I see only one car in the parking lot. Could this be a special holiday we are not aware of?"

"No," said Jenny. "Are we using the correct time?"

"Yes, of course. I can't imagine what's wrong," Adam responded.

"Well," said Eve. "The only thing we can do is try the door and see if it's unlocked"

Adam parked the car and quickly strode up the stairs to see if the church was open. "Come on," he said. "It's only 8:15; maybe the congregation arrives at the last minute. At least, we we'll have our pick of pews."

As they entered the foyer, they looked ahead into the main vestibule, and found it was darkened and appeared deserted. Cautiously, they opened one of the double-doors and peeked inside. No one! The platform was brightly lit though, and they decided to wait until the appropriate time, and see if others joined them. Just as they were seating themselves in the mid-section of the church, two black-robed men appeared and began striding quickly down the aisle on the right. The men mounted the platform and stood side by side behind a tall pedestal stand. Suddenly, the church was a blaze of lights as someone had pulled the switch on three huge chandeliers which pointed the way down the center aisle. Before their startled eyes, hundreds of icons appeared in bold living color. Beginning at the floor and extending about 8 feet in height were bigger than life-sized figures of holy men and women depicted in colorful stained-glass. Christ Jesus, Mary and Joseph were foremost among many saints. Above them on the walls and ceiling were hundreds of faces looking out into the audience. It was very hard to take their eyes from those amazing sights. Later, Eve said that she had started to count them, but gave up after a short time.

Finally, their watches showed it was 8:30, and one of the cantors on the platform began to chant in Greek. When he stopped, the other black-robed man recited verses, some of which were scriptures from the Bible and some other verses that further enhanced the story by relating it in a poetic manner.

It seemed a shame to the foursome that there weren't others in the church to enjoy the beautiful singing. Then, a priest in a cream-colored robe quietly approached their pew and handed each of them a copy explaining what was being enacted on stage. It made it much more meaningful to follow the liturgy which continued for the next hour.

Just before that portion of the service was over, several people entered the sanctuary. Then, another priest clad in a green and gold robe opened a door in the center of the enclosure behind the platform, and began swinging a smoking incense vial hanging from an attached chain. He strode down the aisle, and as he approached the congregation, he swung it in their direction, as they stood to face him and made the sign of the cross. They gestured from their forehead, down to their chest, to their right shoulder, then to the left. Some made the sign in sets of three.

Clarice and Jenny seemed to know what was going on, and participated in the service, even kneeling on the moveable rails in front of their pew. Adam and Eve tried to follow suit, but gave up after a time and just watched.

Finally, the priest walked down the aisle with an elaborate book in his hands. It appeared to have pictures on the cover, and as people were approached, they would kiss one or more of the pictures. At times, various people from the audience would approach and ascend the altar by using stairs on the left side. They then placed a tall crimson glass with a glowing candle inside in front of one of the icons on stage. The majority of them were placed at the foot of the icon depicting Christ Jesus and Mary, His mother. Evidently, the ritual was for special prayers requested or favors granted.

Prayers were recited by the priest for America, our leaders, those in public service, those who were ill or suffering, and many other needs.

God was asked to save and protect all those named by His very special grace. Then, communion was offered to the believers. A bit of bread was dipped into wine and served on a spoon to those who wished to indulge. For those who were not of the Greek Orthodox faith, something called, "Friendship Bread" was offered by an altar boy on each side.

A special half-hour service was held in honor of a member of the congregation who had passed away the year before. Prayers were said by the priests for his soul.

Finally, there was a message from one of the priests in English which encouraged people to examine themselves and determine if there was un-forgiveness in their hearts toward anyone. A scripture was quoted that stated that if we don't forgive others, God cannot forgive us either.

Everyone was invited to share coffee together in a special room on the lower level and fellowship together. As they had a very busy day ahead, they gracefully declined and made their departure.

Later, they pulled up to the dock that housed their boat. There she was, just waiting for them. Her pure white body was trimmed in turquoise and her name in big bold letters proudly proclaimed her given name, "The Land of Dreams." What a sight she was, just sitting there and obviously waiting to be admired. Indeed, she was admired too. Clarice and Jenny were very familiar with the sailboats in their area of the world, and claimed that they had never seen such a royal beauty.

The decision to spend the night aboard ship was rather exciting to them. Adam extended his hands to first one and then another helping them step on board. As Eve showed Clarice and Jenny about, Adam returned to the car for the groceries they had just purchased. Their plans were to have enough food onboard to prepare dinner that evening and breakfast the next morning.

The few steps from the deck down to the cabin were accompanied by squeals of delight as Clarice and Jenny were amazed by the compact area in which they would spend most of the next 24 hours. Admiration for the décor was expressed also as they admired the twin colors of the outer portion displayed again inside.

"Look at this," said Eve, "The cabin door folds to become a serving bar. Another good feature is the pop-up top of the cabin roof. It can be raised to a height of 6'4" and may stay upright even while sailing. Most sailboats' cabins really cramp your style. The roof must be lowered, and then you almost have to walk with your head down and shoulders hunched."

"How uncomfortable," Jenny interjected.

"Yes," Eve continued, "the bunks will accommodate a person 6'6" tall and the mattresses are so luxurious. Just like sleeping in your own bed at home. Five or six can sleep here quite easily, four will find their beds incredibly roomy."

"There is a saying about sailboats that we like." Adam had just put away the last of the groceries. "In a motorboat, you get there in a hurry, in a sailboat, you are already there."

"What does that mean?" asked Clarice.

"Well," said Adam, "I take it to mean that in your mind's eye, the destination is already in sight. Rather charming idea, don't you think?"

"Yes, of course. Sailboats are so much more relaxing too," stated Clarice. "My brother, Andreas used sailing as his hobby. Even though he spent weeks at a time in a whaling boat, there was a lot of tension there. To unwind, he usually took off in his sailboat shortly after coming back into port."

"So, the two of you weren't able to spend much time together?"

"No. Andreas was a driven-man. He had many bad memories that plagued him day and night.

"Bad memories of what?"

"Bad memories of losing his lovely wife, and of interfering in Jenny's life. Andreas expected everyone to share his beliefs, and when they didn't, he reacted with intense anger."

Jenny's eyes misted over as her own memories caught up with her. "I'm sure that he was disappointed in me so often. I just couldn't be the daughter he had hoped for."

"Now, now, my dear. Please don't feel that way. No one should have to live their lives in total subjection to someone else."

Then, seeing the concerned looks on the faces of Adam and Eve, Jenny quickly changed the subject. "Look," she said. "I'm going topside.

It's beginning to rain even though the sun is still shining. Spotting a rainbow means good fortune and I intend to see it first."

"Wait for me," Eve said as she sprang to her feet, "I'm going too."

Hours later, "Land of Dreams" pulled back into the dock. Gentle, warm rains had fallen most of the day. As they spent most of the time on deck, their clothing clung to their bodies. Laughing gleefully like children, they prepared to descend into the cabin and change to warm, dry attire.

Adam proudly exclaimed, "Did you notice that there was no water standing on deck after the rains?"

"Yes, indeed," Jenny responded. "That has always been a problem with sailboats. What's different about yours?"

"This model has a completely walk-able topside, and a self-bailing cockpit system. With this, we never have problems with water standing in puddles."

"Interesting!"

"Yes, this is a rather delicate matter, but another time-saver is the toilet. Instead of bringing water on-board for flushing, this system actually uses the lake water instead."

"That's hard to believe. It must remove much of the labor and time usually involved."

"Pardon me for changing the subject," interrupted Eve, "but is anyone hungry?"

"Oh my, yes," responded Adam.

Clarice and Jenny both nodded in agreement.

"Won't take long," Eve said. "I brought frozen salmon steaks along to grill and will make macaroni and cheese to accompany a fresh salad."

Thirty minutes later, while seated at the roomy pedestal table, and attired in dry clothing, they were all eating hungrily.

"How 'bout that gorgeous rainbow we saw today. It was an incredible prelude to exploring the lake," Eve said with a big smile.

"Have you ever seen a nighttime rainbow?" Jenny asked.

"No! How could that be?"

"Well, one evening, I was walking very close to a local waterfall. The moon was full and as it shone on the cascading water, colors of the rainbow actually seemed to ripple and vibrate as they glistened in the eerie-appearing light."

"Wow! Is that possible?" Adam said in awe.

"Well, possible nor not, I saw it!"

"Adam, it's still too early for bed. Shall we play a game or just talk?"

"Let's take a vote."

"Poker sounds good to me. We can still talk as we play and use toothpicks instead of money or chips."

Two hours later, they were amazed to find that Clarice had all the toothpicks piled in neat rows in front of her. They took a quick vote and decided that she would not have to help with breakfast dishes in lieu of obtaining a prize for her conquests.

"Guess it's time for bed," Adam noted. "I can't afford to play any longer."

"Nite! Nite!"

Monday morning, they were awakened by loud peals of thunder accompanied by a exhibition of jagged lighting that filled the cabin with tinges of greenish-yellow lights.

'Methinks it's time to rid ourselves of our sea-legs and head for shore," Adam noted.

"Sounds good to me, Honey," Eve responded.

After scurrying to straighten up the cabin and pack, it seemed appropriate to find a restaurant for brunch. "How about the one that opened just recently, Adam?"

"Which restaurant do you mean, Eve?"

"You know, the one in that lovely old house."

"Oh yes, I've heard good things about their food. It's called, 'Carlyle Manor' and is in the heart of town."

Very soon, they pulled up in front of a 3-story Victorian-style, turn-of-the-century house. After parking in the rear, and walking around to the front porch, they opened a door which led into an entry hall. The air was permeated by some of the most delicious smelling aromas they had ever encountered. A pleasant-looking white-haired woman greeted them and led the way to a table for four set up in an intimate alcove containing its own fireplace with glowing embers, and a matching reflection from the lit candles on the table. On such a gloomy day, it was the most perfect reception. The delicious lunch that followed more than met their expectations.

Driving home, Eve exclaimed, "Jenny, look at you. Your cheeks actually look sunburned. I guess it's from our boat ride yesterday. Clarice, you too have more color than before. Now, you won't need to apply rouge for a few days."

Adam glanced at Eve and smiled as he said, "My darling, you have a few more angel-kiss freckles on your nose."

"Oh Adam, I forgot all about sunscreen. It didn't seem that warm. You too, got a dose of the sun. Your olive-toned skin is more olive than before."

"Well," he responded, "I suppose we all look a bit more healthy."

The drive home was enhanced for him by the lively chatter of his three lovely ladies. As Adam did not feel any input from him was required, he allowed himself to reflect on the events of the last few days, and of how easily his long-lost family members were beginning to entwine themselves around his heart and emotions.

As the car pulled into the driveway, they all agreed that since it was already 4:00 p.m., they would not require a regular dinner that evening, and a snack of freshly popped corn would probably fit the bill.

CHAPTER IX

While enjoying their individual bowls of popcorn, Eve asked Jenny to tell them of her family. "I think it's time we really understand more about your current lifestyle, Jenny. I assume your children are grown now and living on their own. Is that true?

"Yes, that's true, Eve."

"What do you do personally?" Eve further queried.

"My late husband, Harold, the father of my other two children, was a baker by trade. He owned his own pastry shop and I continue to operate it now with the help of Clarice. Due to our current vacation, the shop is closed until our return. In our absence, it is being remodeled and several new ovens are being installed. Everything needed to be updated."

"What happened to your husband?" inquired Adam.

"Actually, I suppose he just died of old age. He passed away 6 months ago at the age of 86, after just gradually fading away. However, he kept in touch with his bakery to the end. He worked there every day until he was 80, and then turned the total responsibility over to me."

"He was 86 years of age?" Eve asked in a shocked manner. "But, you are so much younger!"

Yes, I was 18 when we were wed; he was 54."

"How did you happen to fall in love with a man who was old enough to be your grandfather?"

"My father, Andreas, made the arrangements. When I was 16 years of age, Harold requested a formal meeting with my father. Harold had been a childless widower for several years and wanted a wife and someone who could help in his shop."

Eve's eyes rolled with amazement, and she asked, "How could your father even think of such a thing?"

"Some of the young females in Greece at that time had few options. They did as their families dictated. I had no mother to try to change his mind, and my father thought it would bring financial security to me and would allow him not to be concerned about me when he was out to sea. His only stipulation was that we would not marry until I reached the age of 18."

Jenny let out a loud sigh and continued her story. "Greek girls usually married at quite a young age, sometimes as early as 14 years old. This was supposed to guarantee their virginity at marriage. Young men usually performed military service before marriage and typically got married around the age of 30. The females married whenever their father or male guardian agreed upon a date. Andreas was being very lenient in allowing me to wait until age 18 to marry Harold."

"So," asked Adam, "you were 17 years old when you met Luke, my father?"

"Yes, Andreas was out to sea for a 6-week period at that time. Luke and I met and, as they say, fell in love at first sight. He was so handsome, charming, and we had such fun together. After only one week, we knew we wanted to be together forever, and were also aware that he could be shipped out at any time. We went to the local court house and were married."

"How did you manage to spend time alone?"

"Luke obtained an R & R, which is a brief military leave of absence, and means time off for rest and recreation. We spent two weeks together in a little rented cottage in a village just 30 miles from home. I told Clarice that I was visiting a friend, so she wouldn't worry about me."

"Oh my," sighed Eve. "What a tragic story. It must have been so hard when Luke got his orders to go to France."

"It was. When he left, we weren't aware that we had conceived a child together." With that, Jenny began to sob. Her head dropped and her shoulders shook as she was forced, once again, to recall her lost love.

As Adam saw her grief, he knelt on the floor in front of her chair and took her hands in his. He too, felt hot tears sting his eyelids. "Oh Jenny," he said. "I'm so sorry that we've been parted for all these years. During the past few days, I've grown to feel so close to you. May I call you mother?"

With that, Jenny's tears actually began to bounce off her bodice, but she looked into Adam's tenderly, serious face and responded, "Oh Adam, how happy that would make me." She threw both arms around his neck and hugged him to her bosom.

By this time, Clarice and Eve were weeping also, and in keeping with the scene, they stood to their feet and embraced one another.

Afterwards, Eve distributed tissues, and the conversation continued. Adam wanted to know how his grandfather reacted to the news of his daughter's marriage and pregnancy.

Jenny continued her story: "Cretan families were very unhappy about a foreign suitor for their daughters, but many of them would also disapprove of a Greek from outside of Crete. Their saying was, 'First a Cretan, then a Greek.' In social life, nothing is more important than preserving the honor of ones' family."

"That seems very prejudiced," Eve noted.

"Yes, well that is just the way it was. My father refused to believe I would ignore his plans for my life and marry someone without permission. He never met Luke as his orders to be shipped out came before Andreas returned. In his fury, my father went to the town hall, and because he was so well known in the community, was allowed to view my marriage record. Evidently, he just took it because years later when I went to make copies, there was no trace of it.

"But, didn't you get a copy of it when you were married?"

"Yes, but that disappeared also. When my father discovered I was expecting a baby, he sent me away. I was placed in a home for unwed mothers. To earn our board and keep, we did laundry, mending and cooking for local wealthy families. When you were born, Adam, I had been sedated. As I told you before, they informed me that you had been stillborn. Two months later, on my 18th birthday, I was forced to marry Harold. That was the initial agreement between the two men, that Harold would wait until I was 18 years of age."

"What a birthday present!" gasped Eve. "How could you possibly tolerate a husband of that age, and someone you didn't love?"

"I had no choice. By that time, I knew your father had been killed, Adam. So, even though there was no longer an official license that could be located pertaining to our marriage, I realized I was indeed a widow. As I had no rights according to my father, and he had promised my hand in marriage to Harold, I had no recourse but to marry him."

"Did you tell Harold of my father?"

"No, I never did. It was a secret that I shut up within myself all those years."

"How could you, as a lovely 18 year-old young woman, stand to be married to a man of that age?"

"I had known Harold and his first wife for many years. Their bakery was the only one in town. When his wife died, I was 12 years of age. I felt very sorry that he was all alone. Before we were married, he asked to speak with me in private one evening at my home. My father was there, but he allowed us to sit in the parlor and discuss the future. Harold told me that he was aware of the big difference in our ages, and that I would probably never be able to love him as a husband. But, he assured me that I would be allowed plenty time to adjust to him and his ways, and that his home had two bedrooms. The first one had belonged to him and his wife, and the second one was to be mine alone as long as I wanted it."

"That's quite amazing. If he was willing to marry someone who did not want to be with him, I'm surprised he didn't insist on his marital rights."

"Harold was actually a very kind and gentle man. He would not have dreamed of violating my rights. Mainly, he wanted a companion and someone to care for his home and cook his meals. We were married for over a year before becoming physically intimate. That happened quite by accident too. One evening, I awoke to a terrible thunder storm. It was the type that shakes the whole house and illuminates its interior. The noise was extremely loud; I became terrified and ran into Harold's bedroom. He jumped up to embrace me and bring me comfort. As the storm continued, I just lay in his arms, feeling his love and protection. We went to sleep holding one another and never slept apart again. Nine months later, we were blessed with twin babies, a boy and a girl. We named them Sarah and Samuel."

"Was he a good father?"

"He certainly was a good father to our children. Actually, he was a father-figure of sorts to me also. I had never known the love of a father, and Harold was a loving caretaker, and later became a wonderful friend to me. Even though I was never sexually attracted to him as I was to your father, Adam, I loved him very much. Losing Harold has been extremely difficult."

"Oh Jenny, I'm so glad you have had happiness, even though it wasn't what you envisioned."

"Adam, you must meet your siblings. They are 30 years of age now, not much younger then you."

"I really want to meet them. Are they married?"

"Yes, I already have four grandchildren."

"Wow!"

All the while, Clarice had been silent. Now they had questions for her too. But...tomorrow was another day.

Tuesday morning at breakfast, they had a discussion about what might be of most interest to all. As Adam and Eve were aware of the local choices, they wrote down a few options, folded the papers over and threw them in the center of the table.

"Who should choose?" queried Eve.

"I think Clarice should choose. She had no chance to talk at all last night," Adam suggested.

"Okay, I will choose." Clarice's right hand reached out and took the paper closest to her. "I see you have five, one for each of our remaining days with you."

As she opened her choice, her eyes lit up. "The St. Louis Zoo. Wonderful!"

"Good," said Adam. "I enjoy our zoo so much. It's rated one of the best in the country, and has more than 3,000 animals there. I understand the San Diego Zoo is still number one, and St Louis is rated number two. Don't forget," he added, "you will certainly need your walking shoes today."

The two ladies disappeared quickly into the guest bedroom to change their clothing.

An hour later, they pulled up in front of the zoo. Adam always preferred to park on the street rather than in the zoo's parking lot. It was a challenge to find a spot nearby.

"Why don't you all get out here, and I'll join you soon. Just take a seat inside the entrance way. There's no need to pay as our zoo is free to all visitors."

"How can they pay for upkeep and expenses?" queried Jenny.

"Our tax dollars allocate funds to sustain it and pay the salaries. This is one of the prides of St. Louis. The state legislation decreed that 17 acres of ground in Forest Park would be allocated to the zoo, and that it would always be free to visitors."

It seemed they had no sooner passed through the turnstile before Adam rejoined them. "Lion country is one of my favorites," he said. "The lions, tigers and panthers are no longer confined behind bars in a building. Now, they are actually out in the open in their customary habitats. It's been noted that they are much more content this way."

As he spoke, they all walked in the direction of Lion Country. It was a bit of a climb from the regular ground level. Adam took Clarice's arm to aid her, but she proved to be quite agile.

"At home, I walk for miles on a daily basis," she said. "Eighty-one is no longer really considered old," she said, revealing her age with a grin.

Ascending to a higher level, they found an amazing sight below. At depths of about 50 feet, all types of huge feline creatures either lay sleepily in the bright sunshine, or prowled about as though looking for food. Sometimes, they would gaze up at their unwelcome visitors, sometimes they totally ignored them. The grounds of their current home appeared as grassy knolls. Safely watching from above was pure pleasure.

Next, they enjoyed the monkey house where the primates were enclosed behind bars. One happy little chimp hung from black steel rods by both feet and chattered happily while watching them as he too, was being watched.

Shuffling on to the next cage, they all laughed aloud while viewing a mother monkey fastidiously groom her child by picking fleas from his coat of fur and devouring them before they could hop away, or once more, be trapped on his chubby little body.

The next cage featured baboons whose claim to fame was their bulbous rear ends, flamboyant in hues of hot pinks and purples. They proudly strutted about as though aware of their unique beauty.

Gasping for fresh air, Clarice groped her way out of doors, thinking she had seen the end of primates for the day. Instead, she was greeted by a huge ape in a ten foot, outdoor cage all alone. As she gazed at him, he returned her attention with a sneer. Then, picking something up from the floor, he drew back his arm, aimed, and threw a huge piece of fecal matter at her. She instinctively ducked, and then understood with gratitude, why the bars of this cage were enclosed in glass. The ugly stream of debris tossed at her split and ran down the inner portion of the enclosure.

Just then, Adam joined her outside and laughed, saying, "Clarice, I'm so sorry. I forgot to warn you. That ill-tempered guy has been here for years. That seems to be the only trick he knows!"

Their next stop was the Reptile House. As they entered, they noted a circular handrail with a drop-off on the other side. Gazing up at them was a huge crocodile widely grinning showing many pointed teeth, and exhibiting a wicked gleam in his eyes.

Adam laughed and said, "If you are ever chased by a crocodile and he catches up with you, don't ever turn sideways. That makes it too easy to snap off an arm or leg."

Eve hastily agreed that she would never turn sideways if chased by a crocodile; she would just keep on running!

Various types of snakes behind glass receptacles either napped or hissed menacingly at them as they, like little children, tapped on the cages. "Wow," said Jenny. "I've heard of king cobras, and viewed their pictures, but have never seen one in real life. Look how he supports himself with the coiled-up section of his body, while swaying back and forth spitting venom. I saw a movie once where the cobra moved to the rhythm of a snake-charmer's musical instrument, a flute I believe. That's certainly not a profession I would choose."

"Just recently," Adam responded, "a local man owned a Black Maumba Cobra as a pet. It eventually turned on him, and bit his hand. He had presence of mind to call the zoo and request anti-venom serum. Luckily, they had some stored up, and his life was spared."

"What a temperamental playmate," Eve said. "I wonder what would possess someone to keep such a dangerous creature in their home?"

"There are people who have a natural fascination for snakes," responded Adam. "And some actually enjoy living on the edge."

"Let's go visit the seals. I enjoy them so much," said Eve. "They flop in and out of the water all day long, and the males try to stake their claim by daring the others to inhabit their territory. Also, they are out-of-doors, and as the day is sunny and bright, it will be much more pleasant than being indoors with all those musky odors."

While walking along outside, Adam told them of a huge gorilla named Phil that had been one of the zoo's most prized possessions for many years, actually from 1941 to 1958. Even after his demise, he remained a local star after being stuffed and put on display in the gift shop.

Soon, they approached a hotdog stand. Across from it was an interesting structure built in the mode of a Chinese pagoda. It was a leftover from the 1904 St. Louis World's Fair. The colors of red and green were rather faded as they had borne the St. Louis sun for many years, and the paint that remained was actually peeling. Turning their attention back to the outdoor walkup restaurant, they ordered a very simple lunch. The round tables with circular benches were a most welcome sight. They had not had the opportunity to sit down for several hours. After eating, they agreed to attend the elephant show next, and that it would be the grand finale for the afternoon.

"This has been a real fast-food day," Eve observed as she placed pizza purchased on the way home on everyone's plate. "Let's all get comfy in the living room as we enjoy our dinner," she said. They had all removed their walking shoes and walked about comfortably in their stocking feet.

"I can't believe we have so little time left to spend with you," noted Clarice. "It's been so enjoyable getting to know both of you, and being made to feel so welcome in your home."

"Yes," said Eve. "It's hard to realize that very soon, Adam and I will be alone again. You have both become beloved members of our family."

"You must visit us too. Then, you can meet our other family members, and view our home, the bakery, and last but not least, the many scenic beauties Crete has to offer."

"We would love to," agreed Eve. "Last night, Adam and I spoke of possibly renewing our marriage vows in Crete with you and your family in attendance."

"Oh my, that would be lovely. We would be so happy to help make the arrangements. Do you wish to be married in church?"

"Absolutely!" Adam and Eve chimed in unison.

Adam went on to say, "Jenny…I mean Mom… You and Dad were married by a Justice of the Peace as we were. At the time, we couldn't plan a church wedding, and we certainly could not afford it. Next spring would be ideal for us."

"Wonderful," Jenny said. "That will give us a year to make the arrangements."

"Okay, that's settled. Now, let's make our plans for tomorrow. What is your pleasure, ladies?"

"Well," said Jenny. "When we purchased a few things at the drug store yesterday, I happened to notice some St. Louis post cards and souvenir key chains. Many of them featured something called, 'The Gateway Arch.' What is it? A local landmark?"

"Yes, Jenny, it is." Adam went on to tell her about some of its history. "It was completed just recently and took 5 years to construct. The huge stainless steel horseshoe-shaped structure was constructed with possible ground movement in mind so it seems to sway a bit when you're at the top. It is the crown jewel of St. Louis and is the world's largest monument standing at 630 feet tall and 630 wide at its base. It sways up to 18" and the foundation is 60 feet underground. It symbolizes the Spirit of St. Louis, the 'Gateway to the West.'"

"You don't mean that people go all the way to the top of the arch?" gasped Clarice.

"Yes, indeed they do. We will travel to the top in a funny little enclosure that looks somewhat like a seat on a Ferris wheel. The car rocks back and forth all the way and it could tend to make you feel a bit queasy. Of course, it is a great adventure. Once the car reaches the top, you disembark and walk slightly uphill in a narrow area with windows on both sides. When the apex is reached, you gradually walk down a slope toward the other side."

"I don't think I want to go," Clarice said nervously.

"Don't worry, it's completely safe. They wouldn't allow you to travel to the top if it weren't," Adam assured her.

"Well, what's the point of going up?" asked Jenny.

"On a clear day, you can see much of downtown St. Louis on one side and the great Mississippi River on the other," said Adam.

"Isn't that the river that gamblers used for travel to New Orleans?" Jenny asked. "I read about that in several books. Although, I assume it's been quite some time since that was allowed."

"Well, enough about history. Dress very casually again, and wear your hiking shoes," Eve suggested. "We will have to walk from a nearby parking lot and will probably have lunch at a riverfront restaurant. Some of the streets in that area are made of cobblestone and make for a rather unsteady footing."

They all went to their respective bedrooms and changed their attire to suit their next adventure.

"Oh, I almost forgot," Adam said. "There is an incredibly interesting museum at the base of the Gateway Arch. You will find that worth seeing too."

"Goodness!" said Jenny as she craned her neck while walking from the parking lot. She held onto Clarice's arm to steady herself while looking skyward to see the top of the arch. "That's an amazing structure. How tall did you say it is?"

"Six hundred and thirty feet," replied Adam.

"Let's take the elevator to the top before viewing the museum. There are just a few people waiting at this time. Then, we can explore the museum until lunch time," suggested Eve.

"Sounds good to me," Adam replied.

Soon, they were on their way to the top, riding comfortably in their own private car. Looking through an array of windows, they were aware of bright sunlight as they walked to the apex. Eve put on her sunglasses. Gazing down at the river on the right revealed sunlit ripples in the gentle waves of the Mississippi River. Several barges were moving downstream. On the left side of the arch appeared many office buildings, hotels, and the ballpark in downtown St. Louis. After 20 minutes, they were satisfied with what they had seen, and took the car back to the lower level, and then walked to the museum area.

Entering the Museum of Westward Expansion, they were amazed to see a four-story movie screen which showed the actual building of the Gateway Arch. The museum itself contained many Lewis and Clark artifacts depicting the westward journey beginning at the Ohio River and traveling all the way to the Pacific Ocean. All in all, they traveled 8,300 miles in three years. The amazing part of the story is that they journeyed through Indian Territory most of the way, and many of the Indians were not sociable.

"Oh my," said Jenny. "Look at those rare Indian peace medals. I remember reading about the pilgrims, Indians and cowboys of America in grade-school. What an interesting history your country has."

"No more so than yours," responded Adam. "There were many invaders through the years in Greece also. One of whom was Alexander the Great, the man from whom we received our surname."

"Yes," said Clarice. "We could tell you many stories that have been passed down from generation to generation. Maybe we'll have time to share some with you and Eve later."

The exhibit included a tepee, covered-wagon, and even an Indian war bonnet covered in feathers.

"It's hard to imagine living in those days," Eve said, as she opened the teepee's flap and peered inside. "No running water or cook stove. How could you live like that? There would be no privacy at all, and besides their children, the elder members of the family also shared their tepee."

Clarice laughed and said, "Can you imagine the four of us living together in those cramped quarters?"

That evening, the compatible foursome decided to take a relaxing swim in the subdivision's indoor pool. All but Clarice splashed about in the water. She preferred to relax in a lounge chair as she gazed fondly at her precious family members. Realizing that their time together was quickly drawing to a close, she knew it was time to share the family secret that had burned in her breast for years. Now, she was the only one who knew this particular bit of information, and the time had come to share it. As she recalled the situation, her heart began to beat more rapidly and she prayed silently for wisdom on how to share it, and that the hearers could tolerate the knowledge, especially her beloved Jenny.

"There's a bit of a chill in the air now. Who's in the mood for a bit of wine, cheese and crackers?" asked Eve. "The day has been lovely, but quite long and tiring."

"Sounds good to me," Adam responded.

The general agreement was that a nice warm shower followed by donning their pajamas and robes would be most comfy. As the May evening had turned rather cool, Adam built a fire in the fireplace for the cozy effect it generated.

Soon, they all sat comfortably with a glass of wine and snacks. The warmth of the fire and the glow on their faces in the dimly-lit room helped exude an aura of well-being in each. It appeared obvious that they would soon retire for the night, when Clarice spoke rather abruptly, almost as though forcing herself to do so.

"There is something I must share with all of you, but Jenny will be the one most affected."

"Why, Clarice. You seem a bit upset," responded Jenny. "Is something wrong?"

"Jenny, there is something I should have told you years ago, but it never seemed to be the right time. Your life wasn't easy, and I didn't want to tell you any sad stories."

"Clarice, please! Go on with your story!"

"Jenny, as you know, your father and I were twins. During our youth, we were very close. He was a good person and extremely fun-loving at one time."

"My goodness," retorted Jenny. "That must have been long before I was born. He always seemed so cold and rigid to me. It was as though I was a terrible burden to him."

"My dear," said Clarice with tears gathering in the corners of her eyes, "he loved you so very much, but felt inadequate to rear a young female child."

"Yes, I know my mother died when I was only 3 years of age, and I was such a responsibility for a sea-going man to handle. Without your help, I don't know what either of us would have done."

"What I have to tell you is regarding Vivian, your mother. She was lovely in personality and looks alike. As a typical Greek girl, she loved to dance. Every festival found her such a delight, a joyous and free spirit. She used to carry you in her arms and dance through the house with you as she sang lively melodies."

"Oh, how I wish I could remember her!"

"Very few people have memories that extend back that early in their youth."

"I remember seeing a musical instrument in our home that she used to play. It was kept in a case; then suddenly it disappeared."

"Yes, that was a lyre. Vivian had a great love of music in every form."

"They never discovered the cause of her early demise, did they?" asked Jenny.

"Jenny, they *did* know what was wrong with her. What I must tell you is that she did not die when you were 3 years of age."

"Oh, when did she die?"

"Vivian had you at age 19. You were told she died at age 22. That isn't correct. She had to leave you at that time."

"Leave me?" Jenny cried out in alarm.

"Yes, she left you, Jenny. She had no choice."

"What happened?" Jenny whispered.

"Vivian was forced to move away by the towns folks."

"Why?"

"She had leprosy!"

CHAPTER X

Current Year—Late Springtime

A few days earlier, Eve had taken a test prescribed by her doctor. It was called the "Mini Mental State Examination." It took only half an hour, but gave more information regarding her mental status. She was told to count backward from ten, say the months of the year backward, and draw a clock while indicating a time of day on it.

When Adam asked Eve about the test, she proudly said, "It was a scholastic exam required of all the students in our nation. They gave me a test on the Gettysburg Address by Abraham Lincoln. I did very well, I am sure. It has always been one of my favorite speeches."

That explained the manner in which Eve had been speaking lately. Just yesterday, when he read an article on Alzheimer's recommended at the doctor's office, there was instant confirmation. It spoke of a term, "salad mix", used for some who were afflicted with Alzheimer's. Those affected often spoke in jumbled terms which did not pertain to what they were asked. They thought their response was appropriate, but it was not.

Adam had asked Eve if she would like to take a walk, and her response was, "Darling, a shopping trip to Macy's sounds like fun."

Such a simple remark, but it did not apply to anything he had asked. Thinking back over the last several months, there had been similar responses. Very rarely, did she initiate the conversation, and when she attempted to answer his questions, she did so with totally unrelated responses. Sometimes, Adam felt as though he were the one who was confused.

Now a decision must be made. Could he be a constant caretaker for Eve? His health was reasonably good, with the exception of arthritis in his knees. What about the times when he would have to go shopping, or run errands? It was almost impossible to take her along. She would just wander off. He could certainly not leave her alone at home. The thought of putting her in a nursing home was intolerable.

There were agencies that had a staff of part-time workers who could be hired for an hour or two at a time. However, each time you requested help, you were very likely to get a different person, one who had no awareness of your loved one's condition, and had to be briefed each time they visited. A variety of different people in their home each time might cause Eve to become more confused than ever.

Having assessed their options, Adam decided to visit a local retirement center. "Family Woods" had received nationwide awards for their multi-faceted types of top-notch arrangements. The initial plan was to provide an apartment for people who could no longer maintain their own homes. It was a step beyond condos which had maintenance-free exteriors, lawn care, and snow removal provided for a monthly fee.

"Family Woods" provided the main meal of the day, nurses to dispense medications, cleaning and laundry services. The apartments were unfurnished and decorating with your own furniture made it seem more like home. This arrangement seemed ideal as Adam could live there too, and monitor Eve's activities each day.

If and when the time came for Eve to have more intense care from health care workers, she could be transferred to the building next door where she would be in a closed ward with professionals to constantly oversee her.

Adam had just stepped out on the front porch that wrapped halfway around their home. He walked down the steps to collect their daily newspaper when he spied their next door neighbor, Melissa Barber. Melissa was a lovely young woman 23 years of age. They had known her since she was a baby, and almost felt she was part of their family. She graduated from college early due to excellent grades, and was now enrolled in a nursing program. Ministering to the elderly had always been a passion of hers as her grandmother had lived with her family until just recently. Melissa's pre-med was being utilized at the facility Adam had just been thinking of.

"Hello Mr. Alexander," she exclaimed. "Beautiful weather, isn't it? If my place of employment were closer, I'd love to ride my bike to work this morning."

"Good morning, Melissa. Yes, it's one of those types of days when you can't seem to stay indoors," enjoined Adam.

Having exchanged these pleasantries, Melissa inquired as usual about Eve. "How is your beautiful wife? I haven't seen her working in her rose garden all summer."

Adam said, "Well Melissa, Eve seems to be extremely depressed, can't seem to keep her mind focused on what she is talking about, and sleeps so much. Her appetite has been affected and she appears to be losing strength."

"Has she seen her doctor?" queried Melissa.

"Yes, I'm afraid she has. I took her to our family doctor recently. After examining her, he recommended a test to determine her ability to comprehend. It didn't take long to discover she is in the early stages of Alzheimer's."

"Oh my," Melissa spoke with great sympathy, "I understand completely what you're going through. Some of the patients where I work have Alzheimer's. Much research is being done to provide a cure, but so far, they have been unsuccessful. However, they have gained more knowledge regarding the symptoms and how to help their families and caregivers deal with the situation."

"Melissa, this is so new to me that I can't begin to formulate a plan. There must be something we can do to halt its progress."

"Sir, I am so sorry. As of now, we can only hope and pray that there are enough funds and interested agencies to pursue a cure."

"You are too young to remember, Melissa, but years ago, there was no vaccine or cure for polio. It is mandatory now that all children get shots to prevent it when they are babies, and polio is now almost a thing of the past.

One of our greatest presidents, Franklin Delano Roosevelt, contacted polio. He was an incredibly brave man, and tried to camouflage his disability and the wheelchair to which he was confined. Due to his brilliance, combined with that of our allies, and primarily Sir Winston Churchill, we won World War II.

There was a time when polio was on the rampage. Children were not allowed to play in neighborhood swimming pools. FDR contacted polio after swimming one day off the coast of Canada; he became chilled and ill immediately due to the frosty temperature of the water. The high fever that ensued turned out to be the prelude to polio.

Not only were people's limbs and walking abilities affected by polio, some even had to live in what was called an 'iron lung.' Their own lungs were affected, and they couldn't breathe without its aide. They had to lie on their backs and were completely enclosed in the iron contraption with the exception of their necks and head. The machine actually breathed for them."

"Yes, Mr. Alexander, I seem to remember that from my history class. President Roosevelt actually passed away before the war ended which caused a tremendous outpouring of grief in our country. He was so loved by his countrymen. The polio must have affected his heart and lungs also. As I recall, he died of a heart attack. What a shame that he wasn't able to see the outcome of his tremendous efforts to help end the war!"

"Melissa, I understand that 'Family Woods' is known for their diverse facilities and aid to people in need. As Eve is no longer able to care for herself properly and running errands and making meals while caring for her is now a problem, I am considering talking to the director there. Would you mind giving me his name, and possibly a referral?"

"I would be most happy to help in any way I can. The director's name is Mr. Lon Cambry. He is a man of great compassion, understanding and knowledge. If you like, I would be most happy to introduce you to him when it's convenient. Do you plan to take Mrs. Alexander with you?"

"I probably won't take Eve the first time. I would like to be free to speak with Mr. Cambry with no distractions. There is a neighbor with whom I leave Eve at times when I cannot care for her."

Well, I mustn't be late for work, Sir. I will pick up some literature that you might be interested in and bring it to you this evening. It might be helpful to read it before making an appointment. Then, you would know what to inquire about. See you later."

Adam stooped to pick up the newspaper, and with a very deep sigh, turned to return to his home and check on Eve's activities.

After settling down in his recliner, Adam opened the newspaper and saw a headline that almost screamed out at him "Alzheimer's Patient Killed on Highway." The attached article went on to say, "Elderly man recently admitted to Family Woods Nursing Facility met his demise while crossing the highway late last night. An oncoming car was unable to stop in time, and the man was tossed up onto the vehicle's windshield and killed. The victim's family could not accept their doctor's diagnosis of Alzheimer's and refused to have him placed in a locked ward. As he was in a regular room, he merely slipped out the door when the nurse's station was unmanned."

Adam heard himself say aloud, "Eve my darling, that will never happen to you. I will always be here to care for you. Then, realizing he was talking to himself he called out, "Eve, where are you?"

CHAPTER XI

Spring—1973 (cont'd)

There was a stunned silence as Jenny and the others felt they were going into shock.

"Leprosy! Oh my God. That's fatal, isn't it?"

"Yes, my dear."

"Why didn't they allow her to die at home?"

"Some people feel it is contagious."

"Is it?"

"They're not really sure. There are scientists in the medical profession who believe it may be caused by a virus. Anyway, they couldn't take a chance."

"How did they know she had leprosy?" Adam asked.

"Vivian started to wear clothing that almost completely covered her up. She had always worn light, airy garments as she was such a free spirit, and didn't want to be burdened down with dark cumbersome garments."

"Was it in the winter time?" queried Jenny

"No, it was during the spring and summer. She would dress you in rather flimsy cotton sun suits as you enjoyed playing outside in the dirt."

"Who, me? I remember always being clad in clean, but drab garments."

"That was because your father dressed you in that manner. Men don't know how to dress a 3 year-old girl."

"Well, then what happened?"

"Vivian's skin began to change. It was rather difficult to see as it happened so gradually. First, I noticed bright red bumps on her neck and hands. The rest of her body was always covered. Then, those spots began to turn white, but looked rather indented."

"Indented?"

"Yes, as though her skin had grooves in it. One day, I entered their home after knocking and not receiving an answer. Vivian was standing at the table containing the water pitcher and bowl used for taking sponge baths. Her shoulders and upper arms were bare. They appeared to be covered with lesions. When she saw me, she gasped and tried to cover her body."

"What did you do then, Clarice?"

"I instinctively reached out for her, and she slapped my hands and turned away. She once again put on that heavy, dark cloak-type garment and sat on the bed and cried with her face in her hands."

"Oh dear. Where was I?" asked Jenny apprehensively.

"You were playing in the corner with a doll and hardly seemed to notice."

"Where was my father?"

"He was out to sea, and had been gone for about 6 weeks."

"Then, he probably didn't know what was happening."

"That's true. He was concerned at that time about the scarcity of sperm whales and was trying hard to earn a living for his family."

"Did my mother finally agree to talk to you?"

"Yes, she was so concerned and frightened about the changes in her body. I think it helped her to finally be able to confide in someone."

"Did you take her to a doctor?"

"Yes, I did. He looked at her and noted that places on her head had turned white and the hair follicles had turned yellow. The hair on her arms where the bad areas had turned the skin from red to white now had white hair growing. Vivian had an olive-complexion and the white patches on her arms were very noticeable."

"What did the doctor say? What was his diagnosis?"

"He said he wanted her to treat all the areas on her body with salve and return the following week. But, when we returned, the condition was even worse. Andreas was due home within the next day or two, and she was terrified that he would see her like that."

"How horrible that must have been to see your body change in that way and not be able to confide in anyone about it."

"Yes, it must have been. She should have told me sooner, but she was so humiliated."

"Well, what did you do?"

"I offered to care for you so she could just rest and try to see if she could get better."

"Did she take you up on your offer?"

"Yes, she did. It seemed that she had not been able to really care for herself properly. Tending to a 3 year-old child and a home takes lots of time and energy."

Eve just sat in wide-eyed rapt attention: "What happened then, Clarice?"

"I remembered that the Bible spoke of leprosy as though it was a rather common thing, and I decided to see what it had to say about it. Surely, I felt, it must have been a punishment on the person who had contacted it."

"Was that the case?"

"If it was, I couldn't be sure that it was true. I did see that the priests would examine the afflicted person and send them out of the camp for a period of time, actually for a whole week. Then, they were allowed to return and be re-examined. If the symptoms had vanished, they were allowed to return to their homes. If not, they were sent to a leper colony. Everywhere they went, if they came into contact with others, they had to cry out, "Unclean! Unclean!""

"Why was that?"

"Because others thought they could catch the disease, and that would give them the opportunity to get away from the afflicted person."

"How was it tested?"

"If their garments began to turn reddish or green in hue, their clothing was burned by fire. That meant it was true that they had leprosy. Then, their homes were tested. If the walls had either of those colors at the baseboard, the walls had to be scraped off and the scrapings burned. The walls were then re-plastered. If the colors bled through after all that, the house had to be torn down and all the materials used to build it were totally removed from the area. That meant the disease had infiltrated the whole home and might be transmitted to the other residents."

"Ghastly," said Adam.

"What happened then?" queried Eve.

"When Andreas returned home, the village physician was waiting for him on the dock and very bluntly informed him that his wife had leprosy and had to be removed to the colony for people in that condition."

"What a homecoming!"

"Yes, Andreas was never the same after that fateful day. He leapt from the boat onto the dock and intended to run home to be with his family, but the doctor caught him by the arm and told him in no uncertain terms that his wife was going to be banished that very day."

"What a lack of tact and understanding!"

"You must realize that people were terrified about contacting the disease."

"Vivian was forced to leave their home right then. It seems the doctor was not discreet, and had told many others of the situation before making it known to Andreas."

"So…did my mother die right away?"

"No, my dear. She died at age 37, when you were 18 years of age— actually, right around the time of Adam's birth."

Jenny sobbed uncontrollably. "Why wasn't I told? I would have gone to her!"

"Your father knew that and he could not allow it. He tried to protect you always."

"Protect me! He stole my life from me. First, he stole my mother, then Adam, my son! Oh, how I hate him!"

"Please, please don't say that. He did what he felt was best for you. You look so much like your mother, and he was pained every time he looked at you."

"Where did my mother go?"

"Vivian was taken to a leper colony. Andreas used to visit her there until she was around 28 years of age. Finally, her condition got so much worse that she would no longer see him. When she heard news that his ship was pulling into the harbor, she told her associates to tell him to leave."

"Oh Clarice," Jenny gasped between sobs, "How terrible for you. Knowing the whole story and keeping up a front for me."

"Then you are not angry with me, Jenny?"

"Of course not, I know what a hard man my Dad was and you could not have gone against his wishes."

"Jenny, do you realize that you called Andreas, Dad? That's the first time you ever called him anything but father."

Jenny put her head down in her arms and sobbed and sobbed. Clarice arose and put her arms around her to bring her comfort.

"Dear Clarice, suddenly I am filled with love and understanding for my father. What a sad and lonely life he must have led. If only he could have shared his grief with me, we might have helped one another."

"Jenny, I suppose the pain never went away. He loved your mother more than life itself, so there wasn't much left over. He was a very angry man—angry with others—angry with life—even angry with God."

"Clarice, I can see it all now. I understand."

"Jenny, do you feel you can forgive him? I realize he's gone, but for your own sake, can you release all the hurts of the past?"

"I'll try. Someone else has been deeply affected by this too."

"Who?"

"Adam, my son."

All the while, Adam and Eve sat almost without breathing as they heard secrets pour out of Clarice and watched them permeate Jenny's heart. The couple was absolutely stunned. Eve glanced at her husband and instinctively knew his heart was filled with pain also. He too, had been taken from his mother, taken immediately after his birth.

Adam rose to his feet and excused himself. "I'm sorry," he said. "This revelation is a hard one for me too. I must sleep on it."

Eve arose and excused herself after inquiring if there might be anything their guests needed before retiring for the night. When they declined, she followed Adam to their bedroom. As he lay there with heart pounding, she wrapped her arms about him and softly whispered, "Darling, I understand, and I am so very sorry. I love you."

Adam declined to respond.

In the morning, the usual banter that had become so normal among the foursome was absent. The red, swollen eyes of both mother and son told the story. Eve tried to offer a few light-hearted casual comments, but the only one who appeared to hear was Clarice.

"Yes, Eve. I think a visit to the art museum in Forest Park would be of special interest to us. Jenny and I always like to expand our horizons by learning as much as possible everywhere we go."

Jenny piped up and said, "Adam, I realize last night's revelation affected you as much as it did me. If you and Eve would prefer to be alone today, there is a bus tour of downtown St. Louis which Clarice and I would certainly enjoy. Please don't feel you must devote all your time to entertaining us."

"Jenny," began Adam, "I mean, Mom, we don't want to be anywhere without you. We are family and soon you will return to Crete. Let's make the most of every moment. Last night's revelation was an overwhelming shock to me, as it was to you. Hopefully, before you depart, we will have made our peace with it. Maybe we should encourage Clarice to share a bit more with us regarding your parents, and my grandparents."

"Thank you, Adam. You're a very compassionate person, and I'm so proud of you."

"Well Eve, let's make our plans for the day. I want them to see one of my favorite displays at the St. Louis Art Museum in Forest Park. You remember the Egyptian mummy with one black toe exposed? For years, every time I revisited, I expected his toe to fall off and disappear, but it remained constant—an ugly black blob."

"Yes, Adam. The restaurant there has a delicious luncheon too, and from that point, we can visit the Science Museum on the other side of the park."

"Clarice and Jenny, they have a wonderful exhibit of the 1904 World's

Fair that was held in St. Louis. Did you know the ice cream cone was invented there? Ice cream vendors ran out of disposable dishes and began to encase scoops of ice cream in cooled, rolled-up waffles. They've been a hit ever since."

"How interesting," said Jenny. "We enjoy them in Crete too."

As they rode along, Adam asked if they would care to hear more about the St. Louis1904 World's Fair. They all responded with an enthusiastic, "Yes!"

And so he began: "The 1904 World's Fair in St. Louis was part of an attempt to show its power to the world. Chicago had an incredible World's Fair in 1893 and was considered the foremost point of interest in the United States because of its influence. Many of the St. Louis dignitaries decided to prove that they were even more influential than Chicago. St. Louis had been founded by the French, thus receiving its name from a very famous French king.

1903 was the anticipated date to open the fair as it would help celebrate the 100th year anniversary of the Louisiana Purchase which took place in 1803. However, there was so much to be accomplished, that the fair was not opened until 1904, one year later. There were 1,200 acres of land in Forest Park allotted to the fair.

Thousands of workers were hired to build structures that would later be called, "The Ivory City of the World." The gleaming white city had over 1,500 buildings built specifically for the grand event, and were connected by 75 miles of roads and walkways which took almost a week to explore. As there wasn't time to build permanent buildings, they were temporary structures made of a substance called 'staff' which consisted of plaster of Paris, and kemp fibers. The only original actual building from that era remaining and in use today is the art museum; the only other structure is the open bird cage which is part of the St. Louis Zoo.

The fair was to help people learn about world events, as they had no radios or TV at that time to inform people. One area was called "The Pike" and consisted of mountains. Tourists were able to walk through places of world interest like, Seville, Paris, Rome, Constantinople, Cairo, and kiss the Blarney stone at Blarney Castle. Deserts were also featured and could be experienced while riding a camel.

One of the most exciting things was the Ferris wheel. It had been a major attraction at the Chicago World's Fair also. It arrived by way of 175 freight cars. The wheel stood at 264 feet tall, weighed 4,000 tons, and had 36 cars which hung on it like giant ornaments. Each car could hold up to 60 passengers each, so that meant 2,160 people could be on-board at a time. The rides cost 60 cents per person, and lasted 20 minutes. That doesn't sound like much admission, but that meant each 20 minute ride could net around $1,300.00 which was a lot of money at that time. Extra revenue was also the result of about 50 marriages that took place on board the cars. One couple was married on horseback inside a car, and another couple stood on top of a car while reciting their marriage vows.

I don't want to bore you with details, but after the fair, in 1906, there was no place to store the huge wheel, and it was dynamited for scrap metal. Later, 4 pound nuts and bolts were found in the area. The only part that could not be located was the 70 ton axel that could not be destroyed, but it suddenly disappeared. It was perplexing for the planners of the fair, and to this day, is still a mystery!"

Adam continued his tour guide explanation: "We are now driving past Art Hill, where the youths of St. Louis (and some of the oldies) congregate on snowy days and ride sleds from top to bottom. Then, with cheeks reddened by the cold, they begin the long climb to the top again, where they repeat the action."

"Note the huge statue of a man on horseback. The rider is supposed to represent Louis IX, the French king for whom our city was named."

Several boats glided across a lake which adjoined a lush green, rolling-hilled golf course. Then, they drove completely around the famous outdoor opera.

"Too bad it's the wrong time of year to attend the opera," Eve said. "We have wonderful evening shows here through the summer months. It is tradition to have a section in the rear for absolutely free seats. As a child, I quite frequently made use of them. We used to take our binoculars, using them made it seem as though we were in the front row. Intermission time was always a treat too, as we got lemonade to cool down. Even though there were huge overhead fans in several areas, they had to be turned off during show time, and St. Louis can be a scorcher in the summertime."

"Eve, my dear," said Clarice, "we have not even asked about you and your past. Please forgive us."

"Don't concern yourself about it, Clarice. Getting things settled for the three of you is my prime concern. We'll talk more at a later time. I want Adam and his mother to be at peace when they part."

"Thank you, Eve. I appreciate your understanding heart."

Early the next morning, Adam and Eve awoke to the delightful aroma of coffee and fresh-baked pastries winding its way under their bedroom door. Slipping into their robes, they quietly left their bedroom and peeked around the breakfast room area. There, they spied Clarice busy at the stove as Jenny was placing four colorful place mats on the dining room table and topping them with the necessary place-settings.

As Jenny sensed their presence, she greeted them with a cheerful look and then a bright smile. "Good Morning! Isn't this a beautiful day? Clarice and I have been awake for several hours, but didn't want to disturb you. We found everything necessary to make a good, healthy breakfast and thought we would surprise you."

"Yum, yum," said Adam. "The smell alone is so delightful."

"Good," Clarice chimed in. "We tried to prepare breakfast and have it ready when you awoke. It looks as though we were successful. As our time with you is growing short, we didn't want to waste any of it."

Jenny chimed in with her agreement. "We both feel so at home here in the St. Louis area with the two of you. It's almost as though we have lived here always. It's not just the sights we've had the pleasure of viewing, it's also the history you share with us everywhere we go. After we eat breakfast, you will have to share your plans for today with us."

Just then Clarice opened the oven door, and with a potholder in each hand, drew out the most incredibly beautiful pastries they had ever seen. She smiled at their amazement and said, "This is the type of pastry we bake at our shop each day. Sit down now. In just a few moments, everything will be ready."

Jenny placed another Greek delicacy on the table. "This is called

Komposta," she said. "It is stewed fruit seasoned with honey, lemon juice, and cinnamon. It's good for the digestive system, and very tasty too." She placed some of their plain yogurt in a crystal bowl, and began pouring the coffee she had brought from Greece. "It is very similar to Turkish coffee," she said. "We brew it until it is quite thick and then sweeten it until it is an enticing sugared brew. Of course, there are those who like to sweeten their own coffee, and do it in a very different manner."

"How do they do it, by using another type of sweetener like honey?"

"No, they use sugar too. They don't actually sweeten the brew, but place a cube of sugar between their front teeth, and as they hold it in place, they drink the coffee and let it swish between their teeth."

"How interesting!"

"Is this a typical Greek breakfast?" Eve asked.

"No, not really. A typical breakfast for us would usually consist of fresh baked bread, cheese, kalamata olives, and a piece of fresh fruit."

"What? No coffee?"

"Oh yes, of course, coffee. That is such a staple to our meals that I sometimes forget to mention it."

"Well," said Adam. "Me-thinks we should stop talking and enjoy this wonderful breakfast."

They all sat down to eat and relished every bite.

CHAPTER XII

Adam began discussing their plans for the day by saying, "The downtown St. Louis area is very interesting. Union Station has been renovated somewhat like a huge shopping mall. At one time, it was the largest and best passenger rail terminal in the world. As you know, people retain memories of certain things that really impressed them when they were young. Well…even though I was extremely young, I remember going there with my grandparents. My grandfather placed me on his shoulders as they waited to greet a returning soldier who was a friend of the family. We approached the train just as it arrived, pulling into the station with its whistle blowing and smoke billowing up from its smoke stack."

"My goodness, Adam, I don't remember you telling me about that," said Eve.

"Actually, the memory just flitted through my mind. There seemed to be acres and acres of people waiting for the military to disembark. What excitement was in the air! I also recall that the young man they went to pick up had been wounded. One leg was in a cast, the corresponding arm was held close to his chest by a sling. The main thing I remember was his huge smile as he caught sight of Gram and Gramps," Adam paused as memories of that time returned.

"Tears were coursing down Gram's cheeks as Gramps slowly approached the soldier, and then, in a very serious manner, performed a military salute. I remember that very well as the thought of losing the security of my perch on his shoulders while being supported by both his hands was questionable at the moment."

"Do your grandparents live nearby?" queried Clarice.

"No, they retired and moved to Florida shortly after Eve and I were married."

"Do you see them often?"

"We try to visit once a year, usually at Christmas time. They live in a city called St. Petersburg. Their home is a small beach cottage right on the Gulf of Mexico, and they seem to be quite happy there. Gramps loves to fish and Gram has many friends and is involved in playing golf and bridge. They both do volunteer work too. Every morning, they deliver meals to several people who are elderly and in bad health and who are unable to do much for themselves."

"Oh! Who pays for the food and who prepares it?"

"It is funded by local businesses, and the community actually has a citizen's fund that is used for that purpose."

"What a lovely idea," Clarice said.

During the animated conversation, they had all been enjoying the bountiful breakfast Clarice and Jenny had prepared for them. Eve rose to clear the table, but Jenny deterred her and said, "Get dressed, my dear. I'll tend to the dishes."

Eve did not protest. Soon they were all ready for their next adventure:

All the way downtown, Adam amused their guests with one story after another of his boyhood. Just as his stories seemed to have reached their climax, Jenny piped up and said, "Oh, look at that beautiful building. It has such unique lines."

"That's Union Station," offered Eve.

"Do trains still use that station?" queried Jenny.

"No, not really; we have Amtrak trains that are used mainly for pleasure jaunts, both locally and long-distance, but their stations are in various other places in the St. Louis area. Look at the pond and fountain across from Union Station. It is called, 'Aloe Plaza.' The fountain and the magnificent bronze sculptured pieces represent the meeting of the Mississippi and Missouri Rivers and were designed by Carl Milles. That small park-like area is a prime spot for people who work nearby to sit on the benches while enjoying lunch in those peaceful surrounding. and cafes, live entertainment, and a large lake with boats all under one roof."

The three ladies exited the car and made their way up the stairs into the Grand Hall which featured a 65-foot barrel-vaulted ceiling of unsurpassed gilt work, stained glass over the entrance, and scale models of trains.

The thing that really caught their eye was the Allegorical Window in the Grand Hall. It consisted of huge stained-glass windows with hand-cut Tiffany glass positioned above the Station's main entry way. There were three beautiful women depicted in full length gowns of yellow, pink and green. Each woman represented one of the main United States train stations during the 1890's. The lady on the right represented the train station in New York, or the East, the middle lady represented the train station in St. Louis, or the Midwest, and the lady on the left represented the San Francisco, or Western train station.

While the trio waited for Adam to park the car and join them, Eve saw something in print about "The Whispering Arch." It indicated that if one would stand under the indentation in the stone that arched in the center over the wide entry hall, another person could stand on the opposite side 40' away and hear what was whispered by the other person as clearly as if they were standing side by side. Of course, when Adam arrived, they tested it on him, and found he was amazed that he could hear what they were whispering about him. Of course, what they said was all very flattering…

A cup of hot tea sounded like a good idea, and they chose the lovely dining area from which they could sit and continue to admire the stained glass windows. As they sipped their tea, Adam continued with his history lesson:

"As you are admiring the ladies representing various train stations, please remember the days when our country depended heavily on the rails. We relied on them both for individual travel and shipment of commodities. That was before huge cargo trucks began to be the preferred mode of shipments. Trucks had access to so many areas that trains could not begin to approach. With trains, a transporter of some sort was necessary to deliver items to their final destination. Next, of course, began the usage of airplanes. Much cargo is shipped in that manner now."

"Adam, even though you are young, you have seen so many changes in your country," noted Clarice. "U.S. history has always been of interest to me, ever since I met your father, that is. Reading about the pilgrims who first settled here, of how they obtained help from the Indians, and then had major problems with them. Then came the era of cowboys and gunfights. After that, robberies that affected people and commodities when stage coaches and trains were used. Some of the robbers were actually considered glamorous, weren't they? Like Billy the Kid, and Jesse and Frank James, those notorious brothers. Then we had the real heroes, like Buffalo Bill and Wild Bill Hickok." It's hard to believe so many men actually toted guns and had shoot-outs at the drop of a hat."

"Yes, Clarice. Our country is rich in history, but so is yours. So often, Greece has been invaded by various other nations. I suppose the conqueror that interests me the most is Alexander the Great. He really blazed his way through history books."

"Yes, of course, and as we previously discussed, we obtained our surname from him," Jenny exclaimed.

"I'm aware of that, as my name contains a double-Alexander, and my full name is Adam Alexander Alexander. It's impossible to forget his influence."

Then, as Adam watched, Eve left the table and walked to one side of the colorful arch, and Clarice and Jenny walked to the other. Once again, they played the whisper game as though they were small children, and he recalled the strange phenomenon about the acoustics that were quite amazing. They were all giggling happily as they continued their experiment. Adam approached the arch also and stood next to his wife as the other ladies continued whispering. He couldn't help but smile as he realized how much fun they were all having together.

Although they observed the outer design of the structure, it was easier to study it by looking at the set-up scale model. The massive Romanesque-style building was designed by Theodore Link in 1894, and was the largest and busiest railroad terminal in the world. In 1940, over 100,000 passengers each day walked to and from a train there.

The ride home from the downtown area was a continuation of one of their delightfully interesting conversations. Eve queried Clarice for more information about Alexander the Great, and Clarice was more than eager to respond. "Where was he born, Clarice?"

"Alexander the Great was born in Pella, a city of Macedonia."

"What was his background?"

"Alexander was a prince, the son of King Philip II and his mother's name was Olympias. His father was assassinated, and then Alexander ascended to the Macedonian throne. Alexander too, was surrounded by enemies at home and threatened by rebellions abroad. He had many of his enemies killed. His father had told him that 'there is no glory without suffering,' and also to 'beware of women, they are more dangerous than men.'"

"Who trained him after his father was killed?"

"He had a very famous tutor, Aristotle, the famous Greek philosopher, who told him Greeks are superior in every way. So, Alexander had absolutely no fear of anyone or anything. Aristotle taught him rhetoric, literature, science and medicine. He was a very accomplished young man who was filled with dreams of his own glory, and many of his dreams came true. At one time, he had 35,000 men in his army. They sold over 8,000 people into slavery. As they plundered many lands, the only structures they spared were temples of the gods, and the house of the Greek lyric poet, Pendar."

"Clarice, you have an incredible memory," said Adam in admiration.

"Yes, I do. But you must realize much of this is what I learned in my primary school classes. They wanted us to realize the amazing things Alexander accomplished. Later, for the sake of interest, I did a bit of research on my own."

"Oh," said Eve. "Please tell us more. As we share his name, we should be well informed."

"Well, let's see," said Clarice as she appeared deep in thought. "Alexander founded the great city of Alexandria at the mouth of the Nile

River. The Persian Empire owned 4/5 of the known world at that time, but when he was only 25 years of age, Alexander destroyed it from Egypt to India. Palestine was included in his conquests. The Greek language became common there, and as you know, the New Testament of the Bible was written in Greek. It is a more concise language than Hebrew. The word love actually has 8 different meanings in the Greek."

"Oh Adam, please learn them and whisper them in my ear, darling."

"Eve, when I think of you, this is what comes to mind: 'How do I love thee? Let me count the ways...'"

They all chuckled together, and then Eve queried Clarice once again, "Did Alexander have any children?"

"Yes he did, and so did most of his military men. He encouraged them to marry Persian women to help unite the East and West."

"I suppose they just left their families behind?"

"In some cases, I'm sure they did. Alexander made the pilgrimage to Egypt as he was interested in the great temple there that was dedicated to the sun god whom Greeks identified as Zeus. Even before that time, he was enraptured with the idea that Zeus was his real father. It seems he buoyed himself up with that notion."

"In which time period did he live?"

"The actual years escape me now, but I think he lived in the 4th century B.C. He died in Babylon at the young age of 33 due to a fever. It was rather amazing that what should have been a simple illness killed him, rather than being killed in battle and dying the death of a hero! Actually, there are those who believe that he actually died of syphilis. He was known to be bisexual. As there was not one single person who could take his place, his empire was left to four of his strongest generals."

"What a tragic story."

"Yes," said Adam. "It truly is tragic. It's amazing that history has entertained so many barbarians that drew a following of others to themselves and brought tragedy to the lives of so many others. And yet, they all eventually met their 'Waterloo', didn't they?"

They decided to spend time at home as it was their last evening together. Clarice seemed to need the assurance that all would part in peace and not carry great heaviness regarding all the painful family history that had been expressed during their week together.

Once again, they had all showered and were clad in comfortable sweat suits. As Eve set out their favorite wine and snacks, Adam stoked up the fireplace. They were becoming accustomed to the feelings of relaxation and warmth exuded by the cheerful, flickering flames.

As Clarice sipped her wine, she said, "If there was some way I could make you all aware of the wonderful man my brother Andreas was before the great tragedy regarding his wife, Vivian, I would do so."

All was quiet. Then, Jenny spoke. "In the back of my mind, there seems to be a memory of a father who carried me about and showed great affection for me. However, during my teen years, he was so abstracted and cold. He rarely looked at me, and when he did, it was to find fault."

"I know darling," said Clarice. "He didn't feel that he could allow you to know the depths of his feelings for you because he had already determined your fate, and knew that if he didn't keep himself from showing his great love, he might relent and not force you to marry Harold."

Adam spoke up and said, "And how could he just tell Jenny I had been stillborn and never acknowledge his own grandson?"

"Adam, your grandfather developed a deep love for you. During the six months before having a hired woman take you to your other grandparents, he spent hours with you each day Of course, you were such a tiny baby and you would not remember it, but he cried and cried when it was time to give you up."

"Where was I during that time?"

"You were in a small town just 15 miles away, and were cared for by the woman who took you to the states."

"Who was she?"

"An older woman who came highly recommended. She was a widow of a seafaring man your grandfather knew. She had no family of her own after her husband died. Her only income came from babysitting several children who lived nearby. Those little children became very precious to her as they were practically her sole contact with others. Andreas was a very stubborn man and thought he was doing the right thing."

This new bit of information was a shock to both Jenny and Adam. Jenny cried out, "Oh, how I wish I could have known my real father—the one who kept himself and his emotions hidden from me. But, I'm so glad to know that he spent time with you, Adam. It makes me realize that he really *did* have a heart."

Eve seemed to fly across the room, sat on Adam's lap with entwined arms around his shoulders and cried out, "Oh, my darling. I pray you are able to make peace with these stories about your beginnings."

Adam gave her a rather bewildered look, patted her head, and said, "I hope so too, Eve. It may just take time. It's been a lot to digest."

Clarice and Jenny stood to their feet as if in one motion and embraced one another. Jenny laid her head on Clarice's shoulder and began to sob. "Oh, how I've yearned for my first-born all these years. All the midwife would say was that the baby was a boy and had lots of dark hair. Even when I gave birth to my twins, it seemed a third child should be present also."

Adam and Eve joined them and the four appeared woven together like a basket. Tears were coursing down their cheeks and a few muffled sobs broke the sudden stillness.

Clarice said, "I feel we need to pray. It's too heavy a burden for any of you to carry. I know, because I've lived with it all these years."

Eve suggested they all be seated close together and hold hands.

"Clarice, you are the logical one to lead the prayer," Adam said. "I just can't do it."

"Yes, I will. As matriarch of the family, it's my place to do so."

As they sat close together holding hands, Clarice began:

"Dear Heavenly Father,

As grateful family members who love you with all our hearts, we need Your wisdom in handling this situation. Please forgive me for holding back this knowledge all these years, but I promised Andreas not to share these secrets until he was gone. It would have just brought more pain to everyone before they could be united as we are at this time. Father, I pray for Your peace that passes all understanding to keep their hearts and minds through Jesus Christ. And it's in His Name that we pray.

Amen"

There wasn't a dry eye in the house!

CHAPTER XIII

Somehow, none of them were ready to retire for the night. As their plane did not depart until the next evening, they were all aware that they still had time to stay up a while longer. They sat silently, gazing into the fire. When the embers had all but died down, Eve stood up and, with a very gentle smile spoke to them of something that just kept coming to her mind. Finally, she said:

"Several years ago, I read about a method someone used to gain peace about a situation where the other party was deceased and their forgiveness could no longer be obtained. It involved a situation that had taken place in their lives shortly before the demise of the other party."

Everyone's attention was fixed on her, and so she continued:

"The person who was being troubled visualized the person who had passed away sitting in her presence. Then, she visualized Jesus Christ sitting there also. She prayed first, and then spoke aloud saying, 'Sophia, I was so wrong to speak badly about you to others. I was not aware of all the facts, and have just recently discovered what made you act in the manner you did. I cannot excuse myself as I was wrong. In the Name of Jesus, and in His presence, I ask both of you to forgive me.'"

They all seemed mesmerized by her story.

Eve continued: "Instantly, the woman felt the terrible burden of guilt lift and her tears of relief brought a quick release in her spirit."

Clarice excitedly responded, "Maybe we can do that too! What do you think?"

"It would be hard for me to visualize my grandfather," Adam said. "I've never seen him."

Clarice excused herself, and returned promptly carrying a rather faded photo encased in an old-fashioned frame. "Here is a picture of your maternal grandparents, Andreas and Vivian Alexander."

The picture portrayed a handsome young couple holding hands and beaming at the photographer who snapped their wedding picture. Andreas was a rugged looking young man with curly black hair, a tanned face, neck and forearms. His blushing bride had long, straight black hair, flashing eyes, a winsome smile, and appeared to be in on an awesome secret.

"My, aren't they a charming couple?" Eve noted.

"Yes," said Clarice, rather sadly. "They were the envy of the town. The love they shared together absolutely animated them."

"Adam, shall we try what Eve spoke of? Do you feel that might help resolve our frustration and pain?"

"I don't know Jen—, I mean Mom…but I'm willing to try."

"Okay, as Eve is the one who suggested it, maybe she should be the conductor."

"Oh no," said Eve. "I think Clarice should be the one as she knew them both so well."

"I'll try," said Clarice. "I talk to the Lord in prayer every day. It doesn't seem spooky to me to speak to Andreas either, as we were formed at the same time in the womb, and were always so close. I understood him so well. And Vivian was a very dear friend of mine too. Let me pray silently and see if it seems right."

Clarice sat with her eyes closed for a few moments. When she opened them again, a sweet smile lit up her face. "Yes, I feel it will help all of us, however none of us have an issue with Vivian. We just need to have peace amongst ourselves regarding the path Andreas chose that has affected us all so deeply. Quite often, I speak as if Andreas is close by anyway. He was part of my life for so many years, and I know that his death was just as though he walked through a doorway and entered another room. When you have faith in God, and lose a loved one who also had faith in Him, your time of separation will be very brief as time is recorded in all of eternity."

"So, Clarice," Jenny responded. "This will not be a séance. It will just be like a continuation of your relationship with Dad."

"Yes, that's the way it will be. And as we all have Jesus in our hearts, He is always here with us."

"I suppose, as his daughter, I should be the first to speak."

"Yes, my dear," Clarice agreed.

"Okay. Father, I must tell you that I've spent many years in anger and bewilderment because of the way you seemed to totally control my life. Now that I've been given all the facts, I can understand somewhat, and I wish to be able to absolutely forgive you."

Then, she went on, "Jesus, You are my Savior, and I know Your Word says that more won't be put on us than we can bear. It also says that if we bring our gift to the altar, but have something against another person, we are to leave our gift and go and be reconciled to that person. As I cannot physically go to my father and speak about the anger I have had towards him for years, I ask you to be the go-between, accept my apologies, and forgive me. Please enable me to accept what has happened and not carry anger and resentment any longer against my earthly father."

Jenny stopped and looked over at Adam as though signaling him to begin speaking. After several moments, he did so:

"Grandfather, I was touched to know that you really cared for me. It's hard to understand why you caused those things to happen. I realize that your culture was so different from ours. My mother was so deeply hurt also, and that is hard to forgive, but I must do so. By faith, I choose to forgive you. As Jesus is Lord of my life, and the precious Holy Spirit lives within me, I know He is always with me, therefore I ask His help, and it is in His Name that I pray. Amen"

The next morning passed by quickly; it was almost time to leave for the airport. Clarice teased Jenny about her luggage's ability to hold all the souvenirs she had purchased for her family. "Are you sure you have enough money to cover the extra weight in your suitcases?" she asked with a grin.

Jenny laughed and replied, "I can't wait to see their faces when they open their gifts. I used the gift wrapping service to make it more interesting for them, and have it take a bit longer to get to the gifts. Little girls enjoy looking at ribbons and fancy paper. Little boys don't even notice. They just rip off the paper in order to quickly reach the concealed prize beneath."

"Let me know when you're finished packing," said Adam. "Then, I'll place your luggage in the trunk of my car, as we must depart rather soon."

Clarice mentioned that they should probably say their personal goodbyes before leaving as so many people would be around at the airport, and they would be too rushed for their farewells to be as meaningful.

They all agreed, and Eve suggested it would be special if they all held hands once again and prayed for perfect peace about all that had transpired, and for traveling mercies for Clarice and Jenny.

As they stood together, it was as though a bond of perfect love flowed from one to the other. Adam was the only one who prayed that time:

"Dear Heavenly Father, I am so grateful to you for the opportunity to meet my family members that You have allowed in our lives. Thank you too, for the new measure of peace You have given me regarding my background. So many questions have been answered, and I am aware that, not only have I suffered from lack of knowledge, but have not had the pleasure and comfort which can only come from other family members, and spending time together. Please bless and keep Mom and Aunt Clarice as they return home. And Lord…thank You for my wonderful, understanding wife, Eve. I am a man most blessed! Amen"

Misty-eyed, they all hugged and whispered sweet terms of endearment to one another.

Eve excused herself and returned with a gift box which she carefully handed to Clarice. Upon opening it, Clarice noted a silken-type fabric which lay in graceful folds. As she drew it from the box, they all saw a scarf of many soft, shimmering hues of rainbow-like tints. The incredibly combined shades were set off by the designer's name discreetly woven in a corner of the scarf.

"Oh my," said Clarice, "we've seen these scarves displayed in some of our most elite fashion magazines at home. You shouldn't have gone to such an expense!"

"Clarice, you are more than worth it," said Eve. "I am so happy to see you attired in your travel suit of soft gray fabric. The scarf will compliment it perfectly. Do both of you plan to wear black again when you return home?"

"Yes, periods of mourning in Greece last for one year. We will fulfill this custom, although it has been such a pleasure to wear softer colors while away. All black attire can become a bit depressing. The only good thing about it is that it is rather slimming," she noted with a smile.

Jenny agreed about the beauty of the scarf, and added, "We both have black garments in our carry-on travel bags. Just before we land in Crete, we will use the restroom and change back into them. Actually, we just have 6 more months to wear black. The summer time which is just ahead is the hardest time of year to wear black, as that color has a way of retaining the heat."

Then Adam turned to Jenny and said, "Mom, I have something special for you. Please close your eyes and hold out your right hand."

Jenny looked a bit surprised, but held out her hand as he requested. He then slipped something on her ring finger. As she felt the pressure, she opened her eyes. Jenny discovered, to her amazement, a very beautiful ring. It appeared as a golden circle with Grecian ivy entwined about the base and circled about three stones which adorned the ring. The middle stone was a creamy, translucent pearl surrounded on each side by an amazing violet-colored amethyst.

"Oh Adam," she breathed softly, "what does this mean?"

"Mom, this ring is what we call a 'mother's ring.' These are birthstones. They are reminders of your three children. The amethyst on either end symbolizes Sarah and Samuel, as they were born in February. The pearl in the center stands for my birth-month of June."

"I shall never remove this ring, Adam. It is so beautiful, and such a reminder of how blessed I am to have three lovely children. But…how did you get it fashioned in such a short time?"

"I ordered it several days ago. The jeweler is a personal friend of ours, and he worked long past his regular hours to handcraft it. You will note the entwined Grecian ivy which makes it symbolic of your homeland too."

"Every time I gaze at it, I will be reminded of you and look forward to our next rendezvous."

"Hopefully, that will be just one year from now when Eve and I celebrate our 10th wedding anniversary by repeating our vows at a second ceremony in Crete. This time it will be a ceremony conducted by a church official, and in the presence of our family members, it shall be an affair to remember."

"Adam," cautioned Eve, "it is time to go. They don't want to miss their flight."

Jenny hugged Eve and said, "Before we leave, I must tell you how happy I am that my son has chosen you to be his wife. The love the two of you share is so obvious, and is a true delight to me."

Clarice interrupted to say, "I certainly agree. You are an amazing woman, Eve. If we had been given the option of choosing a wife for Adam, we couldn't have done any better."

"Come now," said Adam. "We really must go!"

CHAPTER XIV

Summer—1973

"Adam, let's visit the library today. It's Saturday, and I accomplished our errands yesterday and cleaned our apartment too."

"How did you find time, Eve? You were working on a special report yesterday for your next magazine article."

"Yes, I was, but I called a good source necessary to gain more facts, and they promised to mail the data I need, so I can't do any more until I receive it next week. After doing the grocery shopping, I came home, did the laundry and cleaned the house."

"Well, I owe you one, Eve. It feels like freedom not to have the usual chores today."

"We can do research on Greece. We need more information to help with the planning of our trip, so we don't miss any of the most important things to see and do while we are there."

"Okay, Eve. Let's have a light lunch before we go."

"Sounds good to me, Adam."

The table was quickly set with plain yogurt, strawberries, bananas, blueberries and sunflower seeds. Adam could smell the wonderful aroma of raisin-nut bread toasting. An ample section of cream cheese had been patted on each of their blue porcelain plates. Earl Grey tea with fruit flavored ice-cubes sparkled in clear crystal glasses.

"Yum, yum, just what I was hoping for! Shall we indulge?"

An hour later found them leafing through encyclopedias and reference books pertaining to Greece. As the posted signs in the library required their silence, they did much writing of notes back and forth, and spoke in hushed whispers when their excitement became too great to handle.

Eve found a picture of an elderly Grecian man wearing the traditional head scarf trimmed with tear-shaped, black jets hanging from the outer rim, and framed about his face. She pointed it out to Adam and made a quick copy at the patron's copy machine for future reference. She found it was the traditional headgear of the fighting men of Sfakia, and that the jet drops represent the tears that were shed for freedom.

As Eve made copies, Adam continued his research on the mythological Grecian gods. His notes went as follows: "Mt. Olympus in Athens was considered to be the exact center of the world." Then, he listed their 12 major deities:

Zeus—father of the gods of heaven who sired hundreds of mortal and immortal children. He resided on Mt. Olympus, but was born and raised in Dikteon Cave on the island of Crete. He kept order by brandishing thunderbolts.

Poseidon—god of the sea, brother of Zeus. He created islands, calmed seas and earthquakes. Many sailors would lash an icon of Poseidon on the mast of their ships.

Aphrodite, a beautiful seductive female, the goddess of love and lust. She wore a magic girdle that made everyone fall in love with her.

Hera—both sister and wife of Zeus. Protector of women and families.

Ares—god of war. Strong, brave, hot tempered, violent.

Hephaestus—a great craftsman. Zeus asked him to make a woman to punish men. Hephaestus then created Pandora of clay and water. She had a box from which sprang all the evils of mankind.

Demeter—goddess of earth and fertility.

Athena—a powerful goddess of wisdom who was born complete with helmet, armor and spear. She preferred to use wisdom to settle disputes, but would fight if necessary.

Apollo—god of light, son of Zeus.

Artemis—goddess of childbirth and protector of suckling animals.

Hermes—messenger of gods.

Hestia—goddess of hearth.

Some of the lesser gods were:

Hades—god of the underworld

Pan—god of the shepherds

Eros—god of love

Asclepius—god of healing

Hypnos—god of sleep

Heliss—god of the sun

Selene—goddess of the moon

Then, there were other mythical creatures such as the centaurs which had the body of a horse, and the arms and head of a man. They believed that the world was formed from a great shapeless mass called "Chaos."

Wow, all this information made his head swim. How could anyone ever memorize all these mythological creatures? He wondered if many people actually believed in their existence, and if so, how did they equate them with the one true God?

Further reading revealed that vendettas were common in Greece. Cretan's were notorious throughout Greece for them. If a family was insulted in any way, they took revenge on the ones who caused it. The vendettas sometimes lasted for generations and caused hundreds of people to flee the island.

The official language in Crete is Greek.

Adam whispered to Eve when she returned to her seat, "Look Eve, Greeks love festivals, rituals and ceremonies. Modern Greeks have a festival for almost every day of the year."

Eve responded with, "Wonderful, when we visit, we can get in on the joy of each new day. We should probably visit next spring around the Easter season."

In her notes, Eve expanded upon the Easter celebration by noting. "Easter is a celebration of joy, hope, love and eternity, and is the most holy Greek Orthodox holiday. The 40 days of Lent which precede Easter represent Christ's 40 days in the wilderness where He was tempted by Satan just prior to his water baptism and anointing by the Holy Spirit of God to begin His earthly ministry in actuality.

On Holy Saturday, everyone attends church for the midnight Easter service, where each member of the congregation holds unlit candles. Just before midnight, the church is plunged into darkness, except for the everlasting flame. As the clock strikes twelve, the priest lights his candle and calls the faithful to do the same using the flame emitted from his.

As Greek Orthodoxy is the official religion of Greece, 98% of the people are Christians. The church runs hospitals, orphanages, hospices, schools and homes for the elderly. The nuns are trained in the latest agricultural techniques and teach local farmers to better use and conserve their land

The faithful of Greece believe the Greek Orthodox Church is the pure, original Christian Church. They trust the Bible as the source of revelation and religious understanding and practice the seven sacraments given by Jesus Christ. They are as follows:

1) One God
2) The Holy Spirit
3) God's Son, Jesus Christ
4) The birth of Jesus, born of the Holy Spirit and Mary
5) Crucifixion of Christ
6) Resurrection of Christ
7) Ascension into Heaven by Christ.

The marriage sacrament is where two people become one in spirit.

Baptism of babies is required. That is where the priest dips the baby 3 times in water which symbolizes Christ's 3 days in the tomb. He then cuts three locks from the child's hair. After the ceremony, relatives wish the parents, "Na sas/zisi," which means "Life to the baby."

In Greek churches, statues are not permitted as only God is worthy of being worshipped. However stained glass icons which we would call pictures *are* permitted. Greek priests are allowed to remain married if they were married before taking the vows of the church. If they were not married at that time, marriage is not an option.

Eve was amazed to discover that some of the journeys in the New Testament by the apostles, after the resurrection and ascension of Christ took place in Greece. Jesus' apostles and followers fanned out through the Mediterranean area to preach the Gospel, the "Good News" during the 1st century A.D. St Paul, an apostle of Jesus, a Greek-speaking Jew, came to Athens, stood on the Acropolis and preached of God's love and forgiveness. The Greeks were very receptive to his teaching. Paul set up Christian communities until he was later beheaded by the Romans. Due to his influence, most of the New Testament was written in Greek.

The Parthenon was set high on the Acropolis and could be seen anywhere in Athens. It was built to honor Athena, Athen's patron goddess. Although in ruins, it is still magnificent with 50 columns which rise against the azure backdrop of mountains, sea and sky. It once contained a 40 foot statue of Athena. The face was of ivory with jeweled eyes, and the tunic was of detachable gold bars.

After several hours of sharing delightful, almost silent surprises, reading and making notes, Adam and Eve gathered up the books they planned to borrow and data they had compiled. Heading for home in the car, they excitedly shared some of their new information with one another. What an educational day it had been.

Communicating later with Jenny and Clarice regarding renewal of their wedding vows in Greece caused them to realize it would be much more intense than they had originally planned. A simple wedding on the beach was what they had anticipated. Now, they found that it could not be so informal. The ceremony must take place in church, not on the beach. There were very specific guidelines that must be adhered to. Jenny had even called with an important question for each of them.

"Adam, I forgot to mention that a Greek Orthodox wedding requires that the person of Greek heritage be baptized in the Greek church and there isn't time for that."

"Don't worry, Mom. Gram and Gramps realized that my mother was of that faith and had me baptized in the church as a child."

"How fortunate. What about Eve? Even though she isn't Greek Orthodox, she must have been baptized in a Christian church."

"Well, she *has* been baptized. As a teenager, she attended church with a school-chum, accepted the Lord and was baptized."

"So…you both qualify to be married in a Greek church."

"Yes, I suppose we do."

"That's wonderful. I will send information about the ceremony so you will be prepared and know what to expect."

"Thanks, Mom. We really appreciate you making all the arrangements for us."

"You're welcome, my dear. Clarice and I are probably more thrilled about it than you are."

CHAPTER XV

Current Year—Almost Springtime

"Can we really experience a trial run at Family Woods, Mr. Cambry?" asked Adam. "As your facility houses two types of people, retirees who have their own apartments and those who need extra care, it sounds ideal. I understand we can decorate with our own furniture, and Eve and I could share an apartment together?"

"Yes, that's correct, Mr. Alexander. We furnish a delightful dinner each day in our spacious dining room. The other two meals could be prepared by you in your apartment. After the dinner hour, an accomplished pianist plays music of all types and takes requests. We even have a dance floor which you may use if you wish. There are many activities to enjoy on the premises. We also provide field trips and you will have access to vans for your shopping needs."

"Mr. Cambry, I want you to be fully aware of the reason for our need to reside in a facility of this sort."

"Yes, what is that?" inquired Mr. Cambry.

"My wife and I are both in excellent physical health. However, Eve has recently developed other issues."

"What seems to be the problem?"

"Eve has been diagnosed with Alzheimer's."

"Oh, I am so sorry!"

"How are residents with that detriment handled?"

"The responsibility would be completely yours. As you know, residents are free to come and go as they wish. Your wife would be in your care as we don't have the capacity of restraining her if you share an apartment on the premises. However, if you wish to move her to the health center area later, she would be under lock and key at all times."

"Oh my, is that necessary?"

"Yes. Last year one of the gentlemen with Alzheimer's staying at a similar facility walked out in the dead of night. The outside doors were locked, so no one could enter the facility after 8:00 p.m., but he was not observed leaving, and just opened the door from the inside, and attempted to cross the highway on foot. He was hit by a passing vehicle."

"Was he badly hurt?"

"He was killed…"

"Oh, I read about that incident! Is there some way we might possibly do a trial-run without actually making a firm decision about staying here?"

"How much time do you need?"

"Possibly a month. It will take time to put our home on the market, and with realtors showing it to prospective buyers, our lifestyle would be extremely disrupted. At times when I would have to take care of business, I could hire one of your staff to stay with Eve for several hours."

"Well, an apartment has just become available. The previous tenant moved to Tennessee to live with her daughter, and we have been asked to dispose of her furniture. We could easily put a hold on the sale for a month. All you would need to bring would be your clothing and a few personal items."

"I am so relieved. That should take care of the situation."

"It's very unusual sir, to have a person relocate like this to care for a mate who has Alzheimer's."

"Well, Eve and I have been married for over 40 years. I don't intend to leave her alone. She would stay with me if the situation were reversed."

"It's settled then. When would you care to move in?"

"How about next Monday? That will give me four days to pack our clothing and other necessities."

The two men stood up, shook hands, and Adam squared his shoulders as he prepared for the busy time ahead."

As Adam began packing enough clothing for both of them to last for a month, he ran across many items of a personal nature. Speaking aloud to himself, he said, "Oh Eve, I need you so badly. How can I begin to assess what to keep and what to discard? All of our precious memories are bound up in these items. And, here are the pictures we had taken in Greece when we renewed our wedding vows. What a beautiful bride you were. I'll never forget the lovely glow on your face as it reflected on your auburn curls with your green eyes shining."

A sudden noise caught his attention and seemed to come from the guest bathroom. Hurrying down the hallway, he noticed a stream of water ebbing out over the rug. Entering the bathroom, he caught sight of Eve wringing her hands and softly whimpering as she peered into the toilet. The overflow was obviously caused by a large, white object that filled the bowl. Upon closer examination, he found it to be a disposable diaper like the one Eve had been wearing earlier that morning.

"Oh Adam, I'm so glad you are here. I couldn't find the soap powder for the washing machine. Now we will have to start from the beginning."

"Yes, Eve I see that."

As he got the overflow in check by pulling out the diaper and throwing it into the waste can, he turned again to Eve and said, "Come into the bedroom and change your clothing. It's almost bedtime and your warm flannel pajamas will feel so good."

"But Adam, I'm not sleepy."

Finally, she realized that he would not relent, so Eve settled down and accepted help donning her night clothing. She lay down in their bed and seemed to fall asleep immediately.

Feeling extremely weary, Adam sank into the chaise lounge close to the foot of their bed and began trying to assess all their options. Could he possibly care for Eve in a facility like Family Woods where people were free to come and go? He knew the chores and responsibilities of caring for their home and Eve also were too much. Having a daycare worker in twice weekly while he shopped and ran errands was the only time he was away from Eve.

Totally overwhelmed, Adam arose, and donned his pajamas, while mumbling the old familiar phrase made famous by Scarlett O'Hara in the movie 'Gone With the Wind,' "I'll think about that tomorrow!"

On Monday, Adam began to pack their car with the items they would need for the next month while testing the facility of Family Woods. As he returned to their home to help Eve get dressed, he realized she was nowhere to be found. With extreme anxiety, he rushed outside again and finally discovered her sitting on a swing-set several doors away in the backyard of a neighbor's home. He ran to her and found that she was busily picking at the frayed edges of the cushioned seat.

"Eve, what are you doing down here?"

She looked up at him as though she had never seen him before and said, "Can't you see that I am mending this cushion? Who are you and what do you want?"

Suddenly, he felt very old and exhausted. The thought of living with her at the retirement center and being totally responsible was too much for him to contemplate. As he had been told that the facility was open and there would be no restrictions for Eve, he realized it just wouldn't work. What if she wandered out on the highway the way that man with Alzheimer's had done and was killed, how could he ever forgive himself? Very quickly, he made the decision not to accept the trial run there. There must be another solution, but what? Then, he remembered that Dr. Childress had suggested a facility called, "Quiet Haven" where the Alzheimer's patients were closely monitored and resided in closed and secure wards. They would no longer be able to live together, but Eve would be cared for properly, and she would be safe. He called the facility that afternoon and set up a meeting with their administrator.

CHAPTER XVI

Spring—1974

The months seemed to fly by, and now it was time to plan their trip. One Saturday morning, Eve was still sleeping when Adam entered their bedroom with an alluring tray containing her breakfast.

"Wake up, Darling," said Adam as he presented a steaming cup of hot tea and a raisin-filled crumpet on a tray to his sleeping wife. "You must wake up and talk to me. Have your tea first; I can hardly wait to tell you what I would like for you to do."

"Oh Adam, I'm so sleepy. Can't it wait?"

"No, dear, you will really be excited to hear what I have to say. Drink your tea first."

No, Adam! Tell me now. You know I can't abide secrets or prolonged anticipation."

"Now, now, my dear. You must learn the art of patience," he said gleefully.

"No!" Her pillow with a frayed seam was tossed at Adam, and the released feathers gently floated down, covering him and the breakfast tray.

"Now...see what you've done! No breakfast for you!"

"I really don't care," she shrieked, while going for his jugular.

"Well, I suppose you're awake enough to listen. You have always wished to wear a wedding gown..."

"Yes...?"

"As we plan to renew our wedding vows while in Greece, you could actually wear a wedding gown. We could order it from one of their catalogues and it would be ready when we arrive."

"What fun, Adam. Thank you for thinking of such an exciting thing. Now, get the vacuum and clean up the feathers!"

"Yes, dear," he said humbly.

Jenny and Clarice agreed that the time Adam and Eve planned to visit them in Greece would be perfect. They then arranged with their local priest for the renewal of their marriage vows during an actual ceremony by the clergy this time. A justice of the peace had been all they could afford time-wise and money-wise 10 years earlier. Neither of them expected to feel more secure in their marriage than before, but Eve had always wanted to be married by a member of the clergy, and in an appropriate gown.

"Adam, will you love me any more after we recite our wedding vows with a priest?"

"How could I possibly love you any more than I do now? I fell in love with you the moment we met. There's never been anyone I felt that way about before meeting you, nor shall there ever be."

"Not even when I'm old and gray?"

"We shall be old and gray together, my dear, and face those times hand-in-hand."

"You say the sweetest things, Adam."

After breakfast, Eve pulled out the catalogues she had obtained regarding the proper attire for Greek weddings. The more she looked through the catalog at various designs, the more she seemed to realize that the dress could not be ordered ahead of time and delivered to their family in Crete, while awaiting their arrival. What if it didn't fit properly? Would they have a qualified seamstress who could alter it after she tried it on? No, it just wouldn't work. She made a quality decision to order some of the exotic fabric from Greece shown in the book. She would then enlist the aid of a local woman who was a talented seamstress to aid her in the design and structure of the dress.

"Adam, you are so fortunate that you can just purchase a black suit, a white shirt and tie, and you are all set."

"Well Eve, why do women have to be so picky? You could just buy a long white gown here and wear it for our wedding as other women do."

"No! You just don't understand. This is going to be a very special ceremony. It will take place in Greece, and it will be a wedding with a Grecian flavor. As you and your family are of Greek descent, I want it to be just what you would experience if you actually lived there all your life and married a local girl."

"Oh Eve, why would I ever want to marry a local girl from Greece when I have you? You are the love of my life! We could actually renew our wedding vows here if you wish."

"No! That just won't do. Especially not after meeting part of your family—your mother and your aunt. There is no way that I would ever want to renew our vows here. There is so much rich history in Crete and it will be an opportunity to meet the rest of your family, your half-brother and sister, their spouses and children. Also, we talked of renewing our vows close to the seashore, and will be able to do that in the area of the quaint little village where your family lives. I am truly excited about the whole idea. We women just have a way of fussing a bit when we have a problem that must be handled. This is actually not a problem, but a challenge."

"Okay, Eve. I know women must just talk out loud until they figure out what to do. I will try to be more patient and just listen to you, as I realize that you don't really want me to help solve the issue for you."

"Thank you, Adam. You are so understanding. Now, I will just study the books in front of me and write down my observations and share them with you later after you finish your special project from work."

"Whew! Finally got out of that one," quipped Adam.

"Well now," said Eve as she talked to herself. "As I am no longer a young, blushing bride, my choice of color for the gown would not be white, but probably cream, or a champagne tone. This ad says that they have exotic fabrics which are hand-embroidered. A cream design on cream fabric would be lovely. The only real color would be in my headdress and floral bouquet. They should match, of course. What are the most logical flowers to use? Hmmmm! Let's see what this book has to say about the meanings of various flowers. That would be an important consideration…"

As she turned to the pages which depicted flowers easily available in Crete, she noted such a beautiful array of technicolor pictures. "Let's see," she said. "Orchids are very plentiful in Crete; they stand for love and beauty. Lily of the Valley depicts happiness. Orange blossoms mean purity and love. Ivy is for fidelity, friendship and marriage. Queen Anne's Lace (my favorite wildflower) shows trust and healing. Roses bring love, joy and beauty. What a decision to make! I think I'll leave the flower choices for later." Having said that, she placed that special booklet in her folder entitled, 'Our Wedding.'

Gazing down at the golden band on the ring finger of her left hand, she began to visualize the second ring that would accompany it as they renewed their vows. They had been looking at engagement rings recently and so far, the one that appealed to her the most had a brilliant diamond cut in a pear shape design. Adam wanted to buy an entire new set for her, but she declined saying, "My gold band from our wedding is of prime importance to me. If I had to choose whether or not to keep it or get a new ring, I would keep the oldie. As you want to buy me a matching set, I will keep my gold band and get an engagement ring that will enhance and complete it. It would be almost like saying our first ten years together didn't really count for much. Being engaged after being married for so many years is rather exciting!"

After looking at various fabrics, Eve suddenly realized what she wanted for their wedding celebration on the beach. She would purchase exotic embroidered cream-colored fabric, and have it designed as a two-piece outfit. The top would be a peasant design with puffy sleeves in an off-the-shoulder mode. Her skirt of matching fabric, but without the embroidery, would have a gathered waistline and full skirt which swirled down to mid-calf. Her toenails would be painted in the same color as her pink flowers, and her feet would be bare as she walked through the sandy beach area at their reception party. Now, she must decide only the types and shades of her flowers.

Oops! She just realized that if she wore this type of peasant attire, Adam would very definitely look out of place in a suit. Besides, a black suit would be much too hot during that time of year in Greece. Now, he must make a quality decision too regarding what he would wear. She almost hated to ask him as she knew that type of thing just didn't matter to him. It only mattered to her. She would have to obtain more catalogues that featured Grecian men's garments.

Eve decided to tell him right away so he could be thinking about how he would research it. "Be brave," she told herself. "He will probably just bark a bit," however she knew from past experience that he didn't bite. He just pretended to be fierce when interrupted while he was busy. Should she tell him now, or later? Then the phrase, 'Better late than never' came to mind. She decided to wait and liven up their dinner conversation with the matter.

At dinner that evening, Eve waited until Adam had eaten and was feeling rather light-hearted as he had finished his homework. As always, they retired to the living room to enjoy their after-dinner cup of coffee and discussion of how their day had transpired. Eve broached the subject of Adam wearing native garb at their wedding vow renewal. He reacted just as she had anticipated, "What do you mean; I should dress in native garb? That's ridiculous! I'm not a native."

"I know my dear, but do you want to be on a hot sandy beach dressed in formal attire?"

"Well, I suppose if Mom and Aunt Clarice could wear black for an entire year to honor their departed loved ones by traditional mourning, I can handle it for several hours. Besides, maybe I could wear the black head scarf with black jets hanging from it like my grandfather, Andreas did. I have seen pictures of them, and they are very impressive."

"Yes, Adam. That is true, however, remember what the black scarf and black jets stood for. They stand for anguish. The black tear-shaped jets are symbolic of tears of sorrow, which were shed for freedom."

"Oh, why?"

"The men directly affected by battle wore this as symbols of the horrors of war."

"War?"

"Yes, World War II, when the Germans invaded Greece," Eve explained.

"After researching my father's reasons for entering World War II and requesting duty in Greece, it makes me appreciate the way he reached out to help."

"Yes Adam, I found it to be an amazing story. Also, the things that your mother and aunt told us of what their country went through were quite interesting. As you are writing about the history of that time, read me what you have written so far."

"Okay. It is really an exciting story. It involves the battle of Crete. In 1941, during World War II, Greece entered the war when they were rapidly overrun by German troops. The prime minister of Greece named Emmanuel Tsouderos set up their government while in exile in his native home of Crete. Crete was defended by British and Commonwealth forces. On May 20, 1941, German parachutists and mountain infantry men landed near Hanai. The allied troops were forced to retreat after ten days of fierce fighting. The Germans vowed that ten Cretans would die for every German shot. The islanders continued the resistance. In 1945, Germans left behind burned villages and destroyed roads. The island of Crete was ruined economically. In some mountain villages, all the men were killed. The Allied Forces had to retreat and 12,000 men trudged down the coastline to be evacuated to Egypt."

"What a terrible invasion that must have been, Adam."

Now Adam spoke 'off the cuff.' "Yes, my Dad was there at that time. I remember seeing his death certificate which was issued after the war in 1945. It said, 'Luke Alexander served his country in the line of duty as commanded in Great Britain, Crete, and France.' Even though Dad was an American, he was stationed in Great Britain and shipped out from there to Crete. I heard that after the war, a British Commonwealth War Cemetery was marked as a memorial to the Great Britians, Australians, and New Zealanders who died there. It is just a short distance from Soudha town."

"What a lot of interesting history, Adam. One could certainly get lost in the past."

"Now, let's hear what you've learned about Greek weddings, Eve."

"No, not now. Tell me some of the things your Aunt Clarice told you about your grandfather, Andreas. The two of you had several hours to talk the day Jenny and I went shopping for gifts for her family."

"As you probably recall, Andreas was a whaler. He went out in whaling boats and was gone for weeks at a time. They used a harpoon that was anchored to the boat. One of their ways of capturing the whale after being sighted, was by placing a number of small boats between the whale and the open sea. They tried to frighten the whale with noise, activity and small non-lethal weapons such as arrows. Then they attached him to an object such as a floating drum in an attempt to tire the whale out. Sometimes, they used drift nets, which the fishermen called, 'The Wall of Death.' It caught everything in its path, and played havoc with the ocean's ecology and disturbed its natural harmony."

"That sounds as though the whale was outnumbered and didn't have much of a chance."

"Yes, I suppose that's true. You must remember though, he was such a large mammal that it took special measures to capture him."

"A mammal? That means they are actually warm-blooded."

"Yes, whales have their young by live-birth. They are not like fish that produce their offspring by laying eggs."

"It's rather interesting to note that the closest relative on land to the whale is the hippopotamus. Just think about that!"

"Amazing, isn't it? The whale has two blow-holes on his head used for breathing. They actually breathe air into their lungs through a "v" shaped spout. Then, they can stay under water up to two hours after one single breath of air. They eat plankton and fish. The largest recorded mammal was a blue whale that was 30 meters long and weighed 180 tons."

"Let's see, Adam." Eve quickly calculated the whale's size on paper. "At that rate he would have been approximately 98 feet in length and weighed 360,000 pounds! Can that be true?"

"That's what the books say! His tail is actually a horizontal fin called a 'fluke.'"

"I'm sure there were jokes about that. Isn't a fluke also coined as a 'stroke of luck?'"

"Yes, I think so. Where were the whales hunted in that area?"

"The sperm whales were hunted in the Mediterranean Sea. They almost became extinct. In 1964, there were 29,255 killed. Finally, they had to put an international ban on commercial whaling for that reason."

"What did they actually use them for?"

"They were hunted for their meat, but mostly for their blubber."

"You mean fat…?"

"Yes, fat. The fat was needed for lamp oil, and ambergris which is an ingredient used in perfume."

"Why are they called sperm whales? Do they actually extract sperm from their glands?"

Adam laughed. "I think not. Actually, the phrase comes from a very fine oil which is taken from their head called 'spermaceti.'"

"What do you call male whales?"

"The male is called a bull, the female is a cow, and their young is called a calf."

"Interesting! Are they dangerous?"

"They can be, I am sure. They have a row of large white teeth in their lower jaw. Discussing them makes me want to reread the story of 'Moby Dick.,'" Adam said.

"I can understand now why you have been so busy now doing research. It will all be part of the book you plan to write about your heritage."

"Yes."

"How did your grandfather earn a livelihood after whale hunting was banned? He was still rather young when the ban occurred."

"Andreas worked as a diver to gather sponges after he was no longer able to hunt whales. When he began, he actually gathered sponges from the bottom of the sea himself. It was a dangerous way to earn a living. At times, the sponge diver had to reach depths of over 200 feet. Their boats usually had glass bottoms, and they could usually spot the sponges before diving. Many dove in the nude holding a heavy, flat stone to help him descend to the proper level of the sea."

"My, wasn't that terribly dangerous?"

"Yes, I understand that it was. There were many hazards but the main one was staying down deep for too long a time. At that time, some who used diving suits suffered decompression sickness with symptoms of pain, paralysis, and eventually death. They didn't realize how important it was to submerge and resurface slowly. Getting 'the bends' was very common. They later discovered that approximately 10,000 divers died in a span of time of 25 years, and twice that many were permanently disabled."

"How fascinating. You have really done some research, Adam."

"Yes, I have, but Clarice gave me so many more facts regarding sponge diving.

Ships sailed into the Agean and Mediterranean Sea with potential divers on board. Sponges were even used for bathing in the ancient days of Plato. Sponge diving was a great source of income for several of the Greek islands. The waters around the islands were suitable for the sponges to grow in because of the high temperatures. But, suddenly all the sponges became infected. They were never quite sure how that happened, but thought it might be the sudden, extreme rise in water temperatures. Then, of course, the synthetic sponges came into play and took away much of the business for the real thing, because they were much less expensive."

"Anyway, after Andreas grew a bit older, he no longer dove for sponges, but repaired the nets the divers used after cutting the sponges loose from the bottom. As the nets were in constant demand, they were always in need of repair. The divers took them along each time they submerged, and they were critical for bringing the sponges back to the surface."

"It sounds as though the sea was actually Andrea's life."

"Yes, doesn't it? Someone suggested that he become a shepherd as they have so many sheep in Crete, but he was aware that his temperament couldn't take being on land for long periods of time, and not having others to communicate with. Besides, 'once a sailor, always a sailor.'"

Sunday morning found Adam and Eve in church. Since the visit of his family, they continued attending church on Sunday. Their experiences with prayer and peace made them realize that their spiritual lives needed enhancing. The sermon that morning entailed the story of Joseph and his coat of many colors. It was a reminder of how hardships in people's lives can bring them to a much better place if they trust God and act accordingly. It made Adam realize how truly blessed he was to have his beautiful wife, Eve, and to have met his real mother and very special aunt. Soon, they would all be together again as he and Eve planned their trip and renewal of wedding vows through an actual church wedding in Crete.

On the way home they decided to stop for breakfast. As they drank hot tea and awaited their order, Eve said, "Adam, do we have time to learn some Grecian dances? We have to be able to dance at our wedding!"

"Well, I suppose the library could help us. It would be a shame to stand by idly and see others enjoy themselves at our wedding reception, wouldn't it? I'll stop by tomorrow and see what they have to offer that we can order. It is important to learn more of Greek culture and dancing."

'Oh, good! Let's do…"

A week later, they received notice from their local library that the films on Greece and several books were waiting to be picked up. The next two evenings were spent reading and watching films. Then, it was time to share their new knowledge."

Adam said, "Okay Eve. It's your turn. What is your topic?"

"Greek weddings, of course. I don't think I see anything about renewal of vows, but I don't feel that should be a problem, do you?"

"No, I don't. Wait until you hear what I have discovered."

"What?"

"Weddings in Greece are almost always held on Friday or Saturday. They are one of the most important events in Greece, and celebrations sometimes last for an entire week. The trousseau is given by the bride's family to the family of the groom."

"Well, we have everything we need as we have been married for ten years already."

"Oh Adam, we can't possibly invite enough people to celebrate that long. We don't know anyone there, except your Mom and Aunt Clarice."

"I will call my family there and see what they suggest. I'm sure they have a broad outreach of family and friends. We certainly don't want the party to go on that long, and we're not looking for gifts, but maybe some of those people could be invited to our wedding reception."

"Look at this Adam. It says that an old Greek custom was for the father of the bride to choose their daughter's mates. There was no romance involved. Sounds just like a business arrangement."

"Well, that's what happened to my mother. She had no choice."

"Darling, it looks as though things turned out as well as they could under the circumstances. We must be brave and look to the future while being grateful that you and your family have found one another."

"Eve, that is one of the things I love most about you, your understanding heart and going to any lengths to make me happy. Let's retire for the evening," Adam whispered in her ear, "I want to hold you in my arms."

CHAPTER XVII

By the next day, Eve had already changed her mind regarding her wedding dress. A catalog arrived in the mail and the first page to which she turned made her eyes grow large in awe. The dress portrayed was so gorgeous that it literally took her breath. The sleeveless gown had a gently draped cowl neckline. The skirt was fitted at the waist and from the hips fell into soft folds which draped down to the ankles. A slender train cascaded to the floor from the waistline in back. Realizing that it looked familiar, she raced to the living room and held the catalog page up to the vase that Clarice and Jenny had brought to them on their visit. Yes…the gown was almost identical to the one Helen of Troy was wearing. The only difference was the color. The gown on the vase was scarlet, and the one in the catalog was a creamy champagne color, exactly the shade she had envisioned. Viewing the headpiece shown, she noted it was a wreath of flowers, just as she had previously planned. The dress itself was actually called, "Aphrodite, the Grecian Goddess of Love." How much more obvious could it be? This was indeed the dress ordained in which to renew her wedding vows. She had even allowed her hair to grow longer, and her auburn locks now touched her shoulders. By the time they planned to visit Crete, her curls would rival those of Helen of Troy in length. She had begun using a conditioner on her hair which was very simple. It was an item from their refrigerator—pure mayonnaise. The nutritious, natural blend of ingredients caused her hair to actually shimmer with new life.

After dinner that evening, she presented her case to Adam by saying,

"Darling, I discovered a dress in a catalog for our wedding that will allow you to wear a suit as you wish. It is a bit more regal than the two-piece ensemble I previously planned to have made. Also, this one comes ready-made and will not be a challenge."

"Let me see the picture, Eve."

"Close your eyes, Darling. Tell me what it reminds you of..."

Eve gently placed her finger tips over Adam's eyes as he refused to play her little game. "Okay Eve, my eyes are closed. Now let me see it."

"Proudly, she held the picture out at arm's length and awaited his response. "Well Eve, the gown is the same as the one on our beautiful vase from Greece, the replica of Helen of Troy that looks just like you!"

"Oh Adam I am so glad that you see that too. What do you think about purchasing this for my wedding dress?"

"How much is it?"

"Oh my, why do men have to ask such difficult questions?"

"Oh! Oh! Evidently, it is a bit outside our budget for the wedding."

"Yes, it is a bit. But, I will economize. Allowing my hair to grow long for the wedding will save us money. As you recall, I used to get it trimmed every 3 weeks when I wore it short. We will forego eating out several times a week. I will watch my grocery money, and buy more reasonably priced items. There are lots of things I can do."

"Eve, how much is the dress?"

"Well, I won't take an allowance, and my last article for the ladies magazine will be published next month. That will bring in more money too."

"Eve, how much *is* the dress?"

"$950.00."

"Ouch!"

"Oh Adam, I want this more than anything in the whole world! And I already have shoes that will be perfect, my golden sandals. Rather than go barefoot on the beach, these sandals will suit the dress and also be appropriate for the sandy shore too."

"Eve, you know I can never refuse you anything."

"Oh, thank you Darling."

"Eve, I'm home! How was your day?"

"It went very well. The editor of Daystar called a short time ago and said my article on proper grooming for women's job interviews was excellent. Even though pants-suits are now considered as an option for women, they are not nearly as impressive to potential. employers as skirted-coordinated outfits in good taste accented by tasteful mid-high heels and purses to match."

"Why mid-high heels?"

"Some women are a bit clumsy in higher heels. Lower heels are also safer and there are not nearly as many accidents. Besides, they are more appropriate for office wear."

"Do you have photos or sketches to accompany your article?"

"Our friend Liz is an example of perfect grooming. She was kind enough to pose for me. I have photos plus sketches of women with different body shapes and the clothing that will be more flattering to their specific figure type."

"Where did you obtain the sketches?"

"I actually drew them myself. I have a book that tells of the styles that look best on women with various figures."

"Let's see them, Eve." Adam thumbed through the papers that were to accompany Eve's article, and he admitted that her ideas made sense.

"My article on proper grooming for job interviews also indicates the best format for a resume and how to fill out the application form that will be required."

"Do you mean resumes are necessary too? I thought the application form requested all necessary data."

"They contain much of the same information, but the resume is more personal. The application necessary for specific companies is very basic. Another thing that makes a good impression is a cover letter."

"What is a cover letter?"

"It is basically to let your prospective employer know more about you personally. It usually tells of your dreams and goals too."

"Are you going to explain how to write an interesting cover letter also?"

"Yes, I am. Verbal communication is of prime importance too.

Answering questions in a refined manner, listening and responding properly is a must. Body language counts too. Good posture, even while seated is of prime importance. It is best to sit with ankles crossed one over the other, rather than actually crossing the legs. This denotes modesty and femininity. Hands should be lying gracefully on the lap, rather than gesturing while speaking or responding."

"How do those being interviewed know the best way to respond verbally?"

"Well," Eve responded. "Questions about salary, vacations, sick leave, insurance and other benefits should not be inquired about by the one being interviewed until the conductor of the interview indicates that they are actually being considered for employment."

"Why? How will you know if the job would suit you and your needs?"

"The best inquiries would pertain to the job itself and the requirements by the potential employer."

"What about prior knowledge of the company with which you are interviewing?"

"Some knowledge is helpful, but you are not to try impressing them with what you know about their company. They already know everything they need to know about their own company."

"Sounds like a very helpful article for women seeking gainful employment."

"Can you think of anything I've forgotten, Adam?"

"No, my dear. It sounds good to me. Have you been paid for your article yet?"

"No. The check will be mailed at month's end when they pay all their bills. They actually plan to double what I received for my last article."

"Hooray! How do you plan to use the extra money?"

"By opening a 'bridal gown' fund. Good idea?"

As the time drew closer and closer to their trip to Greece, Adam and Eve gave consideration to items necessary to purchase prior to departure. Eve thought it might be fun to buy a few of the native garments while there, but she had not taken time for research. She wondered if their type of attire would suit her personality. A typical man, Adam did not intend to add anything to his wardrobe except a new swimsuit. His old suit was faded and frayed.

"Adam, I certainly hope my wedding dress is delivered soon. I can't wait to try it on. Finding a qualified person to make alterations might be tricky, especially with that fabric. It looks as though it will be quite delicate."

"Have you decided on a headpiece yet, Eve?"

"Yes, I plan to have it fashioned there the day before our wedding. I want a very simple crown made of fresh flowers—probably pink rosebuds and pale lavender baby-orchids with a hint of a cream-colored filler."

"Shall I wear a Grecian wreath of ivy," Adam said in a kidding manner. Eve smiled and said, "No, silly."

"Do I get a boutonnière?"

"We will allow the local florist to make a suggestion, unless you know what you want right now?"

"No, my dear. That's not my cup o' tea. I'll leave that up to you."

After giving Eve a big hug, Adam said, "Well, I'm off to work. Do you still plan to spend several hours this morning at the orphanage?"

"No. I have a deadline on my article for Daystar Magazine; it's complete now except for the typing. I will take it directly to the publisher this morning. After lunch, I plan to visit the orphanage. They have a set of twin girls who are only 6 months old. They need a lot of tender-loving-care. It's amazing to realize how important it is to babies to be held and rocked. They literally nuzzle up to my bosom and almost seem to purr like little kitty cats."

"Eve, you would make such a wonderful mother. Have you thought any more about considering adoption?" Adam asked as he encircled her slender waist with his large hands. His grey eyes seemed more penetrating than usual as he gazed into her deep green eyes, softened now by his adoring attitude.

"Adam, we've discussed this many times. I just can't give up on the hope that one day, we might actually have a child of our own."

"That would be wonderful, but it's been 5 years since we lost our first baby to a miscarriage, and 3 years since our second baby was discovered not to have a heartbeat and had to be surgically removed."

"Please, Adam. I can't talk about it right now. It's too depressing and I have lots to do."

As he reached out to her, Adam gently tucked an auburn curl behind her left ear and kissed her on the tip of her freckled nose. "Bye Honey, I'll see you tonight."

A week later, the much anticipated package arrived via special delivery. As Eve signed for the package and viewed the return address, she felt warm blood begin rising from her solar plexus up into her neck, and finally settle in her cheeks. All aglow with excitement, she ran into the bedroom, quickly ripped the package open, and there amidst the trappings of tissue paper, lay the most elegant gown she had every seen. But…to her dismay, there had been a mistake. The fabric was not the cream-color she had ordered, but a pale, misty seafoam green. "Oh no!" she screamed aloud. "How could they make such a blunder?" She had specifically indicated her choice of colors. Eve felt like throwing herself down on the carpet, while kicking and screaming as a child indulging themselves in a temper tantrum might do.

"I'll bet they even sent the wrong style," she complained to herself. "How could they do this when we must depart so soon?"

As she drew the garment from the layers of tissue and held it up, it appeared to be the style she had ordered. Shaking it loose, and holding the dress up under her chin, Eve gazed into the full-length mirror. She actually gasped as she caught sight of her flashing eyes as they picked up the reflection of the green fabric. What an affinity the two had for one another. Nothing she had ever worn enhanced her large, expressive green eyes as this dress. "My," Eve whispered to herself. "I'm actually beautiful!" And indeed, she was…

Later, while looking up the copy of her original order, Eve discovered the reason for the assumed color discrepancy. The catalog order form indicated a choice of three colors: #2755 Fuchsia, #2756 Cream, #2757 Seafoam Green. In her excitement to post the order, she had placed an 'X' in the wrong box! She had actually ordered the green gown. Now, what should she do? It was several hours before Adam would return home from work. Well, there was nothing to do but try it on. Quickly, Eve slipped out of her garments and turned on the shower. Using a cool spray of water, she shivered a bit, but realized her usual choice of a hot water shower would cause her skin to turn a rosy shade of pink. The misty green color would not be enhanced by a reddened complexion.

"Oh dear," Eve muttered to herself. "I forgot to wear my shower cap. Now my hair will be too curly from the moisture."

After drying off and donning her under-garments, Eve allowed the silken, jersey-type dress to slide over her head and encase the entire length of her long, slender body. The sensation caused by the exotic fabric caused her to almost purr like a contented kitten. Fluffing her red curls with her fingertips, she stepped forward to peer into the mirror.

"Now, I know how queens must feel when preparing to appear in court," Eve thought. What a blend of elegance and casual. Her gown looked absolutely regal, but the feel of it against her skin was comfortably casual, not having the stiff feel you might expect of wedding gown fabric. After the upcoming ceremony, she decided she could wear it as a rather sexy dressing gown as she and Adam relaxed at home in the evenings.

Yes, it looked as though the designer had attempted to match the gorgeous shade of green in the gown to her eyes.

Eve had not intended to allow Adam to view her gown until their wedding ceremony on the beach, but it appeared so completely different than anticipated. Maybe she should get his perspective?

Then, as she peered into the mirror once again, Eve made her final decision. She would definitely keep the green gown, and would not allow Adam to view it until their wedding day. She hung it on a padded hanger, encased it with a cloth cover, and hung it in the back portion of her closet.

When Adam came home, he was pleased to note her exceptionally cheerful mood.

"Well, we've finally made a decision. It seems that April and May are the best times to visit Crete," Eve exclaimed in an excited manner. "The temperatures are very comfortable and vary between 75—85 degrees. Summertime may be as high as 104 degrees. As you know Adam, I can't tolerate that much heat."

"Yes dear, I know that my lovely red-haired bride doesn't think her freckles are very becoming, and doesn't want to accrue more," Adam responded with a grin.

"If we book our flights now in February, we should get a much better rate. Don't forget, we want to spend a day in Staten Island viewing Snug Harbor too."

"Yes, I'm anxious to see where my great-grandfather, Nick Alexander, spent his later years."

"Let's call Jenny and Clarice to make sure the time-frame is convenient for them too. Then, we can make our airline arrangements."

CHAPTER XVIII

Current Year—Summertime

"Hi Eve, I'm home." Adam's voice resounded through their home from the front door. There was no response, and he assumed Eve had left to run an errand before dinner. Entering the hall to hang his coat in the closet, he heard a rather muffled sound coming from the living room. Then, the sound changed and it became one of tinkling glass. Peering around the corner, Adam noticed shattered glass lying on the fireplace hearth.

"Oh no!" he exclaimed. The residue was lying directly under the mantle area where their special vase depicting Helen of Troy had sat for many years. Then, he saw Eve sitting close by on the floor with her head in her hands.

"Eve, what happened?"

"I don't know! I suppose we had an earthquake and it shook the vase off the mantle."

"But, I didn't feel anything. Did you see it fall?"

"Yes, it just seemed to drift through the air." Then, sobbing, Eve cried out, "Don't blame me! It wasn't my fault. You always blame me!"

"Darling, I'm not blaming you. I'm just asking what happened?"

"I don't know. It's so old, it probably just fell apart."

"How could it just fall apart? Had it been broken earlier and just pieced together?"

"Maybe you broke it Adam, and had it repaired. We could have it repaired again."

"Eve, that doesn't make sense. That vase was so special to us. As you know, it was a gift from Mom and Aunt Clarice many years ago. The female depicted on the vase was thought to be Helen of Troy, but there was a striking resemblance to you. Every time I looked at it, I was reminded of your beautiful red hair."

"Don't you think I'm pretty anymore, Adam?" Eve's green eyes appeared very sad behind her gold-rimmed bifocals.

"Darling, no one will ever be as beautiful as you. You are the love of my life now, you were then, and you always will be. You enchanted me from the first moment I saw you and our life together has been a continual source of joy."

Adam reached out and drew Eve to himself. As he patted her white curls, he tickled her ear as he gently nibbled it with pursed lips. Eve giggled at her remembrance of one of his old habits. "Ohhh, you're tickling me, Adam," she murmured as her body relaxed and the memory of the smashed vase escaped her for the moment.

"Why don't you change clothes and we'll go out for dinner, Eve."

While Eve showered and dressed for dinner, Adam swept up the shattered vase. It was never referred to again...

CHAPTER XIX

Springtime—1974

"It seems we've just called to make our reservations and now we're departing next week, Adam."

"Yes. Have you decided what to take? Two weeks out of town is a rather long time to plan for. We shall have to take dressy garments for the parties, and casual things for touring. Of course, you will want to keep your own suitcase private unless you have reconsidered and will allow me to see your wedding gown," Adam said in a teasing manner.

"Of course you can't see it! Why do you think I've kept it hidden all this time?"

"Oh, is that the dress hanging in the rear of your closet?" he asked very casually.

Eve's face turned white and then her cheeks flushed a deep crimson. "Adam," stomping her foot in anger, "how could you do something so despicable?" Then, she began to sob and ran into the bathroom.

Adam, like most men, could not understand why she got so upset. He turned the door knob to the bathroom and found it locked. "Honey, I was only teasing. Is that where you hung your dress? I promise that I never look in your closet. Please let me in. I'm sorry for teasing you like that."

"Go away! I don't want to talk to you. You've ruined the whole trip for me."

He signed and flopped down in a chair. "Whew," he quietly breathed to himself. "When will I ever learn?"

The sobbing ceased and he could hear the sound of water flowing into the wash basin. He could picture Eve applying cold water to her swollen eyes. Ten minutes later, the door opened a crack as she peered out preparing to depart the small enclosed area. As her naughty husband was not in her line of vision, she cautiously opened the door and ventured out.

Suddenly, a long arm reached out and encircled her shoulders. "Darling, I'm so sorry that I upset you so. Is it that time of month?" Adam inquired in a rather pensive manner.

Before he knew it, he was staggering backwards as she pushed on his chest with all her might. "Why do men think they know all about women's hormones, and attribute any little irritation to that cause rather than to their own inconsiderateness?"

"Well, it *is* that time, isn't it?"

"What if it is? That has nothing to do with the matter," Eve said as she stomped her foot.

"I know. I know. Please forgive me for teasing you."

"I'll think about it. For now, just leave me alone. There is a deadline on the story I'm writing and I plan to finish it right now."

Looking down on him as he continued to sit on the floor, she said, "Well, why don't you stand up?"

"Okay."

"Adam, are we still going to visit 'Snug Harbor' the maritime home for retired seamen in the United States," asked Eve. "Didn't you say that is where your great-grandfather, Nick Alexander lived for years?"

"Yes, he was a sea captain on a sailing ship. He was born in 1848 and retired to Snug Harbor in 1918 after many years out to sea. Snug Harbor was opened in 1833. The founder was a man named Robert Randall who had made his fortune from the sea and wanted to repay sailors for their hard life. In those days, there was no Social Security or retirement plans. Many elderly sailors were afflicted with arthritis and alcoholism. Peg-legs were very common due to accidents on board ship."

"What a wonderful thing for Robert Randall to do. I'm sure it was a lovely retreat for elderly sailors."

"Yes, I suppose so. But, they basically gave up all their rights by choosing to live there."

"How so?"

"Many sailors who had spent most of their lives on-board ship were accustomed to a daily ration of grog."

"Grog…what is that?"

"It was a half-pint of rum or whisky mixed with water. There wasn't much in the way of fun at sea, and the grog gave them something to look forward to."

"Was alcohol banned at Snug Harbor?"

"Yes, it was. In the 1830's and '40's, America was in the midst of 'The Great Awakening,' a period of revivalist fervor. Snug Harbor's old, retired sailors were expected to attend morning and evening prayer, and Sunday church services. They also had to observe grace before meals, were not to curse, and to be sober at all times."

"Wow… What a change! When I think of sailors, I think of rather salty language."

"That is probably why they are sometimes called, 'Old Salts?'"

"Could be. That doesn't seem fair to force them to attend church."

"Well, they weren't actually forced to attend, but when the service was going on, they had to sit quietly in their room if they chose not to go."

"Weren't they ever free to go to town where they might indulge in a drink or two?"

"No. However, there was a local tavern called, 'The Little Brown Jug.'" The men were lectured by various ministers on the evils of alcohol, but it didn't change them. Finally, a 7 foot-tall fence was placed as a barrier around the facility, but it didn't really end the problem. It just made it stand out even more."

"Well, I'll be even more anxious to visit since I know much of the history."

"Me too!"

"Well Eve," Adam responded, "We could actually visit 'Snug Harbor' on our way to Greece. We must fly through New York and we would be very close to the area as it is located on Staten Island."

"I wanted to surprise you, Adam, with my knowledge of the complex. Several weeks ago, I did some research at the library and found that a young architect named Minard Lafever designed the first major structures of Snug Harbor in the form of Greek Revival Temples. He intended to convey through architecture the aspirations to civic ideals represented by Classical Greece."

"So…Eve, our trip to 'Snug Harbor' would merge nicely with our trip to Greece. Aside from seeing where my great-grandfather spent the last days of his life, the buildings would be reminiscent of Greece. What do you think, shall we visit before or after our trip to Greece?"

"Oh, let's visit Snug Harbor before we visit Greece. As we will be away for two weeks, returning home will be so pleasant, and we will probably be very weary. If we had another leg of our journey, it might be too tiring."

"You're right, Eve. Let's start planning now. As this is the beginning of a new year, we should be ready to travel around Easter time. I understand Lent and Easter are very special holidays there."

"Aren't we blessed to have a family to stay with? Aside from being anxious to see Jenny and Clarice again, we will learn so much more about the culture by staying with natives of the area."

As Adam always loved to learn the history of places, he told of a recent newspaper article that had caught his attention. "Eve, did you read about Jacqueline Kennedy Onassis becoming involved with 'Snug Harbor'? She discovered that there was talk of tearing down all the remaining structures due to their age and condition? She took a ferry to Staten Harbor and spoke for the many others who were working to save the landmark and said, "Attention should be brought to a place like this. There is no place in all the five boroughs where there is such a sanctuary as this…it must be preserved."

As they packed their garments for the upcoming trip, Adam mused a bit and said, "Wonder what it will be like to meet Samuel and Sarah, my two half-siblings?"

"Well, you've talked to both of them on the phone several times, and they seem to have accepted you to a degree," Eve responded.

"Yes, but I'm sure it was difficult learning that their mother had been previously married, and that she had an older son. But they evidently received the love and support of both parents, and felt secure."

"One never knows, Adam. Your Mom said she never got over loving and losing your father, and being told that their child had been born dead."

"And you, my dear Eve. You never knew your parents. I think we should take time some day trying to learn of your birth too."

"Maybe one day, Adam. Right now, it's the last thing on my mind." She turned and took a dense-looking garment bag from the rear of her closet and placed it at the top of her suitcase over her other garments. Then she shut the lid of the suitcase and locked it.

With a twinkle in his eye, Adam said, "Is that the dress?"

"Yes," she replied stoically. "That's the dress..."

Finally, departure time arrived. Eve packed several days earlier, and had finally included her lovely green wedding gown that made her look like one of those mythical creatures—a mermaid. Every day since its arrival, she had tried it on, and each time marveled at its exquisite fit, the amazing hue as the fabric caught the light, and the way its folds and fine fabric seemed to absolutely caress her entire body. How many times had she been tempted to allow Adam to view her cherished wedding garment, and how many times had she caught herself just in time. The delicate golden sandals were a perfect accompaniment, as were the two golden bracelets that were created to encircle the upper arms, and not the wrists. They appeared to have been formed much like those worn by ancient Egyptians. The only other jewelry planned were the slim, golden hoops which dangled from her ear lobes.

Their flight was to include a two day layover in New York City. Their goal was to visit Snug Harbor in Staten Island, the Statue of Liberty, and Ellis Island.

"Adam, I'm so anxious to visit the place where your great-grandfather retired after years of being out-to-sea."

"Me too, Eve. I've heard the stories about it for years from Gramps.

It will be interesting to retrace his steps and try to imagine what his life there must have been like."

Now, they were actually on the plane en route to New York City, Staten Island and Snug Harbor. To make their flight more interesting, Adam brought along information regarding his great-grandfather who resided in Snug Harbor during the latter years of his life.

After being prompted by Jenny to locate his father's letters and memorabilia to his parents, Adam also discovered letters from his great-grandfather, Nick Alexander. Nick had sailed abroad for many years. Rather than return to his home in San Francisco, he chose to retire at "Snug Harbor" in Staten Island.

Nick's lust for the sea cost him his wife Madeline, and an ongoing, loving relationship with their son Paul. Some women could handle a mate who spent months at a time away from home; Madeline could not. So, the letters were actually directed to his son, Paul, who was Adam's fraternal grandfather. As it always took months for delivery in those days from sea to shore, lines of communication were faulty.

"How strange it seems Adam, that your grandfather Andreas and your great-grandfather Nick were both whalers from opposite sides of the family, and both had the same last name. The sea was their life," Eve noted.

"Yes, I suppose a bit of that heritage comes out in me when I sail. I've always wanted to sail a one-man rig through the Grecian isles, spending a day or two on one island or another. It would be quite a choice though, as there are over100 islands there. When I was 10 years old, I read all of great-grandfather Nick's letters. He spoke of exciting adventures at sea, but in the end, he was a very lonely old man,"

"Didn't he live near his son Paul when he retired from the sea?"

"No, he didn't. My grandfather Paul and grandmother Amy lived in San Francisco, where my father was born. As I told you, Nick went to live at Snug Harbor, a home for retired sailors in Staten Island, N.Y."

"Was he happy there?"

"Well, let's read some of his letters together and see what he had to say."

Adam took an interesting slender, high-glossed, antique-looking wooden box from his carry-on luggage. Opening it, they noted a faded blue ribbon tied around the contents in the box which had darkened with age. A tintype of an elderly man on crutches with only one leg was on top of the stack. A cigar protruded from between clenched teeth and a jaunty cap sat atop his head.

"Who is this, Adam?" Eve asked as she gently turned the photo over. "Oh, here's the answer, the back is signed:

> To my son Paul,
> Nick Alexander

The snow-white hair of the man in the photo streamed down to his shoulders where it joined forces under his chin with a beard of the same length. It was virtually impossible to detect a boundary line between the two. A face of mahogany-hue was highlighted by eyes that blazed like fiery black jets. From his facial expression, he seemed to be daring the photographer to attempt capturing him for posterity.

"Adam, what an intriguing old man Nick was!"

"Yes, isn't he? I've forgotten the main gist of his letters."

"How could you forget?"

"You must remember, it's been over 20 years since I read them. I wasn't really into genealogy."

"Well, let's read them together now."

Directly under the photo of Nick was a record of his birth in Coloma, California in 1849, a bit west of San Francisco.

"Eve, the California Gold Rush took place in 1849, didn't it?"

"Yes Adam, the Gold Rush was from about 1848-1852, I think."

"See here, his parents were listed as Anthony Alexander and Melody Holmes. Isn't that interesting?" Adam mused. "Evidently his parents weren't married, at least not to one another."

The third document was a letter from Anthony to his son Nick:

To my dear son Nick,

Please be aware that your real mother, Melody Holmes and I were not married. We met in San Francisco during the Gold Rush. The first time I saw her, I was in the office of an assayer having my lode of gold weighed. I happened to glance out the window and saw a mystical-looking creature with long hair resembling spun gold being helped down from a stagecoach. Our eyes met through the wavy window pane of the assayer's office, and she has been on my mind and in my heart ever since. I immediately ran out the door, forgetting my gold nuggets which sat on the scale. I took her other hand in mine as she gracefully stepped down.

Melody and I fell in love immediately, but her parents had great social standing in the community, and refused to allow her to be courted by a young, penniless foreigner. True love will have its way though, and we used to sneak out at night to meet. Several months later, she realized she was going to have our child, and had to inform her parents. Once again, she asked that they allow us to be married. They were livid with rage, and continued to refuse to allow her to be my wife. Melody was sent away to have our baby where people didn't know her. My darling Melody died in childbirth. Friends and neighbors were told she died of influenza. The home where you were born allowed me to adopt you as Melody's parents did not want to be involved. They felt recognizing your birth would have cast a shadow on their reputation. Several years later, I married Eve, the woman you always believed to be your real mother. I feel she did an excellent job raising you.

"Oh Adam there was another Eve Alexander!"
"Yes my dear, 'history repeats itself,' as they always say."
"What do you think happened to Nick's leg?"
"Let's continue reading."
A very intense letter from Nick to his son Paul was the next document in the box. It went as follows:

Dear Paul,

The intense pain, anger and anguish I feel cannot really be expressed. I am lying in my berth at sea and have been warned not to move for danger of hemorrhaging. Two days ago, we were chasing a huge sperm whale whose capture would allow us to return home with the coveted spermaceti oil. The chase had been amazing, and we were nearing our prey. The mate atop the ropes of the sail shouted out, "Whale Ahoy!" Several life boats were being lowered as we intended to row towards our coveted prize and spear them with harpoons. As the boat I was to set chase in was lowered, a huge swell of wave flung it aloft. I lost my balance and fell, catching myself between the two crafts, our schooner and the life boat. My left leg was mangled in-between the two. Later, the ship's cook had to use his culinary carving knife to remove the lower portion of the injured leg as it could not be repaired. And no, we did not have a medical person on board. Then, it was cauterized or burned at the stump in order to stop the bleeding. The only medication on-board was whiskey ordinarily kept under lock and key. When the pain becomes too intense for me to bear, they pour some down my throat and I am unconscious once again.

Days later, the letter resumed:

Dear Son,

I am still unable to rise. They feel an infection has set in and I have been delirious with fever. Today, the intense pain has subsided a bit and has been replaced by intense throbbing.

A week later the note continued:

Paul,

When the ship ceases to roll, I am able to stand on one leg and support myself with a stick in my left hand. Another mate on board had a similar loss several years ago, and they call him 'Peg-Leg.' I shall never permit them to call me other than by my given name—Nick.

Your father, Nick

The next document was a statement about the origin of Anthony Alexander:

I was born in Rhodes, Greece and I ventured to America after hearing of the incredible opportunities to acquire wealth through mining of gold. Obtaining passageway to America was not easy, but I made it. Later, I will share that adventure with you.

The last item regarding Anthony's history was a letter that was to be placed alongside his will and given to his son Nick upon Anthony's demise. His last words to his son were:

Dear Nick,

Please know that I loved your step-mother, Eve with all my heart and would never intentionally have harmed either of you in any way.

Your father,

Anthony Alexander

"Oh Adam, that's almost like a fairy tale. It's both tragic and romantic."

"Yes, there's more. Let's keep reading."

The next item was evidently a log depicting Nick's life at sea. A brief portion mentioned his relationship and marriage to a woman named Madeline and a son named Paul, who was born of that union. Their marriage lasted 7 years until Paul was 6 years of age. Then, Madeline divorced Nick and married a childhood sweetheart. However, she evidently allowed Nick to spend time with Paul when he had shore leave. The boy was captivated by the presence of a gift-bearing father who seemed like a pirate. Nick always had exciting tales to relate to a wide-eyed child, and gifts brought from the world-over. Only when he grew older, did Paul learn to resent the fact that his father chose the sea over him. Consequently, Paul opted to pursue a career from the opposite end of the spectrum. He became an actuary, a man who calculates insurance risks and premiums.

"Now, I can understand why your grandfather Paul is such a cautious, methodical person, Adam."

"Yes. Can't you see how I disrupted the lives of him and Grandma Amy? After raising my father Luke, they thought that seeing him through college would put an end to their responsibilities. He went to Great Britain on spring-break, joined the English military, and never returned. Then they heard of my existence, and being the conscientious people they are, they took it upon themselves to raise me."

"Adam they love you dearly. Even though you totally changed their lives, they wouldn't change a thing."

Adam let out a loud sigh, "I know that's true, but I've always felt badly about it."

Eve reached over, hugged him, and said, "Darling, how could I ever have survived without you."

"Well," replied Adam, "this data makes a layover at Snug Harbor en route to Greece much more exciting."

Peering out the plane window, Eve asked, "Darling, shall we visit Snug Harbor today or tomorrow? We decided to visit the Statue of Liberty and Ellis Island too during the short time we will be in New York."

"Well, Eve as our plane lands at 11:20 a.m. today, it might be wise to visit Miss Liberty and Ellis Island this afternoon. Then, we can spend the whole day at Snug Harbor tomorrow and not feel rushed."

"Good idea, Adam."

After checking into their hotel and freshening up a bit, they called for a cab to take them to the New York Harbor. On the way, Eve related facts about America's incredible gift from France to Adam as she read from data she requested from the New York City Chamber of Commerce before they left home.

"That majestic Lady, the Statue of Liberty, was formed of structural steel and coated with copper. Her figure alone is 151 feet tall, her right arm is 42 feet long. From the bottom of the pedestal to the tip of the torch she holds in her right hand is 300 feet. She was sculpted in France by a Frenchman named, Frederic Auguste Bartholdi. It was intended to be a gift to the United States from France in honor of liberty and escape from oppression. They had hoped to have it completed and in place by July 4, 1876 in honor of America's centennial year celebration of our freedom. Actually, it didn't happen until ten years later. Money to produce it was scarce, and the French collected from their citizens and created lotteries to help pay for it. Americans also had benefit theatrical events, art exhibits, and prize fights to help with the cost."

She continued: "There were 350 carved pieces in 214 crates that were shipped to America on a battleship. It took four months to assemble once it arrived in New York Harbor. After her arrival, a huge pedestal stand was formed, and the United States had to provide monies for that also. The seven spikes in her crown represent the 7 seas and continents of the world; the 25 windows in her crown represent the 25 gemstones found on earth. The tablet in her right hand is engraved with our independence date of July 4, 1776 depicted in Roman numerals. It was dedicated on October 28, 1886 by President Grover Cleveland."

"Wow! What a lot of history we shall experience," Adam said with awe.

CHAPTER XX

Soon, the taxi driver let them off at the ferry landing at New York Harbor. In a short time, they were on the ferry and then out to sea. First, they visited Ellis Island and felt a great deal of emotion as they realized that people from all over the world were welcomed to America after a stop-off here. The 3-story museum was devoted entirely to immigration. There were pictures and documents that covered a period of time from 1892-1954.

Spending an hour touring the museum, they were once again on the ferry, heading for the Statue of Liberty. After disembarking and approaching the statue, they ventured inside, and on the ground level, read the famous poem engraved on the inner walls of the pedestal supporting the great lady. It was written in 1883 by an American writer, Emma Lazarus. She donated the proceeds she earned for writing the poem to help pay for the pedestal. Eve read it aloud as they stood gazing upon it:

"Give me your tired, your poor, your huddled masses yearning to breathe free, the wretched refuse of your teeming shore, Send these, the homeless tempest-tossed to me; I lift my lamp beside the golden door!"

As there was just enough time to view the statue from the outside, they wandered a bit through the lower level, and felt satisfied to have enjoyed the amount of time allotted in the area. Then, they had to race for the last ferry of the day so as not to be left behind.

After breakfast the next morning, they were once again in a taxi that raced through the streets, weaving in and out. "Eve leaned over to Adam and whispered, "Honey, I am so glad we don't have to drive on these busy streets." His answering grin and nod indicated that he thoroughly agreed.

The cab driver dropped them off in front of the Snug Harbor Cultural Center which was located on the north shore of Staten Island, just minutes from the Staten Island Ferry. Their air of anticipation was running high. The first thing they viewed was a large fountain containing a statue of Neptune, or Poseidon, the god of the sea sitting on a huge shell surrounded by fish. His long, gray curly locks appeared to blow across his forehead, and in his hands was a trident, an implement that resembled a huge fork. It was symbolic of his power over the sea. With it he was said to have aroused ocean waves, shattered rocks, created storms and earthquakes, and caused shipwrecks.

"Adam, the reason the god of the sea has several names is because Poseidon is his Greek name; Neptune is his Roman name."

"Yes, I know. Neptune is also the name of one of the largest planets in our solar system too, Eve."

"That's true. I had almost forgotten."

Inside the information center, they learned much more about Snug Harbor. It had been termed, "A World Within a Fence." There was a tall iron fence surrounding all the buildings. The Cultural Center was set within an 83 acre National Historic Landmark District containing one of the finest collections of Greek Revival buildings in the United States. The Center continued to exist due to the efforts of citizens who strove to save it from destruction. They had transformed deteriorated buildings of an old seaman's retirement home into a lavish center for the arts. It was very disappointing to discover that there were no seamen living there now. Just one year ago, they had been moved to the city of Sea Level, N.C. where the new Snug Harbor Retirement Center for sailors was currently located.

"Evidently, we didn't do all our research, Adam," Eve noted.

"You're right, Eve. Of course, we are more free now to explore all their facilities without disturbing anyone."

"Yes, this pamphlet says that there were over 100 buildings here at one time. They had dormitories, gardens, greenhouses, dining rooms, barns, dairy, hospital, sanitarium, bakery, laundry, snack bar, library, vaudeville house, church and chapel. There were sheep grazing on the grounds also."

"Can you believe that one man created and paid for this complex? As we discovered earlier, in 1833 a man from Scotland named Thomas Randall, who had earned his fortune from the sea, had it built. He said it was to be open to sailors from all nations. The only stipulation was that they must be at least 65 years of age and have been 'at sea' at least 5 years. However, it seems it was not really a very happy place most of the time. The rules were very strict. They had to attend church on Sunday or else sit quietly in their room while others attended. They were punished when they broke a taboo. The sailors called it 'being on the boo.'"

"It seems they could have made it on their own with their pension." Adam said.

"They had no pension until social security came into effect when originated by President, Franklin Delano Roosevelt. Of course, they would probably have much preferred to have a small place of their own if they could have afforded it. The rules here were very strict. They even had to repeat a pledge and sign it. The pledge is shown here in the brochure. How hard it must have been. It goes like this:

"I _____ _____, having been received as an inmate of the Sailor's Snug Harbor, do hereby agree to abstain from all intoxicating liquors, and to readily and cheerfully perform such labor and service in and about the Institution and Farm as may be required of me by the Governor, without expecting or claiming any reward or remuneration therefore: also to attend church at least once every Sunday in the Sailors' Snug Harbor Chapel, unless excused by the Governor, also to conduct myself in a quiet orderly manner, and to strictly obey all the rules and regulations of the Institution."

145

"My, that sounds very restrictive, doesn't it, Adam?"

"Indeed it does!"

"I wonder how they spent their free time here. It sounds as though they were monitored rather closely. They were encouraged to make things like hammocks, baskets, mats and ship models. I suppose these items were sold to the public. Then too, there was the library where they had many books to read and the daily newspapers."

They had just walked through the dormitories and were struck by the simple décor. The sleeping rooms contained only a single bed, a small chest-of-drawers and a straight-backed chair. A reading lamp hanging on one wall was the only source of light.

Next, they walked into the chapel. It was very plain. The thing that captured their attention was a Biblical scripture emblazoned on the wall behind the pulpit. "Holiness Becometh Thine House, O' Lord Forever."

After several hours of looking about, Eve said, "Adam, there is something we should look for."

"What's that, my dear?"

"We should see if there might be some record of Nick Alexander, your great-grandfather who lived here."

"You're right. Shall we go to the record center?"

"Yes, lets."

After talking to the woman in charge, they found that all the records of seamen who had resided there had been sent to the new facility in Sea Haven, N.C. How disappointing that was. "But," the lady said, "if your relative is buried here, I might be able to help you discover his gravesite."

"We would appreciate that," Adam said.

"Just a moment," she said. "Tell me his name and approximate date of death, and I will look it up for you."

"His name was Nicholas Alexander, and he probably died sometime in the 1920's."

After looking through an alphabetized file, she said, "Oh yes, here it is. He actually died in 1929. His grave marker is #SH5703. I will ring for someone who will be able to find it for you."

"Thank you so much. Your help means a lot to us."

"You are certainly welcome."

She picked up the phone and called for a man to assist them.

As they were waiting for their guide, the lady told them a bit about the former manner of burial there. She said the deceased would be carried in a casket all the way from the church to the graveyard accompanied only by the mortician, a chaplain, and friends of the deceased, if they had any. In the fall of the year, many graves were dug in advance of any future deaths before the ground froze in the dismal, cold winter and made it impossible to do so.

They found Snug Harbor's cemetery by approaching it via a tree-lined road running along the back of the property. The hillside was sparsely dotted with grave markers that proved to be inadequate evidence of the thousands of men who were buried there. Many gravestones had been damaged by vandals. A printed sermon preached in 1856 warned the sailors to prepare for their heavenly voyage. The thought was that not many of the residents were actually prepared to meet their maker.

"Adam, I can understand the rebellion by some of the inmates as they were condemned and threatened with hell if they didn't do exactly as they were told. It reminds me of the way I was treated at the orphanage. The church services there did not teach of God's love, only His wrath. We were made fearful, and felt we could never be good enough to go to Heaven."

"I know, Eve. We certainly never can be good enough to deserve it on our own. That is why a Savior has been provided for all of us, if we will but choose Him."

Just then, an elderly man whose body appeared to be almost bent in half approached them with a map of the graveyard in his clenched fist. "Sir and Madam, if you would care to follow me, I will escort you to the burial site of your family member."

They nodded and followed him.

How sad it seemed to discover the small concrete marker containing only the name, Nicholas Alexander, and the dates of 1848–1929.

After the elderly gentleman shuffled back down the path, Eve said, "Adam, I wish we had something to place on Nick's grave site."

Then, she noticed an assortment of brightly colored wildflowers growing on the other side of the path. Before Adam could stop her, she was in the midst of them picking handfuls which she scattered all around the marker.

"There, that feels better," she said. Adam gently squeezed her hand, and they quietly retraced their steps.

CHAPTER XXI

Finally…Adam and Eve boarded a plane in New York and were headed for their final destination—Greece. After being served lunch, they were beginning to unwind and relax for the long day and night ahead aboard the plane.

Eve snuggled up to Adam and placed her head on his shoulder after raising the armrest between them. "Darling, how do you feel about meeting your step-siblings? Do you think they might be inclined to reject you?"

"It's hard to say, Eve. We've talked on the phone several times since Mom and Clarice returned to Greece, and they are pleasant enough, but I don't really know their true feelings regarding our relationship. Time will tell…"

"Well, I 'm glad we purchased gifts for them and their children. That might help keep us from feeling so much like intruders. The main thing will be the gifts for their children. Doing things for people's children is more important than doing things for the parents. It's hard to believe your step-siblings are just two years younger than you. That would make them around 30 years of age."

"Yes, evidently my grandfather, Andreas, felt he was doing the best thing for Jenny by attempting to assure her future."

"Isn't it amazing how a person's life may be totally slanted in a different direction due to another's actions, Adam?"

"Yes Eve. If Andreas had allowed Mom to keep me, my life would have been completely different. I would have been raised in Greece by a young widow. From what Mom said, she loved my father so intensely that she probably would not have remarried. I would have fit right in there because Mom was 100% Greek, and my father was 50% Greek. I suppose I look enough like a Greek to fit in."

"It will be interesting to see if you feel an affinity for Greece, Adam, and if you might feel it calling to you."

"That may be, but all I know is that I'm glad I didn't grow up there."

"Why? How can you be so sure?"

"I would not have met you, Eve. We were destined to be together."

"Oh, Darling! What a lovely thing to say. Even after 10 years of marriage, you still find me interesting?"

"More than ever, my dear."

The voice of the pilot came over the intercom, "In just 15 minutes, we will be in Athens. Please fasten your seat belts, and prepare for a landing."

"Adam, do you think we made a mistake by not planning to spend time in Athens? We will miss all the interesting sightseeing in that area."

"No, Eve. I'm not really sorry. Maybe we can return another time. The main reason we are here is to renew our wedding vows and visit with Mom and Aunt Clarice. As I wasn't able to get more time off work, that's all the sightseeing we can accomplish at this time. It would have been interesting to relax and take the ferry to Crete from the big island of Greece, but we can't take that extra time either."

After changing planes in Athens, they were now landing in Hania, the capital city of Western Crete. Their eyes caught sight of Jenny happily waving to them. The first thing they noticed was her attire. No longer wearing the somber black of mourning as when she and Clarice left the States, she wore a gray, turtle-dove dress with matching shoes and purse. A delicate silk scarf in hues of mauve, blue and gray was softly entwined around her neck. Happiness and enthusiasm caused her eyes to sparkle and brought a bit of natural color to her cheeks.

"Hello, my dears," Jenny said as they approached her.

After embracing and kissing, they went to retrieve their luggage.

"Clarice decided not to come to the airport to greet you as she is incredibly busy at the bakery preparing specialty desserts. It's amazing how many people leave all the baking to us. More and more women don't care to take the time to dedicate to this age-old craft. The art of baking exotic Greek pastries is quickly becoming a lost art."

"What a shame! Bakeries like yours will not go on forever."

"That's true. By the way, as you plan to renew your marriage vows on Friday evening, we will be closed to the public on that day while busily preparing food for your wedding reception."

"Oh Jenny, we didn't think of that. Please forgive us for only considering ourselves."

"Oh, no," said Jenny. "We knew it all along and even encouraged you to be married on Friday. Friday and Saturday are the most popular days of the year for Greek weddings."

Adam took the opportunity to sneak in a few comments between the women's friendly banter. "You mentioned that festivities usually last a week after the ceremony, but ours won't of course. As we know only you and Clarice, we obviously won't have many attendees."

"You may be surprised, Adam. As the wedding will take place close to the beach just outside our home town, there are many interested people. Your marriage will be something different for them. They all know about you, Adam. I just recently wrote a brief history of my life before marriage to Harold Andropokis for our village newspaper. It was a shock to many people to realize he was my second husband. It gave the villagers something to talk about for some time."

"Sounds as though writing runs in the family Jenny," Eve observed.

Driving southwest from the airport in Hania, it took almost an hour to reach the village where Jenny was born and had lived her whole life, a lovely area just outside Falasarna. They went directly to her home, a quaint one-story building constructed of white stucco with a red slate roof, and sitting on a hillside.

As soon as they entered Jenny's home, the smells of fresh-baked bread and strong Turkish coffee issued a welcome to the weary travelers. Until that moment, Adam and Eve had been so full of excitement, they had not been conscious of hunger pangs. Suddenly, they were both ravenous.

Jenny led them to a bedroom she had prepared for them and poured warm, steamy water that had been heated on the stove into a porcelain basin on the nightstand. As her home had no water-heater, that was the customary way to heat water for baths, dishes and everything they needed hot water for. A delightful green-speckled herbal soap rested inside a dish formed of a large seashell. They were invited to freshen up their face and hands while dinner was being spread on a table covered with a white linen tablecloth.

"Have you ever tried spanakopita?" Jenny inquired.

"Of course. We enjoy it at home quite often, although my recipe is quite simple. It doesn't call for fillo dough. It's just spinach, egg, feta cheese and seasonings, however, we love the crust too when we eat at a Greek restaurant in our neighborhood."

After several sips of a delightful table wine which Jenny called St. Helena, made of golden grapes from Peloponnesus, they almost inhaled a delicious tossed vegetable salad enhanced with feta cheese and kalamata olives, fresh-baked bread, and that delicious spinach pie.

"We will certainly sleep well tonight," Adam said. "Our tummies feel so pampered after this delicious meal."

"Don't forget the dessert," Jenny teased.

"Oh my, Jenny, it was all so delicious, but I couldn't eat another bite," protested Eve.

As it was now dusk, Jenny encouraged them to unpack and get rested for tomorrow. "Clarice is looking forward to seeing both of you so much. Due to her busy schedule and your late arrival, your reunion will have to wait until tomorrow."

"Sounds good to us. Good night, Mom."

"Good night, Son."

Eve gave Jenny a hug and thanked her for her hospitality. Then, Jenny hugged both of them at the same time and called it a day.

"Andropokis's Fournos" (Andropokis's Bakery), the sign above the door looked so familiar. Clarice and Jenny had often told them of the family business. Since Harold Andropokis, Jenny's husband passed away, they were in total charge of it. Baker's hours were not normal, as they had to be up and about long before others began to stir in their beds. So, more than most, they really prized their afternoon siesta, the time when they could truly relax as the bakery closed daily from 2–4 p.m. as did the rest of the town's businesses.

"Ohhh, Adam. Smell that delightful aroma," said Eve as she took a deep breath. Breakfast was to be served at the bakery, and they had worked up a good appetite by walking through the village that morning. "Jenny said we could help with baking too."

"Breakfast sounds good to me," noted Adam, "but baking is not my thing. I'll just watch you ladies."

Hearing their laughter and happy voices, Jenny appeared in the doorway of the bakery's kitchen. "Good morning. Did you enjoy your stroll?"

"Oh yes, Adam and I just can't get enough of this lovely area. The peace and tranquility here is quite amazing."

"Yes," Jenny agreed. "But, it hasn't always been this way. Crete has been invaded by other nations so many times through the centuries. I've been told the story of when the Turks invaded Crete many, many years ago, a group of young women vowed they would not be subject to their whims or cruelty. They went to a mountain top, held hands, and one by one, jumped to their deaths."

Eve gasped and just shook her head.

"Even in my life-span," Jennie continued, "the Nazis took over our country for a period of time. As you know, Adam, your birth was actually an off-shoot of that siege. Your father, who was of partial Greek descent, came here in 1941 to assist in our cry for freedom. As you may recall, I told you that he was in England on spring break from college, and joined the British armed forces to come here and help us."

As Jenny spoke of Luke, her first love, she seemed to be transported back in time, her eyes grew misty, and her features softened. Then, she visibly braced herself, smiled and invited them into the kitchen of the bakery.

Clarice, whose hands were immersed in a huge mound of risen dough, greeted them verbally, "Sorry I can't give you a hug right now, but as you can see, I'm full of flour."

Eve grinned and went behind Clarice and softly hugged her neck. "Oh, how I love you. You mean the world to me. After your visit to St. Louis, you and Jenny were on my mind so often and will always be in my heart."

Jenny took the opportunity to stand behind Eve and place her arms about her slender waist. "Darling Eve, you are as one of my natural children, I love you so much. Adam is blessed to have you for his wife."

"Well, don't leave me out!" exclaimed Adam. He stood squarely behind Jenny and placed both hands on her shoulders.

What a sight they were, a delightful foursome so happy, and so in tune with one another. They resembled an off-balance train. The first one in line was short and stocky, with a mane of white hair that matched the flour on her apron. The second in line was a tall, slender young woman with hair like a flame of fire and bright inquisitive green eyes. Number three was a lovely lady whose black hair was just beginning to show a few streaks of silver. The caboose was made up of a tall, slender but muscular young man with black hair enhanced by a natural cowlick and warm, gentle eyes of gray.

"How very blessed we all are," said Clarice. "I'm so thankful you two have come to visit and also that you have allowed me to share your family, Jenny. Not having children of my own, it makes me realize how fortunate I am to be involved in your lives."

"Oh Clarice," said Jenny. "How could I even begin to visualize life without you? You've always been there for me and my family, through both the good and bad times. You are truly the only mother I've ever known."

Then tears welled up in Eve's eyes. "You are *my* mother, Jenny. Clarice, you are my grandmother. I've never had anyone to care for me as you do. Your letters and phone calls have meant so much to me too. What an encouragement you both are."

"Darling Eve. You are part of our heartbeat. Coming to know you and enjoying your hospitality while we were in St. Louis was such a delight. You made us feel so welcomed and loved."

"Hey, hey! Where do I fit in the picture? Don't you ladies have room for me? After all, if it weren't for me, you wouldn't even know one another," Adam chided.

The first three parts of the train turned as if in unison, and forming a triad circle, they all enveloped Adam in their arms. He came out of their embrace laughing and found himself sprinkled with flour and a few sticky patches of dough.

"I'm so hungry. What time is breakfast served? My tummy is 'whistling Dixie'" said Adam.

"What does that mean?" inquired Clarice.

"There are several theories. 'Whistling Dixie' is a slang expression meaning being idle or doing nonsensical things. 'Dixie' was the official song of the Southern states during the Civil War. Confederate soldiers (the Southerners) would often whistle it to annoy the Union (Northern) troops as their battle lines were often close enough to hear it. To 'Whistle Dixie' means you are engaging in empty threats, or you are all talk and no action. To say, 'I ain't just 'whistlin' Dixie' means you are prepared to back up your threats of physical action," Adam explained.

"Some day you must tell us more about the Civil War in your country," said Clarice.

"It's a sad story, and hard to believe it actually happened," said Eve.

As they walked toward the rear of the bakery, they spied a table set with a white linen cloth and matching napkins. It was enhanced by a vase filled with pink, white and lavender-colored lilacs. Four place settings of blue and white china awaited their dining pleasure.

Clarice set aside the huge container of rising dough, carefully washed her hands, and beckoned them to the table.

Eve buried her nose in the floral arrangement while inhaling deeply. She stood up abruptly and sneezed heartily.

"Oh my," said Clarice. "Don't tell me you're allergic to lilacs. We planned to use them as part of the floral table decorations at your wedding reception."

"I'm okay. I just sniffed up one of the tiny flowers. Lilacs are my favorite flower. The scent brings back some kind of pleasant memory from my childhood. I can't quite recall it, but each time I smell lilacs, it makes me feel so happy and loved."

"We've never discussed your childhood, Eve. You haven't mentioned your parents. Tell us about yourself. Do you have any siblings?" queried Jenny.

"I have no idea, Jenny. I grew up in several homes for orphans in South St. Louis. The state evidently paid for all my needs."

"Oh dear! Didn't they give you any information about your parents when you were old enough to understand?"

"All I know is that I was transferred from a home that burned down. Someone said that all the records were probably destroyed."

"Do you remember the fire?" Clarice asked.

"Yes, I do. It was in an old house, and flames were shooting out from the third floor windows and the roof. Evidently, they had time to get us all out safely."

"Where did you go?"

"We went to the home of a woman who lived in the neighborhood. She was an old lady who made bread and butter sandwiches and hot chocolate for all of us. Later, buses arrived and took us to other homes."

"Were you all able to stay together?"

"No, there were quite a few of us. I don't know how many, but we were split up. My very best friend, Julie and I were separated."

"Did you ever see her again?"

"No. I missed her so much. We used to try to see who could make up the best stories. They had to be verbal as we couldn't write yet. At night, while we lay in our beds, we would whisper them softly to one another so the people in charge couldn't hear. One of us would start the story, and the other would add to it. We knew we would be separated if we were caught talking after lights out, so we were very quiet. Sometimes, we fell asleep before our story ended."

"So...Julie was eventually moved to another home."

"Yes, she was. I never saw her again of course, as we had no control over our destiny." Then in a reflective, musing tone, she said, "It's strange how some people have such an influence on our lives and we never forget them."

"How did Julie influence you later on, Eve?"

"Because of the great love we had for story-telling, I wrote mine down as soon as I was able, and writing later became my career."

"How interesting. Do you specifically remember anyone else?"

"There was a boy who looked so much like me—they teased us all the time about it. He too, had auburn hair and green eyes. Some people said we had auburn hair, others said it was red. It seemed to change with the lights around us. Anyway, we were always getting on one another's nerves. He teased me constantly about having red hair, but his was the same color as mine."

"Did the two of you stay together?"

"Yes, he and I were at the same orphanage until we were approximately 12 years of age. I have no idea what happened to him later either. His name was Steve. Please, I don't want to talk about it any more. It is disturbing and makes me feel like crying."

By the time Jenny and Eve had finished their conversation, lunch was on the table. Clarice had bustled around preparing it and they all gratefully sat down to enjoy the tasty breakfast. The table was set with several types of pastries that had just been removed from the oven. A large platter of various fruits and cheeses made a mouth-watering, colorful display. Clarice and Jenny made their customary sign of the cross while giving thanks for their meal. Adam and Eve bowed their heads in silence.

Adam reached over to take Eve's hand while saying, "One of the things that drew us together was our lonely childhoods."

"Were you really lonely, Adam? You were with your father's parents," cited Jenny.

"Yes, I was, but being told both parents were deceased left me feeling displaced. My grandparents were good people, but weren't thrilled to have a baby in their care. As they had already raised a child, my father, it was a real hardship for them to be on call constantly. Diapers, formulas, pre-school, kindergarten, grade school, high school, college and all in between. They had a good lifestyle in San Francisco where they had both grown up, and were more or less, socialites. When I was eight years of age, they moved to St. Louis after Gramps was transferred there by the company he worked for. As soon as I graduated from college, they moved to Florida. They got a beachside cottage in St. Petersburg and began to move with the 'in-group' retirees who spend their time socializing."

"But, they loved you, didn't they?"

"Yes they did, but devoting another 20 plus years of their lives raising a grandchild had to be very difficult."

"Your grandfather is of Greek origin, isn't he? What about your grandmother?"

"Grams is English. She has blonde hair and gray eyes. Luke, my father inherited Gramp's black hair and Gram's gray eyes. I understand he had a cowlick just like mine. Is that right, Mom?"

"Yes, it is. I tried so many times to smooth it down by dabbing it with water and oil. It complied for a short time, but then, next time I looked, it was standing up again."

Eve jokingly said while running her fingers through Adam's cowlick, "Many times I've considered cutting yours off Adam, but then you would have a hole in your head."

They all laughed.

That afternoon, the bakery closed at 2:00 p.m. as was the custom. All businesses and shops shut down to allow workers to go home for a siesta. At 4:00 p.m., they all reopened.

As Adam and Eve were on a stateside schedule, they decided not to lie down, but rather to do more exploring. The church where they planned to repeat their wedding vows was on their agenda. As it was about 5 miles south of town, they decided to take a bus. Half an hour later, they were walking hand-in-hand on the beach and spied the small chapel where they would soon be united even more, if that were possible. A tall cliff with a winding trail leading to the sandy beach area caught their eye.

"Look at the sand, Adam. It is actually pink in color. Can that be an optical illusion?"

"No, Eve. I remember reading about the pink sand, and wondered if it might be due to residues of pink coral? I don't know and wonder if anyone else does."

"I don't know either, but this will be just perfect, Adam."

CHAPTER XXII

"Eve, I had the most amazing thought," Clarice said. "You mentioned a boy in the orphanage with you whose coloring of red hair and green eyes looked identical to yours?"

"Yes, that's true."

"What was his apparent age?"

"Well...he was probably around the same age as me."

"And how old was that?"

"Approximately 12 years of age when we were separated."

"And his name was...?"

"Steve."

"The names of Eve and Steve have a similar ring, don't you think?"

"I suppose so."

"Have you ever stopped to think the two of you might be twins?"

Unexpected tears began to stream from Eve's tightly shut eyes. "Oh yes, I have. Even though he teased me all the time, there was a definite attachment to him. We seemed to look out for one another. If one of us happened to be scolded for something, the other would attempt to comfort them later. One night when Julie and I were separated for talking after a lights-out warning, my breakfast was withheld the next morning as punishment. As soon as possible, Steve slipped an orange and a piece of dry toast to me as we sat in class."

"Were you able to eat it?"

"Yes, I was. I excused myself and went to the restroom to eat."

"How did you remove it without being seen?"

"I put one item under each armpit and walked very slowly from the classroom."

"So, you made it without getting caught?"

"No, not exactly. Even though I ate it very hurriedly, the smell of a fresh orange is quite distinctive. The teacher sent one of the older girls to check on me as I was delayed, and the girl smelled the aroma. I had just placed the last orange slice in my mouth, and to my dismay, when she walked in, a bit of juice ran down my chin."

Clarice smiled and said, "Could that be why you never eat an orange from our selections of fruit?"

"Why, I never thought of that. I just know that the sight and smell of an orange makes me feel a bit queasy."

Adam placed his arms around Eve and gently drew her to himself, while saying, "Honey, have you really given much serious thought to the possibility of a close relationship with that young boy?"

"Oh Adam, I have. There are times when I awake during the night and feel so alone and frightened"

"Why don't you wake me?"

"It seems so silly, Adam. I wouldn't be able to explain what I was feeling. Even now, I'm not really sure. There seems to be a very empty part of myself that's like a deep gnawing hole, a hole that can't be filled."

Clarice reached out and clasped both of Eve's hands in her own. "I know the feeling, my dear. That is how I've felt since Andreas, my twin brother passed away. We were together during gestation, as children, and then later as lifelong friends. I miss him so much and think of him quite often even though I know I'll see him again in Heaven one day. During our youth, we would quite often begin to say the same thing at the same time. It was as though there was an electronic umbilical cord holding us together."

"Oh Clarice," Jenny said. "I had no idea. How it must have offended you when I spoke sorrowfully about how badly my father seemed to treat me."

"No, my dear, I quite understood. After Andreas lost his Vivian, his wife, he was a completely different man. He became unhappy and bitter. We were no longer on the same wavelength."

"Did you try to encourage him in realizing his life had not ended with Mom's?" Jenny asked.

"Of course, but the grieving went on the rest of his life."

"Well," said Jenny, "I can understand that in a way. Even though I was truly blessed later to have Harold and the twins, Samuel and Sarah, I never forgot Luke and the absolutely perfect relationship we had shared. A love like that seems to be a 'once in a lifetime thing.'"

Again, Adam felt at a loss to completely understand his three ladies. He wondered why males and female psyches were so different. Why would a person pine away for another after so many years had gone by? Even though he loved Eve with all his heart, would he feel like giving up on life if he lost her? Maybe so… He hoped that test was one that he would never have to take. After all, women usually have a longer lifespan than men, and so Eve would probably outlive him.

"Eve," he said gently, "I think we should probably conduct a bit of research and see if we can locate some news about Steve when we return to the States."

Eve's green eyes grew wide with love and appreciation as she took his hand and quietly said, "Yes, lets."

"Good morning, Clarice and Jenny," said Eve as she greeted them in her usual bubbly manner. "Adam and I are here to help you make cookies. Are we on time?"

"Yes, you are," responded Clarice with a smile. "It's now 10 a.m. Jenny and I arrived several hours ago to process the dough."

"What's that lovely smell?" Eve asked.

"It's the almond extract we use for flavoring."

Adam glanced into the bakery's kitchen and spied a huge metal processor with a handle. "Is that the machine you want me to operate?"

"Yes, come see," invited Jenny.

As he approached the apparatus, he noted that it was filled almost to the top with thick yellow dough.

"Look," said Jenny, as she slid a large oiled cookie sheet underneath and cranked the handle. Each turn produced a rounded piece of dough that resembled a cookie prepared for baking.

"Oh great," said Eve. "They're all ready for the oven. We can just watch you fill the trays, Adam."

Clarice placed a hand on each of their shoulders and grinned, "Don't you wish that were true," she said. "This is just the beginning. Now, we must sit down and prepare the cookies for baking."

"What do you do now, decorate them?"

"It should be so simple," laughed Jenny as she carefully washed the huge oblong table with warm soapy water, rinsed and dried it. "Please sit down, and I will show you."

Jenny took the rounded cookie dough, placed it between the palms of her hands, and began a rolling motion. It very quickly became elongated as the shape changed to resemble a healthy looking worm about 4" in length. With a very deft, light touch, and using fingertips of both her hands, the dough took on an oily look and increased in length two more inches. She then created a horseshoe effect and continued to loop one side over the other up to the end until it resembled a two-stranded braid. Then, it was lightly turned over and the underneath portion showed perfect symmetry. Picking up both ends at once, she gently laid it on an awaiting, oiled cookie sheet.

Adam and Eve looked rather mesmerized as Jenny picked up another rounded form of golden dough and repeated the action once again.

"You do that so quickly and it looks perfect," Eve commented as she approached the wash basin to cleanse her hands. Then she said, "Now, let *me* try."

Confident that she could repeat the action Jenny had demonstrated, Eve picked up a piece of dough, rubbed it between the palms of her hands, and dropped it on the table. One end of the dough was thick and chunky, the other so thin it already had a hole in it. Distressed, Eve looked up with a frown.

"Try again," Jenny spoke encouragingly.

"How?" Eve asked.

"Pick it up, press it together and begin again."

Eve did so, and the next time, it was chunky in the middle and the ends were thin enough to see through.

"Oh my," said Eve as she picked up the dough again. This time the lump was extremely oily from too much handling, and the butter in the dough was beginning to melt from the heat of her hands.

Jenny smiled and said, "Watch me, Eve. After you lay it down, use only your fingertips in a light, rolling manner." Once again, Jenny demonstrated the age-old manner of a baker's skills.

"What are we making?" Eve asked.

"They are called koulouria, or the Easter cookie. Even though Easter is past, we are still preparing them as the demand of our customers is always great."

Watching and listening as they continued to make preparation at another work-station were their two helpers, Maria and Sophia. Maria's hands moved quickly and efficiently. In a matter of seconds, she repeated the entire process and placed the newly-formed dough on a large cookie sheet. After each cookie sheet was filled, Sophia brushed a blended-mixture containing milk, egg and vanilla on top of each cookie in preparation for baking.

As Eve's eyes grew wide while watching the knack with which they performed the repetitive action, she began to feel very inefficient.

Clarice realized her feelings of inadequacy and patted her on the shoulder.

Eve sighed and said, "I feel so useless."

"Please don't" said Jenny. "We have been repeating this process for many years. There are many other things that you can help with."

Jenny pointed to an area where previously baked cookies had been set to cool. "All these cookies must be placed in containers. You might like to do that, as we must have the space on the table for cookies that are in the oven baking right now." The plastic container was quite large and would hold many dozens of cookies.

Jenny continued, "The baked cookies are rectangular in shape, and side-by-side placement is standard." Eve found that it held three rows with 8 cookies side-by-side on the bottom. When that row was filled, the cookies placed on top went in the opposite direction. She discovered that the placement job was much easier than shaping cookies for baking. After a time, she had filled a tall container and began a second one. Glancing at

Adam, she noted that he was constantly turning the handle on the apparatus to produce rounded hunks of dough, while adjusting the pan's position to accept more and more. So intent was he on the project, that his tongue appeared to be caught between his lips and front teeth as he concentrated.

Several hours later, a lunch-break seemed appropriate. The cookies had all been baked and stored in containers. For the last half hour, Clarice had been preparing a meal for them. A huge wooden bowl was filled with a healthy-looking salad of many fresh items from produce row. The top of the salad had been sprinkled with large chunks of feta cheese, and kalamara olives were strewn about.

Broccoli-cheese soup thickened with boiled potatoes took priority as their first course. A chicken-vegetable potpie with fillo crust had just left the oven. An overwhelming, enticing aroma steamed from a large pot of perking Turkish coffee. Anticipation was rampant amongst them as they fulfilled their appetites desires.

Soon, the sound of something boiling on the stove caught their attention. Eve stood up to see where the rhythmic bubbling emanated from. She spied tiny spots of red appearing on the stovetop. "What is going on?" she asked.

Jenny laughed and replied, "You hear the centerpieces for our Easter bread being prepared."

"Easter bread… You have Easter bread and Easter cookies?"

"Yes, Eve. We hard-boil eggs and color them scarlet to represent the blood Christ Jesus shed for us. When we form the bread, it is made from 3 long strips of dough that are braided. These represent the Holy Trinity of the Godhead—Father, Son, and Holy Spirit, Three in One. In the center of the bread, we place at least one scarlet egg, sometimes more."

"My, how symbolic the bread is. What type of dough does it have?"

"It's actually a sweet bread. Some compare it to the dough of a Danish pastry. We already prepared many loaves of Easter bread, and make more now to be frozen. There are people who have not yet purchased this very special treat that comes once a year."

"As you make so many cookies at a time, and in advance of the sale, how do you keep them fresh?"

"A napkin saturated in vanilla extract is placed inside the container of cookies, and then a lid is placed on top. This is what keeps them fresh and enhances their aroma."

"Interesting..."

CHAPTER XXIII

"Adam, suddenly I feel quite nervous about meeting your siblings, Sarah and Samuel. It's interesting that you were all given Biblical names."

"Yes, isn't it? I was first and have the name of the very first person ever created. Sarah was the name of the beautiful woman married to Abraham. He was the very beginning of the Jewish race."

"The Bible actually tells us he was the first Hebrew, which later translated to Jewish."

"How could Abraham have been the first Jew? If his parents weren't Jewish, how could he achieve that status?"

"Don't you remember, Adam? He became a Jew through the ritual of circumcision. He was then 99 years of age, the first male to ever be circumcised."

"Ouch! At his age, that must have hurt!"

"I dare say it did, but his heartfelt desire was to please God. He and all the males in his household were circumcised. From then on, the practice has been performed on 8-day old male Jewish babies."

"Why? What does it mean?"

It is a symbol of the covenant between God and Abraham. God told Abraham that he would be a father of many nations, and that He would be his God. Abraham's descendents would be as large in number as the stars in the heavens."

"What about Samuel, Eve. Who was he?"

"Samuel was a special gift from God to a previously childless woman, named Hannah. She promised God that if He allowed her to have a baby, she would return the child to Him."

"How? Did she kill the baby?"

"No, silly! When Samuel was born, she cared for him and took him to the temple as soon as he was weaned. As a child, he helped the priests there. Later, Samuel became a great prophet of God. God also granted Hannah more children after the birth of Samuel."

"You're certainly familiar with Bible characters, Eve."

"As you know Adam, I've been attending a women's Bible study at a neighbor's home. Also, I read through the Bible completely by reading a specific portion each day. We can never learn it all. God's Word is so awesome. We can read the same scriptures many times, and just keep learning more from it. Another thing, I was baptized as a teen-ager when I attended church with a friend who planned to be baptized that day. When they gave an altar-call, I went forward and they invited me to be baptized too if I wished. I felt so brand-new and happy that I wanted to experience all God wanted to give me. When they mentioned that Jesus told his disciples to baptize believers, I decided to be baptized too."

"Yes, we've both been baptized. You remember my telling you that my grandparents had me baptized as a youth in the Greek Orthodox Church, as that was the religion of my mother. Thank you for telling me about Samuel in the Bible. Now, I can talk to Sarah and Samuel about the saints after whom they're named," Adam said.

Jenny had previously arranged to have the three siblings meet without the families of Sarah and Samuel at her home that evening. Eve promised to merely look and listen. Having less people there seemed a good opportunity for them to interact as freely and easily as possible.

The dining room table was set for six with an ice-blue linen tablecloth. In the center of the table was a crystal vase filled with fresh flowers of various hues. Jenny had used place settings of her finest crystal, china and sterling. The sitting room which adjoined it was arranged with three sofas in horseshoe shape, with a huge coffee table in the center. Six wine goblets stood on six hand-embroidered napkins and a snack tray sat in the center. Now, Eve's attention was drawn to the total décor of the room.

Hosts of framed family photos adorned the walls and tables. On tiny easels, stood platters and dishes that were obviously antique and precious to the family. Hand-crocheted doilies were strategically placed on the backs and arms of the sofas. The walls were painted sky-blue which were further enhanced by the hooked throw rugs that contained a variety of colors including the same blue shade as the walls.

As Jenny and Eve surveyed the arrangement, Eve noted that Jenny's olive complexion was flushed, and a fan-shaped area of scarlet blotches appeared on her neck. Another giveaway was her voice which sounded several octaves higher than usual, and trembled from time to time.

Eve had already bathed and was attired in a frothy-looking peach peasant blouse and skirt in a deeper shade of peach. She had come downstairs to help. Seeing and hearing Jenny, and noting the visible tremor of her hands, Eve pulled her aside and said, "Jenny, let's pray about this meeting between Adam and his siblings. I'm sure everyone is a bit apprehensive. As the hostess, you've done an excellent job of preparation. Now, I want to pray that God keeps you calm."

After they prayed together, Jenny exuded a deep sign and said, "Eve, you are such a beautiful, understanding, sensitive, spiritual person. How can I ever thank you?"

"It is always my pleasure to pray, Jenny. This will be a happy time for all of us."

Promptly at 7:00 p.m., Jenny went to the front door in response to a knock and greeted her twins. Clarice was busy in the kitchen, and Adam and Eve stood to their feet to meet Adam's step-siblings. An incredibly handsome young couple stood on the threshold trying to adjust their eyes to the darkened room after intense exposure to the sunlight.

Putting an arm around the waists of each of her twins, Jenny lovingly drew them into the room. Adam stepped forward with his right hand outstretched toward his brother, Samuel. Before Samuel could respond, his sister, Sarah threw her arms around Adam's waist. Her tiny 5'2" frame on tiptoes could not even reach his neck. The black-haired beauty was enraptured by the sight of the man with hair as black as her own. With her luminous black eyes flashing, she looked intently into Adam's clear gray ones. Adam was taken back a bit as he had never been greeted so enthusiastically.

"Adam, my brother!" she trilled. He just grinned and said, "You must be Sarah."

Samuel laughed out loud and said, "Looks as though our sister has extended enough welcome for both of us."

They were finally able to shake hands, and Adam noted that Samuel looked much like a taller, heavier version of Sarah minus the womanly curves. However, his pencil-thin black mustache and goatee confirmed his manhood. Bright white teeth were made more visible due to their gorgeous olive-toned complexions. Both wore clothing in combination colors of black, red and white.

Jenny crossed the room and drew Eve into the family circle to include her. "Samuel and Sarah, may I present to you…Eve…Adam's lovely wife of the past ten years."

Sarah greeted Eve warmly saying, "Your hair is the color I have always admired. In fact, if my complexion were not so tawny, I would have helped it along with a manmade color years ago."

Eve responded by saying, "Sarah, I only wish my skin tones were like yours. Staying out of the sun has always been so difficult for me, as I love being out-of-doors."

"Well," said Samuel, "it's my turn to meet Eve." Turning toward her, he complimented her on her beauty, grace and poise.

"You all make me feel self-conscious, but oh…so special."

Eve and Samuel held hands for a moment, and then exchanged a quick hug.

Clarice ventured in from the kitchen and greeted their guests. She was a homespun sight wearing a large white apron, and her left cheek sported what looked like a smudge of flour. "Please sit down and enjoy a glass of wine. I must return to the kitchen. In just 30 minutes, dinner will be served. I'm running a bit late today as I overslept while taking my siesta. The bakery business has increased a tremendous amount this week due to purchases of extra breads and pastries for the Easter celebration of our regular customers, and also the wedding celebration. Easter celebration goes on for a week or so after the actual holiday."

An hour or so was spent sipping the delicate wine while becoming further acquainted. Then, a delicious, traditional Greek-style dinner was shared. Afterwards, Clarice invited them to return to the living room accompanied by cups of Turkish coffee and a favorite dessert of baklava topped with creamy vanilla ice cream.

Suddenly, Sarah's gaze shifted to her watch. "Oh my, it's almost 10:30. My little girls have a hard time going to sleep without their nightly bedtime story."

As Adam stood to his feet, he and Sarah embraced. Samuel joined them, and the three held hands as Adam said in an emotional voice, "I never realized how wonderful it would be to have siblings. After this evening, I'll always feel part of both of you."

Adam then hugged each of them individually once more, while gesturing for Eve to join them. Suddenly, the little circle of four increased to become a circle of six, as Jenny and Clarice took their places.

The twins wished their family a good night, and joyfully said, "We'll see you Friday evening for your big celebration," blowing kisses as they departed.

"A picnic in a public park sounds like a great way to properly introduce Adam and Eve to the rest of our family in person," Jenny responded to a suggestion by Clarice. "We should prepare the food at our bakery. That way, we can keep track of the menu, and make it a simple picnic luncheon that the children will enjoy too."

"Well, let's take a head count, Clarice. There will be Adam and Eve, Sarah, her husband Mike, their 3 daughters, Samuel, his wife, Maria, and their son, you and me. That makes an even dozen. Samuel will pick up the food after we prepare it, and Sarah plans to bring the games. It is important that you and I arrive early at the park to secure the area in the center of the park. There will be plenty room for all with the three picnic tables and six benches. We will need the benches mainly for eating as the children will be playing most of the time.

"Sounds great. Let's try for Sunday afternoon after church. That way everyone should be free to attend.

At the picnic, Eve and Sarah took the opportunity to meet the other family members and to discuss a few things of the wedding plans. "Sarah, your daughters are simply darling. What are their ages?"

"Darla is seven, Debra is six and Darcy is five years of age."

"I'm so glad we obtained their dress sizes before leaving the States. We had hoped they could wear the garments as our little flower girls. Since we found that neither flower girls nor ring-bearers are part of an Orthodox Greek wedding, they can wear them to the church, and afterwards at the reception."

"What color did you get, Eve?"

"Peach. It's a delicate shade that will be perfect with their black hair and eyes, and their lovely olive complexions."

"Yes, I agree. They will certainly enjoy getting dressed up for such a special occasion. It will make them feel so pretty. Then too, many of their little friends will be there to see them."

"It sounds as though you've all invited many people to attend; it will truly be a gala affair. Of course, we knew no one when we arrived but Jenny and Clarice. Before we return home, we will have many new friends."

"Oh, by the way," Eve continued, "I wish we could have purchased Samuel's son David a little suit, but it's harder to fit boys than girls."

"Yes, I agree, but it was fortunate that they found that navy blue suit for him. I understand that Adam will be wearing navy blue also. That will put them in sync."

"By the way, Adam doesn't know that I have a surprise for him regarding his ring. He will be quite amazed; it will be an addition to his wedding ring." Eve paused to take a breath...

"Oh, what will the addition to Adam's ring look like?"

Eve smiled sweetly and said, "Sorry, but you'll have to wait to see it too. It will be a complete surprise. Anyway, after the ceremony, we would like for your three daughters and David to walk down the hillside adjacent to the church and taverna. David and Darla will both be carrying a white wicker basket full of flowers. Debra and Darcy will be plucking them from the basket and strewing flowers along the hillside until they reach the area where the guests, decorations, music and food will be. As the area will be sloped, do you think that might be a problem for them? I am concerned that they might fear losing their footing."

"No, I don't think so. They all take dance lessons and are quite agile."

Jenny reached into one of the baskets, took out an old, ornate dinner bell and shook it in a lively manner. "Time to eat," she informed her family. Samuel and Adam broke off their conversation about sports and joined the others.

Clarice, that amazing lady, had spread three matching, colorful cloths on the tables and as quickly placed food on top as swirling eddies of winds attempted to remove them as quickly as she placed them there. The wind seems determined to uproot our meal. Please take your seats and enjoy your lunch." She began passing bowls with enticing aromas around the table. The children's parents served them first as they knew which foods each child would eat.

After a prayer of thanksgiving, lunch was served and conversation halted briefly as hunger took over. The only audible sounds were occasional ohs and ahs as they all enjoyed the hearty meal.

"Aunt Clarice, I don't know how you do it," Adam said while licking his lips, "Every single food item you served is better than the one before."

"Thank you my dear. I'm so glad you are enjoying the lunch. It's a privilege for me to be able to prepare it. But, even more than that, it's a delight to spend time with all of you. For a woman whose husband is gone, and who has no children, you all make me feel so blessed to have each one of you."

Then of course, they all felt the urge to line up and give Clarice a big hug, each of which she returned with a happy heart.

Just as they had finished the delicious luncheon and the children prepared to take their games out to play, heavy rains came pouring down. It began as a sprinkle and then turned into a storm. They threw plastic sheets over the picnic supplies and ran for shelter. After 15 minutes the storm abated and they returned to the picnic area.

Jenny laughed and said it reminded her of the day on the sailboat at Carlyle Lake the year before. "Clarice, do you remember our poker game played below deck while the storm raged above?"

"Of course, Jenny. In fact, I brought some cards along today, just in case." She then pulled 4 decks from one of her boxes. "I also have board games for the children."

Jenny then cleared the table and set up the games. After an afternoon of chatting amidst the games, it seemed everyone felt they had a marvelous opportunity to become better acquainted.

In the morning, Adam and Eve decided to tour what some call the "Grand Canyon of Greece." As they rode the bus, Eve began to share more of the knowledge with Adam that she had discovered while doing research at the library before they left the States.

"Adam, have you ever stopped to realize that Greece lies between three continents? Europe to the north, Asia to the east, and Africa to the south. No wonder so many invaders have attempted to conquer them. They have the ultimate location. Do you know that Greece had the first democratic government? America is more like Greece than I realized."

"That's true, Eve. They are basically a Christian nation just as America is. Their national flag in colors of blue and white actually depicts the cross of Christ. Another reason I am beginning to feel very comfortable here is that it almost feels like home."

"Well, of course Adam, so many of your family members live here."

"Yes, and they have all made us feel welcome."

"The bus is stopping now. We seem to have arrived at our destination."

"I'm glad we saved a day to visit Samaria Gorge, Adam. Let's see what the brochure says about it. It's the only national park in Crete, and has the largest, most impressive gorge in Europe. It's 18 km long, and stretches from Xylosalo to Agia Roumeli and takes about 6 hours to cover it all on foot. We had better get started."

In front of them was the entry way and they had to hold onto the rails of a steep, wooden staircase as they climbed lower and lower into the crevice. Afterwards, they waded through streams, while trying to secure their footing, and giggled as they kept sliding off of moss-covered rocks. The air was full of the scent of pines and cypress, and they drank from the fresh mountain stream that flowed down the hillside. Then, the path narrowed and became very slender, as the walls around it rose majestically to introduce them to a very famous area. Sounds were magnified as the wind blew through the breezeway. It was a ten-foot span between tall cliffs called the Iron Gates. Local legends told of water sprites and demons lodging there.

After an hour, Eve said, "Darling, I don't think I can walk five more hours. If we turn around now and go back, we will return to the entrance in only one hour. That way, it will take only 2 hours."

Adam laughed and said, "Okay my dear. Just remember that I told you how long it would take to go through the entire park and you were anxious to get started."

"Women have the option of changing their minds."

On their return bus ride, Eve intrigued Adam with stories she had read concerning the "Bull Leapers of Greece." It seemed that one of their favorite sports was begun by turning a bull loose in a ring. Young acrobats would vault and spring over the bulls backs as they charged. Many times, they narrowly missed the bull's sharp horns. It was thought that this might possibly have been the forerunner of bull fights in Spain.

"All I know Eve, is that neither sport is very appealing. I have heard stories of men being gored by bulls and there wouldn't be much glory in that."

Jenny encouraged them to visit areas in Hanai, one of the nicest towns in Crete. In the town center was an interesting marketplace built in 1911. It contained every type of grocery store, butcher shops, fish markets, and vegetable stands. Next to the market was a place called the Public Gardens. What an area of incredible tranquility.

Outside of Hanai, in a village called Maleme they discovered a famous cemetery, where almost 5,000 Germans are buried who died while invading Crete in 1941 during World War II. It contains a huge cross and a statue of an attacking eagle. Germans bought the plot of land after the war and buried their own troops. Each grave contains a marker and most buried there were in their late teens or early twenties. Two uniformed German soldiers patrol the area day and night.

Another cemetery containing Allies from the war who lay at rest are in a cemetery in Souda. They came from Australia, New Zealand and England to help the Cretans protect themselves and their country.

Adam and Eve were very moved to realize again the futility of war and the terrible waste of lives.

CHAPTER XXIV

What a lot of excitement permeated the air on the Friday they had looked forward to for so long. Eve was invited to use Jenny's bedroom to dress for the wedding ceremony. Adam dressed in the other bedroom, and they were driven to the church at separate times to prevent Adam from an advance viewing of his bride.

The rustic, antique chapel close to Falasarna was situated on a hillside overlooking the Aegean Sea. What a tranquil, isolated area, a perfect spot for their wedding and reception. The only other visible structure was a taverna adjoining the beachside road. Its outdoor tables and chairs were to be part of the reception for those who did not care to sit in the sandy area. There was even talk of a submerged ancient city nearby, but Adam had not had time to dive and search for it, even though he and Eve loved scuba-diving.

Olive trees appeared splattered about, growing at strange angles as though stretching to embrace the sun's enticing rays. The cliff-side, earthen staircase sloped down to the beach and was enhanced by a myriad display of multi-colored flowers strewn on each level. In the foreground appeared the Agean Sea which glittered with the hue of sapphire-studded precious gems. In early preparation for the close of day, huge torches were displayed on stands which would be lit later to illuminate the bridal party as they planned to descend to the beach area where the excited guests awaited the presence of the bride and groom.

Soft breezes gently stirred the garlands of flowers and ivy which cascaded down the sides of the cliff. White-capped waves swirled in the distance amidst the blue/green waters, then grew smaller as they reached a shallow area close to the shore where they gently kissed the sandy beach, and then slowly receded. Countless seashells dotted the shoreline. Sea gulls seemed determined to join the festivities as they competitively dove for brightly-colored fish.

The tides had been considered when making their wedding plans. Low tide often brings residue to the beach and an unpleasant odor. High tide may cause rogue-driven waves. So, the affair was planned around the ebb tide, as the outgoing tide was soft and quiet, and the cove was buffeted by rock to subdue strong winds. Wild goats munching on sea-grass dotted the shoreline, and no one seemed to find them intruders.

As the scheduled time approached, the soft, early evening setting sun cast a rosy hue over all in attendance, and the coral pink sand dunes in the area added to the charm. The whole setting was aided by a flattering glow, the type that soft candlelight aids in inspiring romantic dinners. The actual ceremony was planned to commence at dusk.

Finally, the guests filed into the chapel, almost as though loath to leave the amazing scene while observing the last rays of sunlight. After they were all seated, Adam was instructed to walk to the front of the chapel and await his bride. Turning and looking backward in the chapel, the guests spied the most enchanting sight most of them had ever seen. Almost like a scene from another world, a beautiful fair maiden appeared to be floating slowly down the aisle. This incredible creature attired in seafoam green with a wreath in her hair of lavender orchids, pale peach rosebuds, and baby's breath that matched the bridal bouquet, appeared holding Samuel's left arm. Adam had been deep in thought, but his gaze shifted as he heard the gasps of their guests.

He had been reminiscing of the way Eve looked 10 years ago as a tall, slender blushing bride dressed in a plain navy-blue suit. Her only bouquet then had been a single red rose surrounded by several sprays of tiny white flowers called baby's breath, and encased in a sheet of the typical shiny, hunter-green colored paper that most florists used at that time. The most colorful things about her had been her red hair and green eyes. The Justice of the Peace seemed to sense their nervousness and made a brief joke at which they both obligingly chuckled. The waiting period at that time was 3 days after the blood tests were taken before a marriage license could be issued. Those three days seemed an eternity.

"I now pronounce you man and wife" had sounded so strange to him. He absolutely *was* a man, even before the ceremony. Were the vows only for the woman? Would this new state of being called marriage affect only the bride?

As Adam's mind returned to the present, he found himself amazed to realize that his wife of the past 10 years was even more lovely than at their original wedding ceremony. At 32 years of age, she was now certainly in her prime. How had he rated someone so beautiful, and yet so wholesome, so unselfish and caring?

As Eve slowly approached the front of the chapel where the priest awaited them, her eyes caught those of her husband, and her thoughts were similar to his. Ten years ago in the downtown court house, he had the appearance of a young, innocent god. Attired in his navy blue suit, standing 6'4" tall, with black hair and gray eyes, he exuded an amazing aura. Later, she told him that he reminded her of a young Abe Lincoln— same height—same hair and eye colors, but oh, so much more handsome. For some reason, on that day, even his cowlick was subdued. He had asked a friend from college who had just converted his hair style from an afro to an ivy league cut, how he kept all his hair in place. He was encouraged to apply something that looked and smelled like bear grease on the stubborn area. It worked.

Now, ten years later, she smiled to realize that he should have asked for the brand name of the hair pomade. Even at this distance, she could see his old, familiar cowlick standing tall.

Then suddenly, Eve reached the front of the chapel. A white-robed priest with a silver crucifix hanging about his neck, handed a long, white, lit candle to each of them, while placing it in their left hands. The candles were symbolic of their willingness to accept Christ in their lives. White ribbons tied in bows with streamers adorned the bottom of each candle and hung down gracefully towards the floor. All the while, the congregation stood and observed.

Sarah and Samuel, Adam's siblings, were part of the ceremony also as the engaged couple must have religious sponsors. The male sponsor is called the koumbaro, and the female is called the koumbara. It was a surprise to Adam and Eve that the service would begin with their betrothal, even though they were already married. In America betrothal indicates engagement to be married. Here, the betrothal consisted of the exchange of wedding rings. The priest held their original wedding rings in his hands and blessed them, and handed them to Sarah. Sarah actually lightly touched the ring to the fingertips of Eve and then of Adam, and back again to total three times, finally placing them on the right ring finger of the betrothed rather than the left where wedding rings are worn in the States. The right hands for the rings are chosen as it is the right hand of God that blesses, and the right hand of God to which Christ ascended.

It was noted that all the marriage sacraments were performed three times in a row in honor of The Father, Son and Holy Spirit, and the sign of the cross was done in three's throughout the ceremony also, inviting God to be in charge of their lives together.

It was surprising to Eve that betrothed couples do not repeat vows at the wedding. The ceremony itself indicated the couple's willingness to come forward, be married, and accept God as the Head of their household.

After the exchange of rings, the right hands of the couple were joined together and stayed joined until the end of the ceremony. At one point in time, the right hand of the priest covered the couples joined hands with his own right hand, while the lit candles continued to be held in the couple's left hands.

Then, there was a crowning with the stefana. The stefana consisted of two slender crowns covered with orange blossoms, symbolic of love and purity. The crowns were attached to one another with a long, wide, white, satin ribbon. One crown was placed on Adam's head, the other on Eve's. They had been told earlier that this ritual denotes the glory and honor that God crowns them with. The attached ribbon was a symbol of unity. Samuel then interchanged the crowns on the couple's heads, by moving them back and forth three times.

Following the crowning was a reading from the Gospel, which

described the marriage of Cana in Galilee. It was the first of Christ's miracles, and actually took place at the wedding when He changed water into wine. The newlyweds were invited to kiss the Holy Book, and drink from the same cup of wine. This was not symbolic of communion, but a reminder of their holy union of marriage. The priest told them that marriage is a combination of both happiness and sadness, and that they, as a married couple, are to help complete one another. He quoted from the Bible scriptures that admonish "the wife to be subject to her husband," but did not leave out the part some men would like to ignore, "that husbands are to love their wives as Christ loved the Church and gave Himself for it."

Adam and Eve were admonished to recite the "Our Father" together with the priest and cantor. All the while, they gave glory to The Father, Son and Holy Spirit. They were rather surprised to find that musical instruments are not part of a Greek Orthodox wedding. The only music came from the chanting of the priest and cantor.

Next, the couple walked together around the sacramental table three times as Sarah held the slender train of Eve's gown, and Samuel held on to the long satin ribbon in back of their heads which trailed from the crowns, and hung in an entwined loop. The priest told them that the continuous stream of ribbon was symbolic of God's Kingdom which has no beginning nor ending, and that their marriage would be embarking on an unending journey into God's Kingdom together.

Then, the lit candles were taken from their hands by the priest, and after blowing out the flames, he placed them on the table. "Now, Adam you may kiss your bride," he said.

The priest encouraged them to realize that troubles and obstacles would occur in their marriage, but that The Lord was now a partner. The priest's blessing stated that they should live life together in purity, and to a ripe old age, while keeping God's commandments in their hearts and lives.

After an hour-long ceremony, they realized the culmination of their dream of a church wedding they had shared for some time, had actually become a reality. After greeting all their guests, they turned and retraced their steps down the aisle and out the door to an amazing sight:

Many of the guests had taken off their shoes and were barefoot in keeping with the casual theme of the reception. They loved the delicious feel of the soft, warm sand between their toes. Sarah's three tiny daughters were dressed in peach chiffon, and had fresh flowers stitched into the see-through hems of their gowns. At first, the fancy gowns were thought to be too long for their miniature statures. Now, after being sewn with deep, wide hems which were filled with fresh flowers, it appeared as though the gowns had been fashioned with that intent. The flowers gave their garments an exciting, colorful look and also exuded a fragrant aroma. Their appearance marked the aftermath of the ceremony as they gaily skipped down the earthen staircase strewing tiny wildflowers mixed with peach colored roses from their hand-woven baskets of straw. The flowers were then picked up by the breezes and strewn amongst the guests who were seated on huge, fluffy cushions in shades of pale blue, green and peach. Music filled the air, and the paper lanterns enclosing lit candles also reflected the same hues of blue, green and peach, and seemed to sway with an undulating rhythm.

Clarice and Jenny scurried about giving orders and securing decorations. Long tables held seashells and lit floating-candles encased in colorful earthenware containers. Very soon, guests would serve themselves from the elegant buffet-style meal, and then return to comfortable cushions to enjoy their repast.

As the three flower girls skipped several yards before her, Eve's gaze caught the crowd of guests. "Why," she thought, "is everyone looking at me? Is my skirt in place? Did I smear my lipstick?" She instinctively reached up to smooth down her auburn tresses as the heavenly ocean breezes sought to capture and riffle them about. She seemed to have forgotten her role as one of the main characters in the drama. Then, she lost sight of all the guests who were sitting on the colorful cushions, and who now stood in respect to the bride as she glided down the petal-strewn pathway. All she was aware of was the look of awe on her husband's face. Once again, just as when they began dating, they walked hand-in-hand, their eyes reflecting back to each other their very own image. They truly felt as one…

After the romantic music died down, Jenny read from a poem by Lord

Byron, the famous English poet who loved Greece and died there of fever while engaged in the Greek struggle for independence. Adam had requested the poem in honor of his beloved, Eve. As the poem, "She Walks in Beauty Like the Night" was read, many eyes grew misty with nostalgia and awe.

Eve smiled at Jenny in appreciation of the meaningful reading and noted how lovely she and Clarice appeared in their beautiful new dresses. The materials were hand-fashioned fabric adorned with lace and embroidery that had been purchased locally from the famous shop, Fodheles. No black-attired widows were they on that special day. Jenny's dress was an enchanting shade of deep peach, Clarice's, the heavenly blue of the midday skies. Had they planned in advance to have their attire match the cushioned seats?

Next, Samuel's 10-year old son, David, was encouraged to add his contribution to the party. Even though he was quite young, he had obviously inherited the skills of his great-grandmother, Vivian. Looking very handsome in his navy blue suit, with his black hair gleaming in the firelight, and his black eyes glowing with excitement, he began to strum the lyre. He had worked for weeks to learn a beautiful Greek wedding song. His proud parents beamed and the heads of the onlookers swayed in time with the familiar folk music. David's music swelled the air, and it seemed time for the next phase of the wedding ritual.

As their vows had just been renewed, Adam felt the time was appropriate to give his bride a special gift. Reaching over and grasping Eve's right hand, he placed a second ring on her finger, a ring he could not afford prior to their marriage ten years ago. She gasped in surprised delight as, on top of her original gold wedding band, he gently slid a gorgeous emerald-cut, many-faceted diamond of brilliant hue framed in gold. She then released the clasp on a very slender gold chain from about her neck, and removed an item that had been hanging concealed between her breasts. On Adam's right ring finger, she placed an attachment which locked over his original gold wedding band, a gold filigree reproduction of ivy. Ivy, a Grecian symbol, how perfect!

As the entire party held their glasses of wine up in a toast to the newly-weds, the band played a moving love song. After a beautiful tribute to the

American couple from their Grecian family and new friends, Adam and Eve felt moved to kiss once again. That kiss was so full of love, passion, respect, appreciation, and all the other things that one could dare hope for. The guests just stood quietly, wondering when it would end, but not daring to breathe for fear they might break the spell.

They had been told that the first dance belonged to them, so Adam and his bride complied, all the while gazing into one another's eyes, seemingly oblivious of anyone else.

Then, there was the traditional circle dance around the bride. The Cretan band played the appropriate music and the guests gave a real-live performance of Cretan dancing. Men and women who had appeared so dignified in their special party clothing broke loose, linked arms, and enjoyed indulging in typical Grecian folk-dances. As the bride must dance with anyone who asks her, by the end of the evening, Eve had the opportunity to enjoy many of the guests.

When the dancing finally came to an end, Eve was reminded to glance at the bottom of her shoes. Greek tradition indicated that the unmarried ladies at wedding receptions write their names on the bottom of the bride's shoes. The names remaining after much dancing by the bride were said to be that of women who would never marry. Eve's comment was, "I like our American way of throwing the bride's bouquet over her head, and the woman who catches it will be the next bride. That's a much happier prediction." The name remaining on her left slipper was Sophia, one of the employees at Jenny's bakery.

There was timeout for the amazing assortment of foods spread for the reception. Eve really got a taste of true Greek-style cooking. How she appreciated Jenny and Clarice for all the time and energy spent planning and cooking for their reception. The wedding cake was the traditional light sponge with butter cream icing. Bonbonierres were given to guests as they departed the reception. They are traditional party favors of almonds covered in white chocolate, then encased in small net bags containing an uneven number of the special treats according to custom, and each female received a long-stemmed peach-colored rose.

After hours of socializing, eating and dancing, Adam and Eve decided to call it a day, and retired back to Jenny's home. Jenny told them ahead of time that she planned to spend the night at Clarice's home, so the newly-weds might have privacy, with the entire house to themselves.

Approaching the front door after walking down the pathway, Adam lifted Eve from her feet, and carried her over the threshold. Without missing a beat, he carried her into their bedroom, gently placed her on the canopy bed, and said, "Now, my dear. It is time for some serious reacquainting."

CHAPTER XXV

Sitting comfortably in padded lawn chairs the following day behind Clarice's home, she called their attention to an overhanging tree. "When I was just a child, I planted this tree, so it is almost 80 years old." They all gazed upward as they admired the tremendously tall tree. The bark was shaded in hues of brown, black and gray, and seemed to speak its age.

"Look at the worn, rough bark. It resembles the skin of an aged person. But...look a bit higher." They did and noted the vivid leaves in an amazing chartreuse color of brilliant green.

"The bark seems much like me and my older, mature skin that has endured many seasons. The leaves express new life and growth. We are all to continue to grow and mature as long as we live."

"That's a wonderful analogy, Clarice," said Eve. "Every day of our lives should be treated as a new day, a new day of blessings."

"Yes," agreed Clarice. "Another thing of great importance is the ability to reproduce. Each spring, this tree produces seeds that look like tiny helicopters. The tree not only allows us to experience both the old portions, it also teaches us of new growth. The seeds which flutter to the ground become embedded in the earth and tiny new trees begin to form. No matter how long we live, it is important to be an instrument in aiding others to take root and grow too."

"You certainly do that, Clarice," murmured Jenny. "The way you minister to little children at the home for orphans is such a blessing to them. Even though some of them may never experience the joy of adoption, the love you share with them will never be forgotten."

"Oh, Clarice! You and I have the same type of ministry!" responded Eve. "I too, enjoy little children at an orphanage close to our home. Visiting them is one of the highlights of my week, and being with them brings much more joy to me than my presence could possibly bring to them."

"How true," agreed Clarice. "Remember, God's Word says, 'It is more blessed to give than to receive.'"

Eve continued that line of conversation as she recalled her times with the little children who had no families to call their own. "I wish we could adopt several of them. We have discussed it, but we continue to hope for a child of our own."

"And indeed you could have babies of your own. You're only 32 years of age, aren't you?" Clarice asked.

Adam entered the conversation and said, "Yes, that's true. One of our neighbors just had her first child at age 44."

"Oh, my! Did she have any other children?" inquired Jenny.

"No," explained Adam. "She and her husband had only been married for two years and they realized her childbearing years were drawing to a close. At her age, they took a risk of the baby being normal as women's eggs are beginning to get old by that time and having a mongoloid child is a distinct possibility."

"Well, they were certainly blessed," Jenny exclaimed.

"Yes, they were," said Eve. She then went on to say, "I've seen a fertility specialist and he said my body appeared healthy enough to conceive and carry a child to full-term, but they would have to run special tests to determine our chances of a baby. As you know, we lost two babies before they were born. One was simply aborted after several months, the other died in my womb, but did not abort naturally."

"Oh Eve, what happened?" Jenny inquired with great sadness in her voice.

"Part of my regular exam consisted of the doctor checking with his stethoscope for strength of our baby's heartbeat. At four months of pregnancy, he could not hear one at all. Hoping the baby had possibly just moved a bit, the doctor suggested I return in a few days. I did, and he used special equipment to locate the baby. That was when he realized our baby was dead. The next step was to remove our little one surgically."

Jenny threw her arms around Eve and drew her to herself. "My darling, I'm so sorry to hear what happened to your babies and to my grandchildren."

Adam's arms encircled both of them as he said, "Our doctor sent us to a specialist who ran tests and suggested there might be a problem with our chromosomes being incompatible."

"Chromosomes?" repeated Clarice.

"Yes, it seems there are people whose chromosomes are not compatible."

"What do you know about chromosomes?"

"Well," said Adam. "This is the way I understand it. Most of the cells in the human body contain 46 chromosomes that are arranged in pairs. Each chromosome carries many genes. Genes determine the traits a person inherits from his or her parents. Normally, each sperm from the father and each egg from the mother contains 23 chromosomes, or one member of each pair found in all other cells in the body. When an egg joins with a sperm and fertilization occurs, the 23 chromosomes from each party come together, so the fetus contains 23 from each parent or 46 in total. Each parent makes a contribution to the sex of the child. The egg of the mother always has an X chromosome, the sperm contains either an X or a Y. If a Y chromosome from the father joins the X of the mother, a male child if formed. If an X is in the sperm, the child will be female."

"That's very interesting. Do you know the sex of either baby you lost?"

"No, we don't. All we were told is that genetic disorders may be caused by problems with either genes or chromosomes. He said a person may have a genetic disorder that may not be visible or may carry a disorder without knowing it. Some disorders can be inherited if one parent carries the gene. Some occur at random. Even if a couple has had a normal baby when they are at risk for having a baby with a genetic disorder, they are at risk with each future pregnancy."

"So, what do they recommend?"

"Various scientists are experimenting with methods of creating balances. However, we don't know if they will come up with the answers in time for us to have children together. We've discussed adoption many times, but just can't seem to make that decision yet. It seems ludicrous that a married couple named Adam and Eve aren't able to create just one baby together," Eve said as she gave a faint, rueful laugh.

"Well, let's all brighten up and accept the advice of those who have said, 'Take one day at a time.'" Adam said, as he tried to encourage the ladies with that thought.

Clarice just couldn't get over the emotional pain that Eve had endured after losing two babies to miscarriage. She hugged her and said, "Eve, I can see that you are a very spiritual person. Have you always had a personal relationship with the Lord, or is it a recent thing?"

Eve responded to the question by saying, "My walk with the Lord intensified after our first baby miscarried. It was so traumatic for me, and I cried out to God for answers. Why did our baby die? I couldn't understand why God would take a perfectly innocent child before it even drew its first breath."

"Did God tell you why?"

"No, He didn't, but He gave me peace about it. I had been so distressed, but when I cried out to him, it seemed His arms were wrapped around me, holding me, comforting me.

"And then...?"

"Then, a friend of mine prayed for me, and advised me to read God's Word, the Bible, for comfort."

"How did you know which scriptures to read?"

"She referred me to a portion in John where Jesus tells his disciples about peace."

"Do you remember where it is?"

"Of course, it's in the 14th chapter of the book of John. When depression tried to engulf me, I would refer to it again and again. Eventually, I found I could meditate on the scriptures at will by memorizing them."

"Is that how you grew to know Jesus in a more intense manner?"

"Yes, when I thanked Him for His peace, my heart began to fill with love for Him. Years earlier, I opened my Bible to a scripture in Romans 10:9-10 that said: 'If I believed in my heart and confessed with my mouth that God raised Jesus from the dead, I would be saved.' That was during my teen years when I had a special relationship with the Lord, but later seemed to drift away from Him. When I repeated the words from that scripture, I felt His overwhelming love embracing and filling me. Another thing I noted was that I felt all shiny and new inside, as though I had been forgiven of all my wrong thoughts and actions. Since that happened, I have been so much happier."

Since Jenny had been cooking for them in her home every evening, the decision was made to treat her and Clarice by taking them out to dinner. Adam and Eve wanted to dine in one of the favorites of the local people, rather than to a restaurant frequented by tourists, and allowed their family to choose.

They heard of a favorite drink called ouzo and decided to sample it. When the waiter served it with ice at her request, Eve took a rather large sip as she was quite thirsty. Her eyes grew large, and she said, "Oh, goodness! The flavor is delicious, but it is so strong, and it tastes just like licorice."

"Yes, it does" said Jenny. "The alcoholic content in ouzo is very high, as you might have noticed. It is made of grape stems flavored with anise"

Eve decided to have an appetizer to eat with the brew and chose spanakopita, a dish made with eggs, spinach, cheese and fillo dough. Adam chose grilled octopus. Jenny and Clarice's choice was stuffed grape leaves. On the side was an order of cheese cut in squares and sprinkled with oregano.

"Isn't it wonderful just to sit and relax for a change instead of planning and cooking a meal?" Eve asked.

"Indeed it is. Although, I really do enjoy cooking," Jenny explained. "You will notice a difference in the temperature of the foods served at the restaurant. I served your meals hot as I know that is how you enjoy them in the States, but in Greece, we eat our food lukewarm. The foods served here tonight will not be hot. I hope it isn't distasteful to you."

"No, we want to enjoy things the way the natives do," Eve responded.

An appetizer called saganaki made of cheese set on fire with brandy was served and the traditional cry of "Opa" accompanied the treat.

"What shall we order as the entrée?" Adam asked.

"We enjoy a specialty named parrot fish. It is termed, 'cow of the sea.' by the locals. It is grilled and the scales are left on. You must scrape them off yourself, but the taste is quite delightful. The vegetables served with it are grilled also"

"I want to try that," said Adam.

"Me too," Jenny agreed.

As the waiter passed out locally grown vegetables, he shouted out, "Fresca!" which means "fresh."

After dinner was served and eaten, they all sat with a demitasse-type cup of Greek coffee. Then, they enjoyed a slice of the well-known Baklava for dessert.

The following day marked the close of Adam and Eve's visit to the island of Crete. As they packed and prepared to depart for the airport, the whole family was there to see them off. Jenny's children and their spouses had taken a few hours off work, and the children were allowed to miss school that day too. The mood was one of sadness at the parting which they had realized must come. As they all kissed and wished Adam and Eve a safe flight home, the feelings were entwined with joy at having spent time together, but also sorrow at the thought of leaving their new-found family.

"You must all come to visit us in the States," Eve said, issuing a very sincere invitation. However they were all aware that it would probably be the last time they would be able to actually spend time with Clarice. At the age of 82, they didn't think she would be able to make the trip to America to visit them again, and it would likely be many years before they would return to Greece. Clarice accomplished what she had hoped for by bringing Jenny, Adam, and their families together. Now, she could be in total peace as she had shared all the family secrets and linked them all together forever in love, peace and understanding.

CHAPTER XXVI

Current Year—Summer

The next morning, Adam suggested going out for breakfast. As Eve showered, he hastily threw some of her clothing into a suitcase and placed it in the trunk of their car. He planned to discuss a new environment with her in a manner that would appeal to her sense of adventure.

"Hot, whole-grain pancakes with melted butter and pure maple syrup, that's my choice," Adam read off of the menu. "What would you like for breakfast, Eve?"

"Same thing. The last time we were here, they served singed bread with my eggs."

"Do you mean burnt toast, Eve?"

"Is that what you call it? That person who gave it to me wore a dress that looked like everyone else's who carried food to tables."

"That was the waitress, Eve."

"I don't care what you call her, that's what she did."

Lately, Adam had noticed a big change in Eve's descriptions. Then, he recalled a recent article in a magazine that told of a common change in the speech patterns that were to be expected. It was termed, 'salad mix.' Familiar descriptions might vanish and new unexpected ones take their place.

The whole while they ate breakfast, Eve anxiously looked about as though expecting a visitor. Several times, she stood to her feet as though she had a destination in mind, but promptly forgot it and slid into the booth again as Adam stood up to aid her. After motioning to the waitress for the check, he hastily paid the bill. Then, taking Eve's hand in his, they walked together to the front door.

After driving a short distance, a shop called 'Jan's Coiffeurs' appeared on their right. Releasing the child's safety-lock on the car door, Adam escorted Eve into the beauty parlor. Fortunately, Adam had called in advance for an appointment, and the beautician was ready for Eve.

"Hello, Mrs. Alexander, I'm Jan. How are you today? You're right on time. Let's go to the shampoo bowl area so we can wash your hair."

"Adam, Adam," Eve whispered. "Please don't leave me," while grabbing his right arm.

As they walked arm in arm toward the rear of the shop, Eve's eyes grew larger and the green color grew deeper and more intense in hue. Her breathing sounded heavy and ragged. She was obviously terrified.

"Eve, please don't be frightened, you're just going to have your hair washed so it can be styled. It will be your new look for spring."

"Oh Adam, you always know how to say the right thing. Of course, I want a new look."

As Jan, the beautician, motioned to a specific chair, Eve sat down, but grabbed Adam's hand and clenched it so tightly that his finger tips turned red from the pressure.

"Eve darling, I will sit next to you and hold your hand."

"Do you promise, Adam?"

"Yes, I promise. Have I ever lied to you?"

"No, of course not. I'll be good."

After a refreshing shampoo and conditioner, Jan was asked to recommend an attractive hair style. "Well" she said, "one of my specialties is to design the perfect style for each of my customers. The shape of your face is lovely, Mrs. Alexander, pulling your hair back into a pony tail enhances your high cheek bones. However, it seems a bit harsh. Let me just test the body in your hair and attempt to create a new look for you."

Jan pinned back most of the length in Eve's hair and fluffed out the portion from her scalp to the mid-section of her ears and simulated a wispy bang on one side of her forehead.

Eve glanced into the mirror and smiled at her own reflection. Adam got excited and said, "Oh yes, that's it! That's the way you looked years ago, Eve. I always liked your hair short and fluffy."

Jan agreed and said that Eve would find her hair much easier to care for as the natural curl would probably return if it were trimmed. With their permission, Jan picked up a razor with a long handle, and gray locks began to slide off the protective plastic cape, and onto the floor. In less than 20 minutes, the transformation was complete. A much more youthful face appeared in the mirror. A shimmer gel and blow dryer completed the job. The lines in Eve's face appeared very much diminished, and her hair appeared as a cloud of white, cotton-colored candy, and seemed to form a halo around her face.

Adam reached for her hand and asked if he might be her escort.

Like a wistful coquette, Eve cast down her eyes, and in a very shy manner said, "Yes, I would like that very much, sir."

All the way to "Quiet Haven," Eve plied Adam with questions. "Where are we going? How long will it take? Why can't we just go home, Adam? I'm tired."

Adam found it difficult to keep his mind from going over and over what he must do next. This was going to be the hardest thing he had ever done. If she was terrified just going to the beauty shop, what would she think about being left in a strange place? Not being together after so many years of marriage was almost impossible to consider.

Pulling up in front of the facility, Adam felt waves of anxiety and depression hit him. It was almost as though someone had punched him in the abdomen. Internally, he was literally crying out with grief.

Adam decided not to take Eve's suitcase in before she was settled in at her new home. That could really make her feel like a displaced, unwanted refugee.

"Come, my dear. We've been invited to critique a new facility. Let's look it over and let the managers know what we think."

"I don't really care, Adam. Why don't we let them figure it out for themselves. It has nothing to do with us."

"Come, my lovely lady. I want others to realize how proud I am to be seen with you."

"Oh Adam, you just like to be with me because you think I'm beautiful!"

"How true my dear, how true."

As they entered the building hand-in-hand, the receptionist greeted them and confirmed their appointment. "One moment," she said. "I will make Mrs. Aldrich aware that you're here."

Moments later, a tall well-dressed brunette, approached them with an outstretched right hand. "Mr. & Mrs. Alexander, I'm Mrs. Aldrich. It's a pleasure to meet you. Please follow me to my office and I will attempt to answer any questions you might have."

Before long, the three were back in the hallway, headed in the opposite direction. They passed an atrium in the center of the building, and found its offshoots looked rather like a six-legged spider. Mrs. Aldrich led them down one of the areas which contained a nurse's station at the entry way. A nurse came forward to welcome them, much to Eve's dismay. "Adam, I'm not ill. Why am I here?"

"Eve, this is called a home-away-from-home. We're going to test the facility just as we would check out a potential vacation area."

"But, Adam. I don't need a vacation. Let's just go home. I'm tired."

"I know Eve, but I made an appointment and it would be rude not to keep it. Let's just see what they have to offer."

"Alright, but let's don't stay long. I'm tired…"

Suddenly, Eve began clinging to Adam and said in a tearful voice, "I know you plan to leave me here. Think of all the years we've been married—please don't. I'll do anything you ask, just don't leave me. I know I've been forgetful lately, but I've never stopped loving you. Please Adam, take me home where I can rest. I'm so tired!"

With tears blinding his eyes, Adam placed both arms around Eve's waist and gently drew her to him, "I'm not leaving you, Eve. Let's go home."

Mrs. Aldrich gave them a look of great compassion and understanding, a faint smile and nodded her head as Adam and Eve retreated down the hallway.

Adam called the home health agency that afternoon and arranged for a woman to spend 4 hours with Eve the next day. He then called Mrs. Aldrich and made an appointment to view "Quiet Haven" by himself and visit the Alzheimer's unit as an observer.

The next morning Eve was engrossed in watching a children's program on TV when Adam left her with the caregiver.

Once again, Adam visited "Quiet Haven." Mrs. Aldrich excused herself from a faculty meeting long enough to introduce Adam to Pearl, the unit's director.

"Good morning, Mr. Alexander. I understand you wish to observe our unit today. You are most welcome, but I must tell you that every day here is different. You will notice we have a registered nurse on duty in the unit at all times, two nurse's aides, a cook and me. My main duties are those of activity director. I am also responsible for charting the attentions, non-attentions, and distractions of our guests."

Adam smiled and said, "I appreciate you calling the people who live here guests rather than patients."

Pearl returned his smile and added, "My mother spent the last two years of her life here. After her death, I wanted to help give back a bit of the understanding and love we received here, and this is my way of doing so."

"How commendable. What position did you hold prior to this one?"

"Actually, I was a stay-at-home wife and mother. Years earlier, I obtained a degree in counseling and then marriage and children interrupted my career."

"I'm sure your career choice aided you as a parent."

"Yes, and as a wife also. Many times, I referred back to my text books when we had a marital dispute. Prayer came first though, and there is more information about marriage in the Bible than most people realize."

"Is that right? I didn't know that."

"Yes, that's true. I want you to know that I pray for all the people here in my unit each day too."

"Oh, really? I'm surprised to hear that. Very few people speak of the importance of prayer these days."

"Well, it's so important to me. I pray for God's perfect will in my life, the lives of my family and friends, and then for these dear people who are so confused at times. I can't imagine how difficult it must be for them and their families to have so much disruption and turmoil in their lives."

"Pearl, I can't tell you how much I appreciate your kind and understanding heart. I'm already feeling better about bringing Eve, the love of my life, here to live."

"Mr. Alexander, please feel free to observe what we do here and to ask questions. One thing I wish to point out is this, people with signs of Alzheimer's are much like little children. They don't like to be left anywhere and often become fearful and cry or throw tantrums at being left, but as soon as their caregiver departs, they usually show interest in others and quickly blend in."

Adam nodded, thanked her and took a seat amongst the unit's guests who were listening to some old-time songs and occasionally singing along.

A tiny woman approached Adam as his chair was just outside the circle of residents as they sat facing the middle of the recreation area.

"Are you new?" she asked. "I haven't seen you before. Are you a doctor or do you live here too?"

Adam realized with amusement that they were exactly the same height when she was standing as he was while seated.

"My name is Clara, and we have the same color eyes. Have your eyes always been that color? Are you my son?" she asked.

"No ma'am, you're too young to be my mother, and yes, my eyes have always been gray. What about you? Did you choose to have gray eyes?"

"I haven't really thought about it before now. The only thing I'm sure of is that I'm going home today."

"Oh, are you really?"

"Yes, my son is coming to pick me up."

"How long have you been here?"

"Too long. I live close by, and if they would just return my car, I could drive home by myself."

Just then, a male's voice seemed to penetrate the air waves. He was seated in an isolated area cursing at the top of his lungs. A family member tried in vain to feed him, but he ignored them and continued to shout. A male nurse explained the reason for the outrage. "There is a portion of the brain affected by the disease that will not allow him to have peace."

Sadly, Adam departed.

CHAPTER XXVII

Summer—1974

"Eve, we've been home from Crete for a week now. I think it's time to begin our research regarding Steve, your companion at the orphanage."

"I suppose so, but I'm a bit frightened."

"Frightened, why?"

"What if we can't get any information on him? What if it's true, and he doesn't want to become involved with me? What if it's not true, and I've allowed myself to open up that empty space in myself, and it cannot be filled?"

"Eve, you are a very brave lady. Don't start getting squeamish on me now."

"Okay. I'm ready. Where shall we begin?"

"What was the name of the orphanage where you were last together?"

"I'm not sure, but I think it was on Jefferson Avenue. They transferred me to the home for girls when I was 13. All teenagers had to go elsewhere. We shall have to backtrack in order to find when we were last together and where he went after that."

"You mentioned that your birth records had been destroyed by fire at the original home."

"Yes, that's true. At least, that's what we were told."

"Was there a caseworker that you particularly enjoyed talking with?"

"Caseworker?"

"Yes, didn't someone from the outside speak to you occasionally to determine if you were adjusting properly?"

"No. I don't remember anyone like that. Several people monitored us, and there was a woman in charge by the name of Mrs. Dressler."

"What did Mrs. Dressler do?"

"I don't really know; she had a big office and we didn't see her very often. The others who worked there helped with the cooking and cleaning. Our lessons were done at the orphanage until I was 13. Then I was transferred to a home for teenage girls and we attended public school."

"It must have been a difficult adjustment for you to begin attending a real public school."

"Yes, it was. I used to be very shy. We were monitored so closely at the home."

"Weren't you allowed to express yourself?"

"No, never. When I attended the 8th grade, the students there had known one another since kindergarten, and were a close-knit group. Rumors went about that the girl's home was actually for wayward girls and that we were problems."

"How unfair. Didn't the teachers realize that was untrue?"

"They either didn't know or didn't care. There were 38 students in our classroom, and they felt very overworked. That didn't leave much time to spend with the students on an individual basis."

"How hard were the lessons?"

"Actually, I scored higher than the others in my class because the woman teacher at the orphanage loved her profession, and was very firm regarding the importance of learning."

"So, you had only one year in the public grade school, and then went on to high school?"

"Yes, in those days, grade school took you from kindergarten through 8th grade. High school was from 9th to 12th grade. Then of course, college was college…"

"And, that's when we met. You didn't seem terribly shy to me."

"I know. You made me feel so special right away. That's why we hit it off together."

"Well, my dear. There's always more to learn of loved ones. However, we still don't know where to begin looking for Steve."

"Well, let's drive over to Jefferson Avenue and see if we can locate the orphanage."

"Yes, lets. It's Saturday, and so we have a free day."

"There Adam, that's it!"

"Are you sure? The sign in front says it's a bed and breakfast facility."

"Of course, I'm sure. Evidently, the orphanage went out of business. Let's stop and see how long it's been a B & B."

Adam pulled over to the curb and before he could open Eve's door, she was bounding up the walkway. "Oh Adam, one time I drew a hopscotch on this very walkway," Eve exclaimed.

"Did you get into trouble?"

"I had to clean it off with a scrub brush before we even got a chance to play on it."

"Not much fun, I guess?"

"No, not really. It never felt like a home, just a place to eat and sleep."

Just then, the door opened in response to the doorbell's pleasant chimes.

An elderly gentleman invited them to step inside while saying, "Hello, my name is Alex Sims. How may I help you? Are you interested in spending the night?"

"No," said Adam. "Please allow me to introduce my wife, Eve Alexander. She seems to remember living in this building at one time."

"That's very possible. Our B & B has just been open for the past 5 years. I understand it used to be an orphanage. Actually, it stood empty for several years in-between businesses."

"Do you know the name of the home?"

"Not offhand, but I have a bill of sale that will probably give that information. Please follow me."

Eve's heart began to pound as they followed Mr. Sims down the dark hallway. Her eyes drifted up the shiny wooden staircase which allowed her to view a landing in between two levels of stairs. "Adam," she whispered. "Look, those stair-rails had to be polished every Saturday. That was my job. By the end of the next week, they were always covered again with dust."

Mr. Sims ushered them into a large room that had the appearance of an old-fashioned library complete with a window seat overlooking a flower garden.

"Please be seated," he said. "I'll just be a minute looking through our records." He then busied himself by opening a wall safe hidden behind an oil painting.

Eve gasped and said, "That's the same picture of an area of Shaw's Garden that was on the wall when I lived here. This was Miss Dressler's office."

Mr. Sims placed an old lockbox on his desk, and busied himself leafing through a pile of paperwork. Then he took a deep breath and said, "Yes, here it is, the bill of sale on the property. The name of the orphanage was 'Jefferson Place.'"

"Oh yes," said Eve, "that's right. I remember it now. This was the last place Steve and I were together."

"Mr. Sims, is there some way we could contact the previous owner of this building?" Adam inquired.

"Well, the name of the owner was Virgil Tibbs. There is an address and phone number that belonged to him at that time."

Eve's eyes brightened, and she asked if she could copy the information.

"Of course," Mr. Sims agreed in a gracious manner. "Here are a pencil and paper you may use. By the way, would you care to look over the property? Maybe you might like to enjoy our B & B sometime."

"No, thanks. I don't really care to survey the property. Too many memories, and yet, I'm sure every room looks completely different now as you've decorated it for your business. Thank you so much for allowing us to take up your time."

Mr. Sims. smiled and said he was glad to be of help.

"Hello, may I speak to Mr. Tibbs, please?"

"Who's calling?"

"My name is Eve Alexander. I'm calling regarding a property Mr. Tibbs used to own called Jefferson Place."

"What about it?"

"I lived there for several years, and am trying to locate someone who lived there at the same time."

"Mr. Tibbs isn't well. I don't think he can help you, and I would rather you not bother him."

"Please, I won't take much time. He can probably answer my question immediately."

"Just a minute then... I'll see if he wants to talk to you."

After several minutes, a rather harsh voice responded, "Well, what can I do for you?"

"Pardon my intrusion, sir. I'm seeking information about a possible family member of mine."

"What do you mean, possible? You're either related or you're not."

"That's the problem, sir. A boy who was in the orphanage at the same time as I was could be my brother."

"Could be...?"

With that, Eve started to cry. Although she attempted to muffle the sound, Mr. Tibbs heard her.

"Hey lady! Don't cry about it. What do you want to know?"

Gulping back the tears, Eve said, "All these years I've believed any family I might have couldn't possibly be located. Now, suddenly, it seems I may have a brother who was with me at Jefferson Place."

"Why do you think so?"

"Well sir, it's rather a detailed story. Do you have any record of the children who once lived there?"

"No, I don't. The only person who kept records was a Miss Dressler. She was in charge."

"Do you know how I can locate her?"

"Last time I heard, she was living in a retirement community on South Broadway."

"Do you know the name of it, sir?"

"Yes, it's called, 'Plymouth Pioneers.'"

"Thank you so much, sir. I'll give her a call."

Before Eve could hang up the phone, Adam had the directory on the table scanning through the names of local businesses. As Eve had repeated the name, 'Plymouth Pioneers,' Adam heard her, opened the book, wrote down the phone number and held it out to her.

"Oh Adam, I feel we're really on to something. What if Miss Dressler can help us find Steve?"

"I'm as excited about it as you are, Eve. Before we call, let's talk about it. We should probably ask to speak to her in person. It's been almost 20 years ago since you left there. Depending on her age at the time, she is most likely between the ages of 60–70. Her memory may need to be jogged a bit."

"I agree, Adam. Let's call now and inquire about meeting with her tomorrow."

"Okay, let's do."

They called the receptionist who obtained an affirmative response from Miss Dressler.

"Wake up Adam. Our appointment with Miss Dressler is at 10:00 a.m."

Adam sleepily rolled over and said, "Eve, it's Saturday morning and only 7:00 a.m. Let me sleep a bit longer."

Just as he thought he could drift off to sleep for a bit longer, Adam felt a nudge in his ribcage. "Adddaaam—the least you can do is talk to me about it!"

"Realizing that it was a lost cause, Adam bounded out of bed, hurried to the living room, and flung himself face down on the sofa. Just as he did, he felt a weight on his back and realized that Eve had closely followed.

"Adddaaam—please talk to me!"

"Oh, Eve. What can we say? The appointment is all set up for this morning. Let's talk about it afterwards."

"Oh! Men just don't understand. This is so important to me."

"I know, Eve. That's why we are going to visit Miss Dressler today."

All the way to Plymouth Pioneers, Eve chattered like a nervous squirrel looking for a place to stash some nuts for a delicious mid-winter's meal. "Adam, do you think she will remember me? Will she be able to tell us where to find Steve? Ohhhh my, I'm so excited."

"Well, you sure could have fooled me," Adam said with an impish grin. "Sit back and relax; we're still about 10 minutes away."

"Eve's cheeks were almost crimson due to her high level of excitement. Taking out her compact, she dabbed a bit of powder on her face in an effort to tone down the rosy glow. "Adam, please help me calm down, you know red hair and red cheeks clash."

"Not on you, my dear. It makes you look even more alive and vibrant, if that's possible."

"You're just saying that to make me feel better."

"Eve, have you forgotten, we swore to always be truthful with one another?"

"Okay."

"Now, please wipe that powder off your face, it makes you look like a ghost. You know I like you with a natural glow instead of a made-up look."

A subdued Eve quietly said, "Yes, dear," as she dabbed at her cheeks with a hankie.

At various places along South Broadway, they caught glimpses of the mighty Mississippi River while attempting to gaze between the buildings as they drove past. As they were a bit early, Adam pulled into a park area, one of their favorite places to sit and watch the glistening river quietly glide by. Several swings hung suspended from strong tree limbs furnished by ancient oak trees. Higher and higher they swung in their ongoing contest to determine who reached the ultimate level more quickly than the other. As Eve was lighter in weight and more agile, she always won. However, as the good sport he had always been, Adam tried once more to gain supremacy. And once again—he lost. After a few moments, Adam checked his watch. "Time to go," he noted.

"Do you give up, Adam? Do you admit defeat? Am I not much more able to swing higher than you, and in less time?"

"Of course not. Time just prevented me from making my move."

Eve just chuckled merrily and jumped from the swing onto the awaiting mossy green grass while still aloft.

"Be careful, Eve! You're not a child."

"My heart will always be young, Adam, and I am following my heart."

Hand-in-hand, they retraced their steps to the car. As the complex was just minutes away, they disembarked very quickly. It was 9:50 a.m., and the parking lot had very few cars so they parked right in front of the building. Eve was out of the car and up to the door before the emergency brake clicked on.

Approaching the information desk first, Eve said, "We have a 10:00 o'clock appointment with Miss. Dressler."

"Oh yes, Miss Dressler decided to greet you in our reception room. It's just ahead, and to your left."

Eve's heart began to thump, and she whispered to Adam, "Can you hear my heart beating, Adam?"

Placing his hand on her bosom while inserting a mock stethoscope into his ear, he replied, "Mrs. Alexander, you pass the test. You are very much alive and well."

"Oh Adam," she said while brushing his hand away, "You embarrass me."

Rounding the corner of the hallway, they spied a lovely, well-dressed woman with a crown of snow white braids atop her head. She smiled and rose to greet them with her right hand outstretched. Seeing Eve, she abruptly changed her mind, approached Eve, and then caught her in a warm, loving embrace.

"Oh Eve, I didn't recognize your married name. You are Eve Simmons."

"Yes. Even though your hair has changed from chestnut brown to white, I would know you anywhere too, Miss Dressler."

For a moment or so, they just stood quietly holding one another.

Miss Dressler spoke first. "I've thought about you so many times, wondered where you were, what you were doing, and if you were happy. Please sit down so we can talk."

"Thank you, Miss Dressler. This is my husband, Adam Alexander."

After shaking hands, they all sat down. As Eve looked about, she noted that the room was quite large and decorated in old-fashioned colors of mauve and blue. A gas-lit fireplace created a merry glow amidst the imitation, crackling logs. Adam and Eve sat side by side on a loveseat as their hostess smiled at them from a high-backed blue velvet chair.

"How long have you resided here, Miss Dressler?"

"For the last ten years. The orphanage remained open for approximately that long after you left. Then, it seemed we got less and less children who needed our care."

"Why do you think the decline occurred?"

"It seems the government decided children without families would be happier living in individual homes. They devised a new plan that probably cut costs also."

"Oh, what was that?"

"It's called 'foster care.' Families who passed certain criterion were allowed to take children into their own homes, without actually adopting them."

"And then what?"

"They were raised as part of the family."

"What was the advantage of taking these children in?"

"Well, some people really wanted to care for them. Some had children of their own and wanted to increase their family's size. Some were childless, but did not actually want to adopt."

"How long did the children stay?"

"The actual homes and conditions of the family life were reviewed by social workers periodically. Certain tests were required. The foster children were interviewed apart from the family to determine how they were progressing."

"That must have been a financial deficit for the families," Eve inquired.

"Quite the contrary. The state actually pays for the care of those children. It can be a real money-maker if you care for several."

"Oh, I see…"

"After years of being around others, I found it very lonely when Jefferson Place closed down. As I had never married, I lived in the same rental property for many years. It was a four-room bungalow, and perfect at the time. When I retired, I didn't want to pay to have the grass cut, and it seemed I would be happier around other people. This facility has an interesting social life for me—not too active—just enough. I have my own small apartment furnished with my personal things, a kitchen, and my rent here includes the main meal of the day. I have several good friends and I'm very happy. How about you?"

"Well, Adam and I have been married for 10 years. We are both in the writing profession."

"Do you have children?"

"No, not yet."

"Well, you have plenty time. I'm so surprised to see you again, Eve. What brings you this way?"

"I'm trying to discover my roots."

"Roots?"

"Yes, I really want to discover my heritage, and see if I have a family."

"I can understand that, Eve. How can I help?"

"Do you know who brought me to the home?"

"No. You were already there when I was hired. You were around 3 years of age at that time."

"Do you know anything about a boy named Steve who lived there at the same time?"

"Yes, of course. Your brother."

Eve gasped, "You knew he was my brother?"

"Yes, the records indicated that you were twins, and…"

"Twins!"

"Yes, twins. Didn't you know that?"

"Of course not. We weren't even aware that we were siblings."

"Oh, my, I'm so sorry."

"Why weren't we told, and why were we separated at age 13? I was sent to a foster home where the woman had 5 other teenage girls."

"I truly don't know, Eve. My job was to keep the records, not make the decisions."

"Didn't your records include information about where we came from, and who our parents were?"

"No, not the data I was privy to. My records on each child began the day they came to live at Jefferson Place."

"Who had the earlier records?"

"I'm not sure. Maybe the director of the home."

"One last question, Miss Dressler. Why do you think Steve and I weren't instinctively aware of our kinship?"

"Possibly because boys and girls were kept segregated from one another most of the time. The director felt it was very important to do so. She distrusted relationships between the opposite sex, and wanted no scandal to touch the residents of the facility there."

"What is the name of the director?"

"Mrs. Quail. She was a childless widow of many years. I believe she was about 10 years older than me, and I don't know what happened to her when the orphanage closed down. As I'm 74 years old now, that would make her about 84 years of age."

"Is there someone who might be able to help?"

"I don't know of anyone, my dear."

Eve stood, took Miss Dressler's hand in hers, and kissed her cheek. "Thank you so much. You've been a tremendous help."

Miss Dressler stood also, and accepted Adam's hand which he extended as a sign of their departure.

Once in the car, Adam turned to Eve and said, "We must now search for Mrs. Quail."

CHAPTER XXVIII

Current Year—Summertime (cont'd)

On days when Eve was more like her old self, they had enjoyable conversations. This day seemed to be a good time to actually get feedback from Eve. After her customary afternoon nap, she arose and seemed much more alert than she was earlier that day.

"Eve, how would you like to take a trip?"

"Where shall we go, Adam? How long will we be away? Will I need a new wardrobe?"

"Do you remember when we renewed our wedding vows in Greece? When we were first married, we had no money for vacations but got books on foreign exotic places from the library and attended travelogues. We enjoyed just dreaming together. At that time, you were interested in Greek mythology. The story of Odysseus and Penelope was a favorite of yours."

"Yes Adam, I remember the part about the sirens of the sea luring men to their deaths too. That was the part of the story I found gruesome. If one thinks of mermaids, the tale should be one of beauty."

Adam recalled that Eve loved the folklore of Greece and said many times she would love to visit and explore the areas of which the ancient poet Homer, who was extremely poor and blind, spoke of in his epic poems, "The Iliad" and "The Odyssey." When they spent time there during their ten-year anniversary, after renewing their marriage vows, there really wasn't much time to explore.

"Well Eve, now that we are retired and have the money, I feel we should visit Greece again and try to locate the areas these fables told of. What do you think?"

"Oh Adam, that would be wonderful."

When Eve's symptoms first appeared several months earlier, Adam called a travel agency he located in the yellow pages of their local phone book. Their receptionist had been very friendly, but recommended he make an appointment with one of their specialists after he was made up his mind where they would like to travel and was ready to begin making plans. Knowing Eve's interest in Greece, he planned to surprise her with a trip to celebrate their wedding anniversary. Now, he felt they should go as quickly before her symptoms of Alzheimer's grew more intense.

"Eve, I will make arrangements for us to depart as soon as possible. We need a little excitement in our lives."

In his enthusiasm, Adam glanced at Eve and realized she was not listening. A piece of lint on the cuff of her blouse had her full attention.

"What do you think about my plans for us to visit Greece once again?" Adam queried Eve. A vacant stare was her only response.

Dialing the phone, Adam heard, "Good Morning. Superior Travel Agency."

"Good Morning, Mrs. Dobson, please."

"Hello. Mrs. Dobson, here," a pleasant voice responded.

"Yes. Mrs. Dobson. This is Adam Alexander calling back. My wife and I are very interested in making a trip to the Grecian Islands."

"That is wonderful sir. Shall we make an appointment to discuss it?"

"Yes. Do you have an opening today?"

"No sir, but tomorrow around 10:00 a.m. is available."

"Thank you, I will take that appointment. Oh yes…how long do you think our appointment will be? My wife will need someone to stay with her while I make our plans."

"An hour should be long enough to discuss your ideas, and then we will begin to make plans."

"Excellent. I will see you tomorrow morning."

Arriving at Superior Travel Agency, Adam greeted the receptionist by saying, "Mrs. Dobson, please. I am Adam Alexander; we have a 10:00 a.m. appointment."

"Yes sir, have a seat please and I will tell her of your arrival."

After terminating a brief phone conversation, a tall, tanned, lovely young woman approached the lobby area. Her friendly brown eyes, enhanced by hair of the same color, conveyed intellect and humor. Stretching out her right hand, she said, "Mr. Alexander, I presume?"

Adam allowed himself a brief chuckle as he replied. "That introduction reminds me of Stanley's greeting to Dr. Livingston as they met in the wilds of Africa years ago. Quite formal for the territory, I should say."

"Yes," she chuckled, "it's one of my favorites too, but not many people recognize that quote any longer. It's always enjoyable to work with a person who has a sense of humor."

"Well, we're off on the right foot, Mrs. Dobson."

"Mr. Alexander, if you will accompany me through the jungle area, we shall speak of new adventures."

Winding their way through a maze of offices facing the hallway, which was enhanced by extremely tall green plants in exotic pots, they entered an office that seemed lit up by travel posters of exotic destinations on the walls. "Have you seen many of these places firsthand?" Adam asked.

"Yes sir, all of them" she responded, but before we begin our discussion, please call me Pat. Mrs. Dobson sounds so formal and we must get to know one another in order for your trip to be exactly what you are looking for."

"Very well, Pat it is. Call me Adam." And then, "Please explain some of these posters to me, Pat. They are all quite intriguing."

"The one on your left is called "The Glow Worm Grotto." As you can see, it is completely black with the exception of tiny pin points of light on the sides. The location is in a cave deep underground in New Zealand.

The pin points of light are tiny glow worms, or types of lightning bugs, that just hang on the walls emitting light until they fall off and die. Tourists travel through the darkness in boats."

"And you were there?"

"I was. It was an exciting, but eerie experience."

"The poster to your right shows people laughing and splashing as they enjoy the hot vapors arising from a pool of mineral waters. This is in Rota Roura, New Zealand, and is well known for its therapeutic values."

"I assume you too, splashed through those smoky waters?"

"I did."

"On the back wall, you will find a many times enlarged photo of Ayers Rock in Alice Springs, a section of Australia's Outback area."

"Did you climb it?"

"I did, with the help of chains embedded in its sides. This huge red mountain-like rock is the largest monolith in the world."

"Monolith means one solid rock, doesn't it?"

"Yes. We literally pulled ourselves up most of the way. When we reached the top, there was a sign that said, 'I Made It!' Achieving that climb was certainly one of the grandest feats of my life!"

"Did your husband accompany you?"

"Oh no, my sister and I enjoyed a month-long trip which included Hawaii, New Zealand and Australia after graduating from college."

"You graduated together?"

"Yes. We're twins. Her name is Priscilla, my given name is Patience. As you can see, I shortened it to Pat."

"How long have you been married, Pat?"

"One year. We were grade-school friends and later became sweethearts. Actually, he lived down the street. We lost track of one another, and just became reacquainted two years ago. Well, enough about me."

"Pat, the poster in front of me brings back wonderful memories. I lived in San Francisco until I was 8 years of age. The Golden Gate Bridge is known the world over, of course. We have a picture of it in our living room painted by Thomas Kinkade, the artist who is called, 'The Painter of Light."

"Yes, of course. He is one of my favorites too. Well now, down to business. What are your travel plans?"

"My wife and I have always entertained the thought of returning to Greece."

"Greece?"

"Yes Greece. Have you been there?"

"No, I haven't, although our world-wide contacts can certainly supply us with all the information you might need. I can pull up some data on our computer right now, but it would be to your advantage to allow me several days to research the location. Is there a specific area in which you are interested? Any particular activity you wish to enjoy?"

"Yes, my wife was always interested in Greek mythology, so we would like to visit Mount Olympus where the gods were to have resided. We've owned our own sailboat for many years and enjoy being on the water. A cruise in the Agean Sea, possibly?"

"Well, you've given me some good leads. It's been a pleasure meeting you. I will call you in a few days to set up our next appointment after I have more information to share with you."

That evening as they prepared for bed, Adam asked, "Eve, are you getting excited about the plans for our upcoming trip to Greece?"

No response... Could she be sleeping?

Eve had ceased brushing her shiny white hair and was attempting to entice a colorful ladybug crawling on the dresser onto the tip of her comb. "Adam, look! Remember, these little red and black bugs bring luck. Now, we'll have some too. Do you remember the beautiful red and black dress I wore to your retirement party? This little bug has the same coloring."

"Yes Eve, I remember. You put all the other women to shame when you walked through the door on my arm. I have always been so proud of you for your exquisite poise. And yet, you are always so gracious to others; they flock to you like bugs to an outdoor bug-zapper light."

Then, as quickly as Eve had responded to his comments, she averted her gaze, looked down and once more attempted to lure the polka-dotted insect onto her black comb.

The next evening, they sat on the patio with their faces tilted skyward gazing into the heavens. Eve mischievously said, "Let's lie down among the flowers and count the stars."

They did so, and found the plush green grass almost buoyant under their bodies. The sky expressed its sultry mood in hues of the deepest black velvet, and the stars would appear and disappear as storm clouds covered and uncovered them.

"Eve, what a exquisite aroma, the blend of your garden of roses and lilacs. Maybe we could have a perfume compiled of the blend," Adam remarked.

"Yes Darling," Eve replied. "Now that we have more time we might consider it. All the things we always wanted to do, but were too busy for will be such a pleasure to explore."

Then as they decided to simply lie back, cease talking, and enjoy the starry heavens, they were amazed at the feelings of absolute peace. Not only was the stellar beauty so striking, they also felt the intense love of their creator. It was as though He was cradling them in His arms.

Just as they were thoroughly enjoying their surroundings, Adam felt a slight ping hit the tip of his nose. A drop of rain then migrated across his left cheek. It was a preview of things to come. Before they could sit up, the sky was ablaze with lightning and the ground shook as thunder acted as its accomplice. Screaming, laughing and running, they made their way back into the house.

"Darling, you look like a drowned rat. How could we get drenched in so short a time? I am actually getting cold, Adam, as the air-conditioning hits my wet body."

The beach towels they had used earlier in their sauna were still strung over the laundry room appliances and they used them to wipe off the tiny streams of water running down from their hair, faces and bodies. After taking a warm shower together, they got clean, dry sportswear from their closets and within a few minutes, aside from their damp hair, no one would have ever guessed that just moments earlier, they had been shivering from the cold.

On evenings like the previous one, Adam momentarily forgot that Eve was having problems with her memory. After so many years together, they fit together like 'peas in a pod' and when her moods changed, it made him feel as though he were losing his memory also

The disease of Alzheimer's was one that eventually caused weakness in the body as well as in the mind. The afflicted one could live for many years, but they would forget more and more things. Eventually the disease would end in the ultimate termination—death.

He remembered hearing reports of a Dr. Kevorkian who, years earlier, had assisted some terminally ill people commit suicide. Thoughts of that were very upsetting. A short time ago, an elderly man killed his wife who suffered from Alzheimer's by shooting her as she slept, and then he shot and killed himself too. Was there no answer to this perplexing situation?

Adam allowed his mind to wander and remember all the joyous times they had experienced in the past as they traipsed the woods looking for just the right tree to be taken home and decorated just prior to Christmas each year. After finding one they both agreed upon, he would then use the small hatchet he brought for that purpose and chop down the tree. It was then bundled up, and tied to the roof of their car, to be taken home and decorated. Their ornaments all had very special meaning also. Each time they traveled, they looked for just the right ornament to add to their others, and hang it on their Christmas tree the following year, as a reminder of all their wonderful times together.

Adam suddenly felt he could understand the emotions that a criminal on "death row" might feel. However, he made the difficult decision to appear upbeat. From time to time, he would point out a particular tree to Eve, and comment on its eye-catching appeal.

Adam pondered over memories of the many discussions they had shared in the past. "Adam, I never want to be a burden to you; if I should ever become deathly ill, please don't let them put me on life-support equipment," Eve entreated.

"I feel the same way," was Adams response. "If I can't live a good quality of life, I don't wish to live any longer. Mere existence is not good enough." Then they would hold one another tightly as they vowed to keep their promises.

Trying to evoke memories she might remember, Adam said, "Darling Eve, you have been my life for over 40 years. I remember the day we purchased our sailboat, and christened it, 'The Land of Dreams.' I can still feel the splash of air-borne champagne, and taste the spray of it on my mouth after you lifted the bottle and it literally exploded in your hand as you smashed it into the helm." Eve gave no indication that she heard him.

CHAPTER XXIX

Summertime—1974

"Eve, how would you like to go fishing this morning? It seems to be a perfect day to sit and relax with a fishing pole in hand and enjoy the peace and serenity of our very special lake."

"Yes I would like to go, Adam. Our usual Saturday routine is to clean house and do laundry, but somehow, that doesn't sound very appealing today."

Quickly, they packed their lunch and supplies, and were en route to the lake. Before they reached the turnoff, they passed an old cemetery where the gravestones dated back into the 19th century. A sign on the side of the road said, 'Managed deer hunt in progress.'

"Hurry, Adam. We don't want to be in gunfire range. Oh look, there is a group of may-apple plants. They say mushrooms are often to be found growing amongst them. Let's stop and take a peek. Remember how good fresh mushrooms are when fried in butter?"

"You have just asked me to do two completely opposite things, Eve. First, you want me to hurry out of this area, and then you want me to stop so you can look for mushrooms. What is your pleasure?"

"Well, let's hurry and stop. I will jump out and look about quickly while you wait in the car. If I spot any mushrooms, you can join me."

Adam stopped the car; Eve jumped out, heard a gunshot in the distance and just as quickly, jumped back into the car, saying, "Okay Adam, that's long enough!"

The inner road they traveled was so dusty from other vehicles that a young boy walking along the road just ahead of them in the opposite direction was almost obscured from sight. He appeared to be about 12 years of age, had rather long auburn hair, used a walking stick, and was attired in an oversized sweatshirt with sleeves that dangled over his wrists, and underneath were the usual faded blue jeans. As Eve was a writer by nature, she was already formulating a short story featuring him in her head.

Soon they were walking down the path to the lake, heavy-laden with what seemed to be much too much fishing gear. Eve was entranced by the sights and sounds around them. The springtime path was strewn with luxurious looking golden dandelions and spiked, purple-hued clover. Each side of the path was lined with tall stalks resembling wheat. Even though their parked car wasn't too far from their destination, they noted red ridges on their arms from pressure as they carried the things serious anglers feel critical to their mission of catching the biggest and most choice fish. Just ahead lay the lake, the surface of which enticed them with inviting ripples they felt sure were caused by fish leaping into the air just awaiting their arrival.

They set down their gear and prepared to bait their lines, Eve squealed as she had been watching a v-shaped form skimming through the water close to shore. Swimming just ahead of the strange shape was what appeared to be a miniature, newborn turtle flailing about, possibly in rhythm with underground springs, or to escape a possible predator. Then, the cause of the v-shape appeared in the form of a slithering water snake as he began to surface and swam on the water's surface. The two creatures passed one another side-by-side as though in total unawareness of one other.

Eve squealed again as she stretched out her hand and scraped the bottom of a screen-like boxed apparatus. Enclosed in her hand was a lively cricket which she intended to place on the hook of her fishing line.

"Adam, please put the lid back on the bait-trap. I can't handle my rod in one hand, a cricket in the other, and replace the lid so the others don't escape."

218

Adam stood back, chuckled and said, "Did you ever consider laying your fishing pole down while capturing a cricket?"

As though hearing something new, Eve cocked her red curls to one side, and said, "No Adam, I've never considered that." Then she laughed and said, "I'm not sure that fishing is really 'my thing.'"

"Well, you certainly know how to eat the fish, don't you?"

"That's a different matter all together. Besides, I know where it is possible to purchase fresh fish without the hassle."

"What? And miss out on the challenge?"

"So, who needs it?"

Adam opened a folding chair, pounded a stake in the ground, and perched a huge beach umbrella in its receptacle. "There now, you won't get sunburned, and you can sit in the shade and read or write."

"Thank you, my dear. You know me so well. Sorry I'm such a nuisance."

"Eve, you are never a nuisance. You enliven my life with your very presence."

Adam returned to his fishing and Eve noted that he threw out a heavily weighted, baited line, and then placed the pole in a holder stuck into the ground to free his hands. The telltale bobber was hanging off the line in the center of the pole, nowhere near the water. It gently drifted, moving back and forth in the breeze while the lurking hook was at the bottom of the lake.

"Adam, you've got the bobber in the wrong place, it should be floating on the surface of the lake. Did your line get tangled as you threw it out?"

In a rather condescending manner, Adam explained, "When a fish hits your bait, it causes the line to move the bobber, sliding it up along the pole. That way, you don't have to constantly watch the line. While sitting in your fold-up lawn chair, you get the whole picture. Standing for long periods of time holding the pole in your hands and straining to see if the bobber is moving gets very tiresome."

"I see. That's quite interesting, Adam." Then looking off to her right, Eve said, "Did you notice that black is the 'in-color' today? The bumblebees with their gauze-like wings are black and gold; the dragonflies darting about are black and white; the butterflies are black and aqua, and the purple martin birds are such a deep color of purple, they appear to be black."

"Only you would notice something like that, Eve. It must be the artist and writer in you."

"I suppose so. You remember the shirtless man we passed as we ventured to our favorite fishing spot? When I mentioned he was getting sunburned, he said, "That's not nearly so bad as the way them yeller flies are bitin'. Did he mean they were yellow in color or in their nature?"

"I couldn't really say, Eve. Why don't you ask him as we are leaving?"

"Just a thought Adam, just a thought."

As Eve gazed at the ground in a rather absent-minded manner, she thought about enhancing the story she was currently writing. Then, she spied a tiny movement out of the corner of her eye. Fixing her gaze on the intruder to her thoughts, she discovered it was one of those strange creatures with huge eyes and a curious stance. It was a praying mantis. Recalling things of interest she learned while doing a term paper in biology, she recalled some of the interesting facts pertaining to this curious insect. They are termed 'masters of disguise' and there are more than 1,800 species. Hundreds of the eggs are hatched after several weeks. The one sitting and appearing to gaze up at her was approximately 6" in length. The strange eyes followed her every movement and she felt the hairs on her arm seem to stand up as they responded to the goose bumps caused by fear and excitement. Her thought was that it could actually be called a 'preying mantis' as its front legs were pressed together as it sat in an upright position. She knew that they actually devoured the prey they captured. They are able to dismember animals larger than themselves, eat other insects, frogs, turtles and also one other. Females devour the males while mating with them. She shivered, and instinctively closed her eyes. When she opened them again, the creature had disappeared.

At that moment, one of the huge bumblebees lighted on top of the pen she held in her hand, and she let out a squeal. "Adam, I think I'm ready to leave. Let's stop at the fish market on our way home. That way we can pretend we caught them."

"Sounds good to me."

"Oh wait. Look at that magnificent bird floating aloft with the wind currents. Now he's swooping down. Is it an eagle or hawk?"

"Neither. It's a heron. Note his beak as he turns sideways. He got his prey. See the silvery gleam in his beak? He's carrying a fish."

"Well, he deserves it. It's hard work to catch your own dinner."

"Look at that!"

"What is it now?"

"Look at those two bumblebees flying in perfect formation, one directly beneath the other. What is that hanging down underneath their bodies, is it their stinger?"

"Not sure, but I don't want to find out the hard way."

As they prepared to depart, Eve noticed strange growths on the ground that looked like miniature cabbage plants, and also 3-leafed plants in green, the type that turned into rather metallic shades of bronze in the autumn, and which seemed to say enticingly, "Touch me. Touch me! I'm smooth to the touch, beautiful to look at, and I won't hurt you." Just as Eve bent to pick some for a bouquet, Adam called out, "Don't touch that plant Eve. It's poison ivy!"

Just in time, Eve retracted her hand, and as she did so, she happened to look up and noticed a sky so blue it appeared to have migrated from the Rockies. Clouds of virgin-white appeared in myriads of shapes and sizes. Trees, bushes, and stalks of weeds displayed multiple shades of green.

"What an incredible fairyland God has given us, Adam."

Just then, almost as though nature responded to the compliment, a boisterous wind snatched the multi-colored umbrella off its stand and it began to lift it far above the ground. Even though Adam was tall, he did a 'basketball hero' type of leap and caught it in mid-air.

"Now I'm *really* ready to go," he shouted.

As they loaded up their gear and started for the car, Eve said, "Adam, that young man we saw hiking reminded me of someone I once knew. I've been trying to think who it was, and now I know!"

"Who was it my dear?"

"He looked like Steve, the boy who was in the orphanage with me years ago."

"Well, maybe he has been in Shangra-La, the village that surfaces only once every 100 years, or so. That could be why he hasn't grown any older."

"Oh Adam, please don't make fun of me. This is very serious."

"Well, what do you think, Eve. Would he have stayed the same?"

"Maybe the young man is related to Steve. He was headed up that hillside. Let's drive in that area and see if we can locate him." Then, looking at her watch, Eve said, "It's actually been only an hour, although it seems longer."

Driving through the park area, no one was to be seen. After giving up, they returned to the outer road and were once again, passing the old cemetery. Spotting a slight movement through the trees, Eve saw the young man sitting on one of the grave sites.

"Look Adam, there he is!"

Pulling off the road and parking along the pathway, they sat quietly and tried to determine why he would sit directly on a grave.

"It must be the grave of someone who was very dear to him," Eve said. "Adam, please stop the car, I must talk to that young man."

By the time Adam pulled the car alongside the grave, the young man was lying prone, face down with arms and legs outstretched. The gravesite was fairly new and a few tiny wilted flowers of the garden-variety type were scattered about. His fingertips had penetrated the still loose earth and his nails were coated with mud from the recent rain. So intent was he in his grief, he wasn't aware their car had stopped just 20 feet from him, nor did he hear them walk up from behind. For several minutes, they stood gazing down at him. His slender body was wrenched with sobs.

Unable to help herself, Eve knelt down alongside him, reached out and gently touched his flaming red locks. As she did so, he leapt to his feet in a single motion, and bright green eyes shone above cheeks stained with dirt and tears.

"Who are you? What do you want?" he demanded in a raspy voice.

"We saw you walk past while we were fishing, and as we drove by, we saw you again. It looked as though you might have fallen and we wanted to help."

"You can't help me. Nobody can. Just leave me alone," he said in a painfully defiant manner. "You don't know me, and I don't know you."

"That's true, but we would like to help. May we drive you home?"

"I don't want to go home."

"Why not?"

"I lived with my grandma, and now she's gone." Once again he looked as though he might throw himself on the soggy ground.

"What about your mother?"

"I don't have a mother!"

"What about your father?"

"What father."

"Don't you have a father?"

"He can't help me; he can't even help himself."

"Is he ill?"

"You might say that."

Adam stepped forward, took the young man's arm, and said in a kind, but firm manner, "Get in the car. We're going to dinner. Are you hungry?"

"Tears began to flow down the young man's face, and he confessed, "I haven't eaten for two days."

Eve threw her arms around the muddy stranger and said, "What's your name?"

"Mark."

"What's your last name?"

"Simmons."

Eve suddenly felt faint and gasped saying, "What is your father's first name?"

"Steve."

CHAPTER XXX

Current Year—Springtime (cont'd)

Even though Adam had felt perplexed about placing Eve in the facility known as Quiet Haven, he had not been able to find another place quite as clean or as nice. The week before, he made arrangements for Eve to reside there on a trial basis.

As Adam entered the Quiet Haven facility, he spied Eve sitting in the parlor. Her hands were occupied as she flipped the pages of a "Ladies Home Journal" magazine. He wondered if she might be looking for one of the articles she had previously written for them.

"Hello Darling. What are you reading?"

"It's all about people signing up for the next trip to the moon. Don't you think it's best to travel when the moon is full? That way, your chances of not missing it should be much better. When the moon is just a tiny sliver, the space ship could fly right past."

"Well, Eve. I think the full moon just looks larger because it is completely lit up. Let me explain the process to you. The phases of the moon are caused by the relative positions of the earth, sun, and moon. The moon goes around the earth about every 28 days. The sun illuminates the half of the moon facing it. When the sun and moon are on opposite sides of the earth, the moon looks full from earth, and appears as a bright, round disk." As Adam looked at Eve to see if she understood what he was trying to tell her, he noted that her eyes once again had a blank stare. He let the explanation rest…

Then, Adam gently removed the magazine from her hands and looked at the article she had been reading. Instead of lunar exploration, it was actually about various types of tennis balls. At least their shapes were similar to that of a full moon.

"Eve," he said. "Let's go outside and enjoy that patio area. Their roses are in full bloom now. You can explain the various species to me. The garden we had at home was so lovely. Remember the incredible amount of time you spent looking for various colors and how you got them all to blend together nicely?"

"Yes, Adam. I enjoyed everything about tending to them except for the thorns. Sometimes they even stuck me through my gardening gloves."

"I remember the times you came into the house with tiny pinpricks in your fingers. You asked me to kiss the boo-boos and make them well."

"We had lots of fun, didn't we darling? We talked so often of how the most amazing colors could reside side-by-side in nature and not clash. I can't imagine a dress in colors of red, orange, purple, yellow and pink, and yet, all those colors were in our rose bed, and they enhanced one another's beauty."

Adam took Eve's arm to escort her outside and she turned abruptly and called out to a woman attendant, "Ma'am, please help me! This man is trying to kidnap me."

The attendant turned, saw Adam, and said, "Mrs. Alexander, that man is your husband."

With panic in her voice, Eve cried out, "No, I don't know him. Please help me!"

Adam released Eve's arm and sadly said to the woman in charge, "You had better take Eve to her room. This is obviously not a good time for her." Then, "I'll return tomorrow. Call me if you have any further problems."

The following day, Adam called the nurse in charge of Eve's area. "Hello, this is Mr. Alexander. How is my wife today?"

"She is very quiet—not upset, just quiet."

"What do you think? Shall I visit her today or not?"

"That's up to you, Mr. Alexander. It's hard to know if she will recognize you."

"Well, I think I'll try it," Adam said. "Last night was very difficult. I keep trying to think of something I can do to help Eve, but I can't seem to come up with anything."

Adam made the decision to spend time at their local library in the reading room. It was a pleasure that he and Eve enjoyed together through the years and he was looking forward to a peaceful afternoon. A new journal on Alzheimer's symptoms and hopeful future cures was available now, and it could be found in the area where new releases could be reviewed in-house only, and were not available for loan.

Eating breakfast at a local restaurant featuring pancakes would be a real treat. He could also enjoy reading the daily news over a steaming cup of hot coffee. Already, his mood had lifted a bit as he envisioned a different beginning for the day. Adam even found himself whistling as he ventured out on a typically lovely, spring day. The blueberry pancakes were especially tasty that morning, and he decided to treat himself to eating breakfast out more often.

With his appetite satisfied, and the local and world news absorbed, Adam was ready to delve into the latest research. Never ready to give up, Adam anticipated a new piece to the never-ending puzzle of the dreaded disease of Alzheimer's.

As the library was only three blocks from the restaurant, Adam decided to walk there and back. Leaving his car in the restaurant's parking lot should not be a problem. Crossing the street on foot, Adam realized his gait was not what it used to be. Arthritis in his knees was a constant reminder of that fact. Walking was a big decision, but he realized that *not* walking caused even more stiffness and pain.

Adam queried the librarian about the location of the periodical he was interested in and then, he happened to glance down at some travel magazines. His heart leapt as he noted the very first one was all about the Grecian island of Crete. Immediately, he was transported back in time to that incredible island where he was born. His thoughts however, returned to the week he and Eve renewed their wedding vows there many years ago. Ah yes, how lovely she was then…

As Adam flipped through the pages of the magazine depicting the beauties of Greece, he felt so grateful for the wonderful life he and Eve had shared, their wedding vow renewal in Crete, and the amazing long-lost family of his, some of whom still lived there. A fleeting grin swept over his lips as he remembered many things of long ago.

In the center of the magazine was a perforated cardboard form for easy removal to be sent to a travel agency. It depicted a gorgeous view of glistening waters of the Aegean Sea lapping a deserted beach. The rising sun dominated its background. In his mind's eye, Adam once again pictured Eve, his lovely bride as she stood on the pink-toned sand beach while smiling into his eyes, appearing as a nymph of the sea.

"Oh," he involuntarily muttered, "Why can't we just continue as we were then, Eve?"

Hearing a rather stifled giggle, Adam looked up to see a cute teenage girl looking at him in an amused manner. Obviously, she considered him an old geezer brinking on senility. For a moment, he considered sharing a bit of what he was experiencing, but then thought better of it, and merely grinned back at her.

Adam's mind began to race. He recalled one day last week when he visited Eve at Quiet Haven. The activities director of the Alzheimer's unit had a dozen residents seated in a semi-circle and they were all obviously enjoying themselves watching TV. All but Gretchen, the 90 year-old German lady whose head was resting on the back of the sofa and was obviously in the land of dreams.

The TV show featured a man dancing with a woman in a flared skirt to the tune of "Casey would waltz with the strawberry blonde, and the band played on."

Amazingly, as the director encouraged them with a bright smile, they were all singing along. "How," Adam thought, "could they all remember that old-time song when they couldn't remember what happened 5 minutes ago?" Nevertheless, it was lovely both to see and hear. Eve's cheeks were flushed and her eyes glistened as she too, sang along. When she spied Adam, she stood up, approached him, attempted a curtsey, and said, "Sir, may I have the next dance?"

Adam grinned, took her in his arms, and they twirled about the floor. Several of the viewers began to clap. It felt just like old times.

After the dance, Adam and Eve sat on an overstuffed sofa in the outer area. Eve promptly snuggled up as Adam encircled her shoulder with his arm. Her head rested on his right shoulder, and soon she was sound asleep. Hearing her subdued, dainty way of snoring was soothing to Adam. Having her rest in his arms was such a comfort.

Although Adam appeared to be merely resting while serving as a pillow, his mind was working overtime. If Eve and the others responded to old-time songs and could actually remember them, why couldn't returning to an old familiar place bring back memories too? Returning to Crete, walking along the beach, talking to family members; why wouldn't that work? Instantly, Adam decided to contact the travel agency again and actually schedule the trip for the two of them. As her husband, he could just sign her out for a week or so.

As Adam entered the Quiet Haven facility the next day, he was literally accosted by a woman with shorn blonde hair with gray roots attired in a tee shirt and dungarees. The sequins on her purple shirt spelled 'diva.' She sauntered up to him with an inviting expression on her face, and bright red lipstick glistening on pursed lips. "Hello," she said in her most seductive manner. "Haven't I seen you somewhere before?"

In utter amazement, Adam replied, "No, I don't think so. I'm sure I would have remembered."

Hands on hips, she continued to smile, and said, "I've been waiting for you my whole life. It reminds me of an old song that goes something like this,

'They never met, they never kissed. They'll never know what happiness they missed. But she lived on the morning-side of the mountain, and he lived on the twilight-side of the hill.' But, now I have found you…"

"Yes, I remember that song," he said. "However, I don't know how it could pertain to you and me. I've been married to the love of my life for over 40 years."

At that, the woman cried out, "How can that be? You're the man I've dreamed of since I was a young girl."

"I'm sorry," Adam said, "but you must have me mixed up with someone else. One day, you will probably meet the man who is right for you."

The sound of the woman's sobbing brought an orderly on the scene. She took the woman's arm and said, "Mrs. Deville, your daughter just called and said to tell you she'll be here to share dinner with you this evening."

"Daughter? I don't have a daughter. I've never been married!"

"Well, Karen said she'll be here within the next 30 minutes. Let's go to your room and freshen up for dinner."

"Freshen up?"

"Yes, the chocolate drink you had for a snack seems to have splashed onto your blouse."

Looking down on her purple shirt, the would-be siren said, "You're right." Then looking at Adam she said, "Will you please wait for me until I change?"

Adam looked at her in a sad manner and said, "No, I'm sorry but I can't. I'm here to visit my wife."

"Your wife?"

"Yes, I told you I'm married. My wife is staying here too."

"Oh…what's her name?"

"Eve."

"Eve who?"

"Eve Alexander."

"Then your name is Alexander too? What's your first name?"

"Adam."

"Oh…isn't that cutesy? Adam and Eve." Then, with a tilt of her head and a rather evil smile she said, "How can you be tempted Adam?"

Turning abruptly, Adam walked toward the dayroom.

It turned out that Eve was being showered, so Adam sat down to relax with a magazine as he waited. The woman who had attempted to rescue him from Nancy Deville asked if she could speak with him. He nodded.

"Mr. Alexander, I apologize for that episode. Mrs. Deville's medicine has been changed recently and they are still attempting to obtain the proper balance. She's been here for only two weeks. At first, she was extremely withdrawn. Her doctor prescribed an anti-depressant and it seems to be too abrupt a change for her system."

"I understand," he said. "Don't worry about it. I'm sure she will forget all about me."

Just then, a nurse's aide walked through the other door of the dayroom with Eve on her arm. The green frock Eve wore enhanced the green of her eyes.

"Oh my darling," she said. "You've come to take me home," as she linked her right arm through his left. "The director here has shown me all of the latest fashions. Please buy this green dress for me. Don't you agree that it's my color?"

"Yes, indeed. You look beautiful, Eve. I'm reminded of the 10-year renewal of our wedding vows over 30 years ago."

"How can you say that, Adam? We haven't been married 10 years yet."

"It's been over 40, my dear."

"No, you're mistaken. Look at me, I'm not that old."

Noting that it would be foolish to continue that line of thought, Adam said, "You're right of course, my darling. You're just a spring-chick."

Eve grinned and said, "And you, are my knight in shining armor."

Adam walked her to the front desk and signed her out for the afternoon.

CHAPTER XXXI

Summer—1974 (cont'd)

When the young man said his father's name was Steve, Eve actually felt a tinge of nausea due to the sudden lurch in her stomach. Thinking back, she realized the last names of herself and Steve had never been shared at the orphanage.

"Mark," she said. "Do you look like your father?"

"I guess so. He has red hair and green eyes too."

With that, she leaned against a nearby tombstone, and with downcast eyes, allowed tears to trickle down her face. Then, she slowly slumped down to the ground.

Adam knelt down beside her, and placing a hand on each side of her head, gently kissed her forehead.

After a few moments, Eve regained her composure and said, "Mark, won't someone be expecting you to come home?"

"No way," he retorted.

"We don't want the police to be searching for you. Isn't there someone we can notify, someone who will be worried about your disappearance?"

"No one," he said. "My grandma and I lived together and now she's gone. There is no one else."

"Let's go," Adam said, "we're all very hungry. Would you like to stop by a drive-in restaurant for a hamburger, Mark?"

For the first time, Mark showed some interest. "Yeah," he said.

After they got into the car, Eve pulled down the mirror attached to the sun visor. "Oh dear, look at me, I'm a mess." Then, "Adam is there some clean water left in our jug? I must wash my face and hands."

"Yes, we can splash a bit on a paper towel. I have a bar of soap in the tackle box."

Pulling up to the drive-in window, Adam asked Mark what he would like to eat.

"Oh, a hamburger, fries and chocolate malt should be enough"

"How about two hamburgers?"

"Sounds good to me."

Thankfully, in less than 5 minutes, they were all silently eating. Adam chose a fish sandwich, Eve a salad. In the privacy of the back seat of the car, and after all his food had been devoured, Mark laid his head back on the seat and closed his eyes. Very soon, they heard a faint whistling sound of soft snoring. The gentle hum of the motor and the coolness generated by the air conditioner had lulled Mark into dreamland.

Thirty minutes later, Adam pulled into their driveway and turned off the engine. Immediately, Mark sat up abruptly and looked about in an alarmed manner. "Where am I?" he asked.

"You're at our home, Mark. Forgive us for not introducing ourselves," said Eve. "We are the Alexanders, Adam and Eve. As you will recall, we met today at the lake, and then later in the cemetery. We would like you to spend the night with us. In the morning, we will try to find out where you're from and how we may best help you."

"You can't help me. Nobody can."

"Well, the first thing we can do is get cleaned up. We all need a shower. Let's go inside and we can talk later."

"Okay," he said quietly.

After showering and washing his rather longish flame-colored hair, Mark looked squeaky clean. His knapsack had evidently contained at least one change of clothing, as he was attired in a clean, pale green tee shirt and a pair of much-washed jeans. Looking very awkward, he carried his soiled garments as though wishing to get rid of them.

"Here, Mark," Eve said. "I'll put your clothing in the washer with ours."

Without a word, he handed them to her.

"I'm sure you are very tired, Mark. Would you like to relax and watch TV or go to bed early?"

"I'll watch TV." He flopped down on the sofa.

Eve went to the kitchen and soon returned with a huge bowl of popcorn which she handed to Mark. Tempted first by a tall frosty glass of iced apple juice, he consumed the popcorn in short order.

Minutes after his snack, Mark's head began to droop, and once again, he fell fast asleep. Eve brought in a pillow, and Adam half lifted him and placed his head at one end of the sofa and his feet at the other. Then, he gently removed the lad's shoes.

Early the next morning, Eve peeked around the corner of the living room from the hallway, and found Mark was still sleeping in the same position as the night before. How totally drained both emotionally and physically he must have been, she thought.

Sleeping last night had been difficult for her. Scenes from the past continually raced through her mind. She could hardly allow herself to hope that Mark might be related to the Steve she remembered from the orphanage.

Glancing in at Mark again, she wondered what he might enjoy for breakfast. Of course, pancakes! Within 15 minutes, the delightful aroma caused Mark to wake up salivating. He stretched deeply and sniffed.

"Come and get it." Adam's job was to announce a call to breakfast. Soon all three of them were seated and taking turns spreading melted butter and drizzling pure maple syrup on steaming hot pancakes.

Sipping orange juice in between bites, Mark's cheeks finally began to emit a more healthy glow. His face even looked a bit fuller. After disposing of a 6-stacker of pancakes, he scooted his chair back and sat with hands folded in his lap.

"Why don't we adjourn to the living room?" Eve asked. "We usually attend church on Sunday morning, but it just feels right to relax at home this morning."

"How 'bout a cup of hot tea to polish off breakfast?"

"No thanks," said Mark. "Do you have any milk?"

"*Of course.* We're not used to serving young people. Here you are," Eve said after pouring the white liquid into a glass. "Do you mind carrying it into the living room?"

For the first time, a hint of a smile flitted across his face, and then was quickly gone.

After all three were seated again, Eve asked him to share something about his family. Her opening remark was stated with the tenderness only a woman can emit. "Mark," she said, "we know you've been hurt very badly. Please understand we wish to help you and are not prying due to idle curiosity."

He nodded, and then dropped his head.

Adam conveyed his agreement by extending his right hand toward Mark's shoulder while saying, "Take your time; we really want to do what's best for you."

As Mark raised his head, his sea-green eyes glinted with tears.

Eve took his hand and asked, "How old are you, Mark?"

"I've just turned 13."

Eve smiled and said, "Were you able to celebrate becoming a teenager?"

"No, grandma was too sick to even realize it was my birthday."

"What type of illness did she have?"

"Breast cancer."

"Was she under a doctor's care?"

"At first, she was. After the doctor told her what was wrong, she just gave up. We had very little money, and she used what we had for food and rent."

"Rent? Where did you live?"

"Just a few miles from the cemetery in an old house. It was run down and the rent was extremely cheap."

"Where did you get money for food and rent?"

"We were on welfare. After my father left, there was no money at all."

"When did he leave?"

"Two years ago."

"Where is he?"

"In prison!"

CHAPTER XXXII

All was silent. Adam's face registered shock. Eve gasped in dismay. When she was able to speak, she quietly asked, "In prison! What did he do?"

"I'm not really sure what happened. They called him a murderer!"

"Murder? I can't believe it!"

"We couldn't either, but they pronounced him guilty of involuntary manslaughter."

"On what basis?"

"He left home one evening to cover a story…"

Eve interrupted him, "A story?"

"Yes, he was a reporter for a St. Louis daily newspaper. A police informant probably wanted to get his own name in the news. He may have thought he would become famous for helping unravel a case."

"That's interesting," said Adam. "I'm a reporter for a St. Louis newspaper also. Which paper did Steve work for?"

They discussed the newspapers and found Adam and Steve were employed by competitive news sources.

"Pardon me, I'm sorry to distract you," Adam said. "Please go on with your story, Mark."

Eve nodded her head and said, "Yes Mark, then what happened?"

"My father agreed to meet in a bar that the informant suggested. Dad got there early and had a few beers at the bar while waiting. Later, several people who were there told the police that he probably had a few too many."

"Did Steve...I mean your father, did he usually drink very much?"

"Yes. He didn't drink at home because Ma would pour it down the drain when she found it."

"Did he get mean when he drank?"

"No, he just talked and sang."

"What did he sing?"

"Dad enjoyed show tunes, but most of all, he sang songs written by an old-time composer called, Stephen Foster."

"Stephen Foster?" Adam asked.

"Yes. Have you ever heard of him? Not many people have. Dad said he died around the time of the Civil War and wrote lots of songs about what life was like on Southern plantations before the war began. Some of my favorites were, 'Camptown Races,' 'Swanee River,' and 'Old Black Joe.' My parent's favorite was, 'Jeanie With The Light Brown Hair.' My mother's name is Jean; Dad always sang that to her when he came home feeling good."

"Feeling good?"

"Yes, when he'd been drinking."

Suddenly Eve began to hum and Mark gasped. The tune was that of 'Jeanie With The Light Brown Hair.' Then, with a smile on her face, she began to sing and presently, tears began running down her face. Adam and Mark just sat and listened to the sad refrain.

'I dream of Jeanie with the light brown hair, born like a vapor on the summer air. I see her drifting where the bright streams play, happy as the daisies that danced on her way. Many were the wild notes her merry voice would pore, many were the blithe birds that warbled them o'er...'

Mark seemed stunned. "No one besides my family ever heard of any of those songs. How come you know that one?"

"When I was a little girl, someone we knew used to sing those songs. I've never forgotten them as they always seemed so sad to me. The tunes were catchy, but sad."

"Do you mean a babysitter sang them to you, Mrs. Alexander?"

"No. I mean the gardener at the orphanage where I lived as a child."

"You mean that you were an orphan too? So was my Dad."

Eve choked up again with emotion. Adam, of course, understood because he had heard her sing those same songs so many times. She only sang them as a sort of release of tension when she got upset. After singing the songs, she would cry, and afterwards, she would feel better.

"Well, enough about songs," she said. "Tell me why your father was convicted of murder. What happened?"

"Well, the informant didn't show up. As I said, Dad continued to drink while waiting for him. A woman who knew the man asked my Dad to hold a small package for him until he arrived. Father agreed. After she left, two detectives came in the tavern, flashed badges and took my father outside into an alley. They frisked him and took the package from his coat pocket. My father tried to retrieve it as it had been entrusted to his care. One of the 'so-called' detectives punched Dad in the stomach."

"So-called detectives? Who were they?"

"Dad said they were part of a mob."

"So, what happened then?"

"Dad swung at the detective who punched him, and hit him on the chin. The man fell over backwards and evidently struck his head at a bad angle. The fall broke his neck and he died on the spot!" Mark let out a deep sigh and continued, "It turned out that the guy actually *was* a detective, but he was operating some shady deals that were outside the law."

"So your father was sentenced for killing an officer of the law?"

"Yeah, he was sentenced to 10 years in prison with the possibility of less time for good behavior."

"What was in the package?"

"I'm not sure, but I heard it was 'hot' diamonds that had been stolen from a local jeweler. The woman who gave the package to Dad was under surveillance. They knew she had them and was trying to get them to an informant named Oscar and hoped he would turn them in. She knew Oscar and Dad were drinking buddies. When she arrived, she saw only Steve and gave them to him to give to Oscar. The police already knew Oscar to be an informant and wouldn't think anything of him turning them in for a reward"

"Who was the actual thief?"

"Her husband. She hated his crime-wave and thought if the diamonds were returned to the jeweler through the informant, no one would know who the thief was and her husband would not be arrested."

"How did the detectives find out that she had them?"

"The detective who was killed was her husband's brother, and he knew all about the theft. He and his partner followed her and saw her give the package to Dad."

"How could your father be connected? Didn't the court have all this information?"

"They did, but the judge was convinced that Dad was guilty because he was an alcoholic, we were extremely poor, and that he was the one who had stolen the diamonds and killed the detective in order to keep them."

"My, what a story! Where is the prison where your father is being held?"

"It's not too far, just about a four hour drive from here."

"Oh yes, I know where it is. But, that seems strange, that prison is a federal prison. The accident doesn't sound like a federal offense."

"They said that Dad was sent there because it is also a place for prisoners with medical or addiction problems."

"Was your father ill?"

"No, they said he was addicted to alcohol."

With that, Mark broke down and sobbed. By then, Adam and Eve were teary-eyed too. Their hearts had been touched so deeply by the young man's story.

Adam's analytical mind was sifting through all the evidence they had just heard and was trying to find a solution. They must see that Steve was set free and reunited with his son, but how...?

That afternoon, Mark turned to Eve and asked, "Why are you and your husband doing this for me? You don't even know me."

Eve took a deep breath and said, "Mark, how old is your father?"

"I don't know, probably in his 30's. Why?"

"How old do you think I am, Mark?"

Mark gulped as he remembered hearing someone say that you should never try to guess the age of a female. Young girls always want to be older than they are, and most women want to appear younger. He did not intend to get involved in a guessing game that could prove to his detriment.

"I don't know Mrs. Alexander. You are probably pretty young."

"How young do you think I am?"

"Gosh," he said. "I really don't know...maybe 21?"

Eve chuckled and thanked him. "How kind of you to say that." Then, "I'm probably around the same age as your father."

"Yeah? You look something like him too."

"I do? How do we look alike?"

"Well, you both have red hair and green eyes, and you talk alike."

"Do I have a masculine voice or does he have a feminine one?" she said with a smile.

"Neither one. It's just that the way you say things reminds me of him."

"Like what?"

"Well, when you use the name of the state we live in, you say it different from other people."

"How do we say it?"

"You both say Missouri as though it ends in an 'a'. Other people end it with an 'e'."

"What else?"

"When you told me that you were going to wash the dishes, you pronounced wash as though it contains an 'r' and as though it was spelled warsh. When my grandmother said wash, it sounded like waash with an extra 'a'.

When you talk to others, they can tell what you're thinking by your eyes. Other people look away most of the time, and it makes me feel you know what I'm thinking too. Your eyes are like a thermostat. Hot and cold waves flow from them."

"How so?"

"When you're happy, it's a warm flow, when you're sad or angry, it's cold, when you're interested, your eyes sparkle like ice on trees in the winter time."

"Mark, it seems you've inherited the gift of descriptive gab from your father."

"How do you know?"

"It's possible that I might know your father personally."

"Really, from where?"

"From our childhood."

"Your childhood. Where did you meet?"

"I think we may have been together in an orphanage."

"What makes you think so?"

"Please follow me, Mark."

He followed her as she led him to a large mirror framed in gold in the living room. They both stopped in front of the mirror, and she said," Look Mark, look at our reflections together."

While peering in the mirror, Mark said, "Yeah, I see us. So what?"

Framed in the mirror appeared a woman and young man of the exact same height of 5'8", both had auburn hair and bright green eyes. "Is there a similarity in our appearance?"

"Well, our hair is the same color. You're a female, I'm a male."

Turning his head towards her, he peered intently into her eyes. Even the pale sprinkling of tan-colored freckles on her nose and cheeks looked similar to his. "I guess we look a little alike, don't we?"

"Yes, that's what I thought too."

"Why are you and Mr. Alexander treating me as though you know me?"

"Maybe we feel you and I are related somehow."

"Why? Just 'cause we look alike?"

"Let's let it rest for a while. Adam and I want to get permission to visit your father. Have you seen him there in prison?"

"No. I don't have enough money to go visit him."

"Would you like to see your father?"

"Of course, we communicate by mail, but we really can't say much. They read his mail and I'm sure they probably read my mail to him too."

"Adam plans to make contact with an official of the prison tomorrow and obtain permission to see Steve. Do you want to go along?"

"Oh, yeah!"

After calling the prison, Adam told Mark and Eve that papers would have to be filed requesting permission to visit Steve. Mark could visit because he was a blood relative, but Adam and Eve would have to get special dispensation. The trip from St. Louis to the prison was almost four hours by car. That meant they would probably have to stay somewhere overnight and return the following day. That way, they could visit Steve two days in a row.

The next morning, they called again and were informed that Steve was excited about seeing his son, Mark. Now, it was just a matter of time until Adam and Eve were approved as visitors.

"Mark," said Eve, "you're going to need more clothing. Can we take you back to your home and pick up some things?"

"No, there's nothin' there. When my grandma died, they put me out. I couldn't pay the rent."

"How could they do that to you? Didn't they know it was the only home you had?"

"I guess they didn't care. The day after the funeral, they put a 'for rent' sign on the front lawn."

"Don't you have any other clothing at all?"

"What I had wasn't worth keeping. Besides, they put a new lock on both doors."

"How did you pay for your grandmother's funeral?"

"She actually paid for it herself. Each month for years, she sent a small amount to the local funeral parlor with the understanding that when she died, they would provide a casket, and bury her."

"Adam," Eve said. "You will have to check the validity of what that bank is doing. After all, they surely can't keep what's inside the house. What was your grandmother's name, Mark?"

"Madge Hamilton."

"Mrs. Hamilton…then she wasn't your father's mother?"

"No, she was my mom's mother. My mother left home several years ago; she said it was partly because of my dad's drinking."

"Where is she now?"

"I don't know. Her dream was to go to Hollywood and become a star. The last address we had from her was in Beverly Hills, California."

"Did she get a lucky break?"

"I don't know. In her last letter, she said she was modeling to pay for her expenses and acting classes."

"Why doesn't she keep in touch with you?"

"Because she thinks I don't understand how important an acting career is to her."

"Is she aware that her mother passed away?"

"No!"

"Shall we try to locate her?"

"No!"

"Was your father in prison when she left?"

"Yes, he was. She was so angry about that. Angry at him for killing someone; and angry because there was no money."

"Do you think she loves you?" (Eve just *had* to ask painful that question.)

"She said so, but I don't believe it. I think she just loves herself."

"What about her own mother. Did she love her?"

"I suppose, in her way, she did. She always expected my grandmother to figure everything out. She knew Ma would always take care of me."

"Is that what you called your grandmother?"

"Yeah. When I was young, it was easier just to call her Ma."

"You truly loved her, didn't you?"

"Yes, of course. She was kind, and the only person I could trust."

"You really miss her, don't you?"

"Yeah, and I always will. She never thought about herself, just about me."

"Did she get along with your father?"

"Oh yes, Dad really loved her."

"I assume that he is aware that she died."

"No, I don't think so."

"Why not?"

"Well, she wasn't his mother, just his mother-in-law. Ma and I lived together and didn't associate with many people. I've been so upset with both my parents and didn't really care if I never saw either of them again." With that, Mark heaved a tremendous sigh.

"That's pretty heavy stuff for such a young person to endure."

"That's okay. I'm tough," he said assertively.

Eve didn't mention that she had heard him crying out, "Ma, don't leave me!" in his sleep last night.

CHAPTER XXXIII

Several weeks later, the three of them were en route to the prison. Before leaving home, Eve suggested they hold hands and pray that their visit with Steve would be blessed by God. Many heavy emotions were weighing down on all of them.

Mark had been encouraged to contact the prison to make his father aware of Ma's death. That had been hard. Of course, Steve wondered about where his son would go and who would take care of the 13 year-old young man. When he was told of a married couple who had befriended Mark, he was anxious to learn more of them, and wondered why they had assumed such a responsibility.

Adam prayed before driving to the prison to see Steve. The prayer had been very brief, as Adam assumed his role as 'head of the household.' He prayed first for Mark and guidance for him, then for Steve's release, and finally for the relationship between Eve and Steve, and knowledge regarding their possible relationship to one another. He ended the prayer with, "If we really *are* family, help us to love and minister to one another."

En route to the prison, they all enjoyed viewing the rolling hills covered with green trees and rocky cliffs. Soon these same trees would all be ablaze with the vivid colors of autumn. Once again they felt so blessed to enjoy the wonder of nature in the Midwest. As they spoke of the upcoming fall season, memories of many precious times with his father flooded Mark's mind and softened his heart towards him. Many times, they had visited state parks, pitched a tent and fished and swam in the rivers together. Hiking was another favorite pastime of theirs.

As Adam drove, he looked in the rearview mirror from time to time observing Mark as they spoke together. "Look at that patch of trees. We seldom think of all the brilliant colors hidden inside the green leaves we view all summer long. I understand the colors are there all the while, but only come into view in the autumn when the trees know they must begin getting ready for winter. During winter, there is not enough light or water for photosynthesis. Photosynthesis is a process which occurs when trees take nutrients and water from the ground, and sunlight and carbon dioxide from the air. This combination actually turns into a type of sugar from which the trees are nourished. As the trees know they must rest during the winter, they live off the foods they stored during the summer. So, they begin shutting down their capability to make food, almost like bears in hibernation, I suppose. The green chlorophyll in the leaves that has been present all summer long begins to fade. As this happens, the incredible colors of yellow, orange, red, copper, tangerine, and many others begin to appear."

Mark pondered that for a while and said, "Yeah, I think we were taught about that in my science class at school, but I had forgotten all about it."

Then, Eve turned sideways in her seat to face Mark. She began comparing trees to people: "We are so much like that too. Our bodies cover the 'real us.' Underneath the exterior of our outer frames lies our mind, will, emotions and spirit. Most people work hard to camouflage what's inside."

"Why do you think we do that?" Mark asked.

"Allowing others to see what causes us to tick makes us more vulnerable."

"What does that mean?"

"It means that they could intentionally hurt us if they wish, by having access to the inner, private parts of ourselves."

Mark nodded his head in agreement. "Now I understand why I've never wanted anyone to know me too well. I'm afraid of being hurt. It mostly pertained to my family. I don't want to talk about my mother leaving me to become a movie star, or about my father's drinking problem, or his imprisonment. It's been so hard for me to accept, and it's uncomfortable to discuss. Most folks don't really care, they just want to gossip to others about it."

Eve faced the front of the car again, and pulled down her sun visor with a mirror on the other side of it. This allowed her to look directly at Mark without straining her neck. Mark too, could look into her eyes as they spoke via the mirror, thus enhancing their communication. Seeing the double-vision of their two red heads in the mirror made her aware, once again, of the physical similarities between them.

Her heart seemed to double its rhythm as she anticipated the afternoon to come. She might find that Mark was her nephew if she and Steve could confirm blood-ties to one another. How could they do that? There were almost too many clues to be mere chance. Then too, Mark would feel more at ease living with them until his father was set free if he knew that they truly *were* family.

Their four-hour drive from St. Louis left them all a bit hungry. After stopping at a restaurant advertising home-cooking style food, they had just a few more miles before reaching their destination.

Driving up to the prison gates, they were stopped by a guard who inquired about their credentials. Showing the admission pass they had received by mail, the guard waved them on as the gates opened simultaneously.

Another guard waved and beckoned for them to leave their car in a guest parking area, and soon they were walking into the main building. After presenting the document once again, they were ushered into a huge gymnasium-type room filled with tables and chairs. Five minutes later, a door swung open to admit another guard, followed by a man in prison-garb whose hair was the color of a blazing fire. As he drew closer, they noted that silver streaks throughout his auburn hair caused it to appear to glow like a furnace. However, his vivid hair color was matched only by the intense green sheen of his eyes.

Adam and Eve encouraged Mark to step forward to greet his father before making Steve aware of their presence. At first, it seemed father and son felt awkward as they woodenly shook hands. Then Steve's eyes appeared cloudy, and he reached out and hugged Mark to his chest. Immediately, Mark's arms returned the embrace. Then, he placed his head on his father's shoulder just as a small child might do.

Suddenly, Steve was surprised to find that Mark's attention had drifted. Looking in the direction of Mark's gaze, he saw an attractive couple looking back at him. He noted an extremely tall, rugged-appearing man with black hair and a pronounced cowlick that stood straight up, and alongside him, a tall, slender, attractive, shapely woman with hair the color of his own. Obviously, these must be the people who took his son in after being abandoned due to the death of Mark's grandmother.

With his left arm over Mark's right shoulder, Steve approached them with a smile of appreciation on his face. Eve searched his face for any sign of recognition in his eyes. Obviously, his attention kept returning to his son, even though he appeared grateful for their aid.

Adam suggested Steve and Mark take time alone, and later they could all chat a bit. They agreed, and Adam and Eve retreated to an area containing a sofa with magazines on a nearby table. Even though they both chose a magazine to read, they could not refrain from allowing their gaze to drift to the happy reunion of father and son. Mark seemed to talk non-stop, and then it was Steve's turn. He became very serious about their conversation. Mark's face expressed concern and dismay.

After about 15 minutes, Mark's attention seemed to turn to Adam and Eve once again, and he gestured toward them occasionally. Father and son stood up simultaneously and walked toward Adam and Eve.

As Mark introduced his father to his new benefactors, Steve barely glanced at Adam, but kept his eyes fixed on Eve. She did the same with him, looking deeply into his eyes. Sparks of recognition seemed to flow between them.

Finally…he realized Mark kept saying, "This is Eve."

With that, Steve threw his arms around her and said, "Eve, oh Eve, is it really you?"

Her cheeks flushed brightly, and she responded, "Steve, oh Steve, is it really *you*?" With that, she excitedly and lovingly embraced him too.

"How many years has it been, Eve? I've thought of you often."

"And I you, Steve. We have so much to catch up on."

Unashamedly wiping his eyes, and then, holding Eve's hand in his, he turned to Adam, extended his other hand and said, "Forgive me, I didn't catch your name."

"It's Adam. Adam Alexander. Eve is my wife." Then, "I think we should all sit down and talk. How much visitation time is allotted to you, Steve?"

"Just one hour."

"We plan to spend the night in the area, so we can stop by again tomorrow, if that's okay."

"Okay? How can I ever begin to thank you? Seeing my son after such a long time, and Eve my old friend, is such an intense pleasure."

Eve felt she should withhold the fact that they might be related until tomorrow. The most pressing thing to discuss right now was how to obtain Steve's freedom. She was sure there was much to learn, and many notes to take if they were to do research on his behalf.

They all seated themselves and Steve said, "Before we begin, I must inquire about Jeanie, my wife." Turning to Mark he said, "Have you heard from your mother recently?"

"No, Dad. It's been almost a year since she wrote and there have been no phone calls either. She told Ma that she was too busy with her job and acting classes, so there would be no time to write and no extra money to pay long-distance phone bills."

"I don't understand how she could ignore you like that," Steve said in a distressed voice. "She knew her mother had to be stressed out with the responsibility of raising you and paying the bills."

"Do you think she cares, Dad? She always seemed to be more concerned about her looks than about me. There was never time to play, that I can recall."

"When you were quite young, she really enjoyed you. Then, she entered a beauty contest for attractive married women hoping to gain the title of Mrs. Missouri. She was a runner-up, but all along the way, many people were impressed with her beauty. Their compliments went to her head, and she became totally engrossed in herself and a career in the movies. That was when you were only three years of age. Until then, you had almost her undivided attention. We rented a small apartment and it was very easy to keep clean. We shopped for groceries together. So...she cooked, cleaned and cared for you. Then one day, she decided to shop by herself, so I let her. It seemed we didn't have much in the refrigerator after that, even though I gave her even more money than we had formerly spent. Later, I found stacks and stacks of movie magazines under our bed along with boxes full of every kind of makeup and hair supplies. She changed her beautiful light brown hair to become a phony-looking bleached blonde one day, and a redhead soon afterward. Once, when she tried to return to a light brown hair shade for a change, the dye turned her hair black due to the porous condition caused by intense bleaching."

"I remember that, Dad. When I saw her with black hair for the first time, I actually cried. I was so frightened, and didn't recognize her."

"Well, enough of this kind of talk. You asked how you might help obtain my release. Oscar Hill, the police informant, probably knew about the detective's dishonesty, and that Detective Winchell intended to confiscate the diamonds for himself rather than turn them in."

"Wasn't Oscar summoned as a witness in your trial?" questioned Adam.

"They attempted to do so, but he was nowhere to be found."

"Didn't someone have his address?"

"Yes, but when they tried to locate Oscar, they found he had vacated the furnished rooms which he had rented for several months."

"It seems strange that the police trusted him if he was a newcomer to the area."

"That's true, but he had helped them locate a kidnapped child the month before"

"A kidnapped child? How did that happen?"

"Actually, the child had been taken from nursery school by his own father. They were staying at the same rooming house as Oscar, and the child's picture was shown on TV and posted all over town, while promising a reward. Oscar actually went in person to the police station, and got them to sign a paper stating he would be entitled to the reward when he led them to the child. Several police followed him and he took them directly to the apartment rented by the child's father. They both happened to be there and were taken to the police station. The child's mother was called and they returned the boy to her. The boy's father went to jail."

"Who posted the reward?"

"The boy's grandparents. The very next day, they took Oscar to their bank and gave him $10,000 in cash."

"Wow! I'm surprised he didn't leave town immediately."

"Well, I was too when I heard the story, but it's possible he had already heard about the stolen diamonds and thought he could make even more money."

"What were his plans?"

"He obviously told Winchell, the crooked detective about the jewels being given to me. A cut of 50% had been promised to Oscar for the information, but the detective had no intention of sharing."

"How could he get by with that as Oscar could have reported him?"

"Oscar had a prison record and the detective knew it. He would have twisted the facts and turned him in. Oscar couldn't take a chance."

"But, the detective was dead. How could he have implicated him?"

"Once you have a record, you don't want to get involved with any type of crime."

"So...what do you recommend we do in order to clear your name?"

"The only thing I can think of would be to locate Oscar and ask him to testify on my behalf."

"Where can we start?"

"I've given it a tremendous amount of thought, and I can think of only one possible link to him."

"What's that?"

"The grandparents of the boy who was kidnapped were incredibly grateful to him. They got in touch with Oscar's only living relative, a sister who lives in Tennessee. My feeling is that she may know of his where-abouts."

"Why wasn't she contacted before now?"

"No one believed my story, and I had no money to hire a detective."

"A detective?"

"Yes, that's funny, isn't it? A detective to help get the goods on another detective, and one who is actually deceased."

"So Steve, you're saying that if we contact the young boy's grandparents, they can probably put us in touch with Oscar's sister, and then we may locate Oscar."

"Yes, it sounds simple enough, doesn't it? But, I've never been able to find someone to help along those lines."

"As a starter, how may we contact the boy's grandparents?"

"Well, it's best not to alert anyone about your plans, so…I would recommend you go to the public library to obtain the information."

"Oh yes, of course. They have copies of all the local newspapers on microfilm. If you will just give me the date span of the kidnapping and rescue, I will work on it immediately."

Just then, one of the guards approached their seating area to inform them the allotted time for visitors was over.

Steve gave Mark a big hug and shook the hands of Adam and Eve, saying "Same time, same place, tomorrow."

"We'll be here," promised Eve.

As it was only 2:00 p.m., and not yet time for dinner, Adam drove down the road several miles in the direction they had come. An impressive sign had caught their attention on the way down. It said, 'Animal Kingdom,' and advertised that if you cared to drive through the facility, you could view many animals roaming about in the wild which had originally been captured from all over the world. They all agreed it could be quite enjoyable.

Admission price was by the carload, not per person. Within 15 minutes, they felt as though they were traveling through Africa. All types of wild animals were viewed, however only one kind actually approached their car. A pair of ostriches found them fascinating and one even stuck his head, followed by a long neck, in the front car window. It appeared he was enraptured with Eve's red locks and began to peck on her right ear. Adam sped up and left the huge bird behind. It took Eve a few moments to catch her breath, and soon they were all giggling about the experience.

Two hours later, they felt a bit weary, and drove into the heart of town looking for a clean motel. Their choice was one that had two queen-sized beds. Eve was allowed to shower first and change her clothing. The guys accomplished the same in half the time, and then they went to dinner.

The next day, they returned to the prison for another hour-long visit. This time, it was Eve's turn to make inquiries of Steve.

Just as the day before, the routine was the same. They were waved through the gates by a guard after driving up, and then ushered into the huge reception area to be joined by Steve.

As Steve entered the room, his face lit up catching sight of them, and he waved. Mark's grin of response was heart-warming to watch. After shaking hands and hugging, they all sat down on an adjoining sofa and loveseat. Eve felt her heart racing as she prayed for guidance regarding what to ask. Then, she realized that they had come this far for a purpose, and were obviously to be reunited.

Smiling as she began to speak, she took Steve's hand in hers and began, Steve, let's clarify the evidence of our past together as we see it."

"Eve, I'm sure we spent time together in an orphanage years ago." Then he asked, "Do you remember those days too?"

"Yes, of course. I recognized you immediately yesterday when we met. Looking at Mark was almost like looking at you. Then, Mark told me your last name is Simmons. So is mine; so that seemed to clinch the fact that we were not merely both at the orphanage at the same time, but might even be related to one another."

Then they both began to excitedly relate stories that pertained to their time together many years ago. After verbal confirmation from one another, they both grew very encouraged.

Eve drew a compact from her purse, opened it and held it at arm's length. Then she swiveled about so a reflection of herself and Steve together came into view.

"Wow!" he said. "I see what you mean. We look alike and *could* be related. Same hair and eye color, same freckles, same nose, same complexion."

"And, approximately the same age," Eve observed.

"How old are you, Eve?"

"I would say I'm probably in my early 30's. How about you?"

"The same. How old do you think you were when you were taken there to live?"

"I'm not really conscious of time before that, so I'm not sure. What about you, Eve. Do you have any memories prior to that time?"

"Yes, Steve. I have a couple of conscious memories. One was of lying on the floor in a hallway that had a winding staircase leading up to another level. It seemed there were other children there with me almost as though we were supposed to be taking a nap together. I was lying on something soft like a blanket, and it felt as though it wrapped around my body at the same time to keep me warm, thus giving the sensation of being in a cozy cocoon. A song was playing softly in the background. It may have been a recording because it kept playing over and over again. I have heard some of the words in my head occasionally through the years, but actually realized what it was when I watched the 'Lawrence Welk Show' on TV years later, and heard them singing that very song. Suddenly, the memory of the words and music came back full force. The song was 'Red Roses for a Blue Lady.' It made me feel comforted and sad at the same time."

"Is that your only memory prior to time at the orphanage?"

"No, I remember lying on my back in a dark room and hearing a man and woman talking. I was probably in a baby bed because I seemed to be peering through slender bars and I was elevated above the floor. My room was dark, but I could see beyond the bed and into another room due to its ceiling light."

"What kind of feeling did you have regarding the conversation you heard?"

"Of course, I couldn't understand it, but a man and woman were talking."

"Were you sharing your baby bed?"

Eve laughed rather sadly, and said, "No, I seemed to be alone. However, I understand what you're thinking. If we are as close in age as it appears, could we possibly be twins?"

Steve's expression changed from one of anxious expectation to one of sadness. "How shall we find out, Eve? It's not fair to have come this far and not know the beginning of the story."

"I agree, Steve. There is a part of me that craves to know my roots. Together, maybe we can do some research. But, for the time being, the first thing on our agenda must be to obtain your freedom."

With that, they released one another's hands and noted Adam and Mark as they sat looking back and forth at the two siblings as they spoke. It appeared somewhat like a tennis match where spectator's heads are constantly moving back and forth to catch every volley and return of the ball.

Steve glanced at the large school-type clock on the wall just as a guard approached them. "Time to go," the guard said.

Steve stood up, hugged each of them, and allowed the guard to escort him through the door and back to his cell. His family stood watching until he turned, and gave them a rather sad salute, rather than the customary wave, and then disappeared from sight.

On the drive back to St. Louis, the three of them chattered like magpies. There was so much to discuss.

"Mark, your Dad seemed very happy knowing you will be living with us until he is free to take care of you. How do you feel about that?" Eve asked.

A rather whimsical look flitted across Mark's face; his immature Adam's apple appeared to levitate a bit, and then in a rather husky voice he said, "I don't know where I would be now without you guys. Of course, the best part was being with my Dad. I've missed him so much."

Eve reached over the back of the car seat and patted his hand. "Mark, I'm so glad you're not angry now about your father being in prison. You must realize it's a situation beyond his control."

"Yeah, I know that. It just seems he shouldn't drink so much. That's what got him in trouble."

"Mark, do you think your Dad just enjoys drinking, or do you feel he's got an addiction problem?" queried Adam.

"I think he's addicted. He tried to quit drinking for Mom, but wasn't able to. That's the reason we always lived in apartments and couldn't afford to buy a house."

Eve felt a chill travel up from the base of her spine that made her scalp tingle. The situation was even more grave than she had anticipated. Maybe...just maybe, Steve's incarceration might have helped. But then, she remembered the old adage, 'Absence makes the heart grow fonder.' Does that just apply to relationships, or could it make Steve even more zealous to return to his drinking addiction? Or instead, might the absence of alcohol in prison help remove his need for it? Could abstinence be something Steve's heart desires now? Only time would tell...

CHAPTER XXXIV

Current Year—Autumn

The next day, Adam checked local ads in the newspaper for a different type of facility. There must be a place where he and his beloved Eve could dwell together in peace. Even though he was beginning to realize the enormity of the responsibilities that would be on him, it was a responsibility he must shoulder. He knew Eve would do the same for him if the situation were reversed.

After calling about a few places that appeared to have possibilities, he realized that none seemed just right. But, the final one seemed to offer some delightful features. The ad stated that the facility was charming and home-like. It had the look of a Victorian mansion situated in the midst of acres of ground.

Hastily, Adam dialed the phone number listed and a very pleasant female voice said, "Good afternoon, Friendship Hermitage. How may I help you?"

"Hello, my name is Adam Alexander, and I'm looking for a facility where my wife and I may share an apartment together."

Do you realize this is actually a health-care dwelling?"

"Yes, I do. My wife has been diagnosed with Alzheimer's, and I'm looking for a place that will minister care to her, and where we can stay together."

"Mr. Alexander, we can provide both those things for you. My name is Virginia Holmes, and my husband Frank and I own Friendship Hermitage. By profession, I am an R.N., and Frank is a retired engineer. This is our home and also our business. Does your wife have any physical problems?"

"No, she doesn't. Her overall health is very good. I noticed that her memory began to fail rather rapidly, and she was becoming confused. I took her to our family doctor and he advised screening for Alzheimer's. Once the diagnosis was made, it seemed to progress rather rapidly."

"How old is your wife?"

"Eve is only 63 years old. It's hard to believe the diagnosis; she seems too young for Alzheimer's."

"Sir, Alzheimer's can strike at any age. An Alzheimer's patient in the nursing home where I worked was only 37 years of age."

"37!"

"Yes, 37. It took a long time for diagnosis because they had not considered Alzheimer's due to her age. Anyway, I am always on the premises except for when I must shop or have personal needs. When I am away, a very qualified person is in charge, and a lovely lady who lives nearby can come on a moment's notice if you need to get away. She could stay with your wife until you return."

"Tell me more about your facility."

"We are located in the midst of 6 acres of ground. My husband grows most of our fruits and vegetables. We have livestock too, horses, cows and lambs. Our guests are free to help in the garden if they wish, and also to enjoy the livestock."

"What about our apartment?"

"Actually, the big house is where my husband and I live. There are six cottages on the grounds for those in residence here. Each one contains a sitting room, bedroom, kitchen and bath. They are small, but have all the comforts of home. Oh yes, a tiny screened-in porch is on the back. The porches all face a lake that is periodically stocked for your fishing pleasure."

"What about meals?"

"Each day, a large dinner is served at noon in our home and all are invited. Menus are distributed at the beginning of each week. Breakfast and supper are your responsibility. We found that as people age, a heavier meal around noon is healthier than at supper time. Your kitchen has everything you need, and there is a small town just four miles away where you may purchase your groceries, and other necessary items. Once a month, we change our time-schedule for the day and serve a candlelight dinner complete with wine."

"How far are you from St. Louis?"

"We are only 20 miles from St. Louis so you can drive back and forth quite easily. Next week, one of our bungalows will be vacant. The couple decided to move to Little Rock where they have other family members. Do you have any children, Mr. Alexander?"

"No, we just have one another."

"As you know, our ad is in the paper and we have already had a couple of inquiries. Would you care to visit?"

"Yes, I would. How about tomorrow around 10:00 a.m.?"

"That will be fine, Mr. Alexander. We'll see you then."

"Eve, wake up. We're going to take a drive to the county today."

"Oh good. I'm in the mood for an outing. Where are we going?"

"There's a mini farm and ranch that serves delicious meals in a Victorian style home. Their special today is southern fried chicken with country gravy and all the fixings. They will also serve grilled salmon, which is one of your favorites."

"Yum, yum. I'm hungry already."

"As soon as you're dressed, we'll leave. If we arrive early, we might have time to look around a bit."

An hour later, they pulled up in front of a 3-story house with all the bric-a-brac necessary to qualify it as Victorian. The expansive wrap-around porch containing a hanging two-person swing with gay colored cushions, and several comfortable rocking chairs completed the scene. On one side of the house sat a gazebo with a picnic table and chairs nearby. Gazing beyond the house, they spied a lake surrounded by six charming little bungalows.

"Hello there, you're a bit early. Please come in."

They looked up to see a lovely woman with hair the color of an albino apricot. Adam recalled seeing a woman and her poodle dog parading down the street together one day in St. Louis, and both appeared to have the same hairdresser as their curly locks both sported the same identical shade as the woman in his view.

"Oh hello," Adam replied. "You must be Mrs. Holmes."

"Call me Virginia please, everyone else does. We are very informal here."

"Virginia appeared to be around 50 years of age, and her glamorous attire of cashmere sweater and lightweight wool slacks were the exact same shade as her hair. Her toenails followed suit color-wise, and were exposed by her silver toeless shoes and sterling ear hoops which matched her foot gear. The 4" heels made her almost 5 ½ feet tall.

Eve was evidently smitten by Virginia's hair and even reached out to touch it as if to assure herself that it was real.

Virginia just smiled and said, "Mrs. Alexander, my hair is actually the same color underneath this dye as yours. It has been totally white for almost 20 years and I enjoy livening it up occasionally. Do you like it?

Eve smiled and said, "Oh yes, I do. Maybe I could have mine colored like that too."

"If you like, my hairdresser would be delighted to color it for you. Sometimes, she gives mine a pale blue or lavender tint. I enjoy purchasing clothing to match. For years, I wore a boring nurse's uniform and even one of those strange little hats that won't stay put. They were a must! Now, I amuse myself by wearing whatever strikes my fancy at the moment."

As men don't understand that kind of girl talk, Adam shifted uneasily from one foot to the other, hoping they could soon get down to business.

Virginia seemed to sense his discomfort and invited them into her home. "We will be serving dinner in just one hour. Please feel free to look about in the meantime. The only areas off-limits are the second and third floors, Mr. Alexander. That is where Frank and I reside."

"Thank you, Virginia. Please call us Adam and Eve. It's not necessary to be so formal."

"Oh my, isn't that precious…"

Adam waited until she went through the usual recognition of the symbolic meaning of their two names together.

Then he quietly said, "Thank you. We would enjoy looking over the grounds. See you in an hour."

Walking around the porch swing and to the back of the home, they spied a huge corral-type area which housed several horses. One of them appeared to be prancing as a man spoke gently into the horse's left ear. As they approached the white fence, the man waved and said, "Hello, I'm Frank. I'll be with you in a minute."

Riding horses was something Adam and Eve knew very little about. They had both read the book entitled, "The Horse Whisperer" and it made them wish they had more experience riding. St. Louis was not a big area for that unless you had your own horse and stable.

Frank was tall and lean with salt and pepper colored hair, a weather-beaten complexion, and a wide, friendly smile. He apologized for not shaking their hands as he had just recently cleaned the stable. He then excused himself and washed up, using a jug of water which sat on a homemade shelf jutting out from a huge oak tree.

Returning, he said, "You must be the Alexanders. Ginny told me to expect you."

Adam inquired about how long they had owned Friendship Hermitage.

Frank replied, "Just two years. It's still very much the way it was when we purchased it. We felt it was a good property with great potential and of course, the down-payment took all our savings. Ginny was a nurse, and I was an engineer. We had dreamed of owning our own business for years. This isn't exactly what we had planned, but when we visited the property, we fell in love with it immediately."

"I can understand why," Adam responded. "There is such an aura of peaceful serenity here."

"Yes, nature always provides that. It works out well for us," agreed Frank. "Ginny is an excellent cook, and I am rather adept at making repairs and maintenance. We are very happy here. A neighbor lady comes once a week to clean the cottages of those who need that service. Payment is made at the time by those who order it."

"Is she the one who tends to people who occasionally must be left alone?" inquired Adam.

"Yes, she is. Beverly Wells is a 42 year-old widow. Her two children are grown and married and now she has loads of free time."

As they spoke, the three walked to the house where a wonderful assortment of cooking aromas greeted them. The dining room had four round tables, each one set for four people. Several people were already seated and a few more wandered in a bit later.

The dining room had a comfortable down-home atmosphere and the food was delicious. Afterwards, they talked terms. Eve felt very relaxed there and it seemed right to Adam too.

On the way home, Adam told Eve they must sell their present home in order to move to the country-like location. She seemed very upbeat and agreed.

Adam heaved a sigh of relief.

The next day, the vacant bungalow had been cleaned and was ready for inspection. Adam and Eve returned to view it. When Virginia came out to greet them, Eve said the exact same thing she had said the day before, and once again reached out to touch Virginia's hair. Sadly, Adam nodded his head at Virginia as if to say, "This is the situation." Virginia nodded with complete understanding.

"I'm so glad to see that our queen-sized bed will fit in this bedroom," Adam noted. "We shall have to get rid of some of our furniture, but what we keep will fit nicely. As the rugs and drapes will remain, I won't have much to purchase. Decorating is not my forte."

Deciding what to keep and what to sell acquired from over 40 years of marriage had been a difficult decision for Adam. Most of the responsibility had been on his shoulders as Eve seemed to come and go with thoughts that could be either rational or irrational, depending on the day. At least, their current abode was small enough for Adam to be aware of Eve's whereabouts at all times. Meal times at the "big house" as they called it, were a delight. Virginia continued to wear interesting garments and hairdos to match. Later, they discovered that occasionally, she wore a wig when her hair color didn't match her clothing, and there wasn't time to have it re-colored. Even while cooking, she looked extremely fancy. The only difference in her attire was a large bib-style, lacy apron she wore in the kitchen. The aprons were always pure white and starched, and decorated with lace that was color-coordinated with her outfits.

After cooking what appeared as a banquet meal for 14 people, she still looked fresh and crisp. When asked how she managed to stay so composed and tidy, she would reply, "I'm doing what I love!"

Frank would always grin and give an off-handed humorous remark like, "Sure, Ginny does what she loves. I'm the poor chump who has to plan all the menus so you can eat like kings and queens." He did occasionally make suggestions, but his choice was always fried foods of some sort; Southern fried chicken, battered pork chops, catfish fried in cornmeal…. Ginny allowed a fried entrée only once each week as she realized their guests might be prone to clogged arteries due to their age.

When no one seemed to have sympathy regarding Frank's culinary duties, he would tease about his secondary job as busboy. Occasionally, he helped clear tables if their helper, Beverly Wells was unavailable. Beverly spent at least two hours on the grounds each day, and tried to schedule that time to clean a bungalow, sit with a guest, or purchase groceries and supplies from Ginny's list.

"Frank," said Adam. "Today's dinner must have been your choice. The fried chicken was superb, and Eve enjoyed the fish. Please give our compliments to the chef."

Ginny's lavender locks appeared around the door frame separating the kitchen from the dining room, and then her smiling face appeared. A long lavender skirt with a wide-flared hemline, perfectly matched the long-sleeved gossamer fabric of her blouse with balloon-type sleeves. The guests wondered how she could cook without dipping her sleeves in the country-style, white milk gravy.

In response to Adam's remark, she said, "Thank you Mr. Alexander. I'm so happy you are enjoying it. The recipe came from a very popular restaurant chain in the deep-South. We had to pay for the recipe, but everyone seems to feel it was worth it. Of course, we had to sign a paper stating that we wouldn't share it with anyone else."

"That's fine," said Adam. "I certainly don't care to learn how to cook anything so difficult. But, I do have a question."

"Yes?"

"How do you get such an incredibly golden crust on the chicken?"

"That's my own secret. If you promise not to tell, I'll share it with you."

"I promise."

"Well, then, when the cooking oil reaches the correct temperature, I put a few drops of yellow food coloring in the oil and swish it through before the chicken goes in."

"Isn't that interesting?" Such a simple thing, but it makes sense. Well Virginia, it's time for us to go. Thanks again for a delicious meal."

Adam took Eve by the hand and they took the short walk to their cottage.

Several months went by and all went well. Eve seemed content with their new lifestyle. Even though she did not seem to comprehend much of the conversation that went on in the big house, or what Adam said to her, she would smile and act agreeable. Adam was with her at all times. So far, he had not seen the need to have Beverly sit with her. When they had to purchase groceries or other commodities, Adam and Eve went together. Cleaning their small bungalow was no problem for him either. Neither of them were in the habit of leaving things lying about, and as they never had company, there was no need to make preparation for others to visit.

The fall weather had been extremely balmy, and Eve enjoyed spending time each day playing with, and feeding the farm animals Just sitting at the lake's edge and gazing into the water was so peaceful, and from time to time, they even threw a fishing line in the water.

"Oh Adam, look. The bobber on my line is moving, I think I caught a fish. Ohhhh, I can't pull it in. It must be a whopper. Please help!"

Adam reached for the simple bamboo pole she preferred to use, and felt a very heavy tug on the other end of the line. As he couldn't easily bring it in, he lifted the pole, jerked it into the air, and attempted to throw the catch on the ground behind them.

"Look Eve. See what you caught?"

Eve looked over her shoulder and exclaimed, "Oh my, it's not a fish. What is it?"

"It's a turtle. They enjoy worms too. Shall we have turtle soup for dinner tonight?"

"Ugggghhh! No thanks. Please let him go."

"What makes you think the turtle is a male?"

"Females have more sense. They know they must not take risks so they are able to care for their babies."

"The wind is picking up, Eve. It smells like rain in the air. Let's go before we get soaked."

"Okay, Adam. I'll race you," Eve said as she began a slow trot.

"No fair. You have a head start."

Eve just turned and grinned as Adam scurried to catch up with her.

That evening, after having a snack, Adam got out their checkers. As he set up the pieces on the board, Eve swept them off the table and onto the floor.

"Why did you do that, Eve?" he chided.

"I don't like black and red together anymore. Once, I had a dress in those colors and it makes me sad to think about it."

"Why does it make you sad, Eve?"

"I don't know why, it just does."

"Well then, is there anything else you would like to do?"

"No! I'm exhausted; I'm going to bed."

Adam was concerned. It was only late afternoon, and Eve had slept well the night before. When she got quite tired for no apparent reason, it meant her cognitive awareness was beginning to fade. He could see it in her eyes, and knew another siege of that ongoing condition was looming ahead of them.

"Yes, Eve. I understand. Your nightgown is under your pillow. Shall I help you prepare for bed?"

No answer. She was already lying down, fully clothed. Adam gently took off her shoes, placed the afghan from the sofa over her and closed the bedroom door.

"Eve. Eve. Where are you?"

Adam awoke to find her missing from their cottage. Her clothing from the day before was lying on the bed, and her shoes sat on the floor where he had placed them. The thing that caused great alarm was the open door! His heart began to pound as he realized the sun was just now beginning to come up. Silently, he whispered a prayer while quickly donning his robe and slippers. Hurrying outside, he scanned the faintly lit horizon. There was no sign of her and their car had not been moved. Where could she be?

Adam's mind seemed flooded with his options. Was she playing with the favorite little pet lamb? Had she gone fishing? His heart thumped so loudly that he could even hear it. Was she at the lake? On no, not the lake! Rushing to the water's edge, he spied what, at first glance, appeared to be a floating log. It wasn't a log, it was Eve! But, thank God, she was floating on her back.

"Eve, what are you doing?"

Adam rushed into the water, clothing and all. Scooping her up under her waist, he drew her to his chest. The water-logged garment, and the moss that had attached itself to her, made her feel quite heavy.

"Darling, are you okay?"

"Who are you? Don't you know that mermaids are never to be touched by human hands?" Let me go..."

"Eve, it's me, Adam your husband."

"No you're not my husband. Mermaids never marry. They just swim and play."

Adam would not let her go. He slowly walked her to the bank, up the slight incline, and then guided her into the front door.

"Come, Eve. I'll draw a hot bath for you. You're shivering."

Suddenly, he realized what she was wearing. It was the seafoam green, long gown she had worn when they renewed their vows on a beach in Crete on their tenth wedding anniversary.

"Eve, you're wearing your wedding gown. Why?"

Then he noticed that she had torn the gown while putting it on. The seams had actually been ripped out and her flesh was exposed, as she was no longer the slim, young woman of long ago. Again, he repeated the question.

"Why are you wearing your wedding gown?"

"It's not a wedding gown. Can't you see my green fishtail? I'm a mermaid, and they don't marry."

"Well, whoever you are, you're shivering. I'll fix you a warm bath. Let's take off that wet garment."

"No! Unhand me. Mermaids are to be treated with respect."

Finally, after they were both worn out, she relented and allowed the icy cold dripping gown to be removed. Afterwards, a warm robe, a cup of hot tea, and Eve seemed to be her old self.

Adam was completely exhausted. His hands were shaking and the incredible responsibility dawned on him. What could he do? Their new quarters were lovely, and everything should have been ideal for them. Little did he dream that the lake that had added so much to their delight could also be such a hazard.

Eve had always loved the water. Swimming and water aerobics were second nature to her. Floating on her back was something she was used to. If not for that, she might have drowned.

What could he do? His mind raced with fear. Surely, he thought, there must be something from the past that would prompt her memory. Something to bring her back to herself, and...to him.

CHAPTER XXXV

Summertime—1974

Earlier that morning, Adam had been assigned to a story of concern to the St. Louis community. A man actually flew a small plane under the Gateway Arch. The law was explicit about stating that it was an illegal action.

After gulping down his orange juice and eating a toasted whole wheat bagel while shaving, Adam poured hot coffee into an insulated mug. Kissing Eve and hugging Mark, he was out the door in a flash.

"Mark, as soon as you're dressed and have eaten your breakfast, I want to take you shopping," Eve said.

"Shopping, what for?"

"Clothing, you need some sportswear. Did you bring a swimsuit in your bag?"

"No, my suit from last year was shot. Besides, I've grown a lot since then," he said with a grin.

"I'm sure you have. There's a shopping mall close to our home. It shouldn't take long. I too, have a story I'm working on. You can go swimming if you like when we return."

"Oh…is there a pool nearby?"

"Yes, we have a pool for the residents of our area. You could probably meet some young people your own age there too."

"I'm not in the mood."

"Please sit down, Mark; let's talk." Eve encouraged him to join her at the kitchen table. She went on. "We're going to do all we can to obtain a release for your father. However, you must realize that we have to continue with our lives as we do research to help him."

"Yeah, I know."

Eve continued, "Besides, your father's been away for two years. You continued some type of lifestyle during that time. Now, you must once again begin to make a life for yourself. It's very important to obtain some new friends your age, develop some hobbies this summer, and return to school in the fall. You will be in the 9th grade and school is critically important. We shall have to determine which one you will attend, and how you will get there each day."

Mark heaved a deep sigh, and in a very deep voice repeated his earlier response, "Yeah, I know."

"Well," Eve said, "now that we've got that resolved, eat your breakfast so we can begin our day."

Mark dutifully poured milk from the Dresden pitcher on the table and added honey and a peeled banana to his bowl of hot oatmeal.

After a rather trying time at the department store, Eve and Mark returned home with multiple parcels. Eve suggested he spread his new garments out on the bed in his room so Adam could see them when he returned from work. Mark had resisted her suggestion that he try the clothing on at the store, but at her insistence, he had tried on the shoes. Their purchases included a pair of sandals, tennis shoes, underwear, shirts, sports shorts, socks, jeans, a swimsuit, and a light-weight jacket.

"Okay Mark, I'll leave the room while you try on your new swimsuit. When you're ready, I'll show you where the pool is."

"Am I going alone?"

"Why? Do you want me to go with you?"

"No. I think I can handle it myself."

"Okay, it's just a few blocks away. I need the exercise after our long rides in the car this past weekend. We'll walk there together. I plan to go grocery shopping. By the time you are ready to return, I'll be home."

The walk was an informational one for Mark. He memorized their address and found the area interesting as each house had a different exterior design. The Alexander's home had a delightful English countryside look. Surrounding their home was a traditional white picket fence with several matching trellises which supported blood-red roses whose chartreuse-tipped leaves reached the very top. At the rear of the house was a cozy screened-in porch containing a sofa and two chairs with white wicker frames that sported floral-print cushions in vivid colors of green, blue and yellow. The glass-topped coffee-table also trimmed in white wicker held an old-fashioned kerosene lantern filled with green oil.

"Is your house actually located in St. Louis, Eve?"

"Yes, this area is called St. Louis Hills. We've lived here for five years, and find it to be a pleasant, convenient location."

They rounded a corner and came face-to-face with a large swimming pool containing many people, with an equal number sitting on the sidelines absorbing the sun while conversing with their friends.

"Here's the pool," Eve said. "It seems to be filled with young people. Do you feel comfortable going in the pool by yourself?"

Before Mark could answer, Eve turned aside and said, "Oh, hello David. Are you going in for a swim?"

A blonde-haired young man who appeared to be about Mark's age said, "Yes, Mrs. Alexander, I am."

"I would like to introduce my nephew, Mark. He will be staying with us for several months. Maybe you could show him round and introduce him to some of your friends."

"Of course, I'd be glad to."

"Hello Mark." David extended his right hand and they shook.

Immediately, they struck up a conversation and walked off together. Eve felt tremendous relief as she returned home.

Several hours later, a sunburned Mark walked into the dining room, where Eve was busy typing. "Well, how was it?" she asked with a cheerful smile.

"Terrific! David and I are both pretty good swimmers. All the girls there were sitting around the pool talking, so we were able to swim laps."

"Who won?"

"It was a draw. David invited me to join a local baseball team."

"Oh, what position do you play?"

"Well, I usually pitch."

"My, won't that be exciting? I've always envied women who have children in sports. Adam and I will enjoy watching your games."

Flushing a bit, Mark smiled self-consciously and said, "How do you know they'll want me on their team?"

"I know they will, Mark. I can tell by the way you walk that you're well-coordinated, and will do well in sports. Do you play tennis?"

"No, but I'm willing to learn."

"Okay, first things first. I'm fixing salad, spaghetti and hot bread sticks for dinner. Maybe you could help by setting the table."

"Sure, I'd be glad to."

"After you're finished, you might like to take a shower and put on one of your new outfits. Be sure to rinse your swim suit to wash out the chlorine and hang it up to dry. I have a feeling you'll be wearing it almost every day. And Mark…"

"Yes, Ma'am?"

"From now on, be sure to wear suntan lotion when you go out in the hot sun. Your skin is very delicate, like mine. If you don't protect your skin, you will get badly burned."

"Yes, Ma'am," he said while heading for the shower.

Excitement seemed to ooze from Adam as he flung open the front door. "Eve, remember I told you this morning about a pilot flying a small plane under the Gateway Arch? A sightseer at the Gateway Arch happened to be taking a picture of the arch just as the small plane flew directly under it. I got word of it and was able to obtain the negative for a fair price."

"Great! That will really enhance your story. Have you written it yet?"

"Of course! I spent the afternoon talking on the phone and typing my story. The pilot has been arrested and is being held on bond."

"Where is he from?"

"He flies small seaplanes and helicopters for sightseers in the Ozarks of Southern Missouri as a business. He is evidently quite good because he missed the underneath portion of the peak of the arch by mere inches. Reports I obtained about him indicate he has always been a daredevil. In fact, he did this on a dare."

Just then, Mark walked into the room, and Adam looked a bit surprised, but greeted him with a smile. "Hi Mark, sorry I just burst in with my news of the day."

"Hey Adam, how's it goin'?"

"Great! How's it going with you?"

"Good, come see my new wardrobe."

They disappeared into Mark's bedroom. "Super," said Adam as he surveyed the layout on the bed. "Looks like you'll be set for the summer."

"Yeah. Look at me now, see my new yellow shirt and jean-shorts? Eve picked them out and the fit is perfect. But...the best part of the day was making a new friend. His name is David. We swam together and I'm going to be on a baseball team with him, and...and..."

"Whoa, wait a minute, Mark. Your enthusiasm is overwhelming. I'm so glad you're happy. We shall have to take our turn telling Adam about our successful day after dinner," said Eve. "Everything is ready, let's go eat." She latched an arm through one of each of theirs and directed them toward the colorful screened-in back porch.

After a prayer of thanksgiving for their successful day, and the plentiful food, they began to enjoy their meal and one another.

Eve directed the conversation along other lines. "Mark, I want to make you aware that meat is never served in our home. Adam and I are vegetarians, but not vegans."

"What is a vegan?"

"Vegans are people who eat no animal products. No meat certainly, but no animal products either."

"What's an animal product?"

"That would include things like eggs, milk or cheese. We use those products but don't eat beef, pork or chicken. However, we do eat fish."

"Why don't you eat meat? There's nothin' like a good hamburger."

"That may be true, Mark, but I've never had one. I was told when I was just a toddler, I would spit out the pureed meat they tried to feed me."

"That's really weird. I thought everybody loved hamburgers. What about you, Adam?"

"I used to eat hamburgers. When Eve and I met, she encouraged me to give meat up for a few months and see if I didn't have more energy."

"Well?"

"I have always had great energy and just experimented with it for a few months. My energy level didn't seem to change drastically, but I found the new food plan to be very satisfying and I've never actually missed red meat. However, I occasionally eat chicken when someone else prepares it."

"Tell Mark another reason it helped us not to eat meat, Adam."

"Another reason? Oh yes, it certainly aided our budget. We had so little money when we first married, so it helped a lot as meat purchases raise grocery expenses."

"So...I guess I'll have to give up meat while I live with you."

"I suppose you will, Mark. I find it very distasteful to cook meat for others too. If you really crave a hamburger, we can occasionally take you to a fast food restaurant."

"That's a deal. What you fixed for dinner tonight is good though. What do you call this?"

"It's pasta con broccoli. The salad we just finished and the broccoli in the pasta give you all the vegetables you need for the meal. The pasta supplies starch, and the cheese is pure protein. The bread sticks with butter are a real treat, and the fruit salad gives you another nutrient your body needs for energy."

"Yeah, it was all good. I don't miss not having meat for the time-being."

"Good, let's all take our plates into the kitchen. Then we can sit in the living room with a cup of hot tea and discuss our day further."

"Uggghhh," Mark said. "May I have ice in mine, please?"

CHAPTER XXXVI

The next day, Adam took the time to look up old newspapers at the main library downtown. As it was close to his office, he donated time on his lunch hour because he took snacks with him to eat as he researched microfilm. Very discretely, he took a peanut butter and jelly sandwich and an apple. As he viewed the headlines skipping by on the viewer, he would take a bite here and there. Although it was against library rules to eat while working with the films, he felt sure he could accomplish both tasks without messing up the work station.

After half an hour of viewing flickering articles and pictures, he let out a loud "Eureka" without thinking. In front of him was the story of the kidnapping, the child, a $10,000 reward, and the hero's name along with the grandparent's name, and a picture of the villain. Pictures of the bounty hunter and grandparents of the child were shown on page one. "Good," Adam thought to himself. "This is exactly what I need." Oscar Hill was grinning widely while Jerome Martin, the boy's grandfather shook his right hand, and with his left he reached out for the $10,000 reward check. It even listed the small town of St. James, Missouri as being the grandparent's home. He thought, "It shouldn't be too hard to find the Martins in the phone book." He pushed a button which caused a hard copy of the article to print out for him.

The following weekend found Adam and Eve on the road to St. James. They thought it best not to share this information with Mark until after their meeting with the Martins. Getting him excited too quickly would not be good, and he might speak in a way that would cause the Martins not to give them the necessary information.

After having lunch in St. James, they asked for a local phone book. Immediately, they spotted two Jerome Martins. There was no answer as they rang the first number. After dialing the second one, a woman's voice was heard, "Hello, Mrs. Martin here." How English she sounded with that little lilt to her voice they sometimes have.

"Hello, Mrs. Martin, is Jerome in today?"

"Yes, may I tell him who is calling?"

"My name is Adam Alexander. My wife and I drove out today from St. Louis to meet the people whose grandson was adducted by his father several years ago. Is that you?"

"Yes, it is. Why do you wish to speak to my husband?"

"I'm with the St. Louis paper that did a write-up on the story and would like to do a follow-up."

"We really don't want any more notoriety attached to our family. Our daughter moved away with our grandson, and we don't mention their where-abouts for obvious reasons."

"I understand. Actually, we have no intention of doing another story, the follow-up is for strictly personal reasons. May my wife and I drop by your home and talk to you for a few moments?"

"Give us an hour. Jerome is outside cutting the grass. He's almost finished, but will need to shower and freshen up before you arrive."

"Okay, we'll have another cup of coffee at the restaurant. Please give me the directions to your home."

It turned out that the Martins lived in a charming neighborhood about 20 minutes from the restaurant. Driving through the lush countryside, Eve amused herself by viewing and identifying wild flowers on both sides of the road. Queen Anne's lace, purple coneflowers, painted cups, and sunflowers. On and on, the colorful array caught her gaze and she felt an excitement as wild flowers were some of her most favorite finds. Searching for various types of rocks and wild flowers were two of her passions.

Finding the Martin's home was easy as they had been given explicit directions by Mrs. Martin.

They were greeted at the door by a lovely woman in her mid-fifties with ash blond hair and friendly blue eyes. She made Adam and Eve feel welcome immediately. A husky man with gray hair still damp from a shower entered the room and greeted them warmly also. He invited them to be seated, and his wife offered them a glass of iced tea to help them cool down.

After a bit of small talk, Adam inquired about their grandson.

"He's just fine. His father was convicted of kidnapping by the court as he had already been arrested for cruelty to his family. He wasn't trying to spend quality time with his son, he just wanted to cause trauma to our daughter and frighten their child."

"I'm sorry to hear that," Adam said. "Does your daughter feel their son is safe now?"

"Yes, I think so. If something were to happen to either of them, the law would know the father must be apprehended again."

"Mr. and Mrs. Martin, the reason we are here is to gain information regarding the where-abouts of Oscar Hill, the man who turned in your ex-son-in-law. Do you have any idea how we can locate him?"

"No, we haven't heard from him for quite some time."

"But, you are aware of his sister's where-abouts?"

"Yes, we stay in touch with her."

"You do…why?"

"She is such a pleasant young woman. We hit it off immediately, and we send cards on holidays and notes in-between. Several of her children are fairly close to the age of our grandson, and that created a common bond."

"Does she ever mention Oscar, her brother?"

"No. His name doesn't come up. We just bonded with her due to the children."

"Would you mind giving us her name and phone number?"

"I'm not sure. We don't really know you. If you will wait a few moments, I will call her and get permission to give out that personal information."

"I understand. Just tell her that it is very important that we reach her brother."

"Would you mind telling us why you want to trace her brother?"

"Eve spoke up and said, "My brother was unjustly accused of a crime. Oscar Hill has information that might help clear my brother's name. The problem is that no one has any idea how to locate him."

Mrs. Martin stood up and said, "I will call her now. Would you be willing to speak to her at this time if necessary?"

"Of course. If she doesn't mind us calling her, we will call when we get home. That way there won't be extensive long-distance charges on your phone."

Within a few moments, Mrs. Martin returned holding a piece of paper in her hand, and said, "She gave me permission to share her name, address and phone number with you. Feel free to call her at your leisure."

Adam and Eve stood and graciously thanked the hosts for their consideration.

That evening, Eve called to speak to Oscar's sister. Her face expressed delight as she obtained the woman's response to her queries. She kept saying, "Oh my, that's good news." When she hung up the phone, she turned with delight to Adam. "Guess what?" she said. "Oscar is still in town. He used the $10,000 reward money as down-payment on a home in South County."

"Why couldn't we locate him in the phone book?"

"That's because Oscar is a nickname. His real name is Arnold— Arnold Hill. Let's look in the phone book under that name. She took the phone book down from the shelf in the hall closet. "Look Adam, here's the listing, Arnold Hill. His phone number is the same one his sister gave me."

"Shall we call him now, Eve? Maybe we need to discuss it first. What if he doesn't want to speak with us, would there be any advantage for him?"

"I'm not sure, Adam. I suppose it depends on his sense of right and wrong. It might work against him if he decides to testify on Steve's behalf."

"It might. Let's pray about it and wait until tomorrow."

"Hello, may I speak to Arnold Hill?"

"This is Arnold."

"Do you also go under the name of Oscar?"

"Yes, I do. Who are you?"

"My name is Adam Alexander. You don't know me, but I would like to speak with you in person."

"What about?"

"Do you remember a newspaper reporter by the name of Steve Simmons?"

"Sure. We sort of worked together for a short time several years ago."

"Worked together?"

"Yeah, we worked together on a story for the local newspaper several years ago."

"Are you a reporter too?"

"No. I'm not a reporter, but I was able to gain information for a story that Steve was working on."

"Oscar..., or shall I call you Arnold?"

"Just call me Oscar, everybody else does."

"Well...Oscar, I would like to speak with you soon. Maybe we could meet for breakfast on Saturday morning. Are you free then?"

"Yes, I can make it."

"I understand you live in South County. Do you know where Dohack's Restaurant is on South Lindbergh?"

"Of course. Doesn't everybody?"

"Okay. How about 9:00 a.m.? My wife's name is Eve. She will join us too. I'm tall with black hair, Eve is a redhead."

"See ya then."

Wind-driven rains began pouring down Saturday morning as Adam and Eve approached Dohack's Restaurant by car to meet Oscar. The glow emanating from the restaurant's windows appeared warm and friendly as they pulled into the parking lot.

As Adam had given Oscar a good description of themselves, he stood to greet them. Their clothing dripped water on the floor, and their handshakes were damp. Eve always carried an umbrella in her car, however Adam did not, so she excused herself to visit the restroom and attempted to dry her hair and clothing a bit using paper towels. Adam decided to just drip dry and warm up with a cup of hot coffee.

After ordering and downing their hot beverages of coffee and tea, Adam took on his customary role of reporter and began to interrogate Oscar in a rather brisk manner.

Eve quietly interrupted by tapping Adam on the shoulder and saying, "Dear, why don't we all just relax and eat breakfast before getting into it too deeply."

Adam sighed and said, "You're right, Eve. I'm not here on business; this is a personal matter."

Then they all enjoyed a hearty breakfast and accompanied it with casual banter. Oscar lit a cigarette, took another sip of black coffee and said, "What would you like to know?"

"We're interested in learning more of the reasons behind Steve Simmons being sentenced to prison."

"Sentenced to prison?"

"Yes, you mean you didn't know?"

"No, why was he sentenced to prison?"

"For murder. Actually, the charge was involuntary manslaughter."

"Who did he kill?" Oscar asked in a stunned manner.

"Surely, you must know. He killed a man named Detective Winchell, the detective who frisked him to obtain stolen diamonds."

"Oh no, that's not like the Steve I knew. He sometimes drank too much, but he would never murder anyone."

"Why don't you think so?"

"We spent hours together after work at a local bar drinking and telling stories. He knew I had a record, and I knew about his rather sad life."

"How was his life sad?"

"Steve had no real family...no parents or siblings. He grew up in orphanages and foster homes. He told me about a young son who was living with his wife's mother. His wife had run out on him, and he was a very melancholy guy."

"Did he seem to love his son?"

"Oh yeah...I think his name was Mark. His kid seemed to be upset with him because he drank and thought his Mom left home for that reason. A couple of times he tried to call his kid from the bar, but his son wouldn't come to the phone."

"Did Steve seem to want to stop drinking?"

"Naw, I don't think so. It sorta' helped him chase the blues for a little while."

"How did the two of you become acquainted?"

"I worked for the newspaper too."

"In what capacity?"

"I was a go-fer. I ran errands for everyone in between taking care of the mail. The editor was kind enough to hire me after I got out of prison. They knew I took a bum rap."

"A bum rap?"

"Yeah! My wife ran out on me too. My name was signed to several bank loans and three credit cards were charged to the max. It amounted to a lot of money, and I couldn't pay so they sent me to prison."

"Why didn't they go after her?"

"Well, she had a boyfriend who studied my signature. She gave him my social-security number and other pertinent information, so he posed as me while making purchases and loans. They even bought a car using my ID. After charging about $45,000, they ran off and left me holdin' the bag."

"How long did you serve?"

"Six months. My sister lived out of state, but she kept harassing the governor about my innocence until enough evidence showed up. After my wife and her lover were caught and arrested, I was released."

"Why didn't you testify for Steve?" Eve asked.

"I didn't know about the death of Detective Winchell. Well, I did what I said, I left town and went to visit my sister in Tennessee. When I returned, I got a different job and used part of the $10,000 reward money as down-payment on a home. I had already divorced my wife, met a little southern belle in Tennessee, and we got married last year."

"Evidently, you didn't try to contact Steve when you returned?"

"No, I didn't, I wanted to quit drinking. My new wife and I have a two-month old little girl, and my life has completely changed. I've been 'on the wagon' for over a year now. I knew if I called Steve we would probably meet in a bar and I'm not strong enough yet to resist a beer, and one beer would lead to more. My new family is worth total abstinence from alcohol."

"We certainly understand," Adam agreed with a nod. "But, please tell me about the detective incident."

"All I know is that Detective Winchell's sister-in-law wanted to give me a package to hand to Steve at the bar that night. I told her that I was leaving town that day and wouldn't see him before I left. I guess she took it to Steve herself. I don't know, 'cause I left for Tennessee that afternoon."

"And told no one where you were going?"

"No, I didn't. However, I did leave a note before I left and thanked them at the paper for giving me a chance. Everyone knew I had served time in the pen."

"But they knew the circumstances?"

"Yes, they did."

"You didn't confide your plans to Steve either?"

"No, it was a snap-decision. My intention was to break all ties."

"Oscar, is there anything you can tell us about Detective Winchell? Why would he have rough-housed Steve by trying to take the diamonds and punching him in the stomach?"

"I'm not sure. We both knew him 'cause he was in the tavern a lot too. I heard he was crooked, but was never really sure about that."

"Think hard please. Who else would know more about him?"

"Well, I guess the other detective, his ex-partner might know."

"Is that who would have been with him that night?"

"Probably so. They rode together and were a team."

"Was the other detective—what's his name?"

"Curtis, Detective Curtis."

"Was Detective Curtis crooked too?"

"Not that I know of. Of course, I can't be sure."

How could we locate him?"

"I don't know. Maybe you could call the downtown police department and see if he's still on the force."

"Okay, that's a start. Here's my business card, Oscar. If you think of anything else, will you please call me?"

"Sure. Be happy to."

"Oh, by the way," said Eve. "Congratulations to you, your wife and your new baby daughter."

"Thanks. I really appreciate my new life; I'm so happy now."

"Why did you eventually return to the St. Louis area?"

"It was my home for several years. I wanted to return and not allow myself to be dependent on my older sister."

"How old are you, Oscar?"

"Twenty-one..."

CHAPTER XXXVII

"Hello," Adam responded to the police department's receptionist's voice. "Do you have a Detective Curtis on staff?"

"No. Detective Curtis is no longer with us. He resigned some time ago."

"Can you please give me his phone number?"

"I'm sorry, we're not allowed to give out personal phone numbers."

"Of course, I understand. If I leave my name and phone number with you, will you please call him and ask him to return my call?"

"I suppose so, but he'll want to know why."

"Just tell him it's regarding Detective Winchell."

"Okay, I'll see what I can do."

"Thank you."

The next evening, the phone call they were hoping for came through. Eve answered the phone and a deep, rough, male's voice asked to speak to Adam. Instinctively, she knew who the caller was, and her heart thumped as she called Adam to the phone. After eavesdropping a few moments, she realized a meeting time and place had been secured. It was very hard to wait until Adam finalized the rendezvous plans before she queried him. It turned out that the ex-detective suggested they meet at the bar where his partner had been killed. They wondered why. Could it be that he might remember more about that fateful night by revisiting the actual scene? The appointment was set for 7:00 p.m. the next day.

Expecting to see a man in a long dark trench coat with a hat pulled down over one eye, they were quite surprised by his appearance. Curtis appeared to be around 50 years of age, balding, short and stocky. He had been sitting in a dark-looking booth while sipping from a mug of draft beer. When Adam and Eve entered the bar, Curtis rose to greet them. They wondered later if his instant recognition of them might be instinctive, as a detective's job entailed screening people even before they spoke.

Curtis approached them with a rather quizzical look on his face, and his right hand extended in greeting. "Hello, you must be Mr. and Mrs. Alexander. I'm Jim Curtis."

"Hello, Mr. Curtis. Thank you so much for agreeing to meet with us," Adam said.

"Please sit down. This booth seems to be the most appropriate place to sit and talk. What can I get you to drink?"

"Nothing right now, thank you."

Curtis dismissed the barmaid with a wave of his hand and said, "How can I help you?"

Eve responded first, "Steve Simmons is my brother and…"

'Your brother? I didn't think he had a family."

"Well, that's what we both thought, but we've have just recently been reunited."

"Yeah, I can see the similarity, the red hair and green eyes."

"Yes, well…he said the death of Detective Winchell was an accident—that he just returned a punch that was forced on him."

"That's true. I stood right there and saw the whole thing. The three of us went outside into the alley to talk. Winchell asked Steve to give him the box that his sister-in-law had handed to Steve in the bar. Steve refused. Then, Winchell tried to frisk him and take the box which turned out to contain diamonds. When Steve wouldn't give them up, Winchell punched him in the gut. It seemed to be an automatic thing to return the favor, and Steve let him have it on the jaw. Winchell fell backwards, hit his head on the concrete, and his neck appeared to be broken. He didn't move. I knelt down to help him up; his eyes were open but he wasn't breathing."

Eve gasped and said, "How shocking that must have been for you."

"Shocking for all of us. Steve tried to revive him, but he was a goner."

"How tragic! Did he have a family?"

"No, not really. He and a broad had lived together for about 7 years. She was all broken up over his death."

"I can just imagine. Is she still around?" Adam queried.

"Naw! I don't think so. She planned to leave town afterwards, and probably did."

"Do you think she knew anything about his diamond dealings?"

"Probably not. Winchell kept things to himself. We were buddies for 10 years, but he didn't tell me about it."

"What happened to the diamonds?" Eve asked.

"Winchell was holding them tight when he fell. I had to pry his fingers loose to get the box released."

"Then, what did you do?"

"I turned them in at the station, then they were returned to the jeweler."

"How tragic to lose one's life over something like that," Eve said quite sadly. "And look at the cost to Steve's life too."

"Well, you've told me a great deal," Adam said. Now, we must ask you about another character in the story."

"Who?"

"Oscar Hill. You probably knew Oscar."

"Yes, he was the kid who got a payoff for turning in a neighbor who ran off with his own child."

"Yes, that's correct. He collected a $10,000 reward. Was Oscar involved in the diamond theft? Did he know anything about it?"

"Probably not."

"Weren't you questioned about intent on Steve's part to badly hurt or kill Winchell?"

"Yes. They asked me to testify at the hearing, but it seemed they just wanted to nail somebody for his death."

"Nail somebody…?" asked Eve.

"Yeah, send somebody up the river…"

"Send somebody up the river, what does that mean?"

"It means they wanted somebody to pay for his death by handing out a prison term."

"Oh…why?"

"Because the judge always wanted to be sure somebody paid. Steve didn't have any money and nobody to stand up for him. His son was too young, his mother-in-law was too old, and his wife had skipped town."

"Surely, the state got a lawyer for him?"

"Yes, but he didn't seem to care about the case. He even came late to the hearing. Steve didn't have a chance at all."

"Adam had been growing more and more tense. Finally, he blurted out, "What can we do? People are supposed to be innocent until proven guilty. It wasn't a fair trial."

"Yeah, you're right. I don't know what can be done."

"We can make an appeal to the courts for a new hearing. Would you be willing to testify that it was an accident?"

"Sure. That's one of the reasons I gave up my job as a detective. It was all so unfair what happened to Steve. Plus, some people thought I was crooked too because Winchell and I were partners."

"What do you do now for a living?"

"I'm a P.I."

"You're a P.I. ?"

"Yeah, a private I."

"A private I?"

"Yeah, a private investigator."

"That's interesting. If we were to speak with you as a potential customer attempting to gain Steve's freedom, what would you recommend?"

Curtis's eyelids appeared to go up and down like window shades for a moment or so while his brain processed the question. Then he finally said, "Well, I guess you should request a new inquiry."

"A new inquiry into the possibility of a new trial?"

"No, a new inquiry. There wasn't an actual trial. It was a hearing in the judge's chambers."

All the while, Eve had allowed the men to converse together as she listened. But now, an alarm went off in her head. "Do you mean to tell me that my brother's fate was determined in a judge's chambers, that a judge made the decision on his own?"

"Yeah, that's what I mean. I told you that the whole thing didn't seem legitimate. That's partly why I gave up my career. Nothing I said made a difference. I testified that day, but the judge paid no attention. Later, I heard he was on the brink of retiring and didn't want anything to take extra time."

Eve gasped, and was suddenly speechless. Then she recovered her voice and said, "Why didn't he have a regular trial?"

"Well, he was in jail for about two months. During that time, his lawyer talked him into doing a 'plea agreement.' It was actually an admission of guilt to an act that was not pre-meditated. As there would not be a big expense to the state and an actual trial with a jury was not required in that type of agreement, the judge agreed to accept it. The two lawyers agreed to petition the court with that plea and Steve agreed to sign it."

"I'm surprised he was sent to a prison in Missouri."

"That prison has many medical prisoners. They have mentally-ill inmates and those who have addiction problems. As Steve was obviously addicted to alcohol, he was sent there."

Adam said, "Is that judge still on the bench?"

"No, he retired last year and moved away."

"To whom can we appeal?"

"Maybe the governor. If I can get the records from that hearing, it'll be a good start."

"You're hired! How soon can you begin?"

"How about tomorrow?"

"It's a deal." They stood up, shook hands once again, and parted company.

CHAPTER XXXVIII

When they returned home, they found a nervous young man sitting in the living room, and the TV wasn't even on. Mark had a very strange look on his face. and couldn't even look at them when they spoke to him. Finally, Eve said, "Okay Mark, what's the problem? What happened while we were away?"

Mark's cheeks turned almost the color of his hair, and he spoke softly and said, "Well, there was a problem tonight. As you know, I went to David's home to play baseball with him and some other kids. We were playing, and as usual, I was pitching. Suddenly, I got too wound up, pitched a ball that traveled beyond the batter. We had no catcher, and the ball went through a garage window. When I heard the crash, I took off and ran."

"But, of course," said Adam, "the other players knew it was you."

"Yeah, I know. It was stupid to run; I just got scared."

"Well, the first thing we must do is go to that home, apologize to the owners, and pay to have the window replaced."

"Man! I feel so stupid; do I have to?"

"Mark, this is one of those things you would probably feel guilty about all your life if you don't take care of it now."

"Darn!"

Adam leaned over, took Mark's arm and said, "Come on fella, you can do it."

After they left, Eve sat down and began writing to Steve, giving him an update on their findings regarding his trial.

An hour later, Adam and Mark returned, arm-in-arm, laughing in the way males do when they share in a conspiracy.

Mark said, "It turned out the people weren't even home when I broke their window, and still didn't know about it. They're an elderly couple and acted so understanding. They told us their son had done the very same thing years earlier when he was young."

Adam agreed and said, "I told them that I would personally put in a new window pane. It was a small one of six panes that were side-by-side on the door. Tomorrow, I will take the measurements to our local hardware store, have a new pane made there, and then install it."

"Oh, I'm so relieved," Eve said. "What a lesson you've learned today, Mark. We can't run away from our mistakes, but must face them head-on."

"Yeah," grinned a very relieved young man.

Handing out frosty glasses of iced tea with lemon, Eve said, "Let's sit out on the screened-in porch and discuss our day. As Mark's episode had already been taken care of, they told him of their meeting with P.I. Curtis.

"Man," he said, "it sounds like there's hope for Dad. He never mentioned that there wasn't an actual trial."

"I suppose he didn't stop to give it much thought. Everything happened so fast. He was in prison so quickly after the episode."

"Everyone knows sentences don't happen that fast."

"Well, this one did!"

Does it look as though we can get Dad out of prison with the new information you got today?"

"We feel sure it will help, and P.I. Curtis is very optimistic about our chances."

"Mark, it's so hot outside. How about taking a dip in the pool? Water exercises really help me when I'm feeling stressed out," Eve remarked.

"Water exercises, you mean swimming? How can you exercise in water?"

"Put your swim suit on and let's go. I'll show you how to exercise in water. By the way Mark, do you know how to swim?"

"Of course. Dad taught me when I was only 5 years old."

"Oh yes, that's right. You said you used to visit state parks and fish and swim together."

"Yeah, we had some great times together. Too bad they didn't last."

"You will have great times again, Mark. This time you will appreciate one another even more. Come on, I'll race you to the pool!"

That evening when Adam returned from work, he was full of good news. P.I. Curtis had obtained the court records regarding Steve's hearing and was researching the law to determine their next step. They discussed that for a while, and then Adam delighted them with an idea he had been hatching for a few days.

"In just two weeks, Mark will be in school. The swimming pools will close and summer vacation will be over. It seems we could all use a bit of fun. Eve, what would you think about spending some time in the Ozarks?"

"Wonderful! You're right, Adam, we could all use a break. Shall I call and make reservations at our favorite resort there?"

"Yes, Eve. How long would you like to stay?"

"Three days should be long enough."

"Yes, I think so too. That will enable us to see the tourist attractions, go fishing, boating, swimming and water skiing. There's a special activity we've never taken advantage of that you would both enjoy, I am sure."

"What's that, Adam?"

"Sorry, I can't tell you. It is going to be a surprise. It'll be a thrill a minute, something new to all of us. It will probably require a reservation. Tell you what, I'll call and take care of the whole thing."

"Adam, please tell me. You know I can't bear surprises."

Adam laughed and said he would call the resort from work the next day. Eve just shook her head..."I hate it when you keep secrets."

"Mark, here's a suitcase you can use for the clothing you are going to take to the Ozarks."

Eve had already packed her garments and iced up the food she had purchased for their trip. They might eat out a couple of times, but they usually cooked their own meals in the cabin. She was thankful that this particular resort furnished linens for bed and bath, as some did not.

The five hour ride seemed to go quickly as the three of them always had so much to discuss. One of the biggies was Mark's upcoming school year. He felt both excitement and anxiety at the thought of his first day at a new school. He already knew some of the young people in their neighborhood due to playing on their baseball team, and hanging out at the pool. He and David were now the best of friends, and as David was extremely out-going, he had introduced Mark to everyone in his circle of acquaintances.

Shortly after stopping for lunch, they pulled up at the resort's office. Adam hopped from the car, went inside, and in a few moments, returned with the keys for their cabin. Number 7 sounded good to Eve. They could have stayed in the lodge, but decided to rough it in one of the dozen log cabins spread out over the area.

Thankfully, the cabin smelled fresh and clean. Obviously, it had just been recently vacated and made ready for their arrival. Mark was impressed with the wooden log construction both inside and out. They entered through a large room decorated in Early American style. A matching sofa and loveseat were covered with cheerful shades of apple green, teal blue and watermelon shaded fabric. The arms and legs were crafted of maple. Coffee and end-tables sported the same type of wood. The views on a grouping of four pictures were of outdoor, rustic scenes that were painted of the same area during different seasons of the year. White ruffled, cotton curtains and window-shades complimented the crisply starched, white crocheted scarves on the tables. Lamp-shades of a cane-type twist emitted a welcoming glow emitted by the light bulb beneath. An old-fashioned fireplace comprised of red bricks completed the scene.

"Wow," said Mark as he flung himself down on the sofa. "All the comforts of home!"

"Yes," Eve said. "We've been vacationing here for years. It's where we spent our honeymoon too, as we couldn't afford to travel very far. We usually book a one-bedroom cabin, but this time we requested two bedrooms so we could share it with you."

"Oh yeah, I haven't even checked out the bedroom yet." Mark jumped up to explore the rest of the cabin. "Man, look at this! One room has twin-beds, the other has a queen-size. Which one is mine?"

"The twin-bedded room is yours, Mark. Eve and I have slept together in the same bed every night since the day we were married."

"Well, that's neat. I have a bed to sleep in and one to pile all my clothes on."

"Well, Mark, if that's your plan," said Eve "you can just keep the door to your room closed!"

"That's a deal!"

As Mark walked into the kitchen area, he got excited again, "Look at this, the kitchen table has its own little cubby-hole that opens out onto a deck—that—say, it overlooks a huge lake! We can just walk down the steps and we'll be a few feet from the boat dock."

Adam and Eve smiled at one another as if to say, "We made the right decision to give Mark a get-away before school starts." Later, they also discussed the importance of getting his mind off his father's dilemma for the time-being.

"Let's refrigerate the food, change into our swimsuits, and take a boat ride. As you can see, the speed boat I requested is already at the dock," said Adam. "I got the key when I registered earlier."

"Great! I can't wait to operate the boat," Mark said.

"Sorry, but before you take over, we must have lessons."

"I understand," Mark said grudgingly.

A short time later, they were all scampering aboard the boat. When Adam turned on the motor, Mark's eyes grew wide in awe. In just moments, they were bobbing across the lake creating their own waves. The sounds of the boat slapping the water kept the conversation at a minimum as hearing was difficult. Soon, they were in an area where other boats were going as fast as they. Then, as the wake from other boats grew larger and larger, Adam cut across theirs with the boat he had rented, thus crossing the waves of the other boats on a horizontal level. The noise from the wake was exciting, and the movements jolting.

Soon afterwards, they decided to take a dip in the lake as they approached the shoreline. Climbing from the boat, they were greeted with amazing beauty. Wildflowers, pussy willows, even the weeds were colorful and inviting to the eye. A huge water crane lifted off the ground and took flight. An array of fuzzy honey bees were siphoning the last bit of nectar from fading flowers, now dusty-rose in hue.

Cooling off in the rather shallow water was refreshing. Eve and Mark decided to swim out a bit from shore as Adam secured the boat by tying the rope to an iron rod he carried for that purpose, and which he then plunged into the earth.

Watching Eve and Mark splash water as they raced one another, Adam had to smile. Mark was fast taking a place in their hearts like the son they never had. Thoughts of losing his constant companionship upon Steve's eventual release from prison caused Adam to feel dual emotions. The first, happiness regarding Steve's freedom, the second, a loneliness for Eve and himself when Mark would leave their home.

"Well, snap out of it," he chided himself. "We'll cross those bridges as they occur."

Adam dove from the boat and within a short time had caught up with them. His 6'4" frame allowed him to conquer the distance quickly. Suddenly, the water's depth changed dramatically, and when Mark attempted to touch the bottom and couldn't, he began to flounder about a bit. With a strong arm, Adam grabbed him about the waist and started swimming back towards the boat. When Eve realized what happened, she too turned and headed for the boat. As it was already 4:00 o'clock and they were turning shades of pink and red, the decision was made to return to the cabin.

"So, what's the big secret, Adam?" Eve tried to goad him into revealing the surprise he had in store for them.

Chewing his last bite of breakfast, Adam cocked his head sideways, grinned and declined to answer.

"Adaaaaaammmmmm...tell us. It's not fair. Once we know, we can enjoy thinking about it in advance too."

"All I can say is...grab a towel and put on your swimsuits."

"Yuck! My swim trunks are still wet from yesterday."

"You'll get through it, Mark. Now hurry, we have an appointment."

"An appointment?" screeched Eve. "I haven't had time to shower or fix my hair."

"Believe me, where we're going, you won't need a fancy hairdo."

"Oh sure! You don't care about looking decent. I do!"

"We've got 15 minutes to get to the main pier. I'm leaving in 5!"

Both Eve and Mark ran for their bedrooms to jump into swimsuits as Adam called after them, "I've got enough towels for all of us."

Minutes later, they were in the car rushing to keep their appointment. When they arrived, they saw a speed-boat with a pilot and a two-man crew at the dock. Waving at them, Adam hustled his passengers from the car. As they all boarded the speedboat, the driver said, "Are you all ready for the big liftoff?"

"Lift-off?" Eve inquired.

"Sure, are you going to be first?"

"First for what?"

"To go sailing, of course."

"This isn't a sailboat!"

"No, but you'll be sailing."

"I will?"

"Yes, para-sailing!"

"Hey, I read about that in one of my sports magazines," Mark noted.

"What's this all about?" Eve asked.

"Tell her, Mark."

"Well, it's not the boat that uses sails to travel, it's the person."

"Oh sure. I'm going to have a sail attached, and off I'll go."

"That's right, Eve," Adam agreed.

"First, you put on a harness..."

"A harness?"

"Yes, I'll show you."

One of the mates demonstrated the necessary equipment for them by putting it on himself, and then he helped Adam to gear-up. First of course, a life jacket had to be donned. Then, he aided Adam as he deftly slid into a series of linked straps which formed a harness-type seat, buckled the apparatus in front, and then shifted the colorful fabric attached behind. Next, he attached a wind cone so they could note the direction of the winds while Adam was aloft.

"Now, what are you going to do?"

"I'll let the crew explain it to you."

"Well, Ma'am, your husband will soon be aloft. Our boat has a powerful 115 horsepower motor. We must be sure that the wind velocity does not exceed 15 miles per hour. A 50 meter long, 300 pound test rope is attached to the harness of the person sailing."

"The person sailing...?"

"Yes ma'am, as you can see, your husband is encased in a harness with a parachute-type canopy attached. He will stand on the elevated portion at the rear of our boat. We will increase the speed and at the same time, slowly release the rope attached to him. The parachute-like canopy will expand due to the air-pressure, and your husband will begin to ascend to a possible altitude of 200 feet."

"Two-hundred feet?"

"Yes, he will actually be sitting in the harness rather than hanging, and will just continue to drift higher and higher."

"Then what?"

"Once he achieves the ultimate in height, he will be free to drift and observe the scenery from aloft for about 15 minutes. Then, we will enable him to begin a slow decent by bringing in the rope."

"Can't this be quite dangerous?"

"My crew and boat are top-notch, Ma'am. However, they recommend wearing a helmet, but that's optional."

"Adam?" Eve asked.

"No, I don't want a helmet. I want nothing to block my view."

"What happens when he descends?"

"We will bring him back exactly as he left. Some use the dock for takeoff and return. With our experience, we find it easy to do both from the boat."

Mark actually quivered with excitement. "Can I be next?" he inquired.

"Yes, you may," responded Eve. "I'm going to make sure you're both back safely before I try it."

Just as the pilot said, the ascents and descents went off without a hitch. All three had a full 15 minutes to float aloft in the air and view the surrounding area. Take-offs and landings were all done to perfection. How adept the crew was and how excited the three of them were. In-between flights, they chatted as much as possible. But the big time to express their excitement came afterwards. By lunchtime it was all over, leaving them with wonderful memories of a shared escapade.

CHAPTER XXXIX

The next two days seemed almost anti-climatic. It was a time just to relax and enjoy fishing and swimming together. Eve allowed Adam and Mark to spend the early mornings out in the boat alone to insure more bonding between them. The second morning, they returned with an incredible catch.

The night before, they had set out a trout line and carefully marked the spot on shore where they had secured it. As they knew there were some very large fish in the lake, Adam decided to use a dozen ½-pound sunfish as part of the bait on the 18 hook line as the big fish seemed to relish the small fish for a meal. On the other 6 hooks they pierced crayfish, or crawdads, as they had been told that bait seemed to be the favorite food of bass at that time of year. Imagine their surprise when they found the line almost impossible to retrieve. Adam thought it was probably snagged on the bottom, but when he began to attempt bringing it in, there was an answering tug on the under-water portion.

Mark was allowed to test the line also, and his excitement knew no bounds. "Adam, what do you think we've hooked?"

Casually, Adam replied, "It's probably just a cousin of the Loch Ness monster."

Mark's eyes grew large, and then seeing Adam's smile, he rather nervously grinned back. "What are we going to do Adam? How can we bring that whopper in? Will the boat hold it, or will we topple over?"

After much laborious pulling and tugging by both of them, a huge fish finally appeared on the water's surface. Its body gleamed with a blend of black, brown and yellow hues in the sunlight.

"Wow," said Mark. "It looks like he actually has whiskers."

"Those *are* a type of whiskers, Mark. He's a giant catfish."

Twenty minutes later, they were headed for shore with their prize catch. The resort owner happened to be on the dock making a repair as they approached. When he saw the huge fish, he identified it as a "granddaddy" flathead catfish, and he ran for his camera and set up a hook which hung from a beam on which to display their trophy. The next move was to check its size. They were totally amazed to find that the total weight was 82 pounds and 11 ounces, and it measured 4'2" in length.

"Mark, run up to our cabin and get Eve. She'll want a picture of us with our prize catch."

A few minutes later, Eve and Mark were running together towards the dock. Eve's eyes were as big as saucers as she viewed the huge catfish. "Wow, you guys really did it. How could you bring him in?"

"The two of us together did it. It only took us 20 minutes."

"You mean that you actually timed it?"

"Yep," quipped Mark. "It really put up a fight!"

"I'm so proud of both of you," Eve said fondly.

Adam hooked a thumb under each of his armpits in a stance of extreme cockiness, "Yeah, look at us!" he seemed to boast.

After dinner that evening, they sat outside in the dark, enjoying the sounds and smells of the evening. Fragrant gold and white clusters of honeysuckle along with pink and white lilacs were planted all around the cabin door. The wind whistled through the trees after skimming across the lake. They sat relaxing on lawn chairs which were incredibly comfortable, even though they were crafted of slanted, wooden slats painted white with wide-rimmed arm rests. Sounds of crickets and tree frogs filled the air. Falling acorns hitting the roof made a melodious sound. A coyote howled at the full-moon. Occasionally, they swatted at a hungry mosquito.

Adam began to feel shades of nostalgia as he reminisced regarding evenings out-of-doors with his grandparents in the summertime. They had appreciated watching lightning bugs perform while flashing their ever-ready neon lights. "Have I ever mentioned the story my grandfather Paul told me regarding the story of 'Taps?'"

"No Darling, did you take tap-dancing lessons as a child?"

"No Eve, I meant…"

Yes Adam, I know what you mean. I'm just teasing you. Your grandmother mentioned that your grandfather, Paul Alexander was a bugler in World War I, and played Taps for the unit."

"Yes, he did, and he loved to tell the sad story of how the practice of playing Taps began."

"Tell us Adam."

"Please," said Mark. "I've never heard the story either."

"Well, I understand it has its origins during the Civil War. In 1862, a Union Army captain named Robert Ellicombe and his men were involved in a skirmish in Virginia. During the night, Captain Ellicombe heard the moans of a wounded soldier on the battlefield. Thinking it was one of his own men, he crawled toward the man lying on the ground and pulled him into the foxhole for safety. Alas, it was too late; he discovered the young man had breathed his last.

When a lantern was lit and he gazed upon the face of the dead man, the captain gasped in dismay. The soldier was his own son. His son had lived in the South for some time while attending a university there to study music. Unbeknownst to his father, he had enlisted in the Confederate Army.

Even though his son was classified as the enemy, Captain Ellicombe wanted a military burial. He was allowed to have only one musician, a bugler. The bugler agreed to play from the music score discovered in the dead man's pocket. They called it 'Taps.'

Some feel this is nothing more than a romantic myth, but it appeals to our emotions. My grandfather, Paul Alexander, enlisted in the Marine Corps during WW I at age 17. In school, he had studied the trumpet, and as he was very young, and they were not involved actively in combat but in training, he was commissioned to play the bugle at sunrise and daybreak. In the morning, at daybreak, grandfather played the oldie:

'You gotta get up, you gotta get up, you gotta get up in the morning. Someday, they're gonna murder the bugler, some day they'll find him dead in bed. You gotta get up, you gotta get up, you gotta get up in the morning.' It was to be a wakeup call. Even though it was quite rousing, it was an irritant and they could understand the phrase, 'someday you'll find the bugler dead in bed.'

At night, grandfather played the more somber version of Taps which was like a goodnight lullaby. At military funerals and dedications, Taps is played. It is obviously a very meaningful, emotional song."

"Adam, what a beautiful story. Even though it may be a myth, I love it. I am familiar with the melody but don't know the words. Do you?"

"Yes, I do. Most people know only the first stanza. Grandfather taught me the whole song. It actually has three stanzas."

"Please sing them to me, Adam."

"I would be happy to, my dear"

'Day is done... Gone the sun... From the lakes... From the hills...
From the sky... All is well... Safely rest... God is nigh.
Fading light... Dims the sight... And a star... Gems the sky.
Gleaming bright... From afar... Drawing nigh... Falls the night.
Thanks and praise... For our days... 'Neath the sun...'Neath the stars... 'Neath the sky... As we go... This we know... God is nigh.'

"Oh Adam, how beautiful. It makes me want to cry. I will never hear Taps being played again without being reminded of that story."

Mark's eyes were filled with awe and he was instantly spellbound.

As Eve was still feeling a bit nostalgic and meditated on the atmosphere about them, she asked, "Why don't we hear the same sounds during the daylight hours that we are hearing right now in nature; must they operate under cover of darkness? At the break of dawn, do their voices die or merely rest in slumber?"

Adam did not respond to her query, but jumped as something softly scampered over hairs on his forearm. As he recalled seeing a tarantula lumbering across a blade of grass earlier that afternoon, he suggested they all go indoors and retire for the night.

Soon, they were on their way home again. Each of them relayed the part of their 3-day getaway that most impressed them. It was hard for the guys to choose between their air-borne harness flight and catching the granddaddy of fish, the 82+ pound catfish. It seemed they were all talking at once, and as Adam was the allocated driver, and thus in charge, he made the decision to take control and called the group to order:

"Eve, as they say, 'Ladies First,' it's your turn to tell the highlight of the trip for you."

"Well, that's rather difficult," she replied. "Seeing the two of you together, watching your mutual joy at being out in nature together made it so much more real for me. I am amazed at how you have so quickly become such a precious part of our lives, Mark. Who would ever have dreamed that we could love someone so much in such a short period of time?"

Mark's head drooped a bit, and the only indication that he heard was the sweet shy smile on his face, and the rosy glow on his cheeks.

Adam's eyes began to mist over, and he finally growled at Eve in a very tender manner, "Please Eve, I didn't ask you to expound on love and relationships. I just asked about your favorite part of the trip. Will you please speak on the subject matter requested? Besides," he continued, "I can't see to drive with blurred vision."

Eve patted him on the shoulder and said in the manner of Detective Friday, the star of 'Dragnet' on TV. "Yes, sir!" As she gave a mock salute, she said, "I'll just stick to the facts, sir!"

"Well then...quit horsing around and get to it!"

Like a small child reciting in school about what she enjoyed most about her summer vacation, Eve said in a very sing-song, stilted manner, "What I enjoyed most about our trip was...gazing down from above. You both looked like a couple of ants. I've always wanted to see what earth looked like from the clouds. What an amazing view. The lake's waters rippled like streams of alternating blue and silver. Such a feeling of freedom! I felt absolutely lost in a world of sheer beauty. I used to dream of being able to fly all by myself by just flapping my arms and taking off. Para-sailing was almost like truly living that experience in broad daylight."

"What about you, Mark? What impressed you the most?" she asked.

"Everything! I'm not sure about my favorite though. Our cabin was awesome, the speedboat rides were exciting, the para-sailing scary, but fun. Catching that giant catfish was a real life-changing event for me."

"How so?" questioned Adam. "What was life-changing about that fish?"

"It wasn't just the fish. The thrill of catching him filled me with such joy that I wished I could bring that kind of joy to others."

"How would you like to do that, Mark? How can catching one fish bring lasting joy?"

"Well, I noticed the people around here seem to be so happy to be outside enjoying nature. The couple that runs the resort work hard, but seem to thrive on it. The tourists enjoy being there as a get-away. I noticed people who work in the area are happy to be busy too."

"So, what would you like to do?"

"I would like to learn more about the Lake of the Ozarks area."

"What would you like to learn about the Ozarks?"

"I would like to learn to track various types of fish in the area, and about their habits and nesting spots."

"And then what?"

"Then, I would like to buy my own fishing boat with a huge outboard motor and rent out my services as a fishing guide."

"Have you just come to this decision?"

"Yeah. I woke up in the middle of the night last night as I was dreaming."

"Dreaming...about what?"

"I dreamed I was in a fishing boat and it was full of other people. They all had fishing poles in their hands and were leaning over the side of the boat because they all had big, heavy fish on their lines and were attempting to bring them in."

"Then, what happened?"

"I don't know, 'cause the sound of their laughter woke me up."

"I've heard of dreams determining people's future. I understand that several of the world's most famous inventors would take a nap when they needed wisdom about something they were working on, and felt stumped about what to do next."

"Why do you think I dreamed that?"

"Probably because you observed people enjoying themselves as they fished, and wanted to be a part of their happiness."

"I really do enjoy seeing people happy. I'm tired of being sad and seeing others who are sad too."

Eve said, "I would like to recite something to you that I memorized years ago by another great inventor and botanist, George Washington Carver:

'How far you go in life depends on your being tender with the young, compassionate with the aged, sympathetic with the striving, and tolerant of the weak and the strong. Because, someday in your life, you will have been all of these.'"

"Wow, Eve. I am so impressed!" retorted Adam.

"Okay, Adam. Now, it's your turn."

"I can't begin to top the two of you. Let's just say this has been a very interesting time away."

"It's hard to believe we're almost home," Eve noted. "Sharing our happiness together has caused the hours on the road to fly by."

A siesta after their return sounded like a great idea to all. After several hours, Eve arose first and began cooking dinner. The guys awoke to the delightful aroma of catfish steaming on the grill. Even though the grill on which she cooked it was just outside the screened-in porch, the aroma drifted through to them in the midst of their dreams.

"Oh Adam, I'm so glad you're up. Will you please prepare the veggie-kabobs to place them on the grill? The macaroni and cheese is bubbling away on the stove. Hot break sticks and rainbow sherbet will complete our dinner."

Finally, everything was ready. They sat down to eat, and for a short period of time, there was no conversation as they enjoyed the tasty, wholesome meal.

After Adam and Mark cleaned up the dishes, they all retired to the living room to relax while enjoying frosty glasses of herbal iced tea.

"Tomorrow, it's back to work for me," Adam said in a reflective manner. "I told P.I. Curtis that I'd check in with him when we returned to get an update on Steve's situation."

"Yeah," Mark said. "I guess it's been on my mind a lot, 'cause I dream about Dad every night."

"How do your dreams go, Mark?"

"It seems he dies in a different way every night."

"He dies?"

"Yeah, one night he was in jail and a bunch of angry men on horseback chopped down the bars of the cell and took him out and hung him."

"And...?"

"And, another night, I dreamed he was walked blindfolded to a guillotine and they chopped off his head."

"Was there more?"

"Yeah, one more dream. One night, they put him in an electric chair and I watched when they pulled the switch. He looked directly at me, shuddered, and then his eyes just closed."

"Oh Mark," Eve wrapped her arms around him, "you were actually having nightmares. Why didn't you tell us? We could have talked about it."

"I couldn't. Talking about it would make it seem more real."

"Adam will call tomorrow to find out if P.I. has any more information. This is the last day of our Labor Day weekend. Tomorrow will be your first day at the new school, Mark. Now, let's all relax, take our showers and play a few hands of gin rummy."

"Okay," said Mark. "Then, we'll call it a day."

The next morning, Adam and Mark were both eating a quick breakfast and Eve was hovering over them in a very attentive, motherly-type manner. She felt a bit of relief knowing she could spend a few hours of quiet time at home alone before sinking her teeth into her next writing assignment.

The laundry and a visit to the grocery store were on Eve's list of agendas. After putting a load of clothing in the washer, she made a list of foods they would need for the following week.

No sooner had Eve entered the kitchen with both arms full of groceries, than the phone rang. "Hello Darling. I just talked with P.I. He said he's been in touch with a lawyer, who's in touch with a judge, who's in touch with...anyway, there are some things in the works. He thinks we'll have some good leads very soon."

"That's wonderful, it certainly can't come any too soon for Mark."

"I know. Well, I'll see you tonight, Eve."

"Okay."

CHAPTER XL

At 3:45 p.m., Mark returned from school with his arms full of textbooks. He was absolutely wired with excitement regarding his first day. "David is such a great friend," he exclaimed. "He introduced me to lots of people, both boys and girls. It was his first day at high school too, so we both had to find our way around. It seemed strange to us to have different classes for each subject."

"Which class was your favorite?"

"Probably math. When I'm in business for myself, I'll have to keep track of my clients, know how to charge them, and how to determine the best fishing spots and track them by using mathematical equations."

"Do you have much homework?"

"Not too much. Tomorrow, I have an appointment with my advisor. She's supposed to be able to tell me which subjects to take next semester to go along with the career I'm interested in."

"What are you going to tell her?"

"You know. I told you that I'm going to be a guide for people who want to know where to locate different types of fish, someone to take them to that area by boat, and clean the fish they caught."

"Oh yes. I thought you might have forgotten about that."

"No, I'm serious, I love to be out-of-doors. By the way, my friend David asked if I'd like to go fishing with him and his family next weekend."

"Where do they plan to go?"

"To a clubhouse they own on the Meramec River in Valley Park."

"How long will you be gone?"

"Just for the weekend. We'll leave Friday after school and return on Sunday morning."

"Find out what you need to take along."

"Well, as I'm only 13 years old, I still don't need a fishing license, but I will have to use your fishing gear."

"Ask about the food they want you to take. If they prefer to buy it themselves, we'll pay for your share."

"Okay, I'll tell them."

Immediately after school on Friday, Mark rushed home to gather the gear and clothing he needed for the weekend fishing trip. Eve handed him money to cover his expenses for food and bait. Grabbing a snack to eat en route, Mark gave Eve a quick hug, ran to the waiting car, and was on his way.

When Adam came home shortly after Mark left, he kissed Eve, and then appeared to cock his ear toward the living room. Not hearing anything, he walked through the house with a quizzical expression on his face.

"Does Mark have a ballgame this evening?"

"No. Don't you remember he is spending the weekend at the Flander's clubhouse?"

"Oh yes. It sure is quiet here without him."

"Yes, it is. He just left a short while ago, and I miss him already."

"Well Eve, I guess it will be like old times this weekend with just the two of us. What would you like to do?"

"We could go out to eat tonight, and then to the movies. As tomorrow is Saturday, we can sleep late. Mark will return on Sunday morning."

"Eve, I still can't believe how Mark has fit into our family life so easily." Then, he chuckled and said, "Are you sure you want to help obtain Steve's release from prison? You know Mark will go to live with him then."

"I know Adam. I've thought of that too. Of course, we both want the very best for each of them, but it will be a difficult transition."

"Well, enough of that Eve. Let's get ready to go out for the evening."
"Okay."

Sunday afternoon, Adam and Eve were reading the weekend newspaper while sitting on their screened-in porch. An outside movement caught Eve's attention. Looking up, she spied Mark rounding the corner of the house carrying his heavy gear. As his clothing was full of mud, he obviously intended to rinse his things outside so he wouldn't track dirt inside.

Adam jumped up from his chair as Mark appeared to be over-burdened. Even though Mark's face was sunburned from exposure while fishing, he had a queasy look on his face. His gait was rather halting too.

"Mark, are you okay?" Eve asked in a concerned manner. "You don't look too good."

"I'm fine. It's just that David and I didn't get much rest. When we weren't fishing, we were hiking. We covered miles of territory, and played cards until early morning on both days. I think I'll take a nap before dinner." He appeared to limp a bit, but they attributed it to extreme weariness. Mark showered and lay down for a while.

"Mark, wake up. Dinner's on the table." He just grunted, turned over, and appeared to be asleep again immediately.

Adam tapped him on the shoulder and said, "You've slept for two hours. It's time to eat. If you sleep much longer, you won't sleep well tonight."

"Okay, I'll be right there."

After eating, Mark stood up and began clearing the dished as usual. It seemed to be such a chore for him that Adam said, "I'll take care of the clean-up tonight. Seems as though you're going to need extra time to rest."

"Thanks Adam. I'm bushed."

The next morning, Mark was still limping a bit. "Mark, what's wrong; are you hurt?"

"Naw, just tired."

Still tired? You slept two hours yesterday afternoon and about 10 hours last night. Those fish just wore you out."

"…Suppose so…"

"Here's your lunch for school, Mark. Don't forget to drink your juice. The oatmeal is still hot in the pot. Hey, that rhymes, doesn't it?"

"Okay," Mark said with no acknowledgement of her attempt at humor.

That afternoon, a phone call interrupted Eve's research on her next magazine article. "Hello…yes, this is Eve Alexander." She paused to listen, and then in a voice tinged with alarm, Eve said, "May I pick him up myself, or shall we dial the emergency phone number? What! You've already called for help? All right, I'll drive to the school and follow the ambulance."

Within five minutes, Eve's car was parked outside the main entrance of the school. Almost immediately, she saw para-medics walking through the door carrying a stretcher. On it lay an extremely pale, Mark. Eve flung open the car door and ran to his side. Mark's eyes were wide open in a look of non-recognition.

Stifling an impulse to embrace him, she softly called his name, "Mark?"

No response.

Meanwhile, the doors to the rear of the ambulance were opened and the stretcher slid across its smooth interior surface.

"Are you a relative of his?" one of the para-medics quietly asked.

"Yes, I'm his aunt," she said.

"We're going to take him to the Lutheran Hospital. Do you know where that is?"

"Yes, I do."

"Drive around to the emergency entrance."

Within 10 minutes, the ambulance was pulling up to the door of the emergency room. Eve had been stopped by a policeman for speeding, but after a brief explanation, they gave her a red-light and siren escort all the way to the hospital.

As Mark lie waiting for the doctor to examine him, Eve placed a quick call to Adam. It was fortunate that he happened to be in the office writing a story regarding an interview he had that morning.

Eve sat holding Mark's hand, but he did not respond to her presence. Suddenly, his body began to convulse and his eyes opened wide and rolled back into his head. Slobber appeared on his lower lip.

Instinctively, Eve cried out, "Help! Somebody, please help!"

A nearby nurse ran to them and inserted a wooden tongue-depressor between Mark's teeth to prevent him from biting his tongue. A uniformed orderly wheeled him from the room, and into the area where the main doctor-on-call was waiting. Eve felt extreme panic, but the nurse patted her arm and said. "I'll give you a report as soon as possible."

After twenty minutes, the nurse returned to say they were running tests on Mark, and couldn't tell her anything except that they had given him a shot to control the convulsions.

By the time Adam arrived, Eve had relaxed a bit in the knowledge that Mark was being observed and was no longer convulsing. She shared everything she knew with Adam as they sat close together in the waiting room with his arm around her shoulders.

Several hours later, a doctor approached them and asked, "How did the young man get that deep gash on his ankle?"

"A gash on his ankle? I know nothing about it. What does that have to do with the convulsions?"

It seems the young man suffered an unattended wound. It is infected and there is a possibility that it's a very dangerous one…it might be a staph infection. As you know, he suffered seizures, and he could also slip into a coma, if that is the correct diagnosis."

"What can you do to prevent that?"

"We are pumping him full of antibiotics. That's the only known solution at this time."

"If that doesn't work, then what?"

"We can treat the symptoms only, and pray that it works."

"How soon will you know?"

"We can't be sure. Nights are usually much worse. Especially nights like this when the moon is full."

"A full moon affects healing? That sounds a bit bizarre to me"

"It's true though. I try not to schedule surgeries at that time of the month. Hemorrhaging is more common then also."

"What can be done for Mark tonight?"

"We've given him the maximum dosage of antibiotics for this time period. Now, we will just observe him."

"Is he conscious?"

"I don't think so, but he appears to be resting peacefully at this time."

"Adam, I'm going to spend the night here with Mark in his room."

"I'll stay too, Eve."

"No, please go home. You have a big project at the office tomorrow."

"I don't want to leave you alone here, Eve."

"The medical staff will be here through the night. I just want to stay in his room and be there if his condition changes or he needs me."

"What can you do?"

"If his breathing changes or if he wakes up, I can alert the nurse."

"Well, if you must...I'll come by in the morning, or sooner, if you call me. Can I bring you something from home?"

"Yes, a change-of-clothing please, and don't forget clean underwear. Also, the usual toilet articles that I use daily."

"Okay, dear. I'll see you around 7:00 a.m.—that way I should be on time for work too."

"All the while, they were talking softly in the hallway. Adam looked in on Mark once more before leaving. Mark's breathing was regular and his coloring was almost back to normal.

"Good night, Eve. Please call me if there is any change at all."

"I will. Good night, my dear." Eve stood on her tiptoes, nuzzled his neck with her nose, and put her arms around Adam's waist. "How do people that have no family get along?" she asked. "I appreciate your steadfast reliability so much, Adam."

"You're my everything Eve, and Mark is running a close second."

"You'd better go now, Honey. It's important that you be rested up for tomorrow."

"Good night, Eve." Adam turned and walked out the emergency room door.

Eve and Mark were still asleep when Adam returned the next morning. Mark, lying on his back in bed, was breathing easily, but his cheeks were flushed. Eve was turned sideways in the room's recliner chair. A clean hospital gown had been thrown across her shoulders for warmth during the night.

Adam had checked with the head nurse before entering the hospital room. She indicated that Mark had slept through the night with no problems. It appeared that he was on the road back to health. Now, they no longer had to wear a protective mask over the lower part of their faces that fastened behind their head, or plastic throw-away gloves when approaching Mark's bed. A refuse container box attached to the wall was embossed with a red skull and crossbones indicating the possibility of transference of infection or disease of some sort.

Adam was determined not to leave for work until the doctor issued an 'all clear' for Mark. Fortunately, Dr. Sears had treated Mark the evening before and was on call early that morning. He entered the room shortly after Adam arrived and before Mark and Eve awoke.

"Good morning, Mark, and how are you feeling today?" Dr. Sears' cheerful voice intruded on the dreaming pair.

"I guess there is no time for courtesy in this profession," Adam thought. "The important thing is doing their business properly."

Mark responded to the doctor with a rather weak grin and the usual response, "Fine."

Eve awoke and appeared a bit startled by the unfamiliar voice, and quickly sat up while removing the hospital gown from her shoulders.

A signal from the doctor to the nurse prompted the insertion of a thermometer into Mark's mouth and a blood pressure cuff tightened around his left arm. As both results would take a moment or two, Dr. Sears felt Mark's forehead and then took his pulse rate.

Noting that the results appeared normal, the nurse was dismissed by the doctor, and he sat down on the other chair. Dr. Sears began giving his diagnosis by saying, "Mark is a very fortunate young man. His youth and good health acted on his behalf. Just as I thought, his blood-work indicated a dangerous staph infection. The antibiotics I prescribed were well-accepted by his system. Another day or two of that invasion on his body could have proved lethal. I don't see why you…"

The sound of someone being pushed down the hallway in a wheelchair caught the attention of everyone in the room. Glints of silver shone on the bald scalp of the patient in the chair. After the procession had passed, Dr. Sears continued, "Did you notice that young woman? The metallic sheen on her head was not from barrettes; those were staples."

"Staples?" Eve repeated in a shocked manner.

"Yes, staples. She had a staph infection too which occurred from an injury. While water skiing, the boat pulling her rammed into a buoy on the lake. She was thrown into the air and landed under the boat that was pulling her. Her left arm was almost severed by a section of the propeller. Even though she was taken to a local hospital immediately, they evidently didn't realize how intense the follow-up should have been. They released her almost immediately. A week later, she began having seizures just as Mark did. Finally, someone insisted on more immediate and professional care for her and she was transported here by helicopter."

"So…" Adam noted, "the time lapse without proper care was almost disastrous."

"Yes, this particular staph infection is caused from bacteria which sometimes enters a person's body after an open wound occurs. Symptoms can include seizures and later, a coma."

"What happened to her head?" Mark asked.

"The optical nerve behind her left eye was affected by an orbital abscess. It required surgery. Of course they had to shave her head. Staples were used rather than stitches to close up the incision."

"Wow! You mean that I could have gone through that too?"

"That was a possibility. How did you receive that injury to your ankle?"

"I got hurt while climbing out of a fishing boat. When we pulled up to the dock, I jumped out to secure the line so we wouldn't drift out again. When I did so, I fell against a big hook we used to tie the rope to. It had a jagged edge and it gashed my ankle."

"Didn't you tell the Stevensons?" asked Eve.

"Naw. I just thought it couldn't be too serious if it didn't bleed."

"Didn't it hurt?"

"Yeah, but I didn't want anybody to think I'm clumsy. It's been hurtin' real bad, but when I walked, I gritted my teeth and tried not to let it show."

"Oh Mark," whispered Eve. "Why do the males of the species think they must be so brave? That's probably why women live longer than men; we aren't ashamed to emit a signal for help."

"Well, young man," Dr. Sears began, "your ankle was tended to as you slept. It's cut and bruised and will continue to be a bit sore for a while, but the crisis seems to have passed. You thought because the wound didn't bleed, it wasn't too bad. Bleeding is a good thing sometimes. It actually cleans out the wound. Anyway, you are much better now."

"Great! How soon can I leave?"

"Just as soon as your medicines and the at-home-care kit for your ankle are ready to take along. I want to see you in my office on Thursday."

"Oh yeah?"

"Yeah!"

"Can I go to school tomorrow?"

"Definitely not! Not until your checkup on Thursday. If all goes well, you might return to school on Friday."

"Man! Am I going to miss my game on Wednesday afternoon?"

"What type of game?"

"Baseball. I'm the pitcher."

"Yes, you will definitely miss Wednesday's game!"

"Dr Sears, thank you so much for taking good care of Mark," Eve said. "We've taken so much of your valuable time."

"That's okay. I allocated the time this morning. Before seeing Mark, I made sure the young lady you saw with staples was able to go home today."

"Oh! Is she your patient too?"

"Yes, I performed the surgery on her head. Between the two of you, I've had lots of exposure to staph infections during the past week."

Dr. Sears shook the hands of Adam and Eve, patted Mark on the shoulder and said, "See ya Thursday, Mark."

"Thanks Doc," he said.

Mark realized how the 'art of patience' was acquired through his stay at home after being hospitalized. Eve made sure that he did absolutely nothing but his school lessons, read, and watch TV. By the time his appointment with the doctor was due, he was beginning to feel totally frustrated. Adam and Eve were glad about his frustration because it made them aware that his good health had truly returned. Dr. Sears pronounced him healed and ready to return to school, with the admonition that he was to take it easy, and not play baseball for at least two more weeks. As he could not protest the doctor's orders, he unhappily gave in.

CHAPTER XLI

"Hello, Mrs. Alexander. This is P.I. Curtis."

"Hello Mr. Curtis."

"First, let me say that you and your family are welcome to just call me P.I. rather than by my full name."

"Great, that will make it easier, P.I. Please call me Eve instead of Mrs. Alexander."

"Thank you, I will, Eve. I'm still working with a lawyer on the case regarding your brother's imprisonment. Due process of law takes time. So far, he hasn't been able to procure all the court's records of the swift hearing that took place. Sometimes, people in authority are able to have events and paperwork filed in a manner that makes them difficult to locate."

"That doesn't make sense. For instance, newspaper data can be obtained merely by checking out the date of publication. Then, there is a cross-method too in which you are able to do research using subject matter and/or proper names."

"I understand, Eve, but it's possible that the facts might have been mishandled."

"Where do we go from here, P.I.?"

"As they say, we must just 'keep on keepin' on!'"

"P.I., you may realize that Steve and I discovered quite recently that we are obviously brother and sister, and may even be twins?"

"Really?"

"We would like to find out about our roots. Maybe you can help us with that too. I can tell you about all the places we recalled, and how we were affected."

"Do you want to tell me over the phone, or shall I come by?"

"It would probably be best if you made time to visit us. I've written down some memories, but would like to discuss the matter with you in person."

"Okay, Eve. When would you like to meet?"

"Are you free tomorrow evening? Maybe around 7:00 p.m…."

"Sure. Give me your address."

"Oh, it probably would be best to meet somewhere else. Steve's son was just released from the hospital and is still rather weak. Our conversation might cause him to feel stressed. There's a grill at Grand and Arsenal…"

"Yes, I know the place. Is that where you would like to meet?"

"Yes, see you there tomorrow at 7:00 p.m."

"Okay. Bye."

"Goodbye."

After dinner the next evening, Adam volunteered to do the dishes so Eve wouldn't be late for her meeting with P.I.

"Do you have all the information, Eve?"

"Yes, I do. I made copies today of all my research and plan to leave the data with him."

Eve kissed Adam goodbye and went to the living room where Mark was lying on the sofa watching 'American Bandstand.' with the host, Dick Clark. He was totally engrossed, and said, "Soon as I'm able, I wanna learn how to dance. It sure looks like fun, and they have dances at school."

"Do you have a young lady in mind that you would like to invite?"

"Naw! I just wanna learn how to do everything the kids my age do."

"That's a good idea, Mark. I have to go out for an hour or so now. Is there anything you need?"

"Well, yeah… As you know, I haven't had a hamburger for a long time, and it sounds real good."

"Are you hungry, Mark? We just finished dinner an hour ago."

"Yeah, I know. It's just something I'm hungry for. I know you and Adam don't like 'em, but I do..."

"Of course, dear. I told you that you're free to eat them even though I don't serve them here. Where shall I pick it up?"

"'Steak and Shake' is my favorite, and I love those tiny French fries too. Do you mind?"

"Of course not. I probably won't be home until 9:00 p.m. or later. Is that too late?"

"Naw. I'm not really hungry; I just want one."

"Okay." Eve leaned over and hugged his neck, turned around and left.

Several weeks later after their initial meeting regarding Eve and Steve being siblings, P.I. called again. He had been researching all the data Eve gave him. "Hello Eve. I confirmed all the information you gave me regarding the research you and Adam compiled. My only lead was the name of the director of Jefferson Place, Mrs. Quail."

"Oh yes," Eve felt her breath catch. "What have you discovered?"

"Mrs. Quail was in nursing home in Pacific, Missouri until just recently."

"Oh, where did she move?"

"She passed away last month."

"Oh no! Now what can we do?"

"Well, as she had no children, her only heir was the granddaughter of her closest friend, a young 32 year-old nurse. I have her name, Kay Reynolds, and called her this morning. She agreed to meet with us sometime."

"Wonderful. Do you think she might help in our quest?"

"I'm not sure, but it seems she has some records pertaining to Jefferson Place."

Eve's eyes lit up, and she exclaimed, "Finally. I really feel we may get the answers Steve and I are looking for. When can we meet with her?"

"Her days off next week are Tuesday and Wednesday. Which do you prefer?"

"Tuesday, of course. Make it the time and place most convenient for her."

"It might be best to meet at her home. She stored all Mrs. Quail's things in her basement."

"Oh, my, that could take time."

"Yes, you're right."

The following Tuesday, Eve picked P.I. up at his office, and they drove to South St. Louis where Kay Reynolds lived. She and her husband had renovated a turn of the century 3-story brick home there. As the records in question were in the basement, Kay led them down winding stairs to an area that was dark and smelled musty.

"How long have these records been stored here, Kay?"

"About 8 years. Mom had them first, and shortly after Dan and I moved here, she sold her home and bought a condo with very little storage space."

"Is your basement dry?"

"Yes, it's a bit humid, but no actual water seeps in."

"Good. How many boxes shall we have to go through?"

"Eight to ten, I suppose. We have boxes with our own things down here too, but all of Mrs. Quail's are marked with her name and the number of the box. For example, Quail 1 of 10, Quail 2 of 10, etc."

"Good. That should simplify things. Do you know what's in the boxes?"

"No, not really. Mrs. Quail was of the old-school frame of mind, and accumulated a trousseau for her anticipated marriage. I'm sure we'll find household items as well as papers and letters."

"Oh, I thought she remained single all her life."

"She was actually a widow. During World War II, she met an American soldier. They married before he was shipped to France, but they never actually had a chance to live together. Her mother had collected linens and other household items for her from the time she was a small girl. She couldn't bring herself to use them, but kept them packed away. I understand she went through the boxes from time-to-time, wept, and then repacked them until the next time."

Shelves had been installed in the dark, dreary basement, so the boxes had remained as safe as possible from hint of mold, curious mice or bugs.

Kay furnished Eve and P.I. with barstools which were just the right height to explore the boxes contents without the necessity of lifting them. She pulled an upright ironing board over so the items could be removed from the boxes, the full contents explored, and items of importance placed in an empty box on the floor. The basement lights consisted of just a few naked bulbs offset by short hanging chains.

Eve was both excited and a bit dismayed thinking of the task that awaited them.

"Kay," Eve said. "I don't want to cause any confusion. I hope that we're able to keep things in the proper order."

"Don't concern yourself. I haven't been through any of these boxes. Mom wanted to honor my grandmother's friend by assuring her that her precious memories would remain intact. It's hard to believe they contain anything of value."

"We'll let you know," Eve said. "As we're going through most of the boxes, we can make a list of the contents if you like. As each box is numbered, that shouldn't be too difficult."

"Thank you so much. I really appreciate it."

"No, we truly appreciate you! This is our last possible hope to obtain the necessary information regarding our background."

"Well, okay. This is the day I do my errands. Feel free to take any records you find of interest to yourself. If you decide to leave before I return, just set the bolt on the front door and it will lock automatically."

"Will do," said Eve.

Several hours later, Eve was sitting, pulling items out of the boxes and making lists. P.I. had left to bring lunch back for them when suddenly, amidst all the expensive, yellowed linens, Eve said aloud, "Thank you, Lord. This looks like what I've been searching for."

A metal box with a key inserted appeared under stacks of sheets. As Eve attempted to turn the key in the lock, it stubbornly remained stationary. Fearing it might break off, she moved it carefully to the left and then to the right. No response. Tired and frustrated, she was tempted to cry. Just then, she heard P.I. call down the stairs and say, "Shall we eat in the kitchen, Eve?"

"Yes," she responded, rather happy to submerge from the dreary atmosphere.

P.I. appeared to inhale a huge, juicy hamburger. The aroma made Eve feel a bit queasy, but after a few bites of her specialty veggie salad, she began to revive.

"Have you found anything of interest yet, Eve?" P.I. inquired.

"No, not really! I hope we don't have to come back again tomorrow. It could take two days to explore all these boxes. Isn't it a shame that all these items that were so special to her mean almost nothing to anyone else now?"

"Yeah, that's true."

"P.I., the lock box I tried to open with the key seems to be jammed. What can we do?"

"I noticed a shelf in the basement that contains household supplies. Let's see what we can find."

They went back down the stairs and straight to the supply area. An old standby called, 'WD-40' stood on a dusty shelf. After P.I. sprayed the lock with it, the key turned quite easily.

Eve breathed a sigh of relief as she raised the lid.

"Oh look, it contains medals—how old they are! These must be from World War I—medals earned by her husband and presented to her later."

P.I. became interested as collecting military medals was one of his hobbies. A sharp-shooter medal was there along with a Purple Heart. Directly under that was a letter signed by President Woodrow Wilson applauding Myron Quail for bravery above and beyond the call of duty. It seemed he had snatched a hand-grenade thrown into a trench where he and some fellow soldiers lay. When it landed close to him, he grabbed it, leapt from the trench, and began to run with it. Just as he lifted it in the air to throw it, the grenade exploded, killing him. His buddies were saved.

Underneath the medals and citation for valor, lay a pile of letters from overseas, addressed to his wife, Mrs. Rose Quail, with Private Myron Quail as the author.

Eve felt hot tears spring to her eyes. This made everything so real, another young couple whose lives together were ended by the war. Although, come to think of it, without the war, Adam's parents probably never would have met, and there would have been no Adam.

P.I. was unable to respond to her tears. A typical man, he could not bear to see a woman cry.

Eve shook her head and resolved not to get too involved sentimentally with the box's contents. However, she did sense the makings of a good story, one she could write and submit to her magazine with the permission of Kay Randall. She set the metal box aside and went to the next item of interest.

At 3:00 o'clock there were still four boxes to go. More and more, Eve felt inspired by their contents.

"P.I.," she said. "I think it's time for us to go—let's call it a day. I hope to return tomorrow. There's no need for you to come back though. I certainly appreciate your diligence in locating Kay Randall. I shall leave her a note with my phone number and ask her to call me. Send me a bill and please continue to seek information about how we can obtain Steve's release."

"Will do."

Eve left a note for Kay and drove P.I. home.

Wednesday morning found Eve going through another metal box. This one was rather long and deep. It had no lock. Eve's excitement knew no bounds as she lifted the lid and saw a yellowed parchment-type paper that said in bold print:

"JEFFERSON PLACE"

Her heart beat wildly as she lifted the top page and explored the items below. After paging through several, she came upon a signed document dated August 13, 1956 which was the date she was transferred to live as a foster teenager in a group home. The page that followed indicated that a boy named Steve Simmons had been transferred the same day to a group home for boys in North St. Louis. Nothing more than that. All documents in the box were indications of transfers of children from Jefferson Place.

As she had already asked Kay if she might take documents of interest to make copies, she laid them aside. Kay indicated that she should feel free to take anything she desired, and not be concerned about making copies and replacing them.

Just two more boxes to go. In the second to last, Eve found an old shoe box labeled, 'Brown Shoe' from their St. Louis factory. The items inside were even more yellowed as they hadn't been protected like the documents with a more recent date.

Taped under the lid of the box was a list of names and dates showing when the children were admitted to Jefferson Place. Neatly arranged in alphabetic order, Eve quickly found the data on herself and Steve. Feeling a bit dizzy due to the sudden rush of emotion, Eve sat down on the bar stool, took a deep breath, and began to read:

A court document dated September 12, 1946 indicated the transfer of a set of 3 year-old twins named Steve and Eve Simmons to a local orphanage. An attached newspaper article told of a fatal automobile crash in which the lives of Charles and Trudy Simmons were taken. A freight train struck their car and they were both killed instantly. It was later discovered that it was public knowledge about the dysfunctional signal, but the traffic department had been lax about its repair. The article went on to say that the married couple had moved from England to the area a short time ago. A woman with small children of her own who lived in the same apartment complex of furnished rooms as they, was temporarily caring for the twins so their parents could seek employment.

Eve actually felt waves of shock and sadness envelop her. What could she do? At least she had proof that she and Steve were siblings—but could they live with this scanty bit of knowledge? Evidently, they would have to let it go for a while, at least until Steve was freed from prison. That was her immediate goal. That and doing all they could to be assured that Mark's health would be completely restored.

CHAPTER XLII

"Adam, guess who called today?"

"Who?"

"P.I. Curtis. He discovered that we must obtain an audience with the Court of Appeals to work on Steve's release."

"Oh? I thought he would probably have to go through the governor."

"No. That's only to stay the execution of a convicted criminal. P.I. said we will have to obtain a petition form, have it signed by Steve, and then notarized."

"That's great news, Eve. He has already served two years for his part in an accidental death."

"Do you think we should tell Mark before a date is set, Adam?"

"Probably not. He's been through so much lately recovering from that staph infection. He was able to return to school just last week. Let's wait until we have more information."

Two weeks later, P.I. called again to say the date for audience with the appeals court had been set for 30 days hence. During that time, he would have to obtain data from minutes taken at the hearing in the judge's chambers. It could take time going to the record center. He had been given a form indicating he was eligible to peruse the data in question and make copies.

Adam and Eve both heaved a sigh of relief, knowing that Steve's release from prison was in the works. Previously, they had intended to visit Steve the following weekend and share their progress with him. Before their departure, Mark would be told too. They both felt amazingly lighthearted regarding the news.

When P.I. called later, he mentioned that testimony from the informant, Oscar Hill, would probably be necessary as no one else might be able to attest to Steve's character.

"Eve, we should think about a good place for Steve to live when he is freed from prison, and he will have to decide where he would like to apply for a job. I wonder if he's been incarcerated long enough to be free of the desire for alcohol."

"We'll talk about that when we see him this weekend, Adam. I'm not sure if I should mention the fate of our parents yet. Maybe it should be put on a back-burner until later."

"Maybe so, Eve. Working at freedom will be a biggie to contemplate."

"That's true."

That weekend, the three of them entered the prison's gates together once again, and they were optimistic about it being their last visit. When Steve was set free, he could return to St. Louis by bus.

This time, Mark ran towards his father's welcome embrace. "My son, my son!" Steve cried.

"Dad…I've thought about you every day. We're all believing for your speedy release."

"Me too, Mark. I've wasted enough time here, but there's been plenty of opportunity to think and plan."

"What *are* your plans, Dad?"

"I would like to cover national court trials for the news. I've met people in prison, who, like myself, have been judged unfairly. There's been much to learn from books of the law in the prison library. I enjoy research, writing, and have the desire to help others as you all are helping me. I've been thinking about the two of us living together again. Maybe we could find a place in the St. Louis Hills area too, so you can live in the same district, and wouldn't have to change schools."

"Wow, Dad. That would be great. I know you'll be a success! There's just one more question I would like to ask."

"Ask away, Mark."

"What about your problem with alcohol? Have you been away from it long enough to give it up?

"Well Mark…they say addiction to alcohol is actually a disease—one from which you are never completely free. When a person with certain genes has their first drink, they are addicted to alcohol. With that first drink, John Barleycorn has you in his clutches again."

"John Barleycorn?"

"Yes, it's an old nickname for alcohol. Since I've been in prison, I've been attending '12 Step' meetings."

"What's that?"

"A. A. or 'Alcoholics Anonymous'. It's a program which originated about 40 years ago by a man called Bill W."

"Bill W… Didn't he have a last name?"

"Yes, of course, but it's a program of anonymity. That means that when you attend A.A. meetings, there is a very important slogan you must adhere to. It says:

'What you hear here, who you see here, when you leave here, let it stay here.'"

Mark laughed and said, "It's a cute little ditty. What does it mean?"

"Just what it says. Anonymity is respecting the privacy of others who attend the meetings. Nothing said or done at the meetings is to be mentioned elsewhere. It's not just about keeping the privacy of the attendees from people outside the meetings. We don't discuss one member with another member either."

"That sounds pretty strict to me."

"It has to be. Without anonymity, no one would feel free to tell their story."

"What story?"

"Any story we might wish to tell. It entails very personal things about our lives, mainly things that caused us to drink or want to drink. Sometimes old hurts come up and we discuss them and others are very sympathetic. Quite often, we find others with the same problems or hurts we have, and the understanding and camaraderie can be overwhelming. We don't just discuss problems and situations.

Sometimes, another member has endured the same thing and can give good advice."

"How do you find leaders, or people to take charge?" Eve inquired.

"There is not just one person in charge. We have printed guidelines and take turns leading the meetings."

"What are the meetings like?"

"Well, if I were leading the meeting, I would say something like this: 'Welcome to the Alcoholic Anonymous Meeting of the S.S. (Suddenly Sober) Group. Hello, my name is Steve S.; I am an alcoholic and your leader for today. Are there any other alcoholics here?' Others would usually raise their hands or nod their heads in agreement. My response to them would be to say, "Welcome!" Then, I would ask for all who care to join me in saying aloud either 'The Lord's Prayer' or 'The Serenity Prayer.' I would give a brief testimony of my addiction to alcohol and tell how long I have been abstinent."

"Abstinent?"

"Yes, free from taking a drink of alcohol. Then, I would invite those who wish to share with the others by giving their first name and last initial. They might say I'm an alcoholic, a recovering alcoholic, or a gratefully abstaining alcoholic."

"So, you're never free from alcohol?"

"No, never! According to A.A., you are only as free as the time since your last drink. Then, when the meeting ends, those who wish to may speak with one of the others. We encourage sponsorship."

"How did this Bill W. happen to start these meetings?"

"Bill W. was an alcoholic too. Through a spiritual awakening, he was able to abstain from alcohol, but he realized in order to remain free, he would have to aid others. He could not just keep the wondrous message to himself, but must share it with other alcoholics. In June of 1935, he began making himself available to other alcoholics any time of the day or night. Part of the program he advocated was that in order to remain free, those addicted must take a moral inventory of themselves, confess personal defects, make restitution to those they had harmed, be helpful to others, and believe in, and be dependent on God."

"But," Adam interjected, "some people just can't believe in God. What would an agnostic or atheist do to be free?"

"They were advised to use a 'higher power' for help."

"What is a higher power?"

"It could be people in the group, or it could be their sponsor."

"What is a sponsor?"

"It is a person who has been in 'program' long enough to understand it and who wants to reach out to help others. Every person is advised to have a sponsor, no matter how long they have been in the program. That way, no one has to totally depend on themselves, and cannot become cocky."

"What did you mean by taking the 12 Steps?"

"These are the steps that lead to sobriety. We are encouraged to learn them by heart, and use them as a guideline for our lives. I will recite them to you:

1. We admitted we were powerless over alcohol, that our lives had become unmanageable.
2. Came to believe that a power greater than ourselves could restore us to sanity.
3. Made a decision to turn our will and our lives over to the care of God as we understood Him.
4. Made a fearless and searching moral inventory of ourselves.
5. Admitted to God, to ourselves, and to another human being the exact nature of our wrongs.
6. Were entirely ready to have God remove all these defects of character.
7. Humbly asked Him to remove our shortcomings.
8. Made a list of all persons we had harmed, and became willing to make amends to them all.
9. Made direct amends to such people whenever possible, except when to do so would injure them or others.
10. Continued to take personal inventory and when we were wrong promptly admitted it.
11. Sought through prayer and meditation to improve our conscious contact with God as we understood Him, praying only for knowledge of His will for us and the power to carry that out.

Having had a spiritual awakening as the result of these steps, we tried to carry this message to alcoholics, and to practice these principles in all our affairs.

"When you are released from prison, will this help you to stay sober?"

"Yes, it will. I plan to attend A.A. meetings on the outside too."

"Dad, do you feel better since you haven't been drinking?"

"Absolutely! My head is clear now. I had to do a lot of soul-searching, forgive some people, and must ask others to forgive me too."

"Who do you need to ask forgiveness of, Dad?"

"Of you, my son!"

"Oh, Dad." Mark threw his arms around his father and wept.

P.I. called to say that the U.S. Court of Appeals had made the decision to grant another hearing regarding the death of Detective Winchell. It would be an attempt to clear the name of Steve Simmons, the man convicted of involuntary manslaughter.

The Alexander household was all aglow with that news. "How soon will the hearing take place?" queried Adam.

"I can't be sure," P.I. said. "Once they have granted permission, it should go rather quickly. His lawyer is to let us know as soon as he can get a date set."

Mark just sat with his green eyes all ablaze. His mind was filled with such incredible hope. His most recent trip to visit Steve had brought the two of them closer than they ever dreamed possible. Now, the inevitability was just around the corner that they would be living together again soon. If Steve's trial was found to be an illegal one, he could possibly be home for Christmas.

The hearing date was set for December 5th. Adam and Eve took off work for the day and delivered a note to Mark's teacher expressing the fact that he was to be excused from school. Now, the three of them were seated in the hallway of the courthouse waiting to be admitted for the hearing.

As the clerk invited them to enter the judge's chambers, Eve glanced across the room and happened to spot someone who looked familiar.

Was it? Could it be? Yes, it was Oscar Hill. P.I. Curtis had neglected to tell them that as a focal point of the hearing, he requested that Oscar Hill be allowed to give his testimony because the defense lawyer had not been able to locate him to speak on Steve's behalf during the previous hearing. A testimony would be permitted even though as a general rule, witnesses are not present at a Court of Appeals, nor is a jury involved. The accused party usually argues their own case before the judge.

The prosecuting attorney for the state and Steve's defense lawyer were involved in intense, animated conversation together as they read the paperwork spread before them. As the judge entered, they both approached his desk. The defense lawyer presented information that showed that Detective Winchell was accidentally killed after Steve returned his punch, thus causing him to hit his head on concrete, and thus breaking his neck. Winchell had been involved in graft for years, taken many things including drugs, jewels and other costly items that had been stolen or confiscated by him, and should have been turned in to the police department. The reason he had physically attacked Steve was to snatch the stolen jewels in question and sell them.

P.I. Curtis agreed with the records of thievery by Winchell, and indicated that he had just discovered the dishonest dealings of his partner earlier that very evening, and planned to discuss it with him after they left the bar.

Oscar Hill testified that he was sure Steve was innocent of intent to harm anyone. Even though he had not personally witnessed the incident, it was obviously an accident. If he had been aware that Steve had been accused of such a horrendous crime, he would have stuck around for the original hearing.

After only an hour of deliberation, the judge absolved Steve of any intent to commit a crime, and issued release papers for him.

Steve stood to his feet and said, "Does that mean I won't have to return to prison, that I will be freed immediately?"

"Yes," the judge said. "You are free to go!"

With that, Mark ran to his father and embraced him and with tears streaming down his cheeks, and crying out, "Oh Dad, you're a free man!"

The judge continued, "We do indeed apologize for a wrong conviction, and wish you and your family the very best."

The smiles on everyone's faces lit up the room, and Steve and Mark left the judge's quarters arm-in-arm.

CHAPTER XLIII

Current Year—Autumn

Adam rushed to the airline ticket counter in the hotel. Their second trip to Greece had been an incredible disappointment to him. His hopes of having Eve's mind restored through an attempt to re-live earlier joys had failed. She didn't seem to realize where they were, nor did she care. Her only concern was that Adam might leave her, and at other times, she seemed completely unaware of his presence. Now, he was relieved that he had not notified his step-brother and step-sister of their arrival in Crete. Clarice and Jenny had both passed away, and having his siblings see Eve in that condition would have been very difficult for all of them. Of course, he had hoped that returning to a place that had brought such joy to both of them years earlier might awaken some of her memory.

Their return flight from Hania to Athens would take less than an hour. From there to New York was an approximate 8 hours. As time regressed by traveling west, they would be in the States fairly close to the same time at which they left Greece.

Advance tickets purchased before departing showed they were to return home in three days, and the revision caused by leaving earlier would be very expensive, but it was worth it to him. Staying longer only increased the heartache he felt. All he wanted to do now was to go back home where he could provide a permanent solution for Eve and himself.

The day before he had called the Quiet Haven facility and talked with Pearl.

"Pearl, this is Adam Alexander. We met last year and discussed my wife Eve who has Alzheimer's staying with you at Quiet Haven"

"Oh yes, hello. We haven't heard from you in some time."

"That's right. An opening occurred in a facility where Eve and I could stay together, but that only worked out for several months. Currently, we are in Greece."

"You mean the country of Greece?"

"Yes, the country of Greece. I will discuss that with you later. Right now, I would like to know if you have room in your facility for Eve to stay with you indefinitely."

"It just happens that we do. A private room recently opened up. Would you like me to hold it for you?"

"Yes, please. I will be in touch as soon as we are back in the St. Louis area. That will probably be sometime tomorrow."

"Very well, we will look forward to seeing you and your wife soon."

Luckily, they should be able to depart Crete that afternoon. As they had only three hours to spare, he decided to remain at the airport until departure time. After the embarrassment at their hotel, he packed all their clothing and got an airport taxi.

Their flight home on the major air carrier was assured, but obtaining a flight from Crete to the big island was a problem. Calling the air terminal in Hanai was unsuccessful, so he determined to take all their luggage to the airport and work it out there. He felt such a need to depart immediately and yet, did not understand his desire for haste.

"Come Eve, I've packed our luggage and called for a taxi. Let's go to the lobby and wait."

Eve just looked at him as though she did not hear. He took her hand in his, lovingly kissed her fingertips and said, "I shall always love you, my darling." A faint smile touched her lips.

After removing their luggage from the taxi and paying the driver, they gave him an extra tip to place their luggage in an area next to where they would be free to sit and wait. Adam took Eve by the arm and they headed for a rather secluded area on the airport grounds. Rather than take the risk of Eve becoming disturbed again, he purchased sandwiches, cookies and coffee from a vendor so they did not have to eat in one of the restaurants.

The scenery was very beautiful and there were tables and chairs available. After spreading out their lunch, Adam coaxed Eve to enjoy it be saying, "As soon as you eat, we can take another airplane ride, my dear."

As they ate, they enjoyed watching all the passersby. A friendly man approached them saying, "Sir, you have been sitting here with your luggage all around you for the last hour. What are your intentions?"

Adam responded by saying, "We are waiting for the next plane to depart for Athens. We must be there within the next two hours to be on time for our flight back to America."

"Did they tell you that these flight times are very unpredictable?"

"No, they didn't. We must be on time…"

"Well, Sir, I have a small plane that is going to depart for Athens in just a few minutes. If you like, we can take you aboard also. Even though our plane is small, it will get you there more quickly than the commercial plane."

After discussing the fee, Adam said, "That sounds good to me. We cannot take a chance of being late. I will take you up on your offer."

"Eve, come my darling. We are going to fly with this man to Athens."

Then, it was time to board the plane. Adam gave a sigh of relief to finally be on their way. Now, his responsibilities would not be as great as he could rely on the natural course of events to take them home once more. Only three other passengers boarded the plane; all had swarthy complexions and were clothed in black. Each carried a large tote-bag rather than suitcases. Two of the men seated themselves, and the other man entered the restroom just behind the cockpit. The plane began to taxi and then lifted into the air.

Adam gave Eve the window seat and he picked up a flight magazine preparing for a few quiet moments. He found that his head was beginning to nod as he was finally able to relax. Suddenly, it seemed almost as though the plane was lurching in the air. Could it possibly be changing course, and why? Were air currents causing it to sway back and forth like a small automobile in strong winds?

The stewardess emerged from the flight cabin and her face had taken on a deadly white hue. Panic seemed to ebb from her and her mouth opened in what appeared to be a silent scream. Then, her body began to spiral downward, and she fell to the floor in a dead faint.

Adam jumped to his feet to help but was restrained by a passenger who approached him from the rear. Strong hands brought Adam's arms to his sides and then behind his back where his hands were tied together with what felt like rawhide.

One of the passengers emerged from the cockpit with a gun pointed at him, and Adam realized the fear exuded by the stewardess. Looking over the shoulder of the hooded stranger and into the cockpit, another armed man came into view who was giving orders to the pilot.

Adam's first concern was for Eve's safety, but she was just smiling as though watching actors in a movie. The terrorists didn't seem to notice her, much to Adam's relief. But, where were they being taken? Would they be held hostage? If so, who would pay? Their own assets were minimal now as Eve's care and their trip abroad had almost depleted their holdings. In order to stay at Friendship Hermitage, they had to put up most of the money obtained from the sale of their home, plus pay a monthly fee. Kidnappers would probably ask for hundreds of thousands in ransom. Could there be someone of great importance onboard with mega-bucks? No, they were the only passengers, and the pilot and stewardess did not look like socialites.

With his wrists tied behind him, Adam addressed the man who emerged from the cockpit. "Won't you please release my hands? I'll just sit here quietly with my wife and reassure her. She has a mental disorder and I don't want her to be upset by seeing me tied up like this."

When the gunman assessed the situation, an elderly white-haired couple who just happened to be in the wrong place at the wrong time, he looked at his fellow-perpetrator and commanded, "Release him."

An hour later, they were still in flight. The stewardess had regained consciousness and was busy preparing snacks and drinks at the demands of their kidnappers.

The gunmen were talking excitedly amongst themselves. A detailed map seemed to play a part in their escapade. Adam tried to see where they pointed on the map, but he could not read the foreign script. However, he could tell that they were heading east by following their fingers as they pointed to various locations. How much fuel would this small plane carry, and how far would it take them?

Eventually, the plane began to lose altitude. Adam couldn't tell if it was intentional or not. One of the three men had remained with the pilot and was evidently giving him instructions. From the air, he could see a mountainous area on one side and sparkling blue waters on the other.

Finally, a landing field came into view, and within moments they felt the wheels hit the runway, cruise a short time, and then come to a quick halt. Immediately, one of the men went to the door and opened it. Steps were lowered to the ground and he appeared to view the immediate area before descending. He did so and then beckoned the other two to follow him.

A waiting van carried the three of them away. While pressing one of the speed-dials on his cell phone the pilot was heard to say, "I'm not sure who they were. They certainly knew where they wanted to go and how to get there."

Then, after listening for a moment, he said, "No, I'm still not sure where we are. This looks like a private runway in the middle of nowhere."

All was quiet. Then the pilot evidently responded to a query, "No, my gas gauge is close to empty and we don't have much food left. Well okay, hopefully, your instruments will be able to locate us and send help."

For a few moments, all was silent.

Then, "Okay, call me back."

Adam grew tired of waiting on board, and asked the stewardess if she would sit with Eve for a few moments. "I'm going outside to see what I can discover."

The pilot joined Adam as they exited the plane. Aside from the sandy ground, nothing but a small hut came into view in the immediate area. Cupping his hands over his eyes to screen out the bright sunlight, Adam noted a mountain range in the distance. Somewhat closer, a vast body of water appeared.

After peering in the deserted hut, they realized things were rather hopeless. Both fuel and food were in scant supply. Their only choice seemed to be that of walking, on the chance that they might discover a town where they could seek refuge and obtain food.

Suddenly, they observed what appeared to be a whirlwind of dust in the distance moving closer and closer to them. Soon, they realized its source. The van in which the hijackers had made their getaway was returning. Why? Had they forgotten something? There was nothing left on board ship. Could they be lost?

The stewardess had observed them too, and she began walking down the stairs with Eve following close behind. "What could they possibly want?" the stewardess asked.

"I don't know," the pilot responded.

Pulling the van alongside the plane, one of the men jumped out and commanded the pilot and stewardess to get inside the van.

"Why?" she said. "We can't help you."

At that, the dark-complexioned man commanded the pilot to get inside too. "We can't take a chance of you calling your headquarters to tell them where we are."

"How could I do that? I have no idea where we are."

"Your flight instruments could give the information they need. We can't chance being caught. Get in the van!"

Turning to the girl, he told her to get inside the van also.

"What about our elderly passengers?"

"There isn't room enough for all of us. They will have to stay."

"That's inhumane. You can't leave them here to die."

"Oh no? Watch me. Now get into that van!"

At that, he brandished a pistol which he waved in their faces while threatening to hit them over the head.

"Now, move it! I really don't care about those old people. It's probably time for them to depart this world anyway."

At that, Eve became upset too. "Adam, why are those men so cruel? Tell them to stop."

Adam turned to the man with the gun and said, "So far, you've only committed the crime of hijacking. Do you want to add kidnapping to the charges?"

With that, the man waved the pistol in Adam's face and said, "Quiet old man! We're not kidding you. You and your old lady are staying here."

Then, he swung the tiny flight attendant off her feet and thrust her into the van. One of the others jumped from the van, stuck a pistol in the pilot's ribs and said, "One way or another, you're not staying here alive." The pilot climbed on board the van as did the others, and they were off again in a large cloud of dust.

Adam felt extremely weary, and so devoid of wisdom that he just stood for a few moments with his mouth hanging open as if on a spring that could no longer snap back into place. Finally, an extremely dry throat served as a reminder that he needed to close his mouth and get a drink of water.

Eve's comment of, "Look at that brown whirlwind. It's so pretty, but it keeps moving further and further away," reminded Adam that he would be forced to make a decision soon. How on earth could he and Eve possibly return to civilization?

CHAPTER XLIV

"Well, first things first. Come Eve, let's get back on the plane, we need food and water."

Taking Eve by the hand, and with his left knee throbbing, he walked gingerly up the stairs. Adam led Eve back into the plane. "Sit down, my dear. I'll see what's in the refrigerator" he said as he limped down the aisle.

Several bottles of spring water were sitting out as the flight attendant had intended to serve them before being waylaid. Adam twisted off the caps, gave one to Eve, and then with a grimace induced by pain, sat down next to her. They both sat in silence sipping the rather tepid water.

With a sudden jerk of his neck, Adam awoke abruptly. After the tension caused by the hijackers and their departure, he and Eve had fallen asleep in their seats while sitting up.

Looking out the window, he realized dusk was fast approaching and without power on the plane, there would be no lights available.

"Sit still, Eve. I'm going to look for something for us to eat."

With that, he ventured toward the cockpit. The ignition still held the key and he turned it, but heard only a cranking sound. Then, he remembered the pilot said the plane's supply of gas had been diminished. He found a flashlight in a small supply cabinet. The only food on board appeared to be a few bananas and two packages of peanut butter crackers. Gratefully, he took them back to his seat.

"Look what I found, Eve. Some snacks. We can eat half of this for dinner and the rest for breakfast in the morning."

"But, Adam. I want some ice cream. I'm not really hungry, but something cold would be lovely."

"Yes dear, I know. This is all we have right now."

"Well, let's go back to the hotel. They have ice cream."

"Not now Eve. Maybe tomorrow, we will be able to go. I think we'll have an adventure and just spend the night here."

"Well, okay. Where are my pajamas?"

"Let's not get undressed. That way, we can leave first thing in the morning, and we can have our snack before we go to sleep."

"Okay, Adam."

He peeled one of the bananas, broke it in half, and shared it with her. Then, after opening the peanut butter crackers, they sat in silence munching their scanty meal.

"Adam, I'm finished. Where can I brush my teeth?"

He arose and got their toothbrushes and toothpaste from the overnight bag. Walking her to the toilet, he held the flashlight as she brushed her teeth using the last bit of water left in the bottle. Then, she held it for him.

They were thankful that the seats reclined a bit, and were soon sound asleep with their sweaters curled around their necks for warmth and coziness. Their feet rested on the overnight cases.

Sunlight streamed in the window and shone in Adam's eyes. Turning his head sideways to see if Eve was awake yet, he grew alarmed as he realized she wasn't there. He sprang to his feet as quickly as possible, and walked down the aisle looking for her.

As Adam opened the cockpit door, he saw Eve sitting in the pilot's seat turning a lever back and forth. "Adam, what's wrong? Why can't I fly this plane?"

He realized that a decision would have to be made rather quickly as their food supply was almost totally depleted.

"Come Eve. We are going to take a walk down to the lake. Look outside. See the beautiful turquoise color of the water?" Was it a lake? He couldn't tell, but it stretched out as far as his eye could see.

"Yes, Adam. I see it. Did we pack our swimming suits?"
"I think so. Let's look through our luggage."

Soon, they were walking side-by-side towards the water. After an hour or so, Adam realized that they would not reach the water's edge until the next day. Could he and Eve sleep on top of the sand? Would there be night-creatures that might be a problem? He just didn't know. All he was sure of was this: the desire to live was very strong, and he must protect his mate as she could no longer protect herself. What a task lie ahead...

The next morning dawned bright and clear, just as the former one had. Adam awoke with a stiff neck and back, after lying prone in sand that seemed to stretch out infinitum. Looking up, he was reminded of the small grove of palm trees he and Eve had discovered while pulling their luggage across the sandy terrain. He had heard that sometimes an oasis would suddenly appear in deserts, and was so grateful to have discovered one. His gaze moved to the vivid blue body of water in the distance. He only wished he could calculate the distance they would have to walk in order to reach its shore.

Suddenly, he noted a rather familiar sight. A small sailboat appeared in his line of vision. The sail had been hoisted, and the boat seemed to be striving to free itself from a makeshift dock. In the distance, he could see lightning and hear thunder rolling as the rains pelted down. Thankfully, the storm was headed out to sea and not towards them.

Adam went through their small suitcase and was delighted to discover several protein bars he had stashed for their trip home. After eating the bars, they were able to drink from the spring by cupping their hands in the waters that bubbled up. Much to his dismay, he realized there was nothing he could use to carry water with them. He calculated the journey from the oasis to the sailboat at approximately two hours. Could they make it? He wasn't sure.

Gently waking Eve, he encouraged her to drink water and splash her face with it, eat the nutrition bar, and then drink more water. She sighed, stretched, and did as he suggested, although she seemed very weary after spending the night on the desert floor. Would she be able to walk for two hours? He wasn't sure.

"Adam, why can't we stay under these trees and eat coconuts all day long?"

Of course, why hadn't he thought of that? Coconut milk—a perfect, nutritious drink. They could put some in their suitcase and use them for necessary liquid as needed, but how could they crack them? He noted several huge mounds of rocks in the distance. They could lay a coconut on a stone, and use another stone as a hammer. Even apes in the wild had been known to use that method.

As the coconuts added extra weight to their luggage, Adam decided to leave some of their garments behind. They certainly would not need anything dressy, so that eliminated his suit, several shirts, a pair of shoes, along with Eve's dresses and her high heels. He considered attempting to bury their clothing in the sand, but reconsidered. Just in case someone might be looking for them, that could be a clue. Then he realized that there was absolutely no one but the pilot and stewardess who would even care, and their own safety could not be assured.

What a blessing there were coconuts on the ground that had fallen from the trees. Adam certainly did not feel inclined to attempt climbing the tree to pick them. After practically emptying their suitcase by discarding clothing, Adam made a game called, "Who can fill the suitcase with coconuts more quickly?" This tickled Eve's fancy and she won, hands down. She threw five of the hairy, dark brown ball-type foods in the suitcase, and snapped the lid before Adam even got started.

"Eve, let's share a coconut before we start walking. We will need the energy." Raising a rock high over his head, he smashed it down on a rather hairy looking specimen. The milk flew in every direction, and even spotted his shirt with its white liquid. He used his tiny pocket knife to scrape out some of the meat which he handed to Eve. She made a rather wry grimace saying, "Adam, I like coconut better when it's shredded into tiny slivers and tastes sweet."

"That's the sugared type you buy at the store in a container, Eve. You won't find anything like that out here."

They both selected a small hunk and began chewing. Adam then placed another coconut on a flat rock and used a second rock as a hammer. This time, he was careful to grab both halves before they spilled, and they each drank the milk from their own section.

"Come, Eve. We have five coconuts in our luggage. I understand the nutrition in them could sustain us for some time. Let's be on our way. Where there's a sailboat, there must be people. We need help to get back home."

Eve just smiled as though she might possibly understand, and they began walking toward the boat while using a strap to pull a suitcase behind them through the sand. Adam had tied two of his leather belts together to create a strong strap as they were unable to actually carry their luggage. The others had to be left behind. Pulling it along in the hot sunshine was not easy, but he did it. Amazing what you can do when you have to…

Three hours later, after multiple rest stops, they still had a way to go. "Adam, I'm so tired. Can't we stop now?"

"Sit down and rest a minute, Eve. I know you're tired. It won't be much longer now."

From that vantage point, he realized another hour at the most should take them to their destination. The sailboat had not moved. Could the crew be exploring or fishing? How strange that it just sat there, and no life could be observed on deck. How grateful he was that he had purchased hats and sunscreen before their departure. Eve's wide-brimmed hat protected her head and face, and the long-sleeved light-weight blouse shielded her arms from the unrelenting bright sun.

After another hour of walking and pulling their luggage behind them, they finally approached the vicinity of the sailboat. It looked curiously vacant. Adam shouted, "Ahoy there!" several times to no avail. The only response he heard were the cries of a flock of seagulls which seemed curious about why two people were invading their territory.

"Eve, please sit down on the suitcase. I may have to swim a short distance to board the boat."

Eve nodded, but did not speak.

The water felt refreshing after walking in the heat, and he encouraged Eve to splash her face, but she refused. "That water is dirty," she responded. "Look at the fish swimming in it."

"Eve, please sit down. I'll return soon." After swimming a short distance, Adam ascended the narrow stairs built into the side of the boat, and then lowered the portable stairs which would be much easier for Eve to climb. Soon, he was on board ship, all the while calling out, "Ahoy there!"

As there was no response, Adam descended to the cabin below. No one there either. The area held a bunk large enough for two. Opening the refrigerator door, he found the remains of a huge block of ice. The bottom of the tray holding it was full of water. The edibles were still cool to the touch, and the cabinet contained many non-perishable items. Enough exploring, he thought. "Now, I must bring Eve on board." But he wondered how she would be able to climb the stairs. Alzheimer's had affected not only her mind, but lessened her dexterity too. Still he would find a way.

After going back on deck, he climbed down the portable stairs, and called out to her while wading through the water. "Here I am, Eve. This sailboat was just waiting for us, and it appears to have everything we need."

"Oh Adam, I'm so glad to see you. I was afraid you had deserted me!"

"Never, my darling. Now, you must make a special effort to get on board. I will pull the boat into more shallow water, and then I will lift you up to the stairs. Are you ready?"

A vacant look was her only response…

Using an attached rope, he pulled the boat closer to shore, threw their suitcase on deck, climbed on board, and coaxed her to trust him. Saying a prayer for guidance for him and protection for her, he stretched out his arms. She reached out to him, but was unable to raise her leg to climb the steps. With a sudden burst of superhuman strength, he drew her to himself, lifted her into the air, and hoisted her on board. With sweat running down his face, he abruptly fell backwards in the water. Saying a prayer of thanks, he climbed on board, then helped Eve to the cabin below, and encouraged her to lie down on the bunk and rest. He did the same.

When Adam awoke, the sun was hovering low in the western sky. He quietly went up on deck to see if someone had arrived to claim their boat.

Finally, he realized that no one was coming. He stood and was enraptured while viewing the spectacular sunset. How he wished Eve could have enjoyed it too. When the darkness appeared, he once again lowered himself down the stairs to the cabin below. There was no response from Eve, so he allowed her to continue sleeping. Soon, he too was fast asleep.

At daybreak, he realized the boat had drifted during the night. Eve was sitting up saying, "I'm hungry, Adam. What do we have to eat?"

The cabinet contained food items that resembled K-rations. After their former daily meals of coconut milk and its pulpy white meat, they felt very satisfied to have something more solid to eat. Due to the storm, the boat had been drifting about and land was no longer visible. Adam began looking about for clues to help determine whose sailboat they had confiscated.

Exploring the built-in dresser, Adam discovered maps. The writing was illegible to him as it was all in a foreign language. Suddenly, illumination hit! The map looked identical to the one examined by the terrorists. This one too, had arrows pointing eastward. Could it be that two alternate escape routes had been planned for them? In case one didn't work out, namely the van, maybe the second, the sailboat might. In order to be foolproof, they had obviously not relied on only one plan.

How he wished he and Eve could talk together once more as they used to. He had no idea there would cease to be a rapport between them. How lonely an existence it was now, but at least they were together. Once again, he prayed and asked God for strength and wisdom.

The next morning, they awoke to the sounds of a violent storm, and felt the boat bobbing about with great gusto. Looking over the top of the stairs and onto the deck, Adam noted that they had actually washed out to sea. The land was no longer in sight. The up and down motion of the boat made him feel a bit queasy. For the next two days and nights, they had to hold on to the cabin's walls in order to move about down below. After what seemed like an eternity, the sailboat came to a climatic ending. They had ventured topside when the storm seemed to have abated a bit, and found they were headed toward land.

CHAPTER XLV

Grand Finale...

Drifting aimlessly, the rudder of the wounded sailboat finally scraped the shoreline. It was too dark to determine where they had landed, so they retired below and slept restlessly until morning.

What majestic beauty to behold! A beach of the most pure white sand they had ever seen, just like powdered sugar. The brilliant sun looked down on lush green foliage. They spied magnificent trees bearing precious blooms of every conceivable color and shape. Adam couldn't wait to disembark. As he prepared to clamber down, a sharp pain in his knee prevented him from doing so. Once again, as he was forced to sit down, Adam realized that the warning issued by his doctor proved true. Arthritis pain is intensified by stress...

Finally, Adam stood up once again, took Eve's hand, and together they descended to the shore below. Feelings of pain seemed to vanish as the anticipation of what lay ahead engulfed him. Exploring new places was something he and Eve had always enjoyed.

Proceeding inland on foot for over an hour produced no sign of civilization. No people, homes or roads. However, the wildlife and flora were exquisite. Birds of every size, shape and color flew through the air, rested in trees, chirping and singing as they seemed to welcome the lost couple. Animals, large and small, showed no sign of fear. In fact, everything seemed to welcome them with great joy.

The ground suddenly seemed to be gently vibrating. Could it be an earthquake? No! It was… Could it be?… It was…a dinosaur! Standing as high as a three-story building, it spied them, approached as if on tiptoe, and lowered its head to softly nuzzle Eve's cheek.

Eve responded with glee. Her face lit up in the way of a child opening a much desired Christmas present. Adam was speechless. His first instinct was to protect his beloved, but how do you protect someone from such a gentle creature who obviously meant no harm?

Strolling a bit further, they spotted a lion with a magnificent blondish/red mane and hazel eyes, perched on a hillside. This noble king of beasts began to purr like a kitten. His tummy vibrated with his friendly reaction to them and he approached them with an elegant grace. Amazed, they felt no fear. Nor did they need to be afraid. All wildlife here seemed to be unaware that there should be enmity between any of them. The feelings of peace and well-being seemed supernatural in nature.

Feeling a bit weary, Adam and Eve sat down to rest a bit. Soon, feelings of hunger overrode the desire to sit. No sooner than the thought occurred, the lion king and a gorgeous sleek black panther approached them. They both assumed squatting positions, thus making it evident that they intended to be the mode of transportation for the weary couple.

Adam mounted the lion's back, Eve sat sidesaddle on the panther, and off they went. Soon, they came to a clearing. As far as eye could see, the earth was covered with row, after row, after row of incredibly huge, ripe vegetation of every variety known to them, and many that appeared foreign.

The animal's body language invited them to indulge themselves in the lavish array. Then, they too, partook of the delicious feast. After brunch, they wandered through the area, happily examining and exclaiming over each new discovery.

That afternoon, astride their willing, live taxis, the elated couple went on tour. The most magnificent scenery man could ever begin to imagine greeted them at each new turn. Snow-topped mountains, glistening lakes, sparkling rivers, rolling hills, deep-glazed canyons and marvelous waterfalls enthralled them. It was absolutely breathtaking! Eve said very little, but she obviously enjoyed their escapade. There were no demands placed on her to remember anything or act in a certain manner. All was brand new to both of them.

Nightfall found them outside a huge cavern. Their animal friends nodded as though telling them to enter. They did so, and found that even though it was dark inside, they could see clearly. Beds of soft, green moss stretched before them. They lay down and promptly fell fast asleep.

Adam awoke thinking, "What an incredible dream I had last night." As he opened his eyes, he saw Eve lying next to him, her lovely white hair appearing as a halo surrounded by…green moss! He sat up abruptly and exclaimed, "My God, it wasn't a dream!"

In the opening lay their two friends from the day before. They were awake, just lying there waiting to escort Adam and Eve to breakfast. The next area they visited was an orchard, so huge that it seemed to stretch out into eternity. Luscious fruits and berries provided their second meal in this brand-new land.

After a hearty breakfast, they were led to a waterfall so tall they could not see the top. Prisms of light leaking through the water caused the area to sparkle as though endowed with many-faceted crystal gems. Rainbows appeared at every apex and their colors reflected and bounced off the surrounding rocks and trees. Delighted, Adam and Eve jumped out of their clothing and plunged into the awaiting pool at the waterfall's base.

Lily-pads, frogs and fish enjoyed the splashing that ensued. Giggling like children, Adam and Eve indulged in a game of tag, and then played volleyball with a huge, red pod they plucked from a nearby bush. After the games ceased, they anointed their bodies with a pleasant smelling substance produced by the floating lilies and found it to be the most delightful bath they had ever taken.

Walking up the mountainside later that day, they found the grade an easy one to climb. They stopped only long enough to indulge in some nuts and berries that grew along the way. By chance, they leaned against a tree limb and liquid began to flow from what appeared to be a wooden tube.

The most delicious combination of fruit juices they had ever tasted enveloped their taste buds.

Eve exclaimed, "This must be passion fruit; I feel like a passionate young woman once more."

Her hair was red, her green eyes lively, her complexion glowed, and her figure was once again slim and youthful. It had happened so gradually during their bathing episode that he was unaware of it. It was the way he had seen her for so long a time that it seemed totally natural. The most wonderful thing, however, was the fact that her mind was intact.

He then thought, "What will this young, beautiful woman want with me, an old man?"

No sooner had the thought occurred to him, than Eve said, "Adam, you're no longer limping. Oh my, your black hair is standing up again." She sweetly patted his cowlick in place.

As they gazed into each other's eyes, they saw, as though through the lens of a camera, an image of themselves as they now appeared. They always used to say that they were so in tune, that they were literally a reflection of their partner.

The effects on them were so amazing they had to sit down to catch their breath.

"Eve, we should have known something was different when we tackled this steep mountain trail without hesitation."

"Yes Adam," she agreed, "It's as though we've never been old, that we will be young forever. I think we've discovered the 'Fountain of Youth' that Ponce DeLeon searched for."

Later that day, looking back over the chain of events, they agreed that there were definite healing properties in the waters of the falls. They wondered if they would have to be there on a regular basis in order to maintain their new-found youth.

Their time together became more wonderful than before. Previously, they had been so close to losing what they had together that their happiness grew and grew. They both agreed that, even if the sailboat could be restored to a seaworthy condition, they would probably prefer not to leave this wonderful Paradise they had ventured upon. And, since they had obviously been led here, others might follow.

A short time later, as they explored a different area of their new domain, they were absolutely amazed to see a bright light reflecting colors brand new to them. The lights came from a sword brandished about by a huge... Yes, a huge angel!

Instinctively, they knew that this was the Cherubim of which the Bible speaks, that God stationed 'East of Eden' to prevent the original Adam and Eve from returning to Paradise after their plummet from grace. Could these wonderful water falls that had been given them to restore life, health and youth be restitution for all of mankind? Adam's falls in lieu of Adam's Fall...

As Adam looked adoringly at his beautifully restored bride, he gazed into her brilliant green eyes and quoted a portion of one of his favorite scriptures from the Bible's poetic love story; Song of Songs 8:7

"Many Waters Cannot Quench Love"